The Lost Daughter

The Lost Daughter

LUCRETIA GRINDLE

GC

GRAND CENTRAL
PUBLISHING

New York   Boston

Copyright © 2015 by Lucretia Grindle

Grand Central Publishing
Hachette Book Group
1290 Avenue of the Americas
New York, NY 10104

www.HachetteBookGroup.com

Printed in the United States of America

RRD-C

First Edition: June 2015

10 9 8 7 6 5 4 3 2 1

Grand Central Publishing is a division of Hachette Book Group, Inc.
The Grand Central Publishing name and logo is a trademark of Hachette Book Group, Inc.

The Hachette Speakers Bureau provides a wide range of authors for speaking events. To find out more, go to www.hachettespeakersbureau.com or call (866) 376-6591.

The publisher is not responsible for websites (or their content) that are not owned by the publisher.

Library of Congress Cataloging-in-Publication Data
Grindle, Lucretia W.
The lost daughter / Lucretia Grindle. — First edition. pages ; cm
ISBN 978-1-4555-4878-1 (softcover) — ISBN 978-1-4555-4879-8 (ebook) 1. Students—Fiction. 2. Young women—Fiction. 3. Police—Italy—Florence—Fiction. 4. Missing persons—Investigation—Fiction. I. Title. PS3557.R526L67 2015
813'.54—dc23   2014049905

Rome, 1978
Thursday, March 16

THE ALTAR WAS BATHED in shadow. Behind it a row of candles shimmered, their flames catching the white disk of the host as they guttered and flared.

Oreste Leonardi shifted against the back wall of the church. The gun was digging into his hip. He did not believe. Not deep in his heart the way you were supposed to—not with the soul and fiber of his being. Still, he found it moving, this strange cannibalism. Eat of my body. Drink of my blood. Consume me, and you shall be saved.

He looked to the rear pew where his partner sat. Domenico Ricci glanced back and tapped his watch.

Their charge was up front, on his knees. Candlelight licked his back in its dark suit and caught the silvered hair of his bowed head. There was, Oreste thought, no question about Aldo Moro's faith. He'd grown up with the pope, for Christ's sake—pardon the pun, Father. They'd been little angels, boy servants of the Lord together half a century ago back on the hot white stones of the south. And now, who would have bet on it? One was the father of his church, the other father of his country.

Oreste had actually heard Moro called that yesterday, on the TV news, or the radio. By the end of today it would probably even be true. If they made him president. Which they would. Five times foreign minister, five times prime minister. What else were they going to do with him? He wondered if he would go to the Quirinale, too. If the family would even agree to move into the palace. Or if Moro would commute back and forth, pater patria by day, pater familias by night. Now, that really would be a security nightmare.

Even as he thought it, it struck Oreste again how strange it was, that he should be thinking about keeping the next president of Italy alive. Him. A nobody. Nothing but a policeman, an ordinary cop doing his job. Which was all he'd ever set out to be. All he'd ever wanted, really. The job, and what came with it. A little dignity. A good pension. And look where it had landed him. Thanks to what his mother would have called "an angels' kiss." "Angel's wings," she told him when he was boy. "Angels' wings feather our lips."

Domenico's eyes met his. Oreste shrugged. *Cèrto,* they were tight on time. But so what? It wasn't like communion was exactly something you could rush. *Hurry it along, could you, Father, this redemption thing? We have an appointment at the Chigi Palace.* And what were they going to do, anyway, all those black suits and Andreotti who looked like a gnome? Wait, that's what. They'd hardly start swearing in the government without Moro. After all, he'd put the damn thing together. Jury-rigged it with goodwill and promises. It wasn't exactly elegant, but he'd hauled the Communists out of the cold and, grace of God, lured them into bed with the Christian Democrats. *Lo, the lambs shall lay down with the lions and the hand of peace shall be upon you.* Oreste smiled at himself. For a man who didn't believe, he'd come over all biblical. Must be the time of year. Easter was next week.

The tinny notes of a bell skittered down the aisle. Oreste watched as Moro stood and shook hands with the old woman in the pew behind him, exchanging the benediction. Holding her wrinkled paw in his, he smiled, his long horse face breaking into softness, an almost joy Oreste found himself envying. When was the last time he'd smiled like that, felt it glowing from the bottom of his belly? Maybe he should try harder. Maybe every now and then—on Sunday mornings, say, or Easter—he should forget the world, just for a minute, and make an effort to believe. The idea fluttered in his head, and left. *Get thee behind me.* Believing wasn't his job.

Pushing the church door open, Oreste Leonardi looked left then right, his eyes sweeping the street and the waiting car and the second car with the second group of bodyguards pulled up behind it. He felt Domenico slip past him, caught the signal from the escort and returned it as he heard the familiar intoning, *Go in peace, go in peace,* and looked back at the door in time to see Aldo Moro step from the shadow of God.

On Via Fani the forsythia had begun to open. And the pink stars of the oleander that had been Monica Ghirri's favorite until she discovered how poisonous they were. She'd been just a little girl when a teacher had slapped her hand as she reached for the dusky spear of a leaf. At the time Monica thought it was anger in the woman's voice. Now she understood it was fear.

That was what children did to you. The world looked ordinary, then you had them and it was filled with hazard. She wondered sometimes how any parent stayed sane, burdened with this love and its attendant terror. She could, for instance, perfectly well have let her son and daughter walk to school by themselves this morning. They were old enough, and it was all of three blocks, and what did she think was going to happen to them on a beautiful Thursday in the middle of Rome? It was one of the reasons they had moved to this neighborhood—bought the apartment she and Gio agreed they really couldn't afford—because it was safe. Patrician. An ordered, secure place.

Monica glanced at the bus stop. Two old ladies sat wearing headscarves and, despite the sun, fur-collared coats, each with a small dog on her lap. Beside the bench, a group of Alitalia stewards stood chatting, their travel cases at their feet. One of them, a tall guy with glasses and a mustache—and wasn't that a sign of the times, they'd be bearded next—checked his watch, then looked down the road and shrugged.

Furious honking erupted a few streets away. Something was niggling at Monica, like a stone in her shoe. She stopped, waiting to cross the street, and realized what it was. The flowers on the dining room table. They were wilting. She needed another bouquet, something cheerful, but the flower seller's van wasn't in its usual spot on the corner.

She was looking down the road, thinking he might have moved a block, when she heard the crunch of a fender. A white Fiat had thrown its brakes on, causing the car behind to ram it. *Idiot,* Monica Ghirri thought, *they really ought to improve the driving test.* Then the shooting started.

To be honest, Oreste Leonardi hadn't been thinking about anything. His eyes scanned the familiar road, taking in the intersection ahead, the bus stop that seemed to be filled this morning with Alitalia crew, the woman who, he thought vaguely, was pretty in a too soft kind of way standing by the crosswalk, the opposite corner where— His brain clicked. Where the flower seller's van was always parked.

But this morning, wasn't.

He frowned, suddenly completely aware of Moro behind him, lost as usual in his sheaf of papers. They joked that the backseat was his flying office. *The flower seller's van. Not there.*

Without even being aware of it, Oreste reached for the holster on his hip. He had opened his mouth to say something to Domenico—was just forming the words—when the car in front of them threw on its brakes and instead of speaking, Oreste thought *This is it,* and flung himself into the backseat.

Oreste Leonardi was looking into Aldo Moro's startled face when the first shot hit him. He felt the impact, a sort of dull thud, and then the unexpected frailness of Moro's body as he shoved him down, covering him as the rattle of semiautomatic fire and shatter of glass ripped the car.

The second shot hit Oreste in the back. Suddenly he was aware of words. They came whole, filling his head. Rising, white and perfect, from somewhere deep in memory, when, holding his mother's hand in the shadow of another church, he had believed.

"Deus in adjutorium meum intendi."

Oreste Leonardi didn't know if he said it, or if Aldo Moro said it, or if, in the brief moment before his life ended, they said it together.

"Domine ad adjuvandum me festina."

God, come to my assistance. Lord, make haste to help me.

Part I

Florence, 2010
Tuesday, January 19, to Saturday, January 23

M<small>OMMY</small>!"

The word repeated in its high child's voice. *"Mommy! Mommy!"* It stretched, wailing like a siren. *Mom-mee! Mom—mee!* Until it broke into pieces: *Mom!Me!* And became something else. *Mom and me. Mom is me.* Or nothing at all.

Kristin Carson rocked. Her hand closed over the little white bear, her fingers found the familiar grooves, the dents where his fur was worn completely away in places, exposing the hard nubbled linen of his stuffed-bear skin. Sometimes, when she let go of him, the siren stopped. Sometimes it didn't. And sometimes it changed—blurring into the wind, or the rush of traffic, or the rhythmic swipe of a branch against a roof or windowsill. Tonight it kept pinging back, growing fainter as she surfaced out of sleep, but still there. Like the ping of sonar from something sinking, twelve years down into black water.

If she lay very still, she could do it. She didn't even have to be dreaming, she could will herself when she was wide awake, any time day or night. She could bounce on her toes like a diver on a board, and spread her arms, and lean farther and farther, until she fell. Down into the wound she was so officially, and so expensively, healed of. Go like a maggot to the cut. To the sacred place,

where, under her bare feet she would feel not the striped cotton
bedsheets, faintly damp with sweat and winter, but the basement
steps, their grain soft and dusty and sweet with the smell of lum-
ber, new and still pocked with the heads of silver nails.

Then, if she closed her eyes—and, actually, even if she
didn't—she would see her hand, tiny against the glossed red
paint of the door, its fat worm fingers splayed as it lifted and
banged and beat in time to the words: "Mom!Mee! Mom!Mee!
Mom!Mee!"

Of course, she wasn't supposed to. It was, officially, "bad for
her" to go there. But she liked to. She liked to the same way
she liked picking scabs. Pulling at the covering of dead skin her
body worked so hard to produce. Peeling it back, then flaking
away what was left with a fingernail. Digging until it bled. *Sticks
and stones.* The singsong drifted, thin as a breeze. *Sticks and stones
may break my bones. But words will surely hurt me.*

The memory of sugar swelled the back of her tongue. Her
baby hand itched from the bristly fur of the little white bear that
had been brand-new then, with not only the gold button in its
ear, but the tag, too. "See?" Mommy had asked. " 'Forevermore.'
That's what it says. Because he'll always be your friend. He'll always keep you company." Then she'd closed the basement door.

Kristin sat up. She fumbled for the lamp. The room that swam
into focus was pretty much a box. White walls broken by the
wardrobe's sliding mirrored door that seemed not to throw light,
as it was surely intended to, but to swallow it. Suck in the shadows that streamed across the cheap white laminate bureau and
matching desk and chair. *Welcome to Italy,* Kristin thought. *Design Capital of the Universe, where they also have IKEA.* The room's
single window looked onto a wall. Rain beat the glass. Somewhere near the San Frediano Gate a car alarm was going off.

Theirs was the only student apartment in this particular building, but all the places the program used were pretty much the same. A lot of the girls had made a big deal of fixing up their rooms. In the first few days after they'd arrived, even those who'd been stuck in the dorms had gotten together and gone on shopping expeditions. They'd flocked off like crows, sharing taxis out to the box stores near the airport and coming back with throw rugs and beanbags in bright, startling colors. And with those paper globes to go over lights that always ended up hanging sideways. And with glow-in-the-dark stars that stuck to the ceiling. And wall clocks in animal shapes—cat faces with whiskers for second hands and fish bones for the hours and tails that swung from their bodiless heads.

They'd bought curtains in geometric retro prints, interlocking lozenges of pink and orange, and framed posters from the Uffizi shop. How many fat kissy-faced angels with wings sticking out of their shoulders or stoned-looking naked ladies standing on giant clamshells could there be in one city? Lots, was the answer.

Kristin's roommate, Mary Louise, whose last name was "Tennyson-Like-the-Poet," had bought chains of little blinky lights, too. Not chili peppers or mini howling coyotes, but snowflakes. And instead of the angels or the potbellied shell lady, she'd gone for some sappy-faced Madonna, who, now that Kristin thought about it, looked a lot like her. Dark haired, chubby cheeked, and about as smart. The little white bear frowned. Mr. Ted was Kristin's better half. He didn't like it when she was mean.

"OK, OK."

She kissed the top of his head. His black eyes winked in the lamplight. The tag was long gone, but the button in his ear was still there. She ought to buy him a new ribbon. The one around his neck was pretty ratty. Kristin laid Mr. Ted down beside her.

She tucked the sheet around him carefully, pulling it under his little bear chin.

By now the dream had slushed away like dirty water. She could feel the slick of it though, as if she'd swum through oil. Sometimes the residue had a smell. It wasn't tears, or snot, like you might expect. Or that sore-throaty smell from when you've been crying really hard. It was chocolaty. Not expensive chocolates from a box. But cheap. The smell of those supermarket cookies, the ones that came in plastic trays and had pink or green or sky-blue icing, and the smell had a sickly undertone of alcohol. Not gin, or whiskey, or beer, either. Vodka. People say you can't smell it. But you can.

She sat up, swinging her legs over the bed. The floor was tile, and cold. Rain splatted the window. Wind ruckussed between the buildings, shimmering the bricks next door that were close enough to touch. Kristin knew because her first day here, before she'd unpacked even, she'd pried up the frame and leaned out and held her palm against them, feeling the next-door house, warm as an animal skin.

By November the bricks had been lined with frost. She'd woken up one morning to see them rimmed dirty white, like gums in those ads about what will happen to your teeth if you don't floss. For the last three weeks they'd been silvered with rain. It would freeze, if the wind ever stopped blowing. Which it didn't. There were whitecaps on the Arno. Welcome to Florence, where nobody tells you how fucking freezing it is.

Kristin tapped her phone. Two-oh-five a.m. She listened for a minute. The alarm had stopped. Either the car had been stolen or somebody had made the trek down and out into the street in their bathrobe or with an overcoat over their pajamas to turn the thing off. A shutter was banging. *Creak, thud, creak.* Too far away to be one of theirs, it must be on another floor or across the street. She got up, crossed to the desk, slid open a drawer, and pulled out the Swiss Army knife Santa Claus had left last year in her stocking.

The little computer's screen throbbed as it booted up, making it look almost alive. Like something from outer space, or a heart. Kristin checked the mute button. Her room was at the end of the hall, with the bathroom in the middle, so the bing-bong wasn't going to wake Little Miss Perfect. Tennyson-Like-the Poet slept like a rock. She snored sometimes, too, in short purr, snort, purrs that wandered down the hall. Kristin waited for the screen to be fully lit, then typed in the password and the Hotmail address.

The computer was the first present he sent her. Back then, before she'd heard his voice, she'd imagined it, speaking through the screen. Coming like the sound of the ocean when you held a shell to your ear. She'd suggested Skype a bunch of times. But he'd always said no. Dante, he'd said, wrote to Beatrice.

Kristin clicked on the mailbox. Sure enough, there it was. He had promised she would love the sound of his voice, and she had. He had promised she wouldn't be disappointed when she met him, and she wasn't. He had promised he would know what she was thinking, and would know what she needed, and he did. Always.

She'd told him once that it was magic, the way he made her feel. That it was like she could lean back, and back, and know that she would fall, and that he would catch her. When she'd said that, he'd smiled. And then he'd said, "No, Cara, that isn't magic. That is love."

The mail had been sent just minutes before, at one fifty-seven a.m. Kristin felt a surge run through her. She had a feeling, an almost certainty, that if she opened the door of her room, if right now she stepped out into the hall and looked out of the little window down into the street, she would see him. Standing there. Looking up at her.

That was the miracle of it. No matter what he said, that was magic. The fact that, somehow, in all the world, he had found her. And that now, out there—under one of those red-tiled roofs, while the nightmare unwound, while she banged her baby palm and screamed, "Mommy, Mommy, Mommy"—he'd heard her.

Carina, the message read. *It is late or early and the rain is like stars and I am awake and dreaming of my Beatrice.*

Mary Louise Tennyson sat at the pine table in the main room of the apartment and tried very hard not to be pissed off. Anger, her mom always said, was in you, not in the person you thought provoked you. Only you could make you angry, not them.

Well, maybe. But then again her mom hadn't met Kristin.

What did I do? Mary Louise wondered. Karma. That had to be it. She must have way seriously screwed up in some former life.

Mary Louise had been looking forward to this year in Italy for just about, well, ever. Her mom had promised it to her back when she was a freshman in high school. The deal was, if she got into one of her top three colleges, Smith, Vassar, or Bryn Mawr, on early decision, she could take a year off and her mom would pay. For any study-abroad course she wanted.

Talk about motivation. Mary Louise had never been out of Georgia, never mind across the Atlantic. She'd busted her sweet little tush, and Vassar had come through, and she'd been almost as excited about going on this program as getting in. Who wouldn't want to spend nine months in Florence? Mary Louise was already pretty sure she wanted to major in Renaissance studies, and, apart from anything else, this would give her advance credits. With her AP courses, she'd be sailing come September. Her mom was going to come over, too, at the end, in May, and they were going to travel together, for all of June and July. Go to

Venice, Rome, all the way down to Sicily. Sweet. Then she got landed with Kristin.

Well, no. Not quite landed. She'd volunteered. Which kind of made it worse—the knowledge that she didn't actually have to get stuck doing this. That she'd put on her goodness and flapped her fairy wings right into this mess all by herself.

At first, to be fair, it hadn't seemed so bad. Kristin had been a little weird—kind of hyper—on the plane on the way over. But then again, they'd all been kind of hyper on the plane on the way over. Twenty girls going to Italy for a year were pretty much bound to be at least kind of hyper, if only because it was the first time a lot of them had been to Europe, or lived anywhere other than with their parents or at school. Quite a few of them already knew each other. Sherbrooke College, the school that ran the course, gave its students first dibs on places. Only seven of the twenty who'd assembled at Dulles airport on the evening of last September 6 hadn't gone there, Mary Louise and Kristin among them.

So it seemed like they had something in common, at first. And they were the youngest, too. The only seventeen-year-olds. Mary Louise, because she'd skipped a grade in high school. Kristin, she suspected—no, check that, she knew, because Kristin had told, like, anyone who would listen—because she was a total fuck-up and had gotten thrown out of so many places that she needed these credits before she could even apply to college.

Kristin's father was a famous surgeon. He'd operated on football players, and some guy who'd won Wimbledon. She'd told everyone that, too. And about how he'd paid a fucking fortune, i.e., bribe, to get Sherbrooke to give her a spot on the Florence course. Which was, like, the only place she'd ever even think about going. "I mean, what sort of loser wants to go to Lisbon?" she'd asked, screwing up her nose as if she could smell the salt cod from here, and Mary Louise had thought, *Probably one who wants to learn to speak Portuguese.*

But she hadn't said anything. She'd kind of started to catch on by that time, anyway. She'd seen Kristin's stomach once, just for a second, right after they moved in when she opened the bathroom door by mistake as Kristin was getting out of the shower, before Kristin put the lock on—which she went out the next morning and bought and screwed in herself, presumably in case Mary Louise was really into that kind of thing, or something, and wanted to look, which she wasn't and didn't. Actually it kind of grossed her out. Anyway she'd figured out by then Kristin wasn't stupid. Far from it. She just acted stupid most of the time, like she was about six. Which made it harder—if you were going to in the first place—to feel sorry for her.

Most of the time, it was almost impossible to believe that Kristin was about to be eighteen. Except she wouldn't let you forget it. The Big Day was less than two weeks away. *Countdown to February 5!* Kristin was having a party at some really fancy restaurant. They'd all been invited. Everybody on the course got a printed invitation and the whole deal, which was kind of silly considering they were in class together basically every day. Ms. Hines, the program director, had made it way clear, in case anybody was tempted to, like, have a lobotomy scheduled, that they were all going.

Kristin's parents were even coming over. Or rather, her father and stepmother. She made a big deal of the fact that it was her stepmother because her mother had died when she was little. Although when Mary Louise thought about it—which she didn't often, to be honest—she realized that, while Kristin made, like, a huge thing of it, she didn't ever actually say what had happened, or even talk all that much about her mom. She just referred to "the accident," like you were supposed to ask, but no one did. And she didn't call her mother Mommy, or Mom, or anything like that. She called her Karen. Her stepmother she called the Bitch. Which was nice.

Some of the girls thought the whole thing was garbage. Just a story about having this wicked stepmother. Mary Louise didn't believe that, exactly. She was pretty sure Kristin's real mother was dead. She remembered the lines—just the glimpse of that broken belt, pink and puckered around Kristin's waist. She knew what that was. She'd seen it before. Anyone who'd gone to a girl's school had seen it. Cutters always thought they were different, but they were pretty much the same as everybody else—they just picked up a razor to make life bleed, which Mary Louise actually always thought showed kind of a lack of imagination. Most people figured out, at least by the time they were in high school, the best way to screw themselves was with their own head. Who needed a piece of metal? It was kind of pathetic, actually. But since she couldn't imagine what it would be like to be in the world without her own mom, she'd tried, at first anyway, to be Kristin's friend.

Which had turned out, of course, to be A Big Fat Mistake. Because, basically, the nicer you tried to be to people like Kristin Carson, the more people like Kristin Carson hated you.

If Mary Louise Tennyson had been asked to draw a picture, or to describe it, she would have said her good feelings about Kristin Carson were like a piece of pie—peach, and not that huge to start with. And that every time Kristin did something obnoxious, it was like a rat came along and took another bite out of it.

Take this morning, for instance. They'd made a deal—they each did the dishes every other day. Your turn, my turn. As a concept, it wasn't exactly hard. Mary Louise did the washing up one day, Kris did it the next day. Except she didn't. Not anymore. In fact for the last month or so, she didn't do anything. Except whisper into her cell phone to her supposed boyfriend—whom nobody had, like, ever even seen—then disappear at sunset and come back way late without even trying to be quiet and sleep. Sometimes all day. It was like living with a vampire. One who never took out the garbage, or bought food, or even tried not to hog all the hot water every time she took a bath. She'd used Mary Louise's soap, too. The expensive one she bought at the Farmacia Novella. And left it in, like, an inch of water in the soap dish so it rotted to mush. Fifteen euros down the drain. Mary Louise kept her bath oil and her shampoo and even her toothpaste in her room now, which she kept locked.

Maybe she should start keeping her food in there, too. Except then they'd probably get rats. You never knew in these old buildings. She glanced at the sink. It was full of basically every dish and cup and bowl they had.

"Jesus Christ," she muttered, "what does she think I am, the maid?" No. Don't even go there.

Mary Louise Tennyson sighed and got up. She walked across the room, opened the cupboard under the sink, and pulled out the rubber gloves.

Kristin stood on the steps of the church. The wind whipped her dress around her knees. It was freezing. She should have worn an overcoat. But she didn't have one—just the big poofy parka thing the Bitch had bought her for Christmas.

Mr. Ted wasn't with her, but she felt the pang anyway, as if he could read her thoughts. She shouldn't call Anna the Bitch. She knew there was nothing wrong with Anna, except that she got in the way. And tried too hard. Just like Mary Louise. What the fuck was it? Why was it she always got saddled with these people—the ones who wanted to "care"? Who glommed on, and made you feel like you couldn't fucking breathe, and then, when you tried, when you pushed them away just so you could suck some air into your lungs, looked at you with their big hurt eyes, as though you'd done something really horrible. As though every bad thing that had ever happened to them was your fault.

It made her chest tight just thinking about it. Made her feel like an overinflated balloon, so stuffed with all their caring that she was about to pop and the only thing she could do was cut herself open. Gash, and let some of that shit out so she could breathe.

Wind gusted, rushing up the steps, lifting the hem of her dress and snatching at the flower in her hand. The petals were furled tight and safe, but Kristin cradled the bud anyway, shielding it the way you shield a guttering flame. Which meant she had to let go of the front of her jacket, which blew open as she craned, getting up on tiptoes so she could see the red wink-wink of taillights as his car glided across the piazza.

It made her feel like Cinderella, every time, watching him go. Not the part where the Fairy Godmother waves her wand and Cinders looks down and, voilà! she's dressed for the ball, but the other part. The one where all of a sudden the dress is just a ratty old dress and the little white mice are nothing but little white mice. And there was always the feeling inside—the tightening and the bang-bang, like a thud on a drum—no matter how many times he reassured her, that of course he would be back. Of course he would email her tonight. Of course she would see him again, tomorrow. *Carina, I love you, my little Beatrice.* The bud had no scent, but Kristin raised it to her face anyway, and let the velvet edge of the petals feather her cheek as the black shape winked one last time before sliding back into the city.

The piazza was empty now. Frost glittered the roofs of the parked cars. He always left her here, at the Carmine. It was only a couple of blocks to the apartment, but he said it was more complicated to drive back that way because of the one-way system or something. Which was bullshit. She'd started to say so once, when it was raining and he'd pulled over to let her out. But something had stopped her. It had been the light in his face, a white arc that swept the windshield as another car swung out of its parking place. Her mouth had been open, forming the protest, then the headlights swept across him and he'd looked as if he wasn't in color, wasn't flesh at all, but was black and white, a photograph—something one-dimensional she could put her hand through—and she'd stopped, saying nothing. Not even "I love you," or "Good night." She'd just kissed him, harder than usual, and gotten out, and climbed the steps and watched him slide away.

The high heels she was wearing were open-toed. She'd bought them to go with the dress because he'd said tonight was a special dinner. At least it wasn't raining. Her feet were frozen, but her shoes wouldn't get ruined walking back. And even if it had been pouring and they did, even if every single one of her toes got frostbite, who cared? Because soon it wouldn't matter. In ten days, actually. In ten days everything would be different. A fizz of excitement ran through her. Kristin forgot the cold, and the wind, and picked her way down the steps, holding the rose, and walked back to the apartment.

She didn't realize, at first, that anything was wrong. At first she was just pissed, because Mary Louise never stayed up late. Never. Little Miss Goody-Goody always went to bed by eleven, and here it was almost one in the morning and she was sitting on the sofa staring at the television like one of the Living Dead. She didn't even look up when Kristin opened the door. She just sat there with her mouth open, like she was catching flies.

It was the rose, actually, that Kristin was worried about, which was stupid. What did she think Mary Louise was going to do? Jump up and grab it from her? Demand to know where she'd gotten it? Bite it off its stem and swallow it in a single gulp?

Kristin put her hand around the bud, as if it contained the

whole evening. The way he had looked at her as she had told him about the party and about her father and Anna coming, as she slid the invitation across the table. The way his fingers had rested on the creamy paper as he'd smiled, and said, "Thank you, Carina. I have a surprise for you, too. I also want to give you a beautiful gift."

He'd told her then. And now she wanted to savor it. Alone. Talking to someone, anyone, saying anything at all, would mess it up, like putting your finger in a glass of champagne.

Maybe she could just step back out to the landing, let the door click closed, and come home to bed later, when the apartment was dark. But, to be honest, the idea wasn't appealing. The building's front hall smelled like old food and cats. She didn't want to sit on the stairs in her nice dress, and she had nowhere else to go, and anyway she fucking lived here. She didn't have to talk to or answer anyone. Screw Mary Louise, who did she think she was anyway?

Kristin closed the door. Mary Louise was so engrossed in whatever was on TV—some inane game show, or the Italian news, read by a lady with a boob job and a trout pout—that she didn't even glance up. Kristin could slide across the room. Tennyson-Like-the-Poet wouldn't even notice her.

She'd actually taken a couple of steps and was slipping her heels off so they wouldn't clack along the floor when she saw the wine bottle. And the tipped-over glass beside Mary Louise's fat little socked foot. And realized that Mary Louise wasn't going to bite or grab anything. She wasn't even going to talk, never mind ask where Kristin had been or where she'd gotten the rose from or why she was so dressed up. Tennyson-Like-the-Poet wasn't going to say a word, because she was drunk out of her mind.

Kristin stood completely still. The air in the room was heavy. And now that she thought about it, smelled kind of bad. She looked at the sink, piled with dishes. It had been her turn to do them, and she hadn't. Even so it was weird that Mary Louise hadn't done them, either. She usually did.

Kristin sidled across the rug and opened the hall door. She went to her room, laid the rose on her bedside table, slipped out of her jacket, kicked off her shoes, and changed into a pair of jeans and her oldest sweater—if she was going to get puked on she didn't want to ruin any decent clothes.

Back in the living room, Mary Louise hadn't moved. For a second, Kristin wondered if she was dead. If maybe she'd been dead for a while and rigor mortis had set in while she was sitting there staring at the TV, which might explain how she could watch that stuff, and why her mouth was open. Then she saw the sheen of tears on Mary Louise's cheeks. And the pile of wadded up toilet paper she'd been using to blow her nose.

Kristin leaned over and switched off the TV.

"ML?"

All the other girls called Mary Louise Mary Louise, but Kristin found it too much of a mouthful. Besides, it made her feel like she was living in *Gone With the Wind*. She'd always hated that movie. No one else did, but she thought Scarlett was a dope.

"ML?" she asked again. "Are you OK?"

Tennyson-Like-the-Poet nodded. Then she started to howl.

The sound was high and keening, broken by choked snotty sobs. Kristin stood, staring. She had been in boarding school, had done her apprenticeship in drunks, drugs, and fights, but when it came to grief—the genuine slam-your-face-into-the-wall-no-way-around-it pain of loss—she had been the star, and only, performer. Now, looking at Mary Louise, she felt as if somebody had stuck a foot out in front of her, or pushed her from behind, tripping her up. Then, just as quickly, the swoop of irritation was dowsed by recognition. Whatever Mary Louise was feeling, it wasn't fake, and it wasn't because she was drunk.

Kristin hovered. She stared at the top of Mary Louise's head, at the shine of her glossy dark hair and the hunched shudder of her shoulders. She wanted, badly, to be angry—to feel a groundswell of resentment because her perfect evening had been ruined by Miss Goody-Goody. She wanted to tell Mary Louise she was stupid for drinking too much, or watch her throw up so she could feel superior and stalk off down the hall. She wanted not to hear the echo in the raking rhythmic noise Mary Louise was making of *Mom-my! Mom-my! Mom-my!*

Kristin sat down on the couch. Gingerly, as if the touch might burn, she put her hand on Mary Louise's shoulder. After a second, Mary Louise snorted. Her round face was scrunched and piggy. She squeezed her eyes and groped for the wad of soggy toilet paper.

"Brad," she said, finally.

Brad Boyfriend. Kristin had heard all about him. He was a couple of years older than Mary Louise. He lived down the street from her and she'd known him since she was six. Brad Boyfriend was tall and blond and, if Kristin had to say so herself, pretty hot, at least for someone like Mary Louise. He'd gone to Ole Miss on a football scholarship, and as soon as she got out of Vassar they were going to get engaged and move in together. Or maybe not.

"He dumped me." The words came out on a shriek, as if it was the only way she could say them.

Mary Louise forced her eyes open and turned to Kristin. "It's real," she said, suggesting Kristin had said it wasn't. "I mean, it isn't just a fight. He called me." She nodded at the apartment's telephone. "We just spent fucking Christmas together!"

Now she was spitting the words like they were hot and she had to get them out of her mouth. "He was home for Christmas and we spent it together and he never, he never, said anything. But he's been seeing her, he's been seeing someone else for, like, a year. He said he wasn't sure, but after seeing me again, he knows he loves her. They just got an apartment together."

She screamed the last sentence, then bent forward as if someone had punched her in the gut. Kristin leapt off the couch and
grabbed for what had been the fruit bowl and was now sitting
on the sink drainer crusted with dried spaghetti sauce, just in
time. Mary Louise threw up the bottle of wine, and something
else. Maybe Amaretto. Kristin held her head while she retched.
She took the bowl away, flushed it, and came back with a cold
washcloth that she held on the back of Mary Louise's neck. This
part of boarding school, she'd aced.

It was almost two o'clock in the morning before Mary Louise
finally passed out. On the couch, where Kristin covered her with
a quilt. Earlier she'd made them toast, and spaghetti. And listened to a bunch of long, rambling stories about Brad, who
actually sounded like kind of an asshole. Not that she said so,
for once.

After Mary Louise was asleep, Kristin went into her room.
She picked idly through the stuff on the top of Mary Louise's
dresser—some earrings, a bracelet, a box of soap from the farmacia. Even some shampoo and conditioner. She knew why
Mary Louise kept the stuff there. She'd learned that in boarding school, too. Unscrewing the top of the perfume, which
was in an old-fashioned bottle with a ground glass stopper,
she dabbed some on her wrist. Lifting it to her nose to sniff,
Kristin looked up and saw her own face looking back at her
from the round mirror wreathed in lit-up snowflakes. Her eyes
were blue and wide. Blond hair fell to her shoulders. She
didn't look like her dad, so it must be Karen's face she was
staring into.

Kristin lowered her wrist. She put the bottle back, working
the top in so it wouldn't evaporate. Through the open door, she
could hear Mary Louise starting to snore. The snore was more
hiccupy than usual, like a little kid's snore. At least it meant she
was still alive. There was a note from Brad-ex-Boyfriend-Now-

Asshole stuck in the corner of Mary Louise's mirror. Seeing it Kristin felt a strong urge to take it down and rip it up. Scatter it over the floor in little pieces. Turn it into hate confetti.

Her hand actually jumped, like something out of *Frankenstein*. She'd seen Karen's handwriting only once—on a card she'd found in her father's desk. Looking at the blue slanty letters, she'd felt the same flash fire of rage as she did now, the same desire to reach out and rip up the word *love*.

Kristin's palm itched. She turned out the light, shut Mary Louise's door, and went down the hall and into her own room where Mr. Ted sat in his usual place, hogging the pillow.

"You could at least have hung up my dress." The little white bear frowned. A thread on his nose had come loose and was dangling. "Get a shave," Kristin said.

The dress was flimsy. It slithered around, coming off the hanger twice on the way to the wardrobe. Kristin made space for it, then plucked a piece of tissue paper out of the glossy shopping bag the shoes had come in. She sat down on the edge of the bed and folded it carefully. She'd known how to make origami once, when she was a kid. Been pretty good at it, swans and flowers and cootie catchers that opened like those plants that ate bugs. Venus flytraps. Friends gave them to each other at school, before vacations. You wrote a message on every panel so the words unfolded and closed and unfolded again. *"Here's my phone number," "Stay in Touch," "You are Number One."*

On her bedside table, the rosebud was tight as a fist. She knew it didn't smell, but she held it to her nose anyway, then brushed the petals against her cheek. Kristin closed her eyes, remembering the smell of him. Cigarettes, some faintly lemony aftershave, and earth. Wet earth. The dark kind you found under trees after rain. She looked into the mirror and saw the little white bear sitting behind her, still frowning. Kristin put the flower carefully into the tissue nest she'd made for it.

"Poor old Tennyson-Like-the-P. But she's better off without him. Brad is a loser."

She and Mr. Ted looked at each other for a second in the glass, then she turned around and picked him up.

"You sure?" she asked.

Mr. Ted said he was.

Mary Louise had burrowed into the sofa cushions. Curled under the quilt, she looked like a little animal trying to disappear. Kristin stood looking down at her. She fingered the dulled brass button in Mr. Ted's ear. Then she propped him on the pillow beside Mary Louise's puckered fist and turned out the light.

꧁꧂

The Beautiful Gift—or rather, the Looking Forward to the Beautiful Gift, which was usually the best part anyway, was why she really kind of hated surprises, because you got so rooked out of the Looking Forward, although this time Kristin didn't think it would be, because the real thing would be so Fucking Amazing—fizzed away in the bottom of her stomach. It made her feet itch. Made her feel like she wanted to run. Or walk in little hops. All of which was great, but also presented some problems. On the practical side.

The credit cards Kristin had been supplied with for her year in Florence were her father's. They had her name on them, sure. But the bills went to him. Her father didn't care if she went shopping. She hated to admit it, but he and the Bitch were actually super-generous. They paid all the bills. They also read them. And there were some things you just didn't want to share. At least not with Daddy.

So cash was kind of a problem, at least any decent-size chunk of it. She could get advances on the cards. But cash advances, at least big ones, would cause questions. Maybe prompt a phone call, which she really wouldn't want to answer. She planned on being busy.

Kristin smiled and shaded in the doodle on her pad. He had pointed this out, gently but firmly. And, as usual, he was right. She could have saved up, of course, accumulated cash little by little, if she had time. Which she didn't. The twenty-seventh was coming up fast. It was the weekend right before her party. Which made the Beautiful Gift perfect. Except for the credit card problem.

Kristin finished the doodle and started another one, of spiky flowers and a lightning bolt. She had been chewing over the problem all morning, and was only half listening to the Hines drone on about Botticelli when she heard Mary Louise snuffle and realized she had the answer sitting not five feet away.

Mary Louise felt awful. She felt more awful than she had ever felt. It was easy, for the first few days, to blame the hangover, if only because it put off having to admit to herself—or anyone else, and worst of all, her mom—that Brad had dumped her. The only person who knew was Kristin. And Kristin was being, not to put too fine a point on it, fucking amazing.

There were moments when Mary Louise actually thought that made her feel worse. Not because she didn't appreciate Kristin being nice to her, but because it made her feel even more like her world was upside down. Or better—inside out. Brad—good— was bad. Kristin—mean—was nice. Next the rain would stop and it would be eighty degrees out. Then the Arno would flow backward. If Mary Louise hadn't felt so awful, she would have felt crazy.

She wanted to call her mother, except she didn't. Because her mother had always loved Brad, ever since they had been little and he had lived down the street, and Mary Louise had no idea, none at all, how to tell her that not only was Brad not going to someday be her son-in-law, but that he had moved into an apartment at 101 Larkspur Court in Oxford, Mississippi, with someone called Tiffany. Mary Louise knew because Brad's sister, who was "on her side," had told her. Brad's sister hated Tiffany, and was really mad at Brad, and had sent Mary Louise a picture of 101 Larkspur Court taken off Google Earth to make Mary Louise feel better because "it looked like such a fucking dump."

Sitting at her desk, Mary Louise stared like a zombie. The building was two-story caca-colored yellow brick with 1950s' plate-glass windows and one of those brown roofs that looked like a too-big hat with the rim cut off. It made you hot just looking at it. Not that Mary Louise cared. Because she would have moved anywhere with Brad, including into a fucking dump. Which probably would have been all they would have been able to afford anyway, at least at first. Until Brad graduated and finished law school, or became a pro football player, or a surgeon, all and any of which had been in his plans. Although, let's face it, the football player was the most likely. Mary Louise had already figured she'd have to be the lawyer or the surgeon.

OK, so Brad wasn't maybe the smartest bear in the woods. But he'd been her bear, and she would have taken care of him. How many brains did you need in one family? Just looking at number 101 made her howl, again. Hunched over her computer with a Kleenex almost stuffed in her mouth, she zoomed in on the picture as much as she could, trying to see anything—Brad and Tiffany screwing? Brad on his knees giving Tiffany a ring?—through the front window. There was what might be a person's back—Tiffany, white and naked? Or maybe the edge of a curtain. Mary Louise really couldn't tell.

She was trying to zoom in even more when Kristin pushed open the door to her room, which, if she hadn't been so upset, would have surprised Mary Louise. Partly because it meant she hadn't locked the door. Actually she hadn't locked it at all in the last three days, and nothing was even missing. The New Reformed Really Nice Kristin had even stopped using her soap. And partly because it was after seven p.m., and Kristin was never in the apartment after seven p.m. Because she was always out with Him.

Whoever He was. Which nobody knew. Because nobody had ever even seen, much less met, Him. Some of the girls had started calling him KAAMB. Kristin's Amazingly Awesome Mystery Boyfriend. Or the LIHOM. Legend in Her Own Mind. At first the others had asked Mary Louise about him all the time. Then they'd stopped. Because she never had anything to say. Just that Kristin vanished every afternoon after classes, or if she came home, vanished at sunset. Usually all dressed up. Party Vampire.

More than once Mary Louise had watched her out the window at the end of the hall, the one that looked down on to the street. But she'd never seen anything except Kristin teetering away in high heels. She'd never even seen a car. Finally she got sick of it. Maybe Kristin was working for an escort agency? Maybe she was just fucking nuts. Right now Mary Louise really didn't care.

"You spying on the love nest again?"

Kristin leaned over her shoulder and peered at the computer screen. Mary Louise could smell her perfume. It was gag-me strong. She'd have expected sandalwood or citrus. KAAMB must have bought it for her. Brad had given Mary Louise a tiny bottle of Chanel No. 19, the real thing, for Christmas. He probably gave the same to Tiffany. Mary Louise snorted back tears and nodded.

"I know I shouldn't. But I want to. It's, like, I have to—" Her voice vanished in another snort. "At least, if I do it," she tried again. "I mean, I know he lives there. So, he's still—if I keep looking at it—" She took a deep breath. "I can kind of, feel him. Which is good, even if it hurts. It means he's still—it's like the hurt is him."

She shook her head, unable to put into words this feeling that was like digging your nails into the palm of your hand when you were really afraid so you knew you still existed. "It's kind of like—" Mary Louise tried and failed a third time.

"Picking a scab?"

Mary Louise nodded.

Footsteps creaked in the apartment above. There was a burst of sound, followed by a murmur as someone adjusted the TV volume.

"Yeah," Mary Louise said. Then she asked, "Is that how—I mean, is it?"

They were both staring at the screen, studying the dirty yellowed bricks and the front walk made of round fake stepping-stones. Someone had planted flowers, a scratty line of daisies in the narrow bed under Brad and Tiffany's window. Out of the corner of her eye, Mary Louise could see the ridge of Kristin's cheekbone. If she turned around, she would see Kristin's waist, not a foot away. See her jeans and her T-shirt that hid the belt. The puckered dark pink lines of the scars.

Did Kristin use a razor blade? A knife? A letter opener? There had been a girl at Mary Louise's school who did it, on her legs. Inside the soft jiggly flesh of her thighs. She'd spelled out words. Or letters, anyway. PLK. TS. W, or M, hard to tell. They were probably initials, Mary Louise always thought, but whose? Her parents'? Her boyfriend's? Or where they the initials of no one at all? Of just the whole world that had hurt or humiliated her?

Mary Louise had never asked. Neither had anyone else as they dressed and undressed and filed into the showers and out again after sports. Volleyball. Field hockey. The girl had been a good hockey player. A wing. Fast. And pretty popular, too, when she was dressed. When she wasn't, they'd all just turned their heads. Or looked at their towels, or anywhere but at the marks. Sometimes, when they were new, the letters oozed and ran in the hot water of the showers, spinning pink threads down the drain.

"Yes," Kristin said. Then she reached over Mary Louise's shoulder. The computer gave a ping of protest as she switched it off. "Come on. I have a surprise for you."

When she thought back on it later, Mary Louise thought Kristin must have worked most of the afternoon, or at least for a good couple of hours, cleaning and cooking, and she was surprised that she hadn't heard or smelled anything. Then she wasn't, not really. Because she'd been so busy wallowing in her swill of self-pity, sinking so it covered her ears and eyes and probably made her like one of those people who drown in really cold water—the ones you read about sometimes who are technically dead, or at least can't hear or see or understand anything, until somebody heats them up, or whacks them on the back and they spew water and pop to life again. That's what she'd been like then, she would think later. Half drowned. Wallowing, like a pig in shit. A pig in Brad. And she would wonder, if she hadn't done that, if she'd woken up and spat the water out and noticed anything at all—if she'd done that, maybe things would have turned out differently. Or maybe not.

Kristin had found a tablecloth somewhere. It was pretty. Blue, with little flowers on it. And she had set the table with the plates that matched and even filled a vase with flowers. They were just carnations, from the vegetable guy down the street who dyed them different colors—orange, bright pink, and once, bizarrely, green. But still. The apartment's main room was so clean it glowed. There were candles on the table. And votives on the windowsills and along the shelves of the bookcase and even on the drain board beside the sink. Kristin had even gone out and bought wineglasses. A big globe-y one sat beside each plate, half filled with red wine. From a bottle.

"Oh!" Mary Louise said.

It was like a date.

Kristin obviously hadn't made the food—the only thing she knew how to actually cook was spaghetti sauce—she must have gone out and bought it. But who cared? It was nice to have someone pile her plate with cheese, and olives, and the little ham tortellini that were Mary Louise's favorite. There were the first fresh tiny tomatoes from Sicily, too. The cute, really red ones that exploded in your mouth and squirted seeds if you bit too hard. And the wine was yummy. Not that Mary Louise knew much about wine, but she was looking forward to learning. That was one of her projects for the year. Brad said wine was for pussies. Well, fuck him. It was nice to have someone pour it for her, and clink her glass. It was nice to have someone to talk to. When Mary Louise thought back on that night, she thought that mainly it was nice because Kristin was happy.

When Kristin speared her tortellini, and shook her head while she talked, and jumped up to get the little cakes she'd bought for dessert, yanking the fridge open and blinking from the too-bright light, she seemed like a different Kristin. Or at least, another one. A Kristin who hid inside the Kristin she usually was. A Kristin, maybe, without a red belt. Which made Mary Louise wonder, as she selected one of the little cakes and peeled the paper off, if this was the Kristin her boyfriend saw.

Mary Louise didn't doubt that he was real. She could tell. Kristin was in love. Crazy in love. She wasn't making it up. You couldn't do that with something, someone, you imagined. Not really. Mary Louise speared the cake with her fork. The frosting was very thick and had a sugar crust. She hadn't meant to think about Kristin's boyfriend, any more than she'd meant to ask about him. There was no point, because Kristin wouldn't say anything. She'd smirk that I-have-a secret-that's-better-than-any-secret-you-could-have smirk that made people want to hit her. Sometimes Mary Louise was amazed she still had all her teeth, and a straight nose. Unless her dad had already fixed it. But she'd had kind of a lot of wine, and she was beginning to be just the little tiniest itty bit sick of thinking about Brad, so she just did it. She just put her fork down, complete with the piece of cake, and said, "So who is he?" Just like that.

Kristin's fork was halfway to her mouth. Her arm stopped, as if a gear had jammed, like she was one of those creepy mechanical dolls. She felt herself blink. Mary Louise's round face glowed. Her dark curly hair squiggled off into the shadows of the room. Behind the candles, Mary Louise's eyes looked black. She had a smear of yellow frosting on her chin.

"Dante," Kristin said. Then, miraculously, the fork continued to her mouth, as if saying it had freed something.

The cake had chocolate chips in it. At least the one she was eating did. She'd bought four different ones, pointing to them through the glass at the pasticceria. Chocolate chip, lemon, raspberry, and coffee mousse. The girl had picked them out with tongs and put them in a box that, for no reason Kristin could figure, had a drawing of a pink poodle on it. "Dante," she said again, and laughed.

Mary Louise frowned. She reached down with her tongue and up with her finger and got the frosting smear. "Is that really his name?"

"That's what I call him. And," Kristin added, "he calls me Beatrice."

She felt the fizz. Felt stars threatening to burst out of her and bounce all over the table. She had never said his name. Not even this one, not out loud, to anyone. He had asked her not to, and she hadn't. Until now.

Kristin licked her lips. "He took me out for this really fancy dinner and gave me a rose."

"You love him, don't you?"

Mary Louise was staring at her. Kristin nodded.

"I've never loved anyone before," she said. "Not, I mean. Not like this. The real thing, you know?"

Mary Louise looked down. Then she cut another piece off the lemon cake, carefully, with the side of her fork. "Yes," she said. "I know."

For a second Kristin was afraid Mary Louise was going to cry again. Start sniveling, or howl and blow the candles out. But she didn't. Instead she smiled and stuck the piece of cake in her mouth. "I'm sick of talking about Brad," Mary Louise announced. "Let's do you."

Kristin stared. She did a lot of things, almost everything, really. But she didn't *do* Kristin. Ever. Except with him. And she didn't drink. Or at least, not really. A glass of prosecco, a beer. He teased her about it. *Carina, my little nun.* He'd tweaked her cheek once, which actually she hated, and she'd snapped, "Well, Beatrice can hardly guide you through Paradise if she's smashed." That had made him laugh. Now she knew she'd had too much. Half the bottle of wine. And Mary Louise was still talking.

"I mean," she said, "you guys spend so much time together. You see him every afternoon, or every night, almost. Where do you go? To his house?"

Kristin could feel the stars jumping inside her. She reached for her glass, which still had a little wine in it. "He takes me to museums. Or up to Fiesole. Out to dinner. The movies. Sometimes we go for walks."

"So why hasn't anyone met him? I don't get it." Mary Louise put her fork down and reached for her own glass, which was empty. "I have more in my room," she said. She left the table and came back with a second bottle of red wine. "I mean, you know, when I was with Brad, I wanted everyone to meet him. I thought he was so fantastic, I wanted everyone to agree with me."

"You will," Kristin said suddenly. "Meet him. At my party."

Mary Louise turned around. She was standing at the sink, messing with the corkscrew. "He's coming?"

Kristin nodded. "I gave him an invitation the other night."

"Wow." Mary Louise sat back down. She poured them both more wine. "Well, cheers," she said, raising her glass and clinking it to Kristin's. "To you and Dante. He's older, right?"

"Yeah." Kristin felt a twinge. She was very careful. With the computer. With the napkin she'd kept from the fancy place they went, even with the rose. Especially with the rose. "How did you know?"

Mary Louise shrugged. "If he was our age, you'd bring him around. And he couldn't afford to take you out all the time, to places where you wear heels. I mean, will your parents care? How old is he, anyway?"

Kristin felt herself giggle. "A little younger than my dad. They even have the same car."

Mary Louise looked over the rim of her glass. "And he, what? Works, lives here, in the city? Or is he a prince or something? Does he have some awesome place in the hills? A palazzo?"

Kristin realized they were both drunk. She thought that was funny. "I don't know," she said. "He's really private." She pulled the raspberry cake toward her and plucked the raspberry off the top. "He's a man of mystery." She grinned at Mary Louise.

"You mean you really don't know where he lives? Seriously? Jesus, Kris! You've been with him for, like, months, and you've never been to his house?"

Kristin thought this was funny, too. She started to giggle.

"So where do you guys—" Mary Louise put her fork down. She picked up the remaining piece of cake. "Where do you go?"

she asked, putting the whole thing into her mouth at once. "His office? A hotel?" She licked her fingers, just the tips of them, one at a time like a cat. "I mean, where do you have sex if you don't go to his house? The Boboli Gardens?" She snorted. "The backseat of his car?"

"The Seventh Circle of Hell," Kristin said. And they both howled with laughter.

***

It was the next day that Kristin asked her.

Even if she hadn't wanted to admit it to herself, Mary Louise had kind of known she would. She wasn't stupid. However many Kristins there were fluttering around like moths inside that blond, blue-eyed glass, one of them, the biggest, was always and indelibly Kristin Carson. And when people like Kristin Carson were nice to you—especially if the "you" was someone like Mary Louise—it meant they wanted something. She'd felt it, hovering just out of sight, the night before. So even though it made her sad, she couldn't honestly say she was surprised.

They'd gone to bed late, dousing the candles one by one, those that had not guttered out, leaving bumpy little spires and colored blobs of wax in virtually all their saucers. Mary Louise's mother always warned about candles. Some friend of hers had burned her house down because she'd thought it would be romantic to have real flames in the wall sconces, until one gusted and caught the curtains. *Whoosh!* That's how Mary Louise's mother always said it. *Whoosh!* Throwing her hands up in the air.

Well, the apartment had not gone whoosh, exactly. But it was a mess. Oily bits of cheese, bread crumbs, and hardened blobs of frosting spackled the table. An olive was mushed in the rug. One of the empty wine bottles had tipped over and dribbled. In the daylight the carnations looked brittle and strange, like a kindergarten project made of toilet paper. As she sipped coffee, Mary

Louise rubbed one of the petals between finger and thumb to see if any dye would come off, and thought about Kristin.

She couldn't remember everything they'd said. As they'd gotten drunker it had come in bursts, the words rattling out in fragments that flared and died. They'd talked about their schools, and about what they liked to eat. And their favorite movies. And pets. And the other girls.

It had been sometime around then—after they'd howled over Clarissa Hines's flowered bag dresses that now that it was cold had given way to huge furred sweaters—that Kristin, who had been playing with the wax drips from one of the candles, had stopped talking. Mary Louise had just asked her—or, not really asked, but said, "You don't like anyone here very much, do you?" because Kristin never went anywhere, to the movies or shopping, or did anything, like going to get gelato, or playing what-pair-of-earrings-would-you-have-if-you-could-have-any with them as they wandered along the Ponte Vecchio on Saturday afternoons huffing dragon breath into the frost and jostling each other in front of the jewelry sellers' windows.

"It's not that." Kristin had spoken slowly, each word swinging like a pendulum. "It's just—"

She'd looked up at Mary Louise, and blinked. And Mary Louise had held her breath, her fingers wrapped around the stem of her wineglass, because Kristin's eyes were very blue in the candle light and her hand had stopped moving, pinching the wax, and suddenly Mary Louise knew that Kristin was going to tell her something completely true.

"It's just," she said. "It's just that, sometimes—I mean, most of the time, it's safer to be mean to people than to let them like you. You know?"

And Mary Louise had nodded. Because in that moment, sitting across the table from Kristin with the ghost of whatever it was Kristin wanted from her floating at her shoulder, she had known. That you peeled the scab. You wore the belt. You did what you had to do to keep the hurt alive, not just because it held whoever had left you close—locked them in a private place where only you could be with them—but also because it kept the world out. Kept you alone. And alone was safe.

"How fucked is that?" Kristin had asked. Then she'd laughed, and looked back down at the piece of wax she'd rolled into a little figure.

Now she came into the kitchen, sheepish. Or as close to sheepish as Mary Louise suspected Kristin Carson ever got.

"Shit," she said, hugging her bathrobe around her. "Looks like we had a party." Her hair was lank, as though she'd been sweating in her sleep, and her skin looked kind of shiny. "Is that coffee?" Kristin asked.

Mary Louise nodded. She started to ask if Kristin was OK, but she knew the question wouldn't be welcome, so she just got a mug and poured some coffee from the pot and handed it to Kristin, who held it with both hands like a little kid, then went and sat on the couch, one leg tucked underneath her.

"What time is our first class?" she asked.

Mary Louise frowned. "We don't have any. Today is Saturday."

"Oh, right," Kristin said. "Right." But she didn't look like she remembered. Which was unusual, because while Kristin could be mean—or at least one of the Kristins could be—none of them were disorganized. It was one of the reasons Mary Louise was pretty sure she'd been kicked out of all those schools because she'd wanted to be, not because she couldn't figure out what was going on or couldn't get to classes on time. She started to ask again if Kristin was OK, but before she could say anything, Kristin, who had been studying the rim of her mug, looked up at her.

"That was fun last night," she said. Then, very quickly, "ML, there's something I need to ask you. It's kind of important."

Mary Louise felt the ghost put its hand on her shoulder. "Sure," she said, sitting down. "What is it?"

Four hundred euros was not a lot. It hadn't taken Mary Louise's breath away or anything. But it was enough. Her mom had set up a fund for her. She paid into the account every month, and she was always emailing Mary Louise and telling her to go out and have a good time. But, on the whole, Mary Louise had been saving it for their trip in the summer.

"I can't—I mean, I don't want my parents—my father and Anna, to know," Kristin had said. "And if I use my card for that kind of cash withdrawal, they'll ask and—"

Mary Louise nodded. She was holding her mug, gripping it hard, and she realized that she both wanted to ask Kristin what the money was for, and why she needed it in cash, and didn't want to know the answer. If that was possible. Which it was. Because if she knew the answer, and it was what she was pretty sure it was, then she would have to do something about it. At the very least, she would have to go with Kristin. And probably she would have to tell Ms. Hines. And probably that would mean that Kristin would get thrown out of the program, and if that happened, she wouldn't get the credits and she wouldn't be able to apply to college.

Mary Louise started to say, "Why can't he do it? Why can't Dante do the right thing, for fucking once? Instead of just screwing you. He doesn't even take you to his house." But she didn't. Because something, at some point last night, even though Kristin had been laughing about him, had given Mary Louise the idea that she was afraid of him. That—for all the talk of Dante and Beatrice, and love, and the rose—Kristin couldn't tell him. Because if she told him, he would be angry, and if he was angry he would leave her. And that would be the worst.

A line of pink-brown scars ringing Kristin like a picket fence danced in front of Mary Louise's eyes. She felt sick. Too much wine last night. No food. The coffee. Then she looked at Kristin, huddled on the couch, and remembered the scratchy feel of the little white bear she'd found on the pillow next to her cheek when she'd woken up crying because Brad now loved Tiffany, and nodded.

"Sure," she said. "Sure, Kris. Of course."

Kristin could have cheered. She wanted to jump up off the couch and spill her coffee. But she didn't. Instead she looked at Mary Louise and blinked again. There was something about blinking. It made people think you were taking things very seriously, or at least thinking about them. Kind of like wringing your hands. Or biting your lip. Playing with your hair worked that way, too. But not as much.

"Thanks, ML," she said after a second, being sure to look down into her mug. "Thanks," she said again. "I knew—well, I knew I could ask you. That you'd understand. About my parents, not knowing, and stuff."

"I won't tell," Mary Louise said. "I won't tell anyone. I promise."

⟨≈⟩

It was late. After they'd cleaned up and done the dishes, Mary Louise had gone out with some of the others, like she always did on Saturday, for shopping or to some pizza place or trattoria and a movie. Kristin, as usual, had said no thanks and, not as usual, had stayed in to study. He was taking her out to lunch tomorrow, and she didn't actually want to fail everything.

She was lying on her bed, reading *The Rise and Fall of the House of Medici* with Mr. Ted, when she heard a slithering. The light was on in the hall. Mary Louise must have taken her shoes off and was sliding around in her socks, because Kristin hadn't heard her come in. But she could see her, or at least see the shadow of two feet in the bar of light under the door. And she could see the envelope, which was yellow and had a flower on it.

Mary Louise nudged it farther into Kristin's room with her toe. Then she stood there for a second. After that there was a rustling sound and the feet shadow vanished.

Kristin waited before she put the book down and got up. Turning her back on Mr. Ted, she picked up the envelope, slit it open, and fanned eight crisp new fifty-euro notes in her palm.

Wednesday, January 27

Kristin Carson folded the sweater and placed it in the suitcase. She ran her hand across the wool—lavender, her favorite color— and glanced in the mirror again. She hadn't been sure about the highlights, but the woman in the salon had convinced her, promised the copper streaks would liven up everything, especially her eyes, which people called her best feature, but she'd always thought were kind of dull. Ordinary mid-sky blue. The woman had been right though. They did seem different now. Darker, deeper. Sparked with mystery. Or something.

She fingered her new bangs cautiously, as if the curls were spun glass and might break. It had taken her about an hour to style it this way. Kristin twisted her neck to look at the sides and back, at the strands she'd left rippling down the way the woman had showed her. Putting it up definitely made her look older. Now when people saw them, maybe they wouldn't just assume she was his daughter.

She hadn't seen him since Sunday, the first time since she'd arrived that it had been that long. But he'd been busy. Making special arrangements, he said. Kristin smiled. Already things were different. On Sunday he'd actually picked her up for lunch. He hadn't come up to the apartment or anything radical like that. But he'd driven down the street, and parked right outside.

It was the invitation to her party that had changed everything. The fact that she had given him "the honor," as he called it, holding her hand over the table at the trattoria where they had had dinner, "of meeting her father and stepmother." He made a point of referring to Anna that way, and had frowned when Kristin called her the Bitch, brushing her cheek with his fingers and saying, "Carina, you don't have to be so angry. You're not alone anymore."

The memory of his voice crossed her like wind rippling grass. She thought about what would happen tonight. She hadn't admitted to Tennyson-Like-the-P that they'd never actually slept together, not the whole thing, anyway. That would have been way too embarrassing—not to mention cramping her style as far as the cash went. Watching herself in the wardrobe door, Kristin wondered if she felt bad about that, and decided she didn't. It wasn't any of Mary Louise's business, and anyway it wouldn't be true for much longer. And as usual, he'd been right. It was more exciting, better, that they'd waited.

Kristin smoothed the sweater one last time and closed the suitcase. She lifted the coat off the bed, peeling back the plastic that covered it like a skin, and slipped it on. The idea of introducing him to her father and the—Anna—of walking into her party on his arm, flashed through her head as she did up the wide shiny buttons and ran her hand down the sleeve, stroking the silky nap. Her dad was always talking about how they wanted to meet her friends. Well, now they would. Despite herself, Kristin almost laughed out loud. Just the idea of it filled her with a sort of queasy glee, a high as bright and sharp as jagged glass.

Which was weird—that the idea of shocking them, of drawing blood, so to speak, was still so enticing. Because they weren't bad people. It wasn't as if her father and Anna had been mean to her. Or even unfair. On the contrary, as parents went, they'd been pretty good. Considerate, and generous. And way patient when she got kicked out of one school and suspended from the next. They hadn't batted an eye, or argued or anything, when it came to paying for this year. Instead they'd just been thrilled. That she'd developed an interest in art. That she'd wanted to learn Italian, do something ambitious for once.

Before—she thought of it that way now, before and after him—she'd blamed them. For basically everything. But especially for Karen. And especially Anna. Which—not that it mattered—she knew made no sense at all because her dad hadn't even met Anna until a year after the accident. That was what they called it, the accident, as though it had just happened. As though the basement door had slammed shut all on its own.

The thought still made her chest tight. She shrugged. Who cared what they called it? It didn't matter. And anyway, it wasn't true anymore—the blaming part. Every once in a while, though, she still needed the hurt. The widening of eyes. The tiny, all but inaudible gasp. The punch-in-the-gut dumb surprise at what she had—or hadn't—done. It was like throwing a ball, and having it bounce back.

Without thinking, Kristin ran a hand across her belly. She couldn't feel them under all these clothes, but it was comforting to know they were there. *Forevermore.* Her little stick figures, dancing around her waist.

For a second she closed her eyes and imagined him kissing each one. Anointing them the way you anointed a baby's head with oil. She'd be better, she thought. To her father and Anna. To Mary Louise. She'd be nicer. She would. It was easy, now that she had him.

Kristin glanced at her watch. Five minutes to five. She had to get going. If there was one thing he hated, it was being kept waiting. It would have been easier—duh—if he'd come and picked her up. He'd done it once already, on Sunday. She'd thought of asking, when he kept going over where he'd wait for her, but in the end she hadn't bothered. Things would change, they would. They already were. Why ask for miracles?

Kristin lifted the suitcase off the bed. She looked around the room, checking to see if she'd forgotten anything, and came face to face with Mr. Ted. He felt warm and molded when she picked him up, like Silly Putty, or one of those old rubber Super Balls she used to love. Mr. Ted had gone everywhere important with her. To camp, and on vacations, and to boarding school. He'd stayed overnight to the hospital when she had her tonsils out. She'd always taken him on sleepovers when she was little. Kristin hesitated, then put him back on the pillow.

"Sorry, buddy," she whispered. "Not this time. Somebody has to stay here and watch out for things. Make sure Tennyson-Like-the-P doesn't go all gooey and start calling Brad."

Mr. Ted frowned at the mention of Mary Louise. Kristin looked at him. She really did have to get him a new ribbon.

"No," she said finally, "I haven't told her. It's none of her business," she added.

Mr. Ted glanced at her bureau drawer. The yellow envelope lay inside, empty. Mary Louise had never even mentioned it. She'd never even asked when Kristin would pay her back.

"OK, OK," Kristin said. "I'll leave a note."

Five minutes later, when Kristin Carson closed the front door of the building and stepped onto the street, dark was coming down. It wasn't raining for once, but it was colder than she'd thought. The last of the light folded into a thin sticky mist. She should have brought gloves.

Halfway down the block, teetering on her high-heeled boots, the roller bag bumping behind her, she crossed the street. Kristin hopped up onto the opposite pavement, lifted the suitcase over the gutter, and looked back. The apartment window, the little one at the end of the hall, was glassy and black. She'd forgotten to leave a light on and Mr. Ted was afraid of the dark.

Something quivered in her chest. If she ran, if she went up the stairs two at a time, she could snatch him, and still make it. Still not be late. She glanced left and right. There was no one around, and she'd have to leave the suitcase, or drag it back, and dig out her keys, and—she was being a baby. Mr. Ted was a stuffed bear, for Christ's sake. With a ratty bow, and glass eyes, and a button in his ear.

As she turned away, Kristin caught the flowery scent of the perfume he'd bought for her. It wouldn't have been her choice, but she'd doused it on her coat collar, and even on her scarf. Now she realized he was right. It suited her. Kristin Carson adjusted her grip on the bag and walked quickly down the sidewalk and through the San Frediano Gate.

Wednesday, February 3

"So," Enzo Saenz asked, "what do we know about the girl?"

Pallioti shrugged. It was nothing more than a slight lift and fall of his shoulders and spoke volumes. Of impatience. Annoyance. And something more than a tinge of disdain for the schools that could not keep track of their students, especially when those students were wealthy and American and had parents who were making a fuss. They stopped for the stream of traffic that spilled off the Lungarno toward the Ognissanti.

"Kristin." The unfamiliar name sat awkwardly on Pallioti's tongue. "Kristin Carson," he said.

It was just after nine o'clock in the morning on the first Wednesday in February, and still freezing. Tires spat last night's snow, causing both men to step back.

"Seventeen years old," he went on. "Well, actually, she'll be eighteen on Friday." Pallioti's nose wrinkled at the dirty snow and the leaden sky that promised more. "American citizen," he added. "Arrived here in September with a group from a Sherbrooke College. For a year abroad."

The way he said the last two words suggested that, in his

opinion at least, this particular rite of passage—common throughout the world, but especially in America and England— was of dubious merit. Academically and otherwise.

Maybe, Enzo thought. *Maybe not.* Some minds would never broaden, no matter how many stamps their passport had. Others flowered in a local library. What could not be argued, however, was that the postgraduate year, the gap year, the junior year abroad, the self-discovery sabbatical—whatever you wanted to call it—contributed considerably to the city's coffers. Apartments were rented. Language schools bulged. Visits to the Uffizi and the Accademia tripled. And of course, the students bought things. Gelato. Beer. Shoes. Gloves. Anything with Prada written on it. And postcards. Lots of postcards.

The grand tour wasn't dead. It had simply shifted gears and moved with the times. Or not. Basically it still meant the same thing. *I came, I saw, I shopped.* Sometimes Enzo thought it should be the city's motto. Other times, he realized it was.

The traffic stopped as suddenly as it had begun, dammed at some unseen light blocks away.

"Let me guess," Enzo said as they stepped into the street. "She's studying art history?"

Pallioti's eyes slid sideways. It had become a kind of bad joke, like people ringing up and asking if your refrigerator was running. *I spent a year studying art history in Florence.* He didn't bother to answer. Instead he said, "Her parents landed in Rome on Sunday morning," and sighed, as if the mere idea of a transatlantic flight exhausted him. "Flew up here in the afternoon. The girl was supposed to meet them for dinner at their hotel. When she didn't turn up, they figured she'd appear in the morning. She didn't, and didn't answer her messages. On Monday night they contacted the school. Yesterday they went to the consulate. Her father knows people in Washington. Replaced part of the vice president's brother."

Enzo looked at him as if he'd lost his marbles.

"He's a surgeon. Knees." Pallioti waved his hand vaguely, as if that explained everything. "They're visiting for a week," he added. "The parents. To celebrate her birthday. They have a party planned, for Friday night." Pallioti named one of the more expensive, and pretentious, restaurants in the city. "She shares an apartment." He reached into a pocket and handed Enzo a card with the address on it. "With another student in the program. She hasn't been seen there, and there's no record of her leaving Italy. Or of her flying down to Sicily or Sardinia, or wherever it is they go."

Enzo had a sudden vision of small brightly colored birds, let loose and scattering to the four winds.

"No airline booking," Pallioti said. "No car rental or train booking made online, at an agency, or a station. An alert has been issued, all points of entry and departure, and she's flagged on Europol." He spoke abruptly, naming the EU-wide police database, ticking off the standard procedure that launched a missing-persons investigation—the throwing out of the net that would cover any hotel or hostel Kristin Carson tried to book into, any border she attempted to cross, anytime she slipped her credit card into an ATM, or bought a train, bus, or plane ticket using her own name. The clip of his words matched their pace, which quickened as they shouldered past a few cold-looking tourists and scurrying locals.

"Any chance they're together, this Kristin and the other girl, the roommate?"

Pallioti shook his head.

"None. Unless Kristin's hiding under the bed. I've arranged for the roommate to meet us, with the parents and the teacher in charge." His gloved hands clapped, beating against the cold. "I also called the school in the United States that runs the course. This morning. She, Kristin, didn't attend it, for high school or whatever they call it, so they don't know all that much about her. She signed up for this program more or less at the last minute. When I pushed, they admitted that the recommendations from her own school weren't good. Apparently she's done this kind of thing before."

"What kind of thing?" Enzo asked.

Pallioti shrugged without breaking stride.

"Pulled vanishing acts. Disappeared. According to the woman I spoke to, her record suggests she likes to get people in a stew. Especially if they're her parents. The school wasn't going to accept her because of it, for this course, but—" He rubbed his thumb and forefinger together in the universal sign for cash. "They were having a hard time filling places, the economy and all. And Papa was persuasive. To be fair, they also said they haven't had a problem with her. Until now."

"Until her parents arrived." Enzo stopped abruptly, planting his feet like a mule's. "So, this is a complete waste of time?" He asked. "Another windup?"

Pallioti stopped and looked at him. "Does it matter?"

It didn't, and both of them knew it. What mattered was that the girl's father "knew people in Washington." What mattered was that foreign students equaled cash, and Florence wasn't the only beautiful city in Italy, and February was a dull time for the press, and wealthy blond American girls were like chum to sharks. Especially if they were missing.

Pallioti shook his head, and walked on.

"As of now," he said a moment later, "that's all Guillermo's dug up."

Guillermo, whose very sharp brain was housed in a head as bald and polished as a billiard ball, was Pallioti's secretary, and notorious for his efficiency. And speed. The joke in the office was, if Guillermo called you in the middle of the night he'd tell you what you were dreaming.

Even so Enzo was surprised he'd had time to find out this much. Enzo himself had only heard of the girl half an hour ago when Pallioti had barked down the phone, clearly in no good temper, that "the Americans had gone and lost one of their students." He hadn't added, *"Ancòra."* Again. But Enzo had heard it, loud and clear. It happened, every so often. Along with keys, passports, and train tickets—students got misplaced.

Among the police and carabinieri it was commonly acknowledged that the Japanese kept the best track. The French and Germans were OK. The English and Scandinavians were indifferent, and the Americans were hopeless. Usually these fragments of wandering youth—who were almost always girls and almost always found in the arms of some local Lothario—were none of Pallioti's and Enzo's business. Usually they had bigger fish to fry. But then again, usually, the kid's father hadn't replaced the vice president's brother's knee.

They turned the corner. Wind hit them in the face, splintered with cold. Even Enzo, who was normally impervious to weather and seasons, hated February. He began to turn his collar up, then thought better of it. They were only steps from the American Consulate, and it was arguably bad enough that he was wearing one of his ubiquitous leather jackets. He kept several changes of clothes in his locker, and had offered to at least shave, and even to change into a suit and tie for this meeting with the girl's parents, but Pallioti had snapped that he didn't have time. Which was nonsense. Enzo Saenz could go from unshaven street punk to suited, ponytailed five o'clock shadow faster than most magicians could blink. But that wasn't the point. The point was that it was bad enough that they'd been called out on babysitting duty in the first place, and Pallioti was damned if he'd compound the insult by having his officers gussy themselves up for the American consul who, just for the record, he considered to be a bore and a half-wit.

All of which Enzo knew without a word being spoken because he had worked for Pallioti for the better part of a decade now, ever since Pallioti had first come to Florence and talent-spotted him for the undercover unit he had set up and run—an anarchic and surprisingly effective group that came to be known informally as the Angels. After six years of that, when Pallioti had been promoted and asked to form his new department—an elite squad designed to deal with especially complex, or unpleasant, or simply politically suicidal cases that no one else could be arm-twisted into taking—the first person he asked for was Enzo Saenz.

Since then Enzo had become Pallioti's shadow. His fixer. The occasional Sancho Panza to his Quixote. And once or twice, his bodyguard. The product of a "mistake" made by the daughter of one of the cities more prominent families on a convent school trip to Quito thirty-four years earlier, Enzo Saenz, half Ecuadorian and half Italian, was raised by his grandparents, and had never met his father. Pallioti, on the other hand—son of a Milanese banker and a Florentine mother—was a solid product of the upper middle class. Separated by almost twenty years, the two men were as different, and as alike, as it was possible to be. If, a decade ago, they had been master and pupil, now they were something more equal, and more ill-defined.

"Oh, for Christ's sake!" Pallioti swore under his breath at the sight of the new security wall that had been erected outside the American Consulate. A legacy of the latest terrorist threat, it was see-through, bulletproof, presumably bombproof and, to be fair, not altogether unsightly. It had also, Enzo knew, nothing to do with his boss's current fit of ill-temper.

Alessandro Pallioti was not annoyed about half-witted consuls or bulletproof panels, but simply because he was here. Because, despite the fact that he was one of Florence's most senior policemen, he had been more or less ordered to drop what he was doing and proceed posthaste to what was commonly known as Uncle Sam sul Lungarno to personally express his deep interest and concern over the fact that a wayward teenager had run off for a few days. This was the part of his no-longer-quite-so-new job that Pallioti truly hated, being Band-Aid sticker in chief. It was, he reflected as he reached for his credentials, a strange and cruel trick of fate that he was quite as good at it as he was.

⌒

"The father's name is Kenneth Carson," Pallioti murmured as they were waved through the consulate's security barrier. "Doctor, as I said. Surgeon. Famous. Wealthy. From the east coast. Boston."

Enzo knew Boston. He had visited there once from New York. It was cold.

"And the mother?" Enzo tucked his identity wallet back into his inner pocket and fell into step beside Pallioti as they began to climb the stairs.

"Anna. No other children. She's his second wife."

"So not the girl's mother?"

Pallioti shook his head. "No. According to the school, the mother was killed in a car accident when the girl was small. They suggested, strongly, that it's one of the reasons she gets away with behaving the way she does."

Given that Pallioti's own mother had died when he was a child, Enzo doubted that Kristin Carson, or anyone else, getting a free pass because of a similar tragedy would hold much water with him.

"As I said," Pallioti went on, "the parents arrived Sunday. It's Freedom Day, or some president's birthday, or something. One of those American holidays. In any case the school's on break. There aren't any classes. Which probably explains why they didn't notice she was missing. About half of the girls live in independent apartments and apparently a lot of them have gone off."

Carnevale was coming up. Enzo thought of the birds again. Teenaged ones, this time. With credit cards and hormones.

"So what do we actually know?" he asked. "I mean, in terms of facts?" *Do we have anything more solid,* he wanted to ask, *than a vanishing act?*

They had reached a landing. A woman was making her way down. Suited, glassy-eyed, and nodding, she held a cell phone jammed to her ear. Pallioti stopped to let her pass. A not especially handsome man whose restless soul was betrayed only by the habitual drumming of his fingers, he was both loved and feared by those who worked for him. They were inclined, somewhat to their surprise, to stand up when he came into a room, and were silent when he spoke. Many of them had asked specifically to be assigned to his new unit. He was so immaculately dressed that behind his back they called him Lorenzo. For Lorenzo de' Medici, known as the Magnificent. Now a smile flitted across his face, turning his rather ordinary features sharp and foxlike.

"That," he said, "is what I am counting on you to find out."

Tall, sandy-haired, achingly polite, and possessed of a slightly goofy smile that he frequently used to pretend he was stupider than he was, James MacCready, deputy to the American consul in Florence, looked and sounded like an advertisement for the Ivy League. The fact that he actually came from Indiana, and had gone not to Harvard, Princeton, Yale, or Dartmouth, but to his state university on an athletic scholarship, only enhanced the disguise. Enzo had wondered, more than once, if James really was just a junior diplomat, or if he was something altogether murkier—one of the creatures who slid in and out of the CIA's offices in the aptly named DC suburb of Foggy Bottom. Not that he cared. Unless James MacCready got in his way.

If not exactly friends, James and Enzo were a little more than colleagues. They belonged to the same gym, and occasionally ran side by side, pounding treadmills late into the night, private roads unreeling in their heads. In spring and autumn they sometimes played football—or according to James, soccer—on the same Sunday afternoon pickup team. In a more official capacity, they came across one another from time to time, usually at the city jail where James had been dispatched to explain that, contrary to popular wisdom, Uncle Sam offered no protection from Italy's—or any other sovereign nation's—laws. If you broke them, you were screwed. Whether you had an eagle on your passport or not.

Now, as they took their places around a conference table in a private room on the consulate's upper floor, James MacCready caught Enzo's eye. *All this hoo-ha,* the message that flicked between them said, *over yet another kid who'll probably stroll back in the next hour, unsuitable boyfriend in tow.*

Trying not to smile, Enzo pulled out a chair. He knew that at least half the people gathered in the conference room, certainly himself, Pallioti, and James MacCready, and probably the art teacher and Kristin's roommate as well, would put money on the fact that that's exactly what would happen. Still there was the infinitesimally small, but nonetheless real, chance the girl was in serious trouble. Or about to be in serious trouble. Or dead. Which more or less summed up what he hated about cases like these. They didn't require policemen, they required seers. One glance around the table suggested no one there had a crystal ball.

Dr. Kenneth Carson had placed himself at the head, obviously the seat he was used to. Clean-shaven and blue-eyed, his brown hair peppered a distinguished gray, Kristin's father had the kind of fifty-year-old good looks—at once handsome and completely nondescript—that reminded Enzo of ads for luxury goods. Cars with a lot of walnut veneer. Flight cabins with seats that turned into beds. Credit cards named after rare metals.

His wife, at first glance anyway, was a perfect match. Attractive but not showy, blond and conservatively dressed, Anna Carson sat beside her husband. And across the table from Pallioti, whom she was not looking at. Which was interesting. Because, while everyone else in the room was at least pretending to be intent on what Pallioti was saying—to be listening closely to his expressions of concern for her stepdaughter's well-being and to his reassurance that she had probably not gone far and his description of the alert that had been issued and the fact that the police, even as he spoke, were doing everything humanly possible to find her—Kristin's stepmother was studying her hands.

Enzo liked hands. In his book, they were right up there with legs. Anna Carson's were strong, slightly square, and well proportioned. On her left ring finger she wore a gold wedding band topped by some kind of doubtless very impressive diamond. On her right was a large emerald she was studying with an intensity that suggested she'd never seen it before. Her profile was classic, her nose so perfect that Enzo wondered if its shape was entirely due to nature. Anna Carson's skin was bronzed. From playing tennis probably, or golf. No fake tan, Enzo decided, which probably meant no fake nose either. In his experience women went one way or the other—all natural, or not. So it was weird that her hair was dyed.

It was done well, of course. Expertly. There was no darkness at the roots, and doubtless it had cost a fortune. But it was dyed. Enzo had seen enough people trying, for one reason or another, to be someone else, to be sure. *Maybe,* he thought, *her husband had a thing for blondes.* He gave a mental shrug, made a doodle on his pad, and surveyed the rest of the table.

Apart from Pallioti, himself, the deputy consul, and Kristin

Carson's parents, the only other people present were Clarissa Hines, the Sherbrooke College junior professor of art unfortunate enough to be in charge of the program when Kristin decided to go AWOL, and Mary Louise Tennyson.

Looking at Mary Louise, Enzo realize he owed the girl an apology. He'd assumed Kristin Carson's roommate had been living with Kristin because they were two of a kind. This, however, was patently wrong. One glance told him that if Mary Louise Tennyson had chosen to share an apartment with Kristin Carson, it was definitely not because like attracted like. The photograph of his daughter that Kenneth Carson was currently passing around the table made it more than clear she was blond walking trouble. Half confrontation and half come-hither, with blue eyes and a smile that virtually telegraphed I-dare-you, Kristin Carson was every parent's teenaged nightmare. Mary Louise, on the other hand, had nice girl written all over her.

She would be the one, Enzo thought, *who did not lose tickets and keys. The one who could be relied on to make friends with the fat and the shy. A keeper of secrets and always on time, she was loyal, generous, and everyone's friend because she was safe. Safe because she wasn't desired.* Yet. Mary Louise's eyes, and her dark curly hair and generous mouth, all suggested that one of these days, probably one coming up pretty soon, she'd turn into a bombshell. Most likely without being aware of it, which meant she was destined to break hearts left, right, and center. For now though, round and reliable, she was every teacher's dream. And every bad girl's shill. Which was why she was sitting here, and obviously unhappy about it.

Mary Louise's arms were folded across her chest. Her pretty face was scrunched into something very close to a scowl. Looking at her, Enzo thought that, in her place, and faced with the unenviable choice of either covering for Kristin by lying to the police, the consulate, and her parents, or telling the truth and incurring Kristin's probably undying wrath, he'd be pretty annoyed, too. He made another doodle on his pad, this one of a devil with horns, and placed a bet with himself about how much money Kristin Carson owed Mary Louise. Then he wondered, when it came to it, if Mary Louise Tennyson would lie out of some kind of tribal loyalty, or because she was afraid. And if so, of what.

Pallioti stopped talking. He had removed his black overcoat and sat, impervious, in his black suit. His tie was a deep crimson. Gold cuff links winked at his wrists. He steepled his fingers and let silence fall over the room.

"What I don't understand—I mean, what I think we should try to get a handle on here," Kenneth Carson said finally, "is, when was the last time anyone actually saw Kristin?"

He looked around the table, expectant, like a professor who has just asked a very easy question and is waiting for one of the dunces he's burdened with to raise their hand. Enzo wondered if the man had heard a single word Pallioti had said, or if he'd simply been waiting for his turn to talk.

"I mean"—Dr. Carson raised his eyebrows—"when, exactly, is the last time we can verify that?"

As predictable as the February rain, it was the beginning of the requisite *This could never happen at home because the foreign police are so stupid* lecture. Most parents of missing, drug-addled, or otherwise in-trouble children, usually the fathers—especially those who rarely dealt with them and, having rushed in at the last moment, found themselves burdened with guilt and wonder at the strangers their offspring had become—felt compelled to give it at some point. The lecture did exactly nothing to help their child, but it did make them feel better, or at least direct their anger to any target but themselves. Enzo let it pass. The art teacher, Clarissa Hines, took the bait.

Something close to panic crossed her face—as if she had

looked into the absent crystal ball and seen her career going down the drain. She opened her mouth, closed it, and opened it again.

"Wednesday," she said finally. "Wednesday afternoon." The words were strangled. "At about two o'clock. That was when I last saw her. At the end of the last class."

"A week ago?" Dr. Carson's voice suggested he had just looked at a diagnosis and realized it was far worse than he thought. "Is that right?" he asked. He looked around the table, his eyebrows all but disappearing into his hairline. "How can that be?"

Pallioti did not respond, but Enzo knew what he was thinking. *Let him play it out. Let him get it off his chest. It may tell us something, and even if it doesn't, the faster he gets it over with, the faster we can get on.*

"How can no one have seen Kristin for a week? How can no one have realized anything was wrong until we couldn't find her on Monday?"

The question was met with thick, unhappy silence.

"How can that be?" Kenneth Carson asked again. He turned on Clarissa Hines, his voice rising. "How," he demanded, "can the whole weekend have passed and no one realize my daughter was missing?"

"Because she wasn't."

It was Mary Louise Tennyson who spoke. She had an accent. Southern, Enzo thought, if he had his movies right.

"I beg your pardon?" Dr. Carson looked at Kristin's roommate as if she was a stuffed toy or a small pet, a hamster, possibly, who had just uttered a full sentence. "What did you say?" he asked.

"I said, she wasn't missing." Mary Louise scowled.

"Don't be ridiculous," Kristin's father snapped. "Of course she was missing."

Enzo couldn't decide if Dr. Carson was more annoyed by being contradicted or by being interrupted.

"No, she wasn't." The girl shook her head. "At least, not on the weekend, she wasn't."

"What do you mean?" Kenneth Carson banged his hand on the table. "She disappeared on Wednesday and—"

"I mean—" Mary Louise tightened her arms across her chest, fixed her gaze on Kristin's father, and spoke very slowly and clearly. "I mean," she said, "that Kristin wasn't missing because she didn't expect to be back."

Kenneth Carson began to sputter. Before he could get any actual words out, Pallioti cut him off.

"I don't understand, signorina," he said quietly. "When you say she didn't expect to be back? Do you know where from? Did you speak with her? Did Kristin call you?"

"No," Mary Louise said. "She left me a note."

"A note?"

Unless Kristin's father was as good an actor as he was a surgeon, Enzo thought this really was news to him. News his daughter's roommate had apparently decided to keep to herself until now. Which made him look like an ass. Enzo reconsidered Mary Louise. Maybe she wasn't as nice as he'd thought.

"Why didn't you tell us this?" Kenneth Carson's voice began to rise. "Yesterday. Yesterday morning, you told us you had no idea where Kristin was."

"I don't." The girl bristled visibly. She looked to Enzo like a small, angry black cat. "I don't know where she is," Mary Louise Tennyson said. Then she turned and spoke directly to Pallioti.

"I don't have any idea, because Kristin didn't tell me where she was going. She just said she was gone. Which I kind of figured out anyway, since the apartment was empty. She said she'd be back Sunday or Monday. I assumed she'd called them." Mary Louise glanced at Kristin's parents. "When they told me she hadn't, I called her cell. Yesterday, last night, a bunch of times. I left messages saying her mom and dad were here, and that they were worried and she should call. It didn't say anything anyway." Mary Louise added. "The note. It didn't say anything," she said again. "Just that she'd left."

Kenneth Carson's face colored. He didn't seem like a particularly nice man, but even so, Enzo felt a pang of sympathy. Someone should have reminded him that teenagers were not for the fainthearted.

"This note," Pallioti asked, "you received it, when, Signorina Tennyson?"

"Last Wednesday," Mary Louise said. "Wednesday night. I didn't get back till around nine, so I guess I found it around then. It was on the table. A bunch of us went to a movie," she added, "in the afternoon, after the last class. Then out to dinner. To, you know, start the break. I asked Kris if she wanted to come. But she didn't."

"Was that unusual?"

"No," Mary Louise said after a moment. "Kris didn't do things with us. You know, movies and stuff."

There was something in the words that Enzo couldn't quite put his finger on. Hostility? Disapproval? Hurt feelings? Pallioti leaned forward.

"Do you still have the note, signorina?" he asked. "Or did you throw it away?"

"I have it."

Mary Louise reached in to the small purse slung over her shoulder and produced a folded slip of pink paper. Dr. Carson's hand stretched out. She ignored it and passed the note to Pallioti.

Slipping his gloves on, Pallioti took the paper by the corner. He unfolded it, glanced at it, then handed it to Enzo, who slipped it into a plastic evidence bag he'd produced from the inner pocket of his jacket.

Dr. Carson sat back in his chair.

"Is that really necessary?" He nodded at the plastic bag, his voice petulant. For the first time Enzo saw fear in his eyes.

Pallioti saw it, too. "I'm sure it isn't," he said. "But we like to be careful. As I have told you, Dr. Carson, an EU alert has been issued for your daughter. That is standard procedure. My suspicion, now that I realize that she has been missing for forty-eight hours, rather than a week, as we first thought, is that she will reappear, probably any moment, of her own accord with a perfectly simple explanation. However"—he nodded at the evidence bag—"until that happens, we will take appropriate precautions. Which, I am sure you will agree, is in your daughter's best interest."

Kristin's father opened his mouth. Then he closed it.

The brief message had been penned in bright purple ink, and read: *Hey, ML! Decided to go away for a few days. Back Sun or Mon. Don't be good and have fun!!—K.*

The letters were loopy and flourished. There was a smiley face after the words *have fun*. Something about the way it was drawn suggested it might as well have been a raised middle finger. Enzo stood up and handed the evidence bag to Kristin's stepmother.

"Could you confirm," he asked, "that this is your stepdaughter's handwriting?"

Anna Carson glanced up at him. Her eyes were wide set, a dark greenish-brown. The wrong color. Her skin tone didn't match her hair, either. Definitely dyed, Enzo thought, not sure why this interested him as much as it did.

She took the bag, laid it in front of her and looked at it, one hand fingering a small gold locket that swung from a chain around her neck. "Yes," she murmured, sliding it toward her husband. "Yes, that's Kristin's writing."

It was the first time she'd spoken, and, close as he was, Enzo had to strain to catch the words.

The slip of pink paper had a numbing effect on the room, suggesting as it did that they had been set up. Duped.

James MacCready concentrated on his fountain pen. Clarissa Hines sank further into her sweater. Dr. Carson sat eyeing Mary Louise's tiny purse as if he expected his daughter to hop out of it. Kristin's stepmother returned to the study of her hands.

It was Pallioti who finally spoke.

"Is there anything else, Signorina Tennyson," he asked, "that you might be able to tell us? Did she, for instance, have a boyfriend?"

"The girls aren't allowed to have men in their dorms or apartments," Clarissa Hines announced, as if she believed this might actually mean something.

Mary Louise shook her head.

"No. No," she said again. "Honestly. She didn't have a boyfriend. I swear. I last saw Kris, Kristin, in class last Wednesday. Like everyone else," she added.

Enzo smiled and drew another devil on his pad.

◦◦◦◦

Once the routine list of questions had been asked and answered, Kristin's passport and laptop computer—both of which had been taken by her parents from her apartment—were handed over and signed for, along with information on her cell phone and credit card accounts. Given that she was, technically at least for another day and a half, a minor, this could be done on Dr. Carson's say-so. There were small blessings in the world. On the whole Pallioti was on good terms with the city's investigating magistrates, most of whom he knew well and admired. They were busy men and women, and he preferred, for everyone's sake and if at all possible, to present them with a solid chain of evidence suggesting a crime had been, or was in the process of, being committed. When it looked as if the girl had been missing for a week, he had leaned in that direction. The pink note, however, suggested the opposite. Kristin Carson was acting up. Again. He'd take all the necessary precautions, make sure they had plenty of evidence bags, so to speak, but what he was really interested in was finding her, so the Carsons could have their expensive birthday party and the rest of them could get on with their jobs.

The meeting broke up. Kristin's parents and Clarissa Hines stayed behind to talk with James MacCready, and possibly with the consul himself, who was threatening to make an appearance. Mary Louise took one of the cards Enzo handed her without meeting his eye, mumbled something, and fled. He planned on giving her an hour before he appeared at the apartment in San Frediano. In any event, he didn't have to wait that long. As he and Pallioti came down the last flight of stairs, Enzo spotted her in the lobby, waiting for them.

The American military base in Lucca was the consulate's primary reason for being. A steady trickle of people, many of them obviously armed forces, came and went. None of them paid any attention to the two men and the girl standing in a corner.

The doors behind the security gate opened and closed, letting in gushes of cold air. Enzo suspected that, like spies on foreign territory, all of them would rather talk outside the enemy gates. But the idea of standing on the sidewalk in spitting snow wasn't inviting and it was obvious that whatever Mary Louise had to say was urgent. Where upstairs she had looked defiant and more than a little annoyed, now she just looked scared.

"I'm sorry," she said, barely whispering. "But, look, Clarissa—Ms. Hines—she's not bad, really, and she's in enough trouble already because of this. And, well, I didn't want to drop Kristin in it, either. I mean more than she is, with her dad and all."

She looked from Pallioti to Enzo and back again.

"Ah." Pallioti nodded. "So Kristin does have a boyfriend?"

Mary Louise blinked. Up close it was easy to see that her large dark eyes were glassy with exhaustion. She seemed almost too tired to utter any more words. Watching her, it occurred to Enzo, not for the first time, that secrets sucked blood every bit as efficiently as vampires.

"I take it," Pallioti murmured, "that you think she's gone off with him?"

"I don't know." Mary Louise shook her head. "Honestly," she said. "I really don't know. I didn't tell her parents about the note so I'd have a chance to call her. Give her a heads-up. You know, so she could get back here. Or at least call them and stop them freaking out like this."

The loyalty between kids, even if they didn't particularly like each other, never ceased to amaze Enzo. Inconvenient as it almost always was, it filled him with admiration. And sometimes more than a twinge of jealousy.

"I don't get it, really," Mary Louise was saying. "I don't understand. I mean," she added quickly, "don't get me wrong, Kristin can be a total idiot. Most people don't even like her. But she's not as bad as she pretends to be, and she wants to go to college. Have a life. She gets thrown out of here, out of this program, and she's nixed. Anyway," she added, wiping her eyes with the back of her hand. "I mean, with what happened to her mom, you know, her getting killed when she was little and all, it's not all Kris's fault. Everybody's got stuff, you know?"

Mary Louise studied Enzo and Pallioti for a moment, presumably trying to judge whether people their age could have "stuff." Apparently deciding they could, she went on.

"I really did think, I mean, she was excited about her birthday. About the party. So I thought she'd be back. I can't imagine her missing it. She had her dad invite all of us. She wanted to show off. She'd even invited him. Her boyfriend. It was a big deal. She was looking forward to it. At least I thought so." Tiredness sagged her shoulders. "But maybe it was an act." Mary Louise Tennyson took a breath, the middle-aged woman she would become fluttering across her face. "You think you know people, but you don't. I guess I could be wrong."

For the first time since he had heard the name "Kristin Carson," Enzo felt a hum, something like a string deep inside him being plucked.

"Do you really believe that?" he asked. "That you were wrong?"

Mary Louise looked at him. Then she shook her head.

"No," she whispered. "I don't."

"Tell me," Pallioti asked. "About the boyfriend? Let's start with his name."

"I don't know it."

"You don't know his name?" The question was sharper than Enzo intended. "I'm sorry," he added quickly. "It just seems—"

"I know." Mary Louise deflated as quickly as she had bristled. "I know. It seems weird. It is weird. But honest to God, it's true. I swear. That's why I'm telling you. Because it is so weird. Usually, you know, girls, like, talk about this stuff. And Kristin did, kind of. I mean, she let us all know that she was seeing someone—you couldn't miss it, she went out with him all the time. But she wouldn't tell us anything about him. All I know is he has the same car as her dad, and he called her Beatrice." Mary Louise made a face. "And she called him Dante. Sorry," she added, "but that's all. I never met him. Honestly. And in the last week or so, right before she went away, she totally shut up. She was always really careful."

"Careful?" Enzo felt the string pluck again.

Mary Louise nodded. "Yeah," she said. "Like, she always went to meet him. Away from us. She said he was really private. We used to call him the Mystery Man. Kris told me that stuff, about what she called him—just that once. She said she loved him. That it was 'the real thing,' and that she'd invited him to her party. We'd had some wine. Kris didn't really drink. But that was all she said. That he took her to museums and out to eat and for walks and stuff. I asked her if he had a palazzo, if she went to his house or his office, or what, and she didn't really answer. We were both kind of drunk. If she brought him to the apartment," Mary Louise added, "and I don't know if she did—she made sure it was when I wasn't around. All I really know about him is he's older."

"Older?" Enzo heard the answering hum in Pallioti's voice.

Mary Louise nodded again. "A lot older," she said, looking at Enzo. "Older than you." She turned to Pallioti. "Maybe more like your age. I mean, he's, like, Kristin's dad. She said that. He's in his, I don't know, fifties. I guess"

"If you never met him, signorina," Pallioti asked quietly, "how do you know?"

"Because," Mary Louise Tennyson said, "I took his picture."

The photo had been taken with a cell phone, from above, and through a window. The image showed a large black car parked in the street. A blond girl, presumably Kristin Carson, was ducking into the passenger seat. A man was opening the driver's door. Mary Louise had caught him looking straight up at her.

It had been a rare bright day; the picture's definition was good. The man had a strong-featured, clean-shaven face. Of medium height, broad-shouldered but not fat, even on the little phone screen it was clear that he was handsome. And knew it. He wore a dark high-necked sweater under what appeared to be a suede jacket. His sunglasses were pushed on his forehead, nestling in still abundant curly dark hair that was only slightly silvered with gray. One gloved hand rested on the top of the car door.

There was nothing overt, but the immediate impression was unsavory. The girl, the car, the sunglasses.

"When was this taken?" Enzo asked.

"About ten days ago," Mary Louise said. "Sunday. He came to pick her up to take her out to lunch. Like I said, he never did that, that I know of, anyway. But that time he did. He didn't come up to the apartment or anything. He just parked outside the door."

Enzo handed the phone to Pallioti. "How long," he asked Mary Louise, "did you say this had been going on? This man and Kristin?"

Mary Louise shook her head.

"I don't know. Exactly. I thought at first—well, you know I didn't know Kristin until we got here, really until we got the same apartment." She ran her hand over her eyes. "I don't know," she said. "I've been thinking and thinking about it. Kris was, she was so excited, way back when we first arrived. All, like, you know, when you've just met somebody you really like. But—"

Mary Louise looked at Enzo and shrugged.

"But?"

"But that isn't right. Because she was like that on the plane. On the way over. You know, we all met and flew over together in a group, and when we got here, I mean the second we landed, she started texting and she said some stuff that kind of sounded like she knew him before."

"Before she got here? Before she arrived in Florence?"

Mary Louise nodded. Enzo felt the weight of Kristin's laptop in the bag her father had handed over upstairs. His eyes met Pallioti's over the girl's head. "Why did you take it?"

She blinked, her eyes welling.

"His picture," Enzo asked again. "Why did you take his picture?"

Mary Louise opened her mouth. She looked from Enzo to Pallioti.

"My mom," she said finally. "My mom always told me that if

you feel like there's something wrong, you should do something about it. You know, not just sit there. That afternoon, Sunday—Kris and I had talked about him, for, like, the only time, a few nights before—and I just had a bad feeling. I just—" Mary Louise took a deep breath. "When we were drinking, I asked her, you know, where they went. To make love. Have sex. And she said—she said the Seventh Circle of Hell. And it was funny, you know, because of Dante. But it wasn't. So when I heard her answer the intercom, I was in my room. And after she went out, I was curious, obviously. I wanted to see him. And I went to the window, at the end of the hall, that looks over the street, and I had my phone in my hand, and—"

Tears began to run down Mary Louise's cheeks.

"I couldn't think of anything else to do," she said. "I couldn't think of anything else. It seemed like at least—"

She groped in her bag for a tissue. Enzo wondered if she was still staying in the apartment, if anyone from the school had thought to move her, or if this poor girl had simply been left carrying the whole weight of whatever had or hadn't happened to Kristin Carson.

Pallioti put his hand on her shoulder. "Signorina Tennyson," he asked, "where are you staying?"

Mary Louise made an effort to smile.

"I'm OK," she said, sniffing. "Really. For the last few nights—well, I didn't want to stay there anymore, in Kris's and my apartment, so I moved into one of the others. With some of my friends." Her eyes widened, mistaking Pallioti's concern. "I left a note," she added. "In an envelope on the door. And another one on the table, where Kris couldn't miss it. So if she came back she wouldn't think—"

"That's exactly the right thing." Pallioti's smile didn't reach his eyes. "You don't need to worry about this anymore," he said. "You let us worry about it now."

Mary Louise looked at him for a moment, then she said, "There's something else."

"Go on."

"Up there, in front of her parents." She twisted the sodden tissue. "I wasn't telling the truth. I couldn't. About ten days ago—" Mary Louise stopped. In the silence that followed, Enzo might have congratulated himself on winning his bet, if he'd been in the mood, but he wasn't.

When she started speaking again, Mary Louise Tennyson's words came quickly.

"Kristin borrowed some money from me. Kind of a lot, actually. She said she needed cash, and she didn't want to get an advance on her credit card because her dad would see it. So I used mine." She looked from Pallioti to Enzo. "It was four hundred euros."

"Did she tell you what it was for?"

She dropped her eyes. A blush crept from under the collar of her jacket.

"Well, no," she said. "And I didn't ask. I was waiting for her to tell me. I thought she might be, you know."

"Pregnant?"

Mary Louise nodded.

"That's where I thought she went, actually." She looked up. "That's why I was so careful, about what I said around her folks."

Pallioti nodded. "So you think she needed the money for an abortion, that that's what she's gone to do?"

"She could have told me," Mary Louise said after a second. "I guess I'm mad she didn't. I mean"—she dug her hands in to her pockets—"I know Kris doesn't like me that much, even if we were starting to be, kind of, friends. But even so, I would have helped. I wouldn't have said anything." Hurt etched her pretty face. "I feel like I shouldn't even be telling you now," she added. "But—" Her voice began to teeter dangerously. "When she hadn't called me back by last night, I got scared. That maybe something had gone wrong. And with her parents showing up—"

"You did the right thing. Absolutely the right thing."

Pallioti pulled out his phone. He asked Mary Louise for the address of the apartment where she was staying, confirmed that there was someone there so she would not be alone, and called Guillermo to arrange for a car to come to the consulate and take her home.

"My phone?" she asked.

Still speaking to Guillermo, Pallioti handed Mary Louise's phone to Enzo.

"I have to take it now," Enzo said. "But I'll get it back to you as soon as we download this picture of Kristin and—"

"What picture?"

Between their own conversation and the to-ing and fro-ing in the lobby, none of them had noticed James MacCready escorting the Carsons down the stairs. Now they stood only a few feet away. Enzo didn't think they could possibly have heard what Mary Louise had been saying, but she blanched nonetheless, her dark eyes turning shiny with more tears.

"What picture?" Dr. Carson asked again.

"This picture." Pallioti closed his own phone and reached for Mary Louise's. "Miss Tennyson," he said, "very kindly agreed to wait and answer some more questions for us. She remembered that she'd taken a photo of Kristin and a friend."

"A friend?" Kristin's father was extracting a pair of glasses from his jacket.

"He may have nothing to do with Kristin's disappearance." Pallioti smiled. He handed Kenneth Carson the cell phone. "Do you recognize him?" He asked.

Enzo and Pallioti watched as Kristin's father studied the screen. He frowned, then shook his head.

"No," he said. "No, I've never seen him before in my life. Is he a professor or something? How does Kris know him?"

Pallioti ignored the question, retrieved the phone, and handed it to Clarissa Hines.

"Ms. Hines?"

Clarissa took Mary Louise's phone gingerly, as if it might explode, studied it for a moment, then shook her head. Enzo caught James MacCready's eye as he looked over her shoulder. He shook his head, too.

"Maybe some of the other girls would. But no," Clarissa Hines said to Pallioti. "No. I've never seen him before."

Kenneth Carson was saying something to Pallioti, asking when the photo had been taken and what would happen next, and Pallioti had begun to reply, explaining again about the reach of the databases, but Enzo didn't hear him. He was too busy watching Kristin's stepmother.

In the harsh lights of the lobby, Anna Carson looked exhausted, as if she was about to fall over, the effort of walking down the consulate stairs the final straw. It was jet lag, probably. Or maybe just years of worrying about Kristin. Enzo glanced around to see if there was a chair he could offer her.

"Let me find you somewhere to sit."

The words came before he remembered to translate them into English. She looked at him, then frowned and shook her head.

"I'm sorry," she said. "I'm the original ugly American. I don't speak a word of Italian, or—"

Clarissa Hines was handing her Mary Louise's phone. Kristin's stepmother took it the way someone takes a newspaper or a magazine they aren't interested in. She had started to hand it on to Enzo, their fingers were touching, when he felt her freeze.

"Signora?"

Anna Carson's face went blank. Then she blinked. Her features had the confused look of someone surfacing from deep water.

"Signora?" Enzo touched her elbow, grazing the soft cloth of her coat.

She shook her head.

"Where?" she asked. "I mean, I'm sorry—when was this taken?"

"Outside Kristin's apartment." Enzo glanced at her husband, who was lost in his cross-examination of Pallioti. "The Sunday before last. We'll get a stamp," he added, "when we download it, for the exact time and—"

"No." She shook her head again.

Enzo looked at her.

"No?"

Anna Carson forced a bright, cheerful, and very fake smile on to her face. "No, I have no idea who this man is." She dropped the phone into Enzo's hand. "I've never seen him before in my life," she said, stepping away as she answered the question he hadn't asked.

The Excelsior Hotel stood on the Piazza Ognissanti looking down its nose at its rival, The Grand, which sat almost directly across from it. Since both of them were now owned by the same American chain, Enzo suspected the rivalry was, like more and more of the city, as much marketing as reality. The idea made him sad generally. And in this case, specifically—for his grandmother.

Like many women of her class and generation, his grandmother had marked the major events of her life at one hotel or the other. The occasions had been parsed out evenly, shared between jealous siblings. She had been proposed to in the Excelsior's bar, and celebrated the tenth, and then the twentieth and fortieth anniversaries of the marriage that resulted, in its dining room. The fifth, fifteenth, and thirtieth anniversaries, and the lunch to mark the christening of her only child, Enzo's mother, had been held at the Grand. Until five years ago she had lunched there every Tuesday with her best friend, who had also been her bridesmaid.

On the now rare occasions when his grandfather was out of town, Enzo sometimes escorted her to one of the lobbies for tea. Or if she was feeling festive, or annoyed, to the roof garden or bar, depending on the season, for a martini. He had told his grandparents that he was joining the police, rather than going to medical school as they had hoped for him, over dinner in the safety of the Excelsior dining room.

Now, as he came through the door, he was forced to admit that the much-trumpeted refurbishment was indeed impressive. The inlaid marble floors with their clashing circles and squares, the blue insets of the coffered ceiling, and the chandeliers that hung from them, were undeniably brighter. The carpets were no longer threadbare. The mahogany and brass glowed, and the potted palms had been banished. Which, he thought, explained the sadness in his grandmother's eyes. All this polishing, all this chic efficiency, had left the place empty. Denied their shadows and dusty corners, its ghosts had fled.

At the reception desk, Enzo slipped his identification out of his pocket. The doorman, who had not been replaced in the frenzy of updating, had recognized him. The young woman on duty did not. All she saw were jeans and sneakers topped by a leather jacket and ponytail. She was about to say that deliveries went to the service door, or possibly to ring for security, when he placed his credentials in front of her. She looked at them. Then she looked at Enzo, who smiled and told her what he needed.

According to the concierge, when the Carsons returned from the consulate, Mrs. Carson—who had apparently recovered and was no longer exhausted—had asked about the best places to run in the city. Steering her away from the Cascine, the concierge had suggested she head for the Lungarno Torrigiani, and if she didn't mind hills, the Costa San Giorgio. He'd marked the route on a map. She'd come down ten minutes later, in running gear, and gone out. That had been over an hour ago. No, she had not yet returned. But, he murmured after a moment's hesitation, it had come to his attention that the Carsons had a reservation for lunch. In the restaurant at one o'clock. A table for three. They were being joined by the American consul.

Enzo glanced at his watch, then wandered into a corner where he settled on an uncomfortable settee that had a clear view of the entrance. The old revolving doors had survived along with the doorman. They swung at regular intervals like some kind of circus show, spitting the wealthy and well-heeled into the lobby or spinning them out into the gray morning. Enzo resisted the impulse to take out his phone and check with the computer lab, see if they had found anything on Kristin Carson's laptop.

Given that he could he could observe two, if not three, things at once and remember them in more detail than most people remembered their names, he refrained largely because it wouldn't do any good. The police geek squad was impervious to harassment. And everything else. Nestled in the heart of the labyrinth that was the building's basement, breathing their own air, running on their own time, they took pride in the fact that no one had yet discovered the threat or bribe that could move them. If there was something to find on Kristin's computer, they'd find it, in their own sweet time and not before. When they did, they'd text him. Enzo leaned back and concentrated on the doors. He suspected Kristin Carson's stepmother was not going to be delighted to see him.

~

When Anna Carson did finally come into the hotel lobby she was behind a family with two teenagers, boys, bickering and giving each other little shoves, and looked so different from the woman Enzo had seen at the consulate a few hours earlier that he almost missed her.

The unreconstructed male in his brain couldn't help registering the fact that her running clothes, spandex leggings and a windbreaker, were a distinct improvement over the almost dowdy skirt and sweater she'd been wearing that morning. It wasn't tennis or golf. As the concierge said, Anna Carson ran. And seriously. Legs like that didn't shuffle for fun. Her hair was pulled back. Despite the weather, she was wearing sunglasses.

Enzo caught up with her just as she put her hand on the stair banister.

"Signora Carson?"

She looked up, startled, then almost too late, remembered to smile. It was nothing more than a slight upturn of her lips.

"I'm sorry," she said. "Of course. From the consulate this morning—I've forgotten your name." She shook her head in a silly-me gesture that Enzo found entirely unconvincing. "I'm not very good with names."

"Saenz." Enzo held out his hand. "Enzo Saenz."

Her skin was cold from the outdoors, her fingers hard and lean. The rings were gone, consigned, doubtless, to the safe in the suite her husband had reserved for the week.

"You'll have to excuse me." Anna Carson dropped his hand and looked down at her leggings and shoes. "I've just come in from a run." She made an effort to laugh. "Stupid, isn't it? But it helps me relax. All this with Kristin, it's so— My husband is up in the room," she added. "If you've found something I should call him—"

Enzo shook his head. "I'm not here about Kristin," he said. "Exactly."

"Then—" Her eyes widened, and again Enzo registered the fact that, like her skin tone, they didn't match her hair.

"I came to see you." He nodded toward the uncomfortable settee were he'd been sitting. "I wondered if we could talk a minute."

Anna Carson opened her mouth. Then she shook her head and smiled again, if anything more stiffly.

"I'm sorry," she said. "But I'm rather damp. If I don't get out of these things, I'm going to get cold. And we have a lunch reservation. With the consul. So I'm late already. Really, Mr. Saenz, if this isn't urgent, it would be better if my husband—"

"Signora Carson."

She stopped talking.

"It's about the man," Enzo said. "In the photograph."

"The man?"

Enzo nodded. "The man Kristin was getting into the car with."

"Oh," she said. "Yes." As if she remembered, but only vaguely.

She was fiddling with the sunglasses now, turning them over and over, her fingers running like a rat on a wheel. Enzo resisted the impulse to reach out and cover her hand with his own.

"I wondered," he said, "if there was anything you could tell me. About him?"

"Tell you?" Her hands stopped moving.

Enzo nodded.

"Me?" She shook her head, the smile widening. "Why would I be able to tell you anything about him?"

"Because you recognized him."

She tried and almost succeeded, but Enzo saw the shot hit home.

"You recognized him," he said again. "The man in the picture, on the phone. I was standing beside you. I saw you."

"That's ridiculous." The smile froze. "Ridiculous."

"I don't think so." Enzo waited a moment, then he added, "I think you know who he is."

"Why on earth would I know who he is?"

"I don't know." Enzo didn't take his eyes off hers. "I was hoping," he said, "that you'd tell me."

Voices and footsteps clattered around them. Enzo could sense the concierge and the young woman at the reception desk making an effort not to watch them.

"Signora Carson." He dropped his voice, wishing now that he had found somewhere else, somewhere more private to talk to her. "If you're in trouble—" He reached out, his fingers brushing her arm. "I can help you. And I will. But only if you talk to me."

Anna Carson's eyes seemed to darken, to turn the color of moss and earth. She stared at him, still as an animal in a beam of light.

Enzo let a heartbeat go by. Then two, then three. He was about to try again when she put the sunglasses on.

"I'm sorry," she said, "but I really have no idea what you're talking about. Now." She moved her arm deliberately out of his reach. "If there's nothing else, Mr. Saenz, I really do have to get going."

Anna Carson smiled. Then she turned on her heel, and walked away.

<hr />

"I can't do that! For Christ's sake, Enzo."

James MacCready leaned back in his chair. Carefully. In the last few days the rollers had taken on a life of their own. He'd asked for maintenance, or a new chair, but neither had been forthcoming. He shook his head. "I can't just go around digging up dirt on American citizens."

"Yes, you can."

Enzo was standing in the doorway of MacCready's office where he'd appeared without warning, like something conjured out of a lamp. James MacCready looked at him and sighed.

"All right," he said. "All right, yes. Strictly speaking, I can. I'm the federal government. Better than that, I'm the State Department. I can do whatever the fuck I want. Or at least find out whatever the fuck I want. You're right. You. Are. Right. Score one for you." James laced his hands behind his head. "Why do you want to know anyway?"

Enzo shrugged.

"A hunch."

"A hunch?" MacCready laughed. "Oh, come on. Drop the enigmatic cop routine. You don't have hunches, Enzo. I know you."

You don't know me, Enzo wanted to say. *We've drunk beer together; it isn't the same thing.* Then he wondered if it was. He stepped into the room and closed the door.

"She knows him."

The deputy consul frowned. "What do you mean, she knows him? Who knows who?"

"The man her stepdaughter was getting into the car with. Anna Carson knows him."

"Uh-huh. And how do you figure that?"

Enzo looked at him.

MacCready rolled his eyes.

"Oh, I see. She told you, did she?"

"No. She didn't tell me. That's why I want you to run a background check on her."

James MacCready made a face. "Run one yourself."

"I will," Enzo said. "But it could take weeks."

James sighed. It was true. As far as official channels in the United States went, background checks from foreign law enforcement might be dealt with in a day. Or in a week, or in two months, or not at all. Plainly speaking, it was a crapshoot. James swung his feet onto his desk and crossed his ankles.

"So," he said, "you're saying you really think Mrs. Perfect Doctor Wife knows this guy? The fifty-year-old Lover Boy in the phone picture?"

Enzo nodded.

"So why wouldn't she tell you who he was?"

"I don't know." Enzo crossed to the window and looked through the venetian blind. "I can think of a number of reasons," he said, moving the slats aside. "But all they'd be is guesses."

"What if you're wrong, and she doesn't know anyone?"

"Then I'm wrong and she doesn't know anyone. What is it you say? No harm, no foul?" Enzo dropped the blind. "I'm not asking you to dig for dirt, Jim. I'm just asking you to run her details, a routine check, see if anything comes up. Any criminal record other than a parking ticket."

"Oh, well. I'm glad you don't want those."

"When a kid disappears family are the number-one choice."

James rolled his eyes. "The 'kid' hasn't 'disappeared.' She's gone off on a little screw-fest to annoy her daddy. And even if she hasn't—which fifty bucks says she has—the woman was four thousand miles away. What do you think she is? A time traveler?"

Enzo shrugged. With the light behind him, James MacCready couldn't see his eyes, but he remembered they were an odd color. A brown so light it was almost golden. Very weird. Kind of like Enzo. Who, despite the fact that he had the irritating habit of being right all the time, James liked. He swung his feet off the desk.

"How long has she been seeing him?" he asked. "The girl? Kristin Carson, I mean. This guy? Do we know how long she's been with him?"

"Not really. Certainly the whole time she's been here. The other girl, the roommate, thinks Kristin might have known him before she got here. It's hard to tell because she didn't talk about him."

MacCready's eyebrows jumped, disappearing momentarily under his thatch of blond hair.

"I thought seventeen-year-old girls talked about everything."

Enzo nodded. "Exactly."

James picked up an elastic band, pinged it at the mug that held his pens, and said, "So what do you think this is? I mean, what are you suggesting? The guy has a thing with the stepmother? You think we're talking kidnapping, extortion? Some weird sex thing? What?"

"I don't know." Enzo smiled. "That," he said, "is what I'm hoping you can get a line on."

James sighed.

"OK," he said after a minute. "So we have a seventeen-year-old girl maybe missing. Maybe. Personally, like I said—I think that's horseshit, especially since she's done it before. But I guess you're right, we can't dick around with it. If I do this officially—" MacCready jerked his head in the vague direction of the upper floor where the consul had his offices. "Put in a request to run a criminal background check on the stepmother, he'll hear about it."

"Which means the Carsons will hear about it."

"Bingo," James agreed. "They're tight as ticks. The Carsons'll pitch a fit, and he'll ride my ass—start screaming about privacy and sovereignty and due process. He's really into due process these days."

Enzo started to point out that that was ironic, given extraordinary rendition and all. But in the interest of transatlantic cooperation—and getting what he wanted—he decided to leave it alone. Instead he asked, "Can you call someone?"

James MacCready's handsome face creased into a frown. "So you really think this is something? I mean, something more than a teenage girl running off with somebody old enough to be her father because, well, she wants to freak out her father?"

Enzo looked at him.

"Right," MacCready said. "Right. OK." He looked at his watch. "Give me a couple of hours. I'll see what I can do. I'll call you.

Who knows?" he added, shaking his head. "Maybe Mrs. Doctor Perfect is one of those low fliers with ten warrants out on her."

Enzo smiled, but neither of them laughed.

Enzo Saenz listened for the soft sound of the bolts dropping into place. When he was satisfied that the combination lock had reset itself, he turned and surveyed the room, performing the nightly ritual of taking inventory, listing the objects that summed up his life.

A pair of brown leather sofas faced one another, their arms creased and dented from supporting either his head or feet. There was no television and no sound system in the loft, just piles of books, stacked more or less neatly on the bare chestnut floor. Stainless steel and marble let off a shimmery, almost ectoplasmic glow in the kitchen area. A blue plate hovered on the glass dining table. At the far end of the room, the futon bed was covered in a red quilt.

Spidery arms of reading lights threw webs of shadow across a collection of framed photographs—most of them landscapes—that hung on the far wall. Several were by the same photographer, Seraphina Benvoglio, and several others by friends of hers. One, a study she had called *The Winter Line,* took pride of place above the bed. In it, a gravel road headed by gateposts stretched away between the snow-crusted ridges of plowed fields.

The photograph had cost Enzo more than he had wanted to spend, but he hadn't hesitated, knowing the moment he saw it that he needed it. Much as he had felt, from the first moment he saw her, that he needed Saffy herself. Which was stupid, and pointless, and therefore entirely safe. A coward's passion if ever there was one. Because Seraphina Benvoglio was not only happily married with a young son, she was also Pallioti's sister.

He slid out of his jacket, hung it up, and flipped on the lights.

The loft took up the top floor of what had once been a medieval warehouse at the edge of the Oltrarno. Now it was an apartment building, one of several in the city owned by his grandparents. When he joined the police, Enzo had told them that he intended to live, not off of their generosity, but off his salary. They had bridled a bit, then accepted his terms. With one exception. His grandmother had convinced him, finally, to let her give him a home. It would, she had insisted, be doing them a favor—save them the fuss of converting, dealing with a management company, leasing to potentially awkward tenants. She'd had the good grace to attempt sincerity, but both she and Enzo knew that was rubbish. Their only child, his mother, had drifted, bumping up against Florence and floating off again, all her life. His grandmother was simply trying to break the pattern, give her only grandchild an anchor. Finally it had seemed not only unkind, but stupid and churlish not to accept the gift.

It was past ten p.m. Enzo crossed the room and raised the blinds. The night roofs of the city stretched beyond the glass that made up the east wall. On the opposite bank of the river, the Duomo and Santa Croce glowed like spaceships fallen to earth. An outdoor table sat on the terrace, icicles hanging from its rim, surrounded by a skeletal set of metal chairs. The cat sat on one, looking cross. She jumped down as Enzo slid the door open and came pattering in, making her bird noise, demanding to know where he'd been, and when, exactly, he was planning on feeding her.

"I told you," he said. "You wanted to stay out. It snows, don't blame me."

She switched her tail. He'd left food in her hutch on the terrace, but she considered the hutch down-market, a doss house of last resort. Which Enzo thought a little unfair. The hutch wasn't any old upturned box. It had cost him a small fortune. He'd even had it insulated. She stalked into the kitchen, throwing him an evil look. Her eyes, a paleish golden brown, were almost the same color as his. Sometimes he wondered if they were twins.

The cat had arrived almost a year ago. She had come over the roofs, dropped down onto his terrace, and informed him that she was home. He really should, he thought as he went to refrigerator, give her a name. He couldn't just go on calling her "the cat" forever. Or perhaps, actually, he could.

Enzo spooned her some rabbit, apologizing that it was not something more interesting, put the bowl on her mat, and poured her some milk. Then he retrieved a beer. As he reached for the bottle, he registered the fact that there were several things alongside it that could be turned into something enticing. He wasn't entirely undomesticated, and in the ordinary course of things found cooking—the chopping and measuring as well as the eating—a pleasant punctuation, a sort of formal end to the day. But tonight the idea wasn't even tempting. He wasn't hungry. He was worried about Kristin Carson.

She hadn't turned up—at her parents' hotel, or at her apartment or, as far as the police could tell, anywhere else. Hospitals, clinics, jails, and now morgues were being checked. As the hours had ticked by with no sign of her, Enzo had sensed Pallioti becoming as uneasy as he was. When, having finally decided he'd done all he could, Enzo had dropped in to announce that he was on his way home, he'd found Pallioti standing at his window, staring morosely down onto the snow-sodden piazza. Leaning in the doorway, Enzo had started to say something about the girl's stepmother, then decided against it. What he had—or rather didn't have—was so vague that it would just make him sound as if he was clutching at straws. Besides, it was Pallioti who believed in hunches, who seemed sometimes to stare into thin air and pluck solutions out of it, not Enzo. Enzo believed in evidence. Facts. All the boring little concrete bits and pieces. And as far as Kristin Carson's stepmother was concerned, there weren't any.

"She's only a little girl," Pallioti had said finally, not turning around. "She's really not more than a child."

The statement hadn't required an answer, so Enzo hadn't offered one, just watched his own reflection nod in the glass. Now he opened the beer and a bag of almonds and slid a copy of the photo Ken Carson had provided of his daughter out of the file he'd brought home. Pallioti was right, she was a child. A very pretty one and, from the looks of her, one drifting in that dangerous place—a girl inhabiting a woman's body and all too eager to put it to use.

As was standard procedure in a missing-persons case, the photo had gone out that morning to all police stations, customs points, hospitals, and transit authorities. After hearing what Mary Louise had to say, the alert had been widened to include clinics, dentists, and even veterinary offices—Enzo shuddered at the thought, but it had been known to happen. Europol had been updated. The geek squad, after taking its sweet time with her computer, had finally called and told him they had come up with nothing. Having combed Kristin's files, hacked her email and dismantled her Facebook page, they had found no trace of a boyfriend, elderly or otherwise, and no clue as to where she might be. The police didn't have Kristin Carson's cell phone records yet—the Americans were a pain in the ass on that front. They'd done better with the banks. Her credit card history, unfortunately, offered little reassurance.

Enzo dropped the files he'd brought home on the counter, opened the top one, and pulled a copy of credit card printouts from the papers. Kristin's parents had thoughtfully provided her with both a MasterCard and a Visa, neither of which had been used since Tuesday, January 26. That afternoon, however, she had, as the Americans would say, gone hog wild. Basically, as soon as she'd finished her morning of declining Italian verbs and listening to a lecture on the symbolism in Piero della Francesca's late works, Kristin Carson had gone out and spent the better part of twenty-five hundred euros. Which seemed like a lot for a girl worried about getting a cash advance.

Her first charge had been made in the department store Coin. Visiting, Enzo had confirmed that she had purchased a black cashmere coat, a pair of leather boots, and a large amount of lingerie. He had then trailed her back across the river to a boutique in the Borgo San Jacopo. There she had bought a black dress, a pair of black wool trousers, a black sweater, and two pairs of very expensive and very high-heeled shoes. The final charge, made just after five p.m., had been from somewhere called Carlo Bay Diffusion, which turned out not to be the surf shop or music emporium its name suggested, but a hairdresser, where she had a cut, a deep pampering conditioner, and something called double depth highlights. All of which took the better part of three hours and had been booked by telephone on the previous Friday.

Enzo ate another handful of nuts. In his humble opinion, Kristin Carson's purchases read like the checklist for a dirty weekend. All that was missing was a stop at one of the sex shops behind Santa Maria Novella. Certainly none of the purchases sounded like they'd been chosen by a girl about to slink off and terminate a pregnancy. Who took a black lace garter belt and three pairs of black stockings to have an abortion?

No. The four hundred euros she'd borrowed from Mary Louise, which wouldn't be enough anyway, was never intended for a doctor's office. The sex shop was, of course, a possibility. But he thought it more likely that the cash was intended to pay for whatever she might otherwise have put on her cards after she left. In other words, she needed it to be sure that she couldn't be traced exactly the way he'd traced her this afternoon—to guarantee that once she walked out of the apartment in San Frediano, she would leave no trail.

Enzo laid out a line of almonds and ate them one by one,

tossing them into his mouth like a trained seal. As he did, he wondered if Kristin had thought of that all by herself. Or if someone else—someone older and more experienced—had suggested it to her. Enzo flipped open a second file and fanned the contents on the counter.

On top were a handful of printouts Guillermo had put together from a routine web search. Most of them concerned Kenneth Carson's general fame as an orthopedic surgeon who had worked miracles for a number of well-known athletes. One, a profile that had appeared some four years earlier in a publication called *Runner's World*, showed several pictures of him. One was with his first wife, Karen, who, it noted, had been tragically killed in a car accident, and their then seven-year-old daughter, Kristin. There was another with his second wife, Anna, a web design executive who, the caption said, had met him when he miraculously healed her knee, thus allowing her to resume her passion for the marathon. Enzo rolled his eyes. He seriously doubted anyone had a "passion" for running twenty-six point two miles, although it probably explained why she looked as good as she did. He put the pile of clippings aside and reached for an enlargement of the photograph Mary Louise Tennyson had taken with her cell phone.

Blown up, the picture was a little muzzy, but good enough. The time and date stamp confirmed that it had been taken on Sunday, January 24, at eleven forty-six in the morning. Enzo smoothed it on the counter, reached into the refrigerator, and opened another beer.

There was no question that the girl getting into the car was Kristin. Her head was bent, but now, in a larger format and thanks to the shadow of the building, there was no glare on the glass and her profile was visible through the windshield. Pre–Carlo Bay Diffusion, Kristin's hair fell to her shoulders. She was wearing sunglasses, a blue jean jacket, and jeans. Entirely different from the clothes she'd purchased just a few days later.

The car itself was a black four-door BMW that appeared to be in good condition. He'd get somebody to check, but he thought it looked new. The angle was such that Enzo couldn't see into the backseat, or make out whether or not anything was sitting on the rear shelf. He could, however, see the roof, the hood, the blue-and-white disk of the BMW badge, and part of the front license plate. It had not been obvious on the phone's screen, and was not crystal clear in the enlargement, but it was there—the first two letters, the three-number sequence, and possibly part of the third letter. Enzo squinted. He could make out a B or an R. The following numbers were obscure. He'd ask the photo technician to see if he could improve the resolution, but it probably wouldn't yield much.

Earlier in the afternoon, after finishing his tour of boutiques and hairdressers, Enzo had paid a visit to Kristin and Mary Louise's building. Most of the block was residential, apartments or small town houses. But there was a salumerìa a few doors up. There was also a bank with an ATM around the corner. And a Laundromat two doors down on the opposite side. Noting that it was open on Sunday, he went in. Between the chipped blue letters that spelled WASH 'N DRI, Enzo had an excellent view of the window where Mary Louise had to have been standing when she took the picture. It was almost directly above the street door. Going out, he'd stood for a moment on the pavement. It was not a busy street, but it wasn't a dead one either. On Sundays people walked dogs and, shortly before noon, came home from church and went out to lunch. January 24 had been uncharacteristically fine. It was more than possible that someone might have noticed Kristin's suitor, and the car. A big shiny BMW might blend in on the Costa San Giorgio or up at Bellosguardo. In this part of town it would stand out like Cinderella's coach.

Pallioti's officers were all busy, so Enzo had arranged to borrow two of the Angels. The sort of people they kept contact with tended to have good memories. If they got lucky and asked the right questions in the right places, they might just get another letter or digit off the license plate. It was a lot to wish for, but wishing never hurt. Enzo smoothed the enlargement with his thumb as if he could polish it, and turned his attention from the car to the man.

Closer inspection did nothing to change his initial impression. The guy was handsome, and knew it. His suede jacket still looked expensive. His black high-necked sweater, his sunglasses, and what Enzo could now see were driving gloves—complete with open backs and snaps at the wrists—still smacked of the self-consciously slick. The haircut looked expensive, too. It was not quite styled, but it wasn't a barbershop chop. Square, even features topped a generous mouth. Kristin's Dante had white teeth. And he was smiling. Definitely. In fact he was looking straight up into the camera, grinning.

Suddenly Enzo knew why. It was not because he was about to drive off with the blond seventeen-year-old. It was because he was having his picture taken driving off with the blond seventeen-year-old.

On the other side of the river, Anna Carson stood in the shower of her suite's master bedroom on the sixth floor of the Excelsior Hotel. She could hear her husband in the sitting room. He was talking to somebody in the States, giving them hell in fast, agitated clips.

Bracing her hands against the marble wall, she let the water beat down her back. It didn't work. She couldn't get the policeman's face out of her head. *Policeboy,* she thought. *Policepunk. No, Policechild. That was even better. He was young enough to be her son, for God's sake.* She closed her eyes and made him very small and very inconsequential.

Anna bent one knee, then the other. She stretched her calves and bounced on her toes. Her legs ached, from tension mostly. It was the only thing about hitting fifty she'd really minded. Her muscles seemed to be on some kind of vendetta. Going running this morning had probably been stupid, or at least going as fast as she had, but it was the only thing she'd been able to think of that would get her out of the hotel and allow her some time alone. She hadn't followed the concierge's advice. Too late, it had occurred to her that asking him at all had been a mistake. She was rusty, no question about it. Like an abandoned engine, her brain had seized up, willful neglect making sure certain parts no longer worked. She'd had the wit, at least, to stay away from the Cascine. *Never do the opposite, it's too obvious.* The words came back like an unwelcome prayer.

She'd decided on the Piazzale Michelangelo, and by the time she hit the stairs beyond San Niccolò she'd been going a good forty minutes, fast all the way, and her calves were screaming. Driving up the long flights of stone steps, she hadn't slowed but had pushed harder, as if the pain might mean something. As if she could run away from—or at least outpace—the picture on that girl's phone. The tiny image that had slithered in through her eyes and lodged itself inside her like an incubus.

Slowing at the top of the steps, she found she was shaking, and actually wondered if she ought to be afraid. If her heart was out of control and her body was about to follow it. If, right there, she would start to spasm and twitch. Jig and writhe until she died like some poor medieval peasant, racked with Saint Vitus' dance.

Catching her breath, Anna had crossed the road beside the dumpy café, climbed the last few yards to the Piazzale Michelangelo, and seen the city laid out below her. She didn't really know Florence all that well. She'd visited only once or twice, a long time ago, and always, it seemed, in the winter. Maybe in spring, or summer, or autumn, it was beautiful. Standing up there this morning it had looked like nothing more than a jumble of roofs with an inky green ribbon threading through it, a broken maze with no center. She'd closed her eyes, felt herself still trembling, and wondered if she was making a wish, and if so, what it was. Then she'd unzipped the pocket of her windbreaker and pulled out her cell phone.

Anna turned off the shower and stepped out. Ken's voice had stopped. She heard him rustling in the bedroom, then a *whump* as he threw himself down on the bed. In a matter of minutes, if not seconds, there would be snoring. She stood on the mat, digging her toes into the deep nap. Naked and dripping, steam rising from her pinked skin, she stepped across the tiled floor, sat down on the edge of the tub, and held on with both hands as if she might fall off.

"Ciao," Kristin's message had said after barely one ring. "Wait for the tone," she'd added, her voice faux sexy and terribly young. Then "Tell me everything."

As if she could know what that meant. Another time Anna might have laughed.

The beep had sounded. She'd taken a deep breath. She did it again now. Then she looked up into the fogged bathroom mirror and whispered the words she'd left on her stepdaughter's voice-mail. *"Sono io,"* she'd said. It's me. *"Ho veduto la foto."* I've seen the photo.

Thursday, February 4

Enzo Saenz looked at his watch. Just after eight a.m. Perfect.

Kristin and Mary Louise's apartment was no more than a ten-minute walk from his own. He had been sorely tempted to come straight here last night, but only inexperienced burglars broke in when any thump, scrape, or flash of light was sure to be noticed. The hours when people were getting ready for work, or coming home from it, were infinitely preferable. Contrary to popular wisdom, true wickedness, Enzo thought, did not always—or even often—happen after dark.

He could, of course, have followed normal procedure, told Pallioti about his conversation with Anna Carson, and his visit to James MacCready, and his—what? What was something that was beyond a hunch? What did you call something you absolutely knew, despite the fact that there was not one single shred of evidence to suggest that it was true? An obsession? Which policemen were absolutely not supposed to have, and which every really gifted one he'd ever known operated on.

Whatever you want to call it, he could have told Pallioti that he was as sure as the day is long that Kristin's stepmother knew her stepdaughter's boyfriend, and that he needed a warrant to search the girls' apartment without the Carsons knowing about it. All of which was certainly possible, but would take time. Enzo didn't want to take time. And he didn't want to go on the record. Because he might find nothing. There might be nothing here to find. The only way to know was to look. Which was what he was extremely good at, and now intended to do. Enzo Saenz had spent a decade undercover in the Angels. Apart from anything else, he preferred, if at all possible, to come and go unnoticed.

He slipped into the building as a couple, dressed for work in almost matching suits, came out. The young woman held the door for him, smiling, somehow getting the impression that he had something to do with maintenance, or possibly one of those guys who always seemed to be reading meters.

Actually getting into the apartment took, perhaps, another two minutes. Enzo could have been quicker, but he waited to make sure there was no one in the stairwell, then waited again outside the door. Mary Louise had left a note for Kristin, explaining what had happened and where she was. The envelope was still pinned below the tarnished brass knocker. Even so Enzo stood still as a cat on the landing, reassuring himself that Kristin had not ignored it and come home overnight, that he was not about to come face to face with her.

He needn't have worried. The apartment was empty. So much so that when he stepped inside he paused, reluctant to disturb the stillness. There was a confusion of smells. Dry burned dust from the heating system, the mildewed odor of stale food, and something else that made Enzo's skin prickle.

He circled the main room—a combination kitchen and living space—slowly, sticking to the perimeter. Two windows looked out over the back of the building. The shutters were open, revealing silver sky, part of a wall, and a cracked mosaic of roofs. To his right a corridor stretched down to another small window, the one where Mary Louise must have been standing when she took her picture. Three doors opened off it. Enzo pulled on a pair of gloves and pushed the first one.

The room was obviously Mary Louise's. It was little more than a white-walled box, but she had done her best to make it habitable. A pink spread was smoothed across the double bed, two matching pillows at its head. On the far wall a string of lights framed a poster of one of Duccio's Madonnas. Enzo wondered if she had chosen it because it looked like her. Another string of lights wound around the mirror above her bureau. He flipped a switch. Tiny snowflakes glittered and winked, catching a display of jewelry—bracelets, a bowl of earrings, and a necklace—arranged next to a group of picture frames. One held a close-up of a terrier of some kind. The next showed Mary Louise standing between two people who were obviously her parents. In the third she had her arm around a girl. Wearing bikinis, they posed on a long white beach. In another she stood in a long dress that could almost be a wedding gown beside a tall boy who posed awkwardly in a tuxedo. *Prom,* Enzo thought. He had heard about this particular, and apparently vital, American ritual, a sort of combination of themed disco party and wedding rehearsal. Notes on heart-shaped pieces of pink paper were stuck to Mary Louise's mirror. One read, *M L, we LOVE you!!! Have-a good-a time-a in Italia! Mom and Dad.* Another, written in a boy's dark block print over a phone number said, *Hey, Girl, Don't forget this number—Kisses, B.*

Enzo saw himself smile in the glass. He made a quick survey of the desk on the far side of the bed, then switched off the snowflakes and closed the door.

The bathroom was next. He lingered there long enough to examine the cupboards, the shower, and the space under the sink. None held what he was looking for. He hadn't expected them to. He stepped back out into the corridor. He had known somehow that the third door, the one at the end of the hall, would be Kristin's, and found himself surprised that the knob turned easily under his hand. For some reason he'd assumed he'd have to pick it. He waited for a second before he stepped inside.

The air in the room felt thick and slightly chilly. A stale scent of flowery perfume mingled with something that might have been hairspray. Dull gray light fell from the small window on the far wall. The bed was a double, the spread rumpled and pulled haphazardly over two pillows.

Enzo turned on the light. A couple of books were piled on the top of the bureau. There were no notes on heart-shaped paper stuck to the mirror, or anywhere else. No posters. No snowflakes. The only thing that suggested the room might be inhabited by anyone with any character at all was a small moth-eaten white bear that sat on a pillow at the head of the bed. Its chest had been rubbed bald from years of being held. The red ribbon tied around its neck was frayed. Enzo leaned down and picked it up. The stitching on the bear's nose was coming loose. The brass Steiff button in its ear was dull. Glass eyes winked up at him from a face so serious it appeared to be frowning. Enzo heard Pallioti's voice—*She's only a little girl. Really not more than a child.*—and felt a wave of sadness.

For the next ten minutes, he went through the room. With quick, delicate hands he examined the contents of the bureau and bedside drawers, the papers piled on the desk, the pockets of the jackets and pants that were hung in the wardrobe and strewn over and around the straight-backed chair in the corner. He unfolded the glossy, stiff shopping bags that had been shoved in the back of the wardrobe and shook them out. He reached inside the scuffed cowboy boots and looked under the bed, then went carefully through the wastebasket. After that he stopped and stood, trying to think like a seventeen-year-old in love.

Further exploration yielded nothing inside the pillowcases, no slits in the mattress, and nothing underneath it. Enzo circled the room, aware of the bear's eyes following him. He slid the bureau out, then tested the wardrobe ceiling for loose tiles. Then he looked again at the room. The few pieces of furniture were arranged exactly the same way as Mary Louise's. With one exception. The desk. Where Mary Louise's desk was in the obvious place, under the small window that looked out onto the wall of the neighboring building, Kristin's was pushed hard into the corner so the window was to her left and she was staring at the wall. Enzo stepped across the room, slid it sideways, and saw the heating duct.

Bending, he saw that the slats of the grate were rimed with dust, but not the edges of the frame. Scratch marks laced the screws that held it in place.

Fifteen minutes later Enzo Saenz turned off the Borgo San Frediano and headed for the river with a spring in his step. Being a policeman in no way diminished his pleasure in being right. Within seconds of removing the grate and reaching into the heating duct in Kristin Carson's bedroom he had felt what could only be a shoe box.

It was heavier than it should have been, so much so that it had briefly occurred to Enzo that perhaps he shouldn't take the lid off without the assistance of a bomb disposal unit. Then he'd told himself not to be melodramatic. The chances that Kristin Carson was secreting supplies of plastique in her bedroom were minimal. Still, he'd held his breath. Then smiled in satisfaction. The box revealed a dried red rose, several paper cocktail napkins, and a brand-new Toshiba netbook.

The rose and the cocktail napkins he'd set carefully aside. The netbook he'd opened and switched on. Enzo got the password—*Amore*—on the second try. A quick look suggested that virtually all the files were emails. If they turned out to be evidence—of anything other than seventeen-year-old passion and adult sleaziness—well, he knew where to find them officially when he had a warrant. Right now all he wanted to do was read them and find Kristin Carson. Reaching into his pocket, he'd pulled out a memory stick. It took only a minute to copy the entire hard drive.

While the computer gave up its secrets, Enzo made a note of the names and addresses of the bars the cocktail napkins had come from. He knew them. They were all of a kind—large, ritzy in a bland sort of way, and expensive. The sort of place frequented by the sort of tourists who prided themselves on being stylish. In short, a great location if you didn't want to be remembered.

The rose told more or less the same story. Carefully wrapped in a piece of tissue paper, its drying petals puckered in a bud, there had been no point in lifting it to his nose. As a token of love, it was tawdry—the sort of thing that would impress only a starry-eyed teenager.

As he repacked the box, replacing the contents exactly, Enzo found himself developing a strong dislike for the man in the photograph. He could at least have bought her real flowers. He could have taken her somewhere nice.

He slid the pathetic little treasure back into its hiding place, then screwed the grate back over the duct and finally replaced the desk against the wall. Enzo Saenz took one last look around the room, then he switched out the lights and left the apartment.

"Hi," the first message said. *"Has anyone ever told you you have the most beautiful eyes in the world?"*

Enzo looked at the date. April 20, 2009. Ten months ago. If Kristin had replied, she hadn't saved the message. Which suggested she hadn't—because she'd certainly saved everything else. There were almost six hundred emails in the folder. Giorgio, if that was his real name, which it probably wasn't, may have started off a bit rocky—with the Internet equivalent of "What's a nice girl like you doing in a place like this?" but he'd hit his stride fast enough. By late May there were as many as five emails a day, assuming all of them had been saved. Maybe more. Enzo clicked on another at random, this one in early June, from Kristin.

I miss you so much. Things have really sucked recently. If it wasn't for you, I don't know what I'd do. See? You're bringing out the poet in my soul :)

He scrolled back to the second email in the list, sent on April 22.

I am sorry to bother you. I'm not harassing you or trying to stalk you, but I wanted to contact you again because I read the poems you posted on your page, and I was so moved. Your words touched me deeply. I would like to read more.

Your page. Facebook. Enzo hadn't seen Kristin's page, he'd only heard it referred to by the computer geeks when they'd phoned saying there was nothing unusual on it. He'd bet even money some of that "nothing unusual" included an email link, and poetry. Which Giorgio had spotted, and fastened on when the *you have beautiful eyes* line hadn't worked, even on a seventeen-year-old. So he'd tried again. Appealing to artistic vanity, the old hidden inner soul. Worked every time.

Enzo clicked on the next mail. April 23. Kristin had waited a day, but she'd taken the bait.

Thank you so much for your kind words about my poetry. I will be posting some more poems soon. I hope you'll enjoy them.

A day later she'd asked him where he was from.

Florence, the home of Dante.

Before they ran him out of town.

I love Dante! Kristin had replied.

Then I will call you Beatrice :)

Enzo felt a wave of depression and pushed his chair back. Was this really all it took to snare a lonely teenager? Yes. He already knew that. He'd seen it a billion times before. Social networking sites were a mecca, a happy hunting ground for every horny, lying sleazebag on the face of the earth. The last statistics he'd read suggested that as many as forty or fifty percent of the postings were made under false identities. You could talk, all right. You could even fall in love. In your own head. Because the truth was, you had no idea who you were talking to, or falling in love with.

He scrolled through a few more of the emails quickly, then came to one that stopped his heart.

I am so sorry to hear about your mother. I know what it is like to grow up alone. I feel as if I can reach out and touch your loneliness.

It was possible, of course, that Giorgio was the guy's real name. That somewhere in this dismal correspondence he had told her that he was, what? At least a good twenty, and Enzo would bet it was closer to thirty, years older than she was. It was possible that all of this was, if not perfectly innocent, at least not illegal. There was no law that said two lonely people of whatever age couldn't talk to each other over the Internet.

But nothing about it felt right. Enzo doubted it would have felt right even if the girl wasn't missing. The cash. The secrecy. Dismissing his—what now seemed slightly deranged—fantasy about Signora Carson, Enzo thought again of the scentless rose and closed the file. He ejected the memory stick. He needed to get it down to the basement and get the geek squad to take the hard drive copy apart and see if they could at least trace the server paths to try to get some line on who this guy was. Maybe when they found him, he'd answer the phone. Maybe he'd hand it to Kristin, who'd explain where the two of them were and why she was torturing her parents. Maybe there were unicorns in the Apennines and mermaids in the Arno.

There was no smoking in the fancy new police building, a fact that was much lamented, and probably just as well, because anyone lighting a match in the outer room of Pallioti's office would have blown up.

Pausing in the doorway, Enzo felt a pang of alarm, then relief. An import/export case he had been working on—partially refined heroin packed into the legs and lamp bases of artisanal furniture, giraffe tables, and elephant chairs shipped from Thailand—had flared. Between putting out that fire, and visiting the computer labs—where he'd called in every chip he had to get them to put a rush on looking at the netbook's hard drive, something they'd promised to get to, well, sooner rather than never— he'd lost track of time. He had no idea what was going on up here in the real world, but if it had involved finding Kristin Carson's body, the atmosphere would be altogether different. Low, sober, and morose. This was electric.

Guillermo, whose head had been bent far too industriously over the keyboard, looked up and widened his eyes, which were round, very blue, and generously lashed. His eyebrows rose in a pantomime gesture of alarm.

"Warning," he muttered. "All personnel to battle stations."

The comment might be apt, but it wasn't very helpful. Enzo was about to ask what on earth had happened, when the office door flew open.

"For Christ's sake, will you get ahold of—"

Pallioti stopped in mid-sentence, glaring first at Guillermo, then at Enzo. His reading glasses had slipped on his nose and he was holding one of his fountain pens, which was as likely to mean he had been beating it against the edge of his desk as writing down great thoughts.

"Where the hell have you been?"

Enzo had turned his cell phone to mute before going into Kristin's building. Then on going down to the labs, he'd turned it off. The geeks couldn't actually insist that all pagers and phones were killed in their presence, but they gave strong hints. Now he slid it out of his pocket and saw that there were a slew of messages. The first three were from Guillermo. The last several were from Pallioti.

"Never mind that now," Pallioti snapped. "You'd better have a look at this."

Before Enzo could ask what "this" was, Pallioti disappeared back into his office. By the time Enzo joined him he was brandishing a copy of the enlarged photograph from Mary Louise Tennyson's phone.

"I don't know how I could have been so stupid. I should have seen it immediately."

Enzo was inclined to be sympathetic, but he had no idea what

Pallioti was talking about. The photograph didn't seem to have changed since last night. Kristin was still getting into the car, part of the license plate was still visible, the man was still smiling.

Pallioti sank into his desk chair, reached for his pen, and began beating his little tattoo. The taps were so sharp and so measured that Enzo sometimes wondered if they were Morse, or some other secret code known only to Pallioti.

"Well, don't you recognize him? No," Pallioti muttered, staring toward the window. "Why would you? You were hardly even born."

Looking at his boss, Enzo began to wonder if it was him, or something in the water. The computer techs barely grunted at the best of times, and both Guillermo and Pallioti seemed to be speaking gibberish. The most intelligent conversation he'd had so far today had been with the cat. He looked at the enlargement, and shook his head.

"Should I?" he asked. "Recognize him?"

Pallioti dropped the pen abruptly, took off his glasses, and rubbed the bridge of his nose. Today's cuff links were lapis and matched his tie.

"No," he said quietly, when he finally looked up. "No, you shouldn't. But I should have. Before I did."

"Why? Who is he?"

The prickling Enzo had felt on entering Kristin Carson's apartment ran down his neck again.

"Antonio Tomaselli."

Enzo frowned. The name sounded familiar, but he couldn't put his finger on why.

"1978." Pallioti stood up and went to the window. He dug his hands into his pockets. "March 16, 1978."

Pallioti was not quite right. Enzo had been born, but he'd only been two. Not that that made much difference. He knew about it, all the same. There wasn't an Italian of a certain age—

and certainly not a European policeman of any age—who didn't. It was the day Aldo Moro, leader of the Christian Democrats, the man known as the Father of Italian Politics, had been kidnapped by the Red Brigades.

Italy's answer to the Baader-Mienhof Gang, ETA, and the Red Army Faction—their own homegrown version of the left-wing terrorist groups that had swept across western Europe in the 1970s—the Brigate Rosse, or simply BR as they preferred to be known, had been almost single-handedly responsible for the Anni Piombi, the Years of Lead. A decade during which so many bullets had been fired, banks robbed, judges and union leaders and policemen kidnapped and kneecapped and just plain killed, that the numbers were still squabbled over to this day. Fourteen thousand, fifteen thousand, or ten thousand acts of violence. Seventy-five, sixty-five, or a hundred fifty dead. Not that it mattered. The net result was the same. A failed reign of terror that resulted not in some dreamed-of Utopia of the Proletariat but in deaths, maimings, arrests, and ransom demands. Ironically it had been the BR's pièce de résistance, the kidnapping of Aldo Moro, that had finally turned the country against them. And achieved, however briefly, what Moro himself had been trying to achieve for most of his long career—the uniting of the political jigsaw that was Italy.

Pallioti's back was stiff. He appeared to be staring down into the piazza, but Enzo didn't think he was seeing the fountain, or the fogged windows of the restaurant on the far side of the square, or the glassy damp paving stones. There was not a policeman in Italy who did not remember exactly where he had been when Moro was kidnapped. Or what he had been doing fifty-four days later when, after the biggest manhunt in Italian history, his body was found and their failure was broadcast to the world.

The prickling on Enzo's neck was replaced by a cold feeling. When Pallioti finally turned around, his face was drawn.

"I recognized it last night," he said. "Or thought I did. I called someone, a friend. In Rome. Emailed him a copy—" He gestured toward the picture in Enzo's hand. "He confirmed an hour ago. He's sure. It's Antonio Tomaselli. Fifty-four years old last August. Born in Ravenna, educated at Padua. His father's dead, his mother's in a home outside Mestre. His only sibling, a brother, was killed in a factory fire. That may have been one of the things that drove Antonio into the BR, who knows? What we do know is that he was convicted in the Moro kidnapping for being part of the group that carried it out—ran the apartment, engineered the People's Trial, all that. They were never able to prove," Pallioti added, "in court at least, exactly who killed Aldo Moro. He was shot more than once. There were conflicting reports, confessions." He nodded at the enlargement. "Tomaselli was certainly one of the candidates. Not that it matters," he said smiling sourly, "who actually pulled the trigger."

Enzo shook his head. "I don't—" Then he remembered. There had been an amnesty, of sorts.

Pallioti nodded.

"Antonio Tomaselli was caught, in 1978. In 1981 he was convicted. He served twenty-eight years. His behavior inside was exemplary. He was released ten months ago."

Pallioti crossed to his desk, sat down again, picked up his pen and began to tap it.

"None of which," he said, "necessarily means anything. He may be entirely innocent, and have done nothing wrong. All we know for sure is that the girl knows him. Well enough," he added, "to get into a car with him ten days ago. We don't even know if she's with him now. Or if she is, what the hell he's doing with the seventeen-year-old daughter of a surgeon from Boston, Massachusetts." Pallioti looked up and smiled. There was no warmth in his face. "Maybe," he said, "Signor Tomaselli just likes little girls."

And maybe, Enzo thought, *"Giorgio from Florence" was someone else altogether. And maybe pigs with wings would flutter above the unicorns and the mermaids.*

Anna came around the corner without breaking stride. When she had been here two days ago with Ken and the terrified art teacher, she had not taken much in. They had been in a taxi and she had been exhausted. Now she glanced up and down the street and registered the lights in the salumeria, and the coin-op laundry, and the tall rows of houses.

It was late afternoon and foggy. Already the streetlights glowed in dull orbs, highlighting the sleet that ran down the chipped plaster facades and the tracks of rust that dribbled from the shutters, making the buildings look like aging tarts wearing cheap mascara. It was a typical student neighborhood, the sort of place friends back in the States would rave about as "authentic," *which meant "grubby,"* Anna thought sourly. For a moment, she felt a longing for the safe, comfortable, boring suburban street she had called home for the eight years she had been married. For the spreading trees and lumpy sidewalk, the manicured lawns and wooden houses. She pushed it away. Blocked it with the memory of his voice.

The call had come at breakfast. She'd come down before Ken, which was lucky, because she wasn't sure how she would have explained it otherwise. Even without him there, she'd stood up and stepped away from the table, turning her back on the room.

The number had shown on her BlackBerry screen as *Unknown.* Of course.

It would be a land line, in a bar or a phone box, if they still had them. Or in this day and age, a pay-as-you-go disposable.

The chatter of conversation, the clink of cutlery and china rose behind her, and for a split second she had contemplated not answering, dropping the phone on the overpatterned carpet and grinding it with her heel until it cracked and broke, and was silenced to nothing. Then she thought of Kristin.

At first she'd heard only the empty buzz of miles, and wondered if it was better, or worse, this hovering silence. Then his voice came, like a remembered touch.

"Ciao, Carina," he'd said. *"Da quando non ci si vede."*

Hey, Sweetheart. Long time, no see.

Anna glanced at her watch. She crossed the street, reached into her pocket, and pulled out the spare set of keys. It was half past three.

Getting ahold of them had been pathetically easy. All she'd had to do when they visited the school this morning was wait until Ken was grilling someone before she sidled up to Clarissa Hines and mumbled some nonsense about Kristin's dress for the party. The poor woman had given her the building's security code and handed over a set of keys to the apartment so fast she seemed almost grateful—almost as eager as Ken himself to buy the idea that Kristin might actually show up for her birthday bash tomorrow night. It was, Anna reflected, and not for the first time, amazing what people could believe when they really wanted to.

She punched the code and pushed open the front door. Standing in the dingy stairwell, she fumbled for the light, then when it snapped on stood blinking in the sudden glare, breathing in the damp smells of mildew and cooking. The girls' apartment was on the third floor. Anna had passed the second landing when she heard the street door open. Two women came in, their words bouncing and echoing up through the stairwell as they stood discussing the shocking cost of children's clothing. Keys in hand Anna opened the door and stepped inside Kristin's apartment before they even suspected she was there.

She paused, listening to the click of heels on the stairs. A door opened and closed on the floor above, followed by the creak of footsteps, then the low gabbling of TV. The shutters were open in the apartment's main room, filling it with gray watery light. Anna let her eyes adjust to the well and ebb of shadows before she stepped into the corridor.

Opening the door to her stepdaughter's bedroom, Anna Carson felt a pang of something like shame. Long years of habit made it hard to ignore the barrier of privacy, the fact that she had never snooped on Kristin, and rarely gone into her room uninvited, even when she was a little girl. Maybe I should have, Anna thought. Maybe she didn't want to be left alone as much as she insisted. Anna took a deep breath, then stepped inside. The single window looked out to a wall. She flipped the light.

It was hardly the den of a teenage girl away from home and having the time of her life. The room looked like a cell. Or a cheap motel room. It looked like one of the loneliest places she'd ever seen. Anna sat down on the bed, and felt something move. She started to jump up, then stopped when she saw the little white arm. Mr. Ted must have been here on their previous visit, and she must have been too tired to have noticed him. She had only been in the room for a minute, to fetch Kristin's computer and passport. Now her sitting had knocked him behind the pillow. Fishing him out, Anna looked into his frowning face and felt a sudden, heart-thumping panic.

The little Steiff bear had been Karen's last present to her daughter, the thing she left with her seven-year-old—along with cookies and Coke—before she locked her in the basement, drank a bottle of vodka, and drove herself into a tree. *Forevermore*. The tag had been gone for a long time, but the brass button was still in his ear. Anna smoothed the loose thread on Mr. Ted's nose. Kristin had never gone anywhere without him. She even used to take him to school in her backpack, his little head sticking out of the top where the zippers met. Now meeting his black glass eyes, Anna Carson allowed herself to wonder for the first time if her stepdaughter was dead.

"No!" She said it out loud. "No."

If she stepped too close to that whirlpool she'd never get back. Anna stood up and slid open the wardrobe door.

As usual Kristin's clothes were a mess. Things hung every which way. Shoes were piled on the floor, boots shoved to the side. A silk dress Anna didn't recognize had slid off its hanger and lay pooled on the floor. She picked it up, fixed it back on a hanger, and then got down on her hands and knees to find what she was looking for. The bright red backpack with Kristin's initials embroidered on it was part of the luggage set they'd given her for this trip. Anna tugged it out from the very back of the wardrobe and, holding it up, wished it wasn't so new, or so red. An Alitalia tag, from the flight Kristin had taken to get here in September, dangled from the back strap. She pulled it off, then laid the pack on the bed, unzipped it, and turned to the bureau. Opening the drawers felt like another violation. *"Don't!"* Kristin had always screamed. In her room, in the bathroom, even in the changing cubicles at the country club swimming pool. Anna heard the echo, like a stone dropped far away. She took a breath and told herself, again, not to be stupid.

She had seen her fiftieth birthday come and go, but for all that, Anna Carson was not much bigger than her stepdaughter. It was, she supposed, partly thanks to genetics, and partly thanks to the running that Ken referred to—only partially joking—as her "addiction." More than a dozen marathons in as many years had kept her leaner than she had any right to be. Kristin was as tall, and thinner through the hips and chest than she was, but Anna didn't think she'd have a problem finding things that would fit.

Winter helped. Kristin favored bulky sweaters, ethnic stuff. Anna chose two and laid them on the bed. Then she pulled out a pair of fashionably slouchy boyfriend jeans and a pair of camouflage pants. Socks and underwear came next. After she'd made her selections, Anna untied her running shoes and peeled off her leggings and thermal top. She folded her own clothes into the bottom of the backpack, packed the things she'd chosen on top of them, then pulled on the camouflage pants. She found a black turtleneck in Kristin's middle drawer, then put one of the sweaters on over it.

A belt and a scarf were easy. Shoes were more difficult. Her feet were a size bigger than Kristin's and she couldn't afford to hobble. She was about to give up, dig her own running shoes out and put them back on, when she noticed the cowboy boots. Kris had complained after buying them online that they were too big, by which time she'd worn them too much to send them back, and had shrugged and said she could always put on an extra pair of socks. Anna grabbed one and stepped into it. Perfect.

Looking at herself in the mirrored door, she saw an aging, boho graduate student. She pulled her hair out of the ponytail, braided it quickly, then tucked it under a gray wooly hat she'd found on the top shelf.

Satisfied with the overall effect, Anna went down the hall to the bathroom. In the cabinet that was a complete mess, and therefore obviously Kristin's, she found several lipsticks, some gray eye shadow, and a too-black mascara. Anna daubed her eyes, then painted her mouth a purple pink that didn't suit her, or Kristin—or anyone who wasn't a corpse, for that matter. Now all she needed was a jacket. She had noticed Kris's new parka—goose down, and if she remembered correctly, costing a small fortune at Barney's—still hanging in her closet, obviously abandoned, like the backpack, for something more chic and Italian. Back in the bedroom Anna slid it off the hanger. The fabric was beautiful, dark olive green and satiny. She stood holding it, her hand fastened on the collar, suddenly paralyzed by the memory of another jacket, much smaller, but also expensive. Also smooth and shiny. The first gift she ever bought her stepdaughter, almost exactly eight years ago.

It was bubblegum pink. With silver piping and a hood trimmed with white rabbit fur, and personally, Anna thought it was hideous. Not Kristin, though. The minute she saw it, the little girl had fallen in love. Hanging on Anna's hand in Saks Fifth Avenue, she had pleaded and whined and reminded Anna that she had promised, absolutely promised, that this stepmother-stepdaughter shopping trip was all about her, all about whatever special treat she wanted to pick out for her birthday.

Looking at the jacket, Anna had known Ken would have a fit. That he would say his daughter looked like some kind of cheap Barbie doll. Then again, she'd thought, Ken would dress her in Brooks Brothers if he could. If they made clothes for little girls instead of dour suits and club ties for middle-aged men.

So she had handed over her credit card, knowing, even as she did it, that it was absolutely against her better judgment. That she was falling for the oldest trick in the book—the new wife being manipulated into buying her stepdaughter's favor.

But it had been worth it. When Kristin threw her arms around her, squealing. And afterward, at their special lunch—Kristin's choice at The Creperie on Newbury Street—when the little girl kept peeking into the bag, stroking the fur collar as if it was a pet. Anna had known she would shrug off the money, and the crap she would take from Ken, if only for Kristin's smile. Which was radiant, but too rare, and almost never bestowed on her.

She'd been a fool, of course, and even half realized it at the time. But for a few days she'd actually deluded herself that somehow the gift had sealed something between them. That maybe it had taken away some tiny bit of the hurt that had hovered like a storm cloud over the little girl since her mother's death.

So a week later, when Ken was away at a conference, leaving them alone together for the first time, and the school called to report that Kristin had asked for a bathroom pass and vanished, Anna had not only panicked, she had defended her. Determined to stand up for her stepdaughter even as the headmistress pointed out that this had happened before, Anna had insisted that whatever had happened was not Kristin's fault, and that the police be called, and that they organize a search team. Lunchtime that winter afternoon had found her, not at home making Kristin the grilled cheese sandwiches she then professed to love and later decided were gross, but wading through the bog along the Concord River, certain the next thing she would see would be not more golden bulrushes rippling in the late sun or a flight of green-backed mallards, but the shiny satin and muddied fur of the pink jacket.

Which was, in fact, found at about the same time. In a Dumpster, smeared with you wouldn't want to know what, behind a mall two towns away.

Kristin herself was inside the mall. In an outlet of GapKids, where she was nabbed for shoplifting. By the time the dots were connected and her parents notified, she was being held in juvenile detention by a social worker and a cop.

Ken came roaring back from New York, on the way calling his lawyer, who obligingly made the whole thing vanish and charged them the better part of a thousand dollars for it. Anna, having given righteous lectures to both the school and the police, apologized profusely, and went home with her tail between her legs feeling like a hysterical idiot. Which was nothing compared to how she felt that night, when Ken—after reassuring his daughter that they loved her, and that they really, truly wanted to understand—had asked Kristin why on earth she had done something like this?

Sitting at the kitchen table drinking hot chocolate, Kristin had looked at her father, her beautiful blue eyes welling with tears, and replied, sadly, that she was sorry but she "really, really needed a new jacket."

At the sound of the words, Anna, who had been standing at the stove making Kristin's favorite dinner, cheeseburgers, had felt something inside of her stop. Later she thought it was like the moment when you see someone you love raise their hand and understand that they're about to hit you.

"I mean, Daddy, I couldn't wear that queer pink thing Anna made me buy," she'd heard her stepdaughter say. "It was so gross! She made me wear it and everybody laughed."

Standing in the dim light of the bedroom, Anna blinked, amazed that after all this time the pain was still there. Not as searing as it had been at first, but there nonetheless. Like a thorn covered by a hard callus.

She put Kristin's green down parka on, trying not to notice that her hands were shaking. Then she picked up the backpack, fitted it over her shoulders, and buckled the waist belt. The last thing she did before she left the room was grab Mr. Ted and stuff him into her pocket.

⌒

"So, yeah, I saw her." The big man's face split into a grin. "A fox," he said. "That blond hair, it was fake blond—I can always tell— but pretty. You know, with those stripes. Streetlights, whatever. Sometimes they're pink, or even green. Hers wasn't like that, though. She looked like that actress, you know the one? All in black, and her hair twisted up."

Enzo did not know which actress Benny was talking about and he didn't care. Knowing Benny, it was probably the star of some movie he saw in his head. Probably several times a night, on rerun. Not that it mattered. All that mattered was that it really did sound like he'd seen Kristin Carson.

Benny Ibrahim, which was almost certainly not his name, was
well known to the police, and particularly to the Angels. He was
harmless enough, a big North African guy who sold counter-
feit sunglasses and cheap gloves with MADE IN ITALY tags that
came from Morocco. For a while Benny had lived in the Cascine,
which was where Enzo had met him. They'd gotten to talking
and found they had a few things in common. Benny, for instance,
didn't like drugs, and he didn't like men who hit women. A few
years ago, he'd tipped Enzo off about a particularly unpleasant
Bulgarian trafficker. The information had been good and the bust
that followed significant.

Even after that Benny didn't feel real warm and fuzzy about
the police. They tended to confiscate his gloves. But over the
years he'd come to the Angels a couple of times. Personally
Enzo thought it was a good deal. He was perfectly happy to
turn a blind eye, no pun intended, to a bunch of fake Ray-Bans
in return for information on immigrant teenagers who thought
they were coming to work in sunny Italy as chambermaids and
found themselves paying for their tickets by turning tricks in
motorway rest areas. It had been his suggestion that one of
the Angels looking for Kristin have a word with Benny, who
sometimes worked the area around the Carmine. It was worth
checking if he'd been around a week ago Tuesday. As it turned
out, they got lucky.

Benny had folded up his pitch, and been wandering down toward Piazza Gaddi, when he'd noticed a big black car pulled up
on the opposite side of Lungarno Santa Rosa. It had struck him
as strange because it was too early and the wrong part of town
for curb crawlers, and there was no reason to stop there. Then
he'd seen the girl. The fox. All dressed in black and hauling a
suitcase on wheels.

Sleet splatted against the plate-glass window of the café they were sitting in. Tiny ice crystals twinkled briefly in the pink neon light of the sign, then slid away. The Angel who had found Benny had already bought him a sandwich and a coffee while they had waited for Enzo. Now she got up and went to the bar again.

"OK," Enzo said. "So what else?"

Benny shrugged, his big shoulders hunching in the black woolen jacket that matched the watch cap pulled down almost to his eyes. He knew the routine. The details were what you got paid for.

"Well, if I'd known I was looking for her—"

Enzo waved his hand in an OK-come-on gesture.

"OK, OK." Benny smiled. "Like the man said, hindsight is a beautiful thing."

Enzo resisted the impulse to roll his eyes. Benny occasionally waxed poetic. Putting up with it was the price of admission.

"She didn't look forced," the big man said suddenly. He shook his head. "She didn't look like, you know, she was scared. If she had been—" One of Benny's more endearing fantasies was that he was some sort of superhero, drifting through the Oltrarno protecting young women in peril. Once he'd hit a pickpocket who was stealing a girl's bag and scared the girl so much she fainted.

"The car?" Enzo asked.

As much as he agreed, he really wasn't in the mood for one of Benny's soliloquies on the evils of men and the vulnerability of young girls. After hearing the news about Antonio Tomaselli, Enzo had told Pallioti about his visit to Kristin's apartment. Pallioti had heard him out, saying nothing, and Enzo had felt a pang of relief that he had not decided to share his apparently increasingly loony fantasy about Anna Carson. Given what they now knew, it would make him look like one of those conspiracy theory nutcases who thought 9/11 had been planned by the Israelis, and Jim Morrison and Elvis were running a diner in Havana. Instead he'd followed Pallioti's advice and hightailed it back down into the labyrinth, where he'd spent the better part of the last few hours in the computer labs watching the geeks re-create the hard drive of Kristin Carson's netbook and pry it apart again.

As for Anna Carson, she was probably guilty of nothing more than thinking Antonio Tomaselli's face reminded her of somebody else's. It happened all the time. The admission, even to himself, left Enzo with an unaccustomed punch of embarrassment. He was sorry he'd wasted James MacCready's time, and would buy him dinner for it.

There was not a shred of doubt in Enzo's mind that Giorgio and Antonio Tomaselli were one and the same, which made him all the more eager to catch this slimeball—even if he was, as Pallioti posited, possibly perfectly innocent. Of an actual by-the-book crime, maybe. Of manipulation, nasty little sex games—with however willing a victim—and basically of general slimeball-ness, Enzo thought, no way. The emails pretty much nailed him cold on those fronts.

Giorgio had first noticed Kristin on Facebook where, stupidly but not uncommonly, she'd posted a Hotmail address for use by new friends. That was one of the things Enzo really hated about Facebook—what it had done to the word *friend*. That from now on one of the most beautiful words in any language would carry, at best, the hollow ring of false intimacy. At worst, the stink of outright lies.

By May he was sending her presents. One of the first had been the netbook, which had been delivered, not to her home, but to an address at somewhere called Mailboxes Etc., where he had thoughtfully suggested she acquire a mail drop. The emails suggested he'd taken care to do this by snail mail—still the most untraceable method of all—sent to her boarding school. There would be a little cache of letters and cards somewhere,

Enzo thought, under a drawer liner or in another heating duct, probably tied with a ribbon. All of which explained why they hadn't picked up anything on the original laptop. No history of connections. No Hansel and Gretel trail of bread crumbs. The netbook—along with a new email address—and Skype had taken care of that. All set up so they could talk freely. Have, as Giorgio put it, some real privacy. In July he'd mentioned the course in Florence, and sent Kristin the link.

Parsing the emails had made Enzo feel like he was watching a snake slithering through tall grass. A very well-prepared snake. Because it was clear, at least to Enzo, that before he ever contacted her, Giorgio aka Antonio Tomaselli knew an awful lot about Kristin Carson. He knew where she lived, and went to school, and what she looked like, all of which he could have figured out from her Facebook page. What was a little more puzzling was how he had known about her mother. Because he had.

It was skillfully done, Enzo had to hand it to him. He'd let Kristin actually tell him about her mother's death. But, reading the emails, it was easy to see he'd been priming her. Fishing for it the whole time, lacing his comments with sympathy and understanding that was so pointed that eventually she'd poured out the whole story. All the details of the night when Kenneth Carson, who was chairing a panel in Cape Town, South Africa, had left his seven-year-old daughter home in the States with her mother, his wife, Karen. Who, suffering from clinical depression rebooted by a recent miscarriage, had proceeded to drink the better part of a bottle of vodka before, probably in a half-baked effort to protect her child, locked her in the basement with a new teddy bear and a six pack of Coca-Cola and a package of cookies, then picked up the car keys and headed out to the parking lot of a local recreation area where she'd unbuckled her seat belt, got up a good run of speed, and driven herself hell-bent-for-leather into a tree.

The accident had happened around one a.m. Karen wasn't found until the park personnel arrived the next morning. She had no ID on her. By the time the police figured out who she was and that she had a child, Kristin had been in the basement for almost twenty hours. When they finally got to her, the little girl's hands were raw from clawing the locked door.

Reading the description she had written to Giorgio of how she'd felt waiting for her mommy to come home had made Enzo queasy. It had made him feel far more like a Peeping Tom, the worst kind of voyeur, than his earlier pawing through her underwear drawer. The queasiness had turned to rage when Giorgio responded with his own confession. He had never told anyone else, he wrote, but his mother drank, too. And she, too, had died young. When he was only eight. Just a year older than Kristin. It was a sign, he'd said. He'd known from the first time he read her poems that he could also read her heart.

Benny stirred the cappuccino that had been placed in front of him and nodded.

"The car," he said. "Right, the car was big-ass. A Beamer. Black. You know, fancy. When he saw her coming, before she got there, he popped the trunk. Opened it up like a smile. That's what I remember." He laughed and sipped the coffee. "That big-ass car looking like it was grinning."

Enzo tried not to think of jaws, and what they did when they closed.

"You don't remember any of the license numbers? Anything like that?"

The geek squad had promised they would start running possible combinations as soon as they had time. Another digit would help. The province seal would be a ten strike. But even Enzo had to admit it was asking for pennies from heaven.

Benny shook his head.

"What about the driver?" Enzo asked. "Did he get out? Did

you see him? Any idea if there was more than one person in the car?"

"Yeah." Benny nodded. "He got out. He was a real gentleman. Gave her a kiss, put the bag in the trunk, held the door. Like I said, it wasn't like he forced her or anything."

"What did he look like? What was he wearing?"

"Tall. Dark hair. He was wearing some kind of jacket. I wasn't really paying that much attention, you know? And it was getting dark. He was definitely waiting for her, though. He lifted the case in, closed the trunk, then they hopped in and, sayonara." The frothy milk left a line on Benny's upper lip as bright as the whites of his eyes. "The whole thing didn't take more than a second or two."

"OK." Enzo stood. "Thanks." He clapped Benny on the shoulder and slipped a twenty-euro note under edge of the sandwich plate. "By the way," he asked, as he turned toward the door. "I know it was getting dark. But the suitcase, you didn't get a chance to see what color it was?"

If Benny said black, or leather, or canvas, they'd have to think again.

The big man's face broke into its familiar grin.

"Red," he said. "I told you. She was a fox. That case." Benny Ibrahim shook his head and laughed. "That suitcase was as red as a cherry."

⟨⟩

"So, Bambino Mio, how was your day?"

Giulia Saenz rolled her eyes as she spoke the American TV show greeting. Enzo smiled. He plucked an olive out of a bowl in the center of the long table and bit it in half, watching his mother as she stood at the stove.

Giulia had been no more than a girl, younger than Kristin Carson was now, when she got pregnant and married his father.

At barely twenty, she left her marriage—and everything she'd ever been—and took off, pausing only to hand her son over to the safekeeping of her parents.

Three decades later, she was a woman who turned heads. With her cloud of dark curly hair, her smile, and her wide-set eyes that, unlike his own, were an ordinary brown, Enzo doubted his mother had ever been what was conventionally considered pretty. She was tall, and moved with a faint awkwardness, as if her body was somehow unfamiliar. Her features were too strong. Her mouth was too wide and her nose too prominent.

For as long as he could remember, Giulia had lived a life best termed alternative. She'd dabbled in every trend the counterculture of the time had to offer. Enzo wondered if youth had suited her, and suspected not. He guessed her restlessness had been less rebellion than an effort to survive—a way of marking time until she finally grew into herself. He wasn't sure, at fifty-two, if she'd done that yet, and chose not to think too closely about what that might mean. For either of them. Traits traveled in blood and bone. Enzo had been aware of various men in her past, but none lasted long, and there had been no one at all in the last few years. Giulia had never remarried and, although she rarely mentioned him, she had never stopped using his father's name.

"What do you think?" She nodded toward the far wall.

Like Enzo, Giulia had been given her house by her parents. She was their only child and they had never made her a black sheep. Never cut her off or cast her out, even when she had disappeared for years at a time. Instead his grandparents knit what ties they could, one of which was this farmhouse outside Greve. His mother had gutted and remodeled it over the years, when she was around. She leased the small vineyard and the several acres of olives, and had stripped one of the barns and turned it into a studio where she periodically made increasingly large, and to Enzo's eye increasingly bizarre, pieces of what she called fabric art.

Her latest creation took up most of the far wall. He suspected it might be some sort of seascape. Bits of the blue and green felt she made and dyed herself undulated in waves, interspersed with scraps of livid pink, and slices of something metallic that looked suspiciously like pieces of old tin cans.

She was smiling when he looked back at her.

"Never mind," she said, reaching for a bottle from the wine rack. "Tell me about your day. Week. Month."

After a lifetime of sporadic contact and sometimes outright absence, in the last few years Enzo had found himself visiting Giulia, when she chose to be in Greve, more or less regularly. Occasionally he brought one or both of his grandparents, but usually he came alone, sometimes announced, sometimes not. Often they cooked and ate together. From time to time, he simply stood in her studio and watched her work.

He reached for the corkscrew. Giulia put two glasses on the table. Enzo poured, the sound of the wine lost in a rattle of wind. It was a nasty night. Taking his glass, he went to the fireplace, picked up the poker, and jabbed at the big log. A flame jumped and died.

"Tell me about the Red Brigades."

He said it without turning around. A moment later he heard rather than saw her pull out a chair and sit down.

"What about them?"

Enzo glanced over his shoulder. His mother was wearing her habitual jeans, red high-topped sneakers, and one of her own sweaters—what looked like a loosely held-together pile of wool the color of autumn beech leaves. In the shadowed light, with her long boy's legs and half-pinned-up nest of hair, she might have been any age. Or no age at all. As eternal as the Medusa.

"Did you know any of them?"

She picked up her glass, took a sip, and shook her head.

"Not personally. If you mean did I know anyone who was running around toting machine guns, no. But, yes, of course." She glanced at him. "I mean, back then, everyone knew someone who knew someone. Or said they did." She shrugged, pushing up the sleeve of her sweater. A set of silver bangles clinked. "It was the times," she added. "What it was like. If you were young, and like-minded."

"And were you? Like-minded?"

Giulia smiled. Her mouth was the one physical feature they shared.

"Of course," she said. "Everyone was. Well, everyone I knew. Everyone on the Left, more or less, at least at first."

She stopped talking. Something passed behind her eyes, and for a moment Enzo wondered who she saw when she looked at him.

"You have to understand," she said finally, "everything was different then. Italy was different. Europe was different. We were different. The war hadn't been over very long, really. What? Twenty, twenty-five years? And a lot of people felt, well, that promises had been betrayed."

"Had they been?"

"It depends what you thought you were promised."

She looked into her glass, studying the dark inky liquid.

"The university system was collapsing," she said a moment later. "There had been so much hope, and then there was so much anger. We were educating people so fast, promising them a different life. But there was no different life because there weren't enough jobs. The country didn't grow as fast as the promises did. So, yes. Some people, young people mostly, thought they'd been betrayed—been promised a better life, then had it snatched away, when in fact, it couldn't be promised because it wasn't there to be offered. It had to be built and that takes time. But—" She reached for an olive and shook her head. "When you're young," she said, "you don't want to hear that. You just want everything. Now. *Vogliamo tutto e sùbito!* We want everything and right now! That was the Red Brigades' motto." She laughed. "We thought it was wonderful. But it seems so childish now. A sort of tantrum by spoiled infants."

Spoiled infants with guns, Enzo thought. He wondered if that was what Aldo Moro had tried to explain to them—that "everything now!" is nothing but the outraged wail of children and martyrs. In itself the message would probably have been unwelcome, more so since it was delivered from the sullied state of adulthood. No wonder they'd killed him.

"Some people—well, a lot of people, really," his mother was saying, "blamed the state. And, of course, NATO. And the Americans." She sipped her wine. "Thank God we have the Americans to blame. I don't know what Europe would do without them."

Enzo had a quick vision of James MacCready.

"Anyway." Giulia tucked stray hair behind her ear and smiled. "We all quite enjoyed feeling betrayed and hard-done-by and righteous. Imagining we were just like Che, spouting Marx and frantically understanding the proletariat. But of course Italy wasn't Cuba, and the proletariat didn't want to be understood. They just wanted stability, and jobs. So—" Her shoulders jumped under the russet wool. "A lot of shouting went on, especially in the universities. About Mao, and Lenin, and Marx. The usual, really. Then some people decided to take it a bit more seriously." She lifted her glass again. "They modeled themselves on the Partisans, the Brigate Rosse. Did you know that?"

Enzo shook his head.

"I don't know," his mother added, "what the Partisans made of it. I should think people were careful not to ask them."

She stood up, went to the stove, adjusted the gas, and took the lid off a pot. A garlicky smell flooded the room. Enzo relinquished the poker and reached for his own glass. There was nothing remotely alternative about his mother's taste in wine. She kept a very good cellar.

"It was a nice idea," she said, reaching for a wooden spoon. "To play at being heroes. Don't get me wrong," she added. "Some of them, the BR—no, a lot of them, probably most of them— really did want, believe in, a better, fairer society. They just misunderstood how to go about getting it."

Enzo watched his mother drop the spoon in the sink and put the lid back on the pot. He remembered the wool her sweater was made of, remembered the day he had watched her lift it out of the dying vat, limp and dark and dripping like something drowned.

"They made the mistake," she said, turning around and looking at him, "of thinking that just because you happen to have a conviction it's a good idea to act on it." A smile flickered across her face. Enzo couldn't see if it reached her eyes. "That's the problem with convictions—at least I've always thought so—that you have to test drive them to know if they're any good. And by the time you find out they're not—well, it can be a bit late. It's a hazard of youth. Believing." Giulia folded herself back into one of the kitchen chairs, tucking a leg under her.

"That and having the courage to act," she added, reaching for her glass. "A lot of the BR were awfully young. Most of them. That was part of the tragedy. Noble ideals. Courage of convictions. Living the word. I think sometimes about the university professors, who did all the preaching, and—"

She shook her head. Enzo thought she was going to add, *"Who should have known better,"* but she didn't. Instead she said, "There's something terribly childish about notions of purity. Don't you think? That's what makes them so dangerous."

Enzo prodded the log with his toe. It rolled backward, sending up a fizz of sparks.

"Where were you?" he asked.

"When Moro was killed or when he was kidnapped?"

He realized he hadn't even had to tell her what he was talking about. It was like JFK's assassination in the States, before 9/11 all you had to ask people of a certain age was *"Where were you?"* and they knew you were talking about Dallas. Now he supposed that, at least for his generation, it would mean the Twin Towers. Or something more horrible that hadn't happened yet.

"In Paris. I saw it on the news, walking past a shop that sold televisions. The cars in the road. That body lying there with its arms flung out—the driver or one of the guards, I can't remember. They killed them all," his mother said. "All the police who were guarding him. Gunned them down. The others were still in the cars. Only that one poor man fell into the road. I didn't know what had happened, just then, standing in the street. But I knew it was Rome. There wasn't a sign or a caption or anything. I just knew. And oddly," she added, "I wanted to come home."

Enzo felt himself returning her smile. "Did you?" he asked.

Giulia stood up and lifted a set of plates down from a cupboard.

"Yes," she said. "As a matter of fact, I did. It's strange, but at times like that, when something horrible happens, it's what you want to do."

Enzo watched as she laid the table, aligning the silverware. Reaching for the pepper grinder and the salt dish. Fetching linen napkins out of a drawer and folding them on the bread plates. The kitchen of the farmhouse bore no resemblance at all to the rather formal dining room of his grandparents' apartment, but the gestures were familiar. He remembered something he had read in some magazine he had picked up on a train or at the dentist's, a wailing lament about how, in the end, all women became their mothers. The piece had seemed to take it for granted that this was a bad thing. It had offered no opinion on whether the same was true of men and their fathers.

He went to the oven, opened it, and lifted out the leg of lamb that was spitting and hissing. Giulia was slicing a loaf. Enzo set the meat to rest, then reached for the carving knife and the whetstone and began stropping the blade.

"Some of them are out now, aren't they?" She didn't look at him as she asked.

Enzo turned to the meat. Browned slices, pink at the core, peeled away from the bone.

"That's why you want to know, isn't it?"

They had an unspoken agreement, their own Chinese Wall. Enzo never talked about the details of his work, and she didn't ask. He reached for the long pronged forked, picked out slices, and arranged them on the plates. Neither of them spoke as Giulia poured more wine and they sat down to eat.

◦◦◦

By the time Enzo left, the sleet had stopped. Chased by a strong gusting wind, clouds shredded above the twisted branches of the olive trees. A smattering of stars appeared in the rips, cold and far away.

His mother kissed him, then she laid her hand against his cheek, studying his features as if she was memorizing him.

"Be careful," she said, "of the Brigate Rosse." She watched him for a moment, then added, "Not all of them were dangerous, even then. But some were, the true believers."

Enzo felt his mother's palm, the brush of her fingers like a memory against his cheek.

"You won't understand them," she said. "It's not that you're not clever—but your generation doesn't have those kind of idealists. Not anymore. So you won't know them. You won't recognize them. But the real ones, even after all this time, they won't have changed."

He leaned down and kissed the smooth, bronzed skin of her forehead.

"Goodnight, Mama," Enzo said. "Sleep well."

She dropped her hand and smiled.

"Sogni d'òro." Golden dreams.

He was halfway down the path, had reached for his keys and was pushing the automatic lock and hearing the answering ping from the car, when she called to him.

"Enzo."

Her voice sounded like a bird's trill in the dark. Enzo stopped. Giulia stood in the doorway of the farmhouse, the big sweater rolled up to her elbows, the silver bangles catching the light.

"Your father," she said, "sends his regards."

Friday, February 5

Somewhere deep inside, Enzo Saenz harbored the suspicion that, having been abandoned by Giulia, he probably shouldn't love her, much less like her. And almost certainly shouldn't care what she thought.

The fact that he felt all three—and that he had forgiven, and even understood, her—was more worrisome than he cared to admit. If only because it was one more piece of evidence, along with the shape of their mouths, that they were, in fact, the same. And therefore suggested that he was capable of doing what she had done. Abandoning. Running. Disappearing. He thought of it as a genetic flaw or hereditary disease. A tiny fragment that might one day become unmoored and drift into his blood and his organs, contaminate his liver and heart.

It was just past dawn. He made himself a plate of eggs, then decided it was going to be a long day and added bacon. It was a trope well-beloved of in-the-know travel writers that Italians never ate breakfast. Enzo lost track of how many articles he'd read in airline magazines advising visitors to Italy to sally forth in the early hours to the nearest café where they would catch real Italians starting their day by swilling brandy and knocking back espresso before stumbling off to work on empty stomachs. Most of the people he knew considered breakfast the best meal of the day. Many even used a French press.

He ground beans, poured water, and pushed the knob down on his own pot. As he poured his first cup, the cat rubbed against his legs, then invited herself onto his lap. He sat stroking her and sipping the hot black liquid. A second later when the phone chirped and jumped on the table, he was so certain it was Pallioti that he didn't even bother looking at it before answering.

James MacCready's voice came as a surprise. "Hey, my man. How about a cup'a joe?"

James had the uniquely American ability to say things like this without even a trace of irony. Even more amazing, when he did it he didn't sound like an idiot.

"Seriously, where are you?" MacCready asked, before he could answer.

Enzo looked at the phone. Where the hell did James expect him to be at six fifteen in the morning? Out in hot pursuit of drug runners and lowlifes, making Florence safe for humanity? Running laps? Doing a hundred pushups?

Seriously," James said again. "You on your way in? How 'bout we meet up? In an hour, say? Have, as our British chums say, a little chatski?"

Even this early the café James suggested was crowded. Bankers and businessmen milled at the bar. Every time the door opened several thousand dollars' worth of leather briefcases swooshed in and out. Enzo was probably the only person in the place, at least on the far side of the counter, who wasn't wearing a black suit.

He staked out a table, and waited. It was nearly half past seven when James MacCready wove his way through the crowd, his camel overcoat flapping, making him a stalk of corn in a field of crows.

"Hey," he said by way of greeting. "Sorry about the early hour, but I needed to talk to you. And I didn't want Dickhead dropping in. I'd rather it wasn't on the phone, either."

Enzo assumed Dickhead was the American consul. James had a variety of names for him, depending on his mood. Or the consul's recent behavior. The phone was one of James's fetishes. He didn't trust anything but landlines, and nobody had those anymore. It had crossed Enzo's mind more than once that James was lonely, and that the whole can't-talk-on-the-phone thing was just an excuse to meet up for coffee or get somebody to buy him a beer.

"So," he said, biting the top off a sugar packet and emptying it into his cup. "About our little problem."

Enzo started to say he'd made a mistake, that James had been right and the idea of Kristin Carson's stepmother being involved in her disappearance was desperate. Or just plain silly. And either way, wrong. Then he changed his mind.

"Is she?" he asked. "A problem?"

A smile twitched James's lip. For a split second, he looked almost sinister.

"Like I said, or maybe I didn't," he added. "I have this friend. A good guy, in New Jersey." James reached for a second sugar packet. "Anyway I thought it was better, you know, than calling DC. Would look more run of the mill—and my guy was happy to do it. So he ran a routine check on Anna Carson of 237 Monument Street, Concord, Massachusetts. White female, born Manhattan, May 11, 1960. Social Security number blah, blah, blah. No problemo."

Enzo waited. James picked up the tiny silver spoon on the edge of his saucer and began to stir.

"And?" he asked finally. "That was it? No problemo?"

James MacCready shrugged, his overcoat falling back to reveal a tiny American flag pinned to his suit lapel.

"More or less," he said.

"Nothing?"

Mobile phone paranoia was one thing, but dragging him over here to buy two cups of overpriced coffee to tell him nothing was entirely another. Enzo scowled. Which made James smile.

"Hold your horses," he said, taking a sip. "So my friend, he does this check, and she comes back clean as a whistle. Right? Anyway," James went on, "no outstanding warrants. No previous arrest record. Not so much as a goddamn parking ticket. My friend calls me and tells me our Mrs. Blond Perfect is indeed perfect. That's at about six p.m. last night. Our time." He put the cup down. "So that's all fine and dandy, right?"

Enzo nodded.

"Right," James said. "Until midnight, one o'clock this morning—my cell rings. Hauls me out of la–la land where I'm having a really nice time with some hot girl I last saw in high school. So I jump up, and there I am in my underwear thinking, shit, they've found the Carson kid in pieces in a garbage can. Or Dickhead has gone and started World War Three. Or there are riots out at the base because of God knows what, or—"

"But no?"

James shook his head.

"But no, indeed," he agreed. "Guess what? Or rather who? It's my friend from Jersey. And he wants to know what the fuck I'm doing, because he's just had one weird phone call."

James pushed the cup away. He leaned toward Enzo, dropping his voice. "He's leaving the office, right? Closing up for the day, and the phone rings. So he grabs it, thinking, OK, it's probably his wife telling him what to get for dinner or something, and well—" James MacCready leaned back. "All I have to say," he said, pointing at Enzo, "is, You. Are. The Man. You don't just hit the jackpot, pal. You win the whole freakin' lottery."

Enzo frowned. James MacCready glanced over his shoulder. Then he leaned forward, lowered his voice again, and said, "The call came from some guy from the Federal Marshal's Office."

"The federal marshals?"

James nodded. "Uh-huh. Wanting to know why my friend wanted to know about Anna Carson."

Enzo thought for a moment. James MacCready was watching him.

"Like I said," James said, finally. "It looks like you hit the sweet spot, my friend. Because this guy was real interested. Within hours of filing an ordinary background search from a police station in Jersey, the federal marshals know about it. And they want to know what he wants to know about Anna Carson, and why he wants to know it."

"So what the hell does that mean?"

"Well," James said. "That was the very question I asked myself."

Before Enzo could ask if his self had come up with an answer, James smiled his twitch of a smile.

"Think about it," he said. "For a start, it means the search is flagged. Right? Anybody anywhere runs a routine check on Anna Carson, the feds know about it. I wondered if it was some kind of mistake, you know, like the do-not-fly lists, or some screwed-up Terrorist Watch thing. But that's Homeland Security."

"And this was definitely the federal marshals?"

Enzo was scrolling back through his head, trying to sort through the tangle of US federal agencies. There was the FBI, the ATF, the Treasury, the behemoth of Homeland Security, and a host of others. As far as he could remember, the federal marshals were responsible for court security, for arresting federal fugitives, for moving high-profile prisoners, and—

Watching him, James MacCready nodded.

"Right" he said. Then he added, "Look, I don't know about you, but unless you think Mrs. Blond Perfect is a high-value prisoner they've misplaced—in which case I think they would have mentioned it—or a federal fugitive from justice, in which case I think they would also have mentioned it—not to mention the fact that a warrant as long as my arm would have turned up—or, unless you think she's done a runner before giving evidence in a mob trial, which is possible, but personally, I think they might also have said something. Then that leaves only one possibility."

He leaned back, looking pleased with himself.

"Think about it," James said. "It's what the federal marshals are famous for, right? Sort of like the Mounties. They claim they've never lost a man. Or in this case, I guess, a woman. My friend calmed them down," he added. "Made them dry up and blow away. Told them he was doing background checks for a local charity that works with children." James shrugged. "It's a federal law—easiest thing to say, for women—some after-school program or something. If it's a guy, go for a gun license. They don't ring any alarms, you know? Anyway," he added, "my friend thinks it was a babysitting call. You know, just making sure their little Bundle of Joy is A-OK."

Enzo stared at him. "Let me just get this straight," he said finally. "What you're telling me is, Kristin Carson's stepmother is in the Federal Witness Protection Program?"

James looked back at him.

"Hey," he said, raising his hands, "I'm not telling you anything."

"Which means she probably isn't really Anna Carson."

"Or at least she hasn't always been."

"So who the hell is she?"

James MacCready laughed. "Well, if she's in Witness Protection, we don't know. That's kind of the point. My friend didn't ask," he added. "Not that they'd have told him." James looked at Enzo. "You absolutely sure you don't know?" he asked.

Enzo was already zipping his jacket. He looked up.

"Why would I know?"

"Just a hunch." James MacCready's blue eyes were suddenly shrewder than his thatch of blond hair and all-American boy talk suggested. "Same hunch that tells me you think this thing is a little more complicated than a roaming teen. The girl, Kristin," he asked. "You think she's dead?"

Enzo shook his head. "I don't know. Honest to God." He looked at James. "I don't. I don't know what to think."

"So what have you found out?"

"Nothing good."

"This is about the guy. The guy in the picture, right? The guy Mrs. Blond Not So Perfect After All recognized. You going to tell me who he is?"

Enzo hesitated. Before he could answer, James smiled. "You owe me dinner," he said, and turned toward the door.

~

Enzo Saenz stepped onto the street feeling like a fool. He had started to call Pallioti to tell him about Anna Carson, or whoever she was, then thought better of it. Eating humble pie, particularly when you might choke on it, was best done in person.

He broke into a half trot, shouldering his way through the flood of office workers who swarmed up onto the pavement chattering so loudly he didn't hear his cell phone, just felt it start to jump like a demented cricket in his pocket. Feet still moving, he pulled it out, saw it was Guillermo, and put it to his ear.

"Get to the Excelsior," Guillermo barked. "Now. Lorenzo's already on his way."

Good morning to you, too, Enzo thought. If he'd been in a different mood, he might have smiled, and marveled at Guillermo's mind reading. Again. Or paused to wonder how on earth Pallioti could have gotten ahead of him so quickly.

"Is he bringing her in?"

Enzo could imagine this scene, exactly how thrilled Kenneth Carson would be to be informed that his wife was being escorted to the Questura for questioning. He was probably bellowing down the phone to the consul right this second. Demanding that the marines be deployed to protect his family from the depredations of the Italian police. MacCready must have already known. No wonder he'd been smiling. He was probably at the Excelsior now.

"Bringing who in?" Guillermo asked.

Enzo's feet slowed. "Anna Carson. Bringing her in for questioning. Isn't that why Pallioti's—" Enzo didn't get to finish.

"I'm sure he'd love to," Guillermo snapped, cutting him off. "In fact I can almost guarantee you nothing would thrill him more. If he could find her."

Enzo stopped dead. A woman ran into him from behind, shook her head, and stepped around him down into the street, picking her way through a crust of slush.

"What?"

"You heard me. Dr. Carson's having trouble keeping track of his women. He ought to put those chip things in them."

"What do you mean?" Enzo asked.

"I mean," said Guillermo, "that he called here in hysterics fifteen minutes ago because his wife is missing."

❦

"How did this happen?"

White lines pinching the edge of Pallioti's nose were the only visible sign that he was angry. Enzo, who had just relayed the bare bones of his conversation with James MacCready, took a breath. Pallioti dismissed whatever he'd been about to say with a wave of his hand.

"It doesn't matter," he murmured. "We don't have time."

They were standing in the sitting room of the Carsons' suite. Behind the half-open doors of the bedroom they could hear the sound of running taps. Kenneth Carson had excused himself, said he needed a glass of water. Enzo wondered what he was taking with it. Some kind of sedative probably. Not that he blamed him. His teenaged daughter had driven off with a man old enough to be her father and who had just served the better part of thirty years in jail for being a terrorist and possibly a murderer—not that they'd shared this piece of joy with him yet—and his wife had disappeared. In Kenneth Carson's place, Enzo would probably take something, too.

He glanced at the sitting room's unmade sofa bed, the rumpled pillows, sheets, and blankets spilling onto the rug, and wondered if they were a one-off or a regular occurrence.

"I snore. At least I do when I've been drinking."

The answer came from the bedroom door where Kenneth Carson stood running his hand through his hair. The man at the head of the table, the captain of the surgical team who had been so visible at the consulate forty-eight hours ago, was gone. Now Dr. Carson just looked scared. And hungover.

"Why don't you start at the beginning?" Pallioti said gently. "Tell us everything you can remember. When was the last time you saw your wife?"

Coffee had been delivered. Enzo crossed to the tray and poured a large cup, black, and added extra sugar.

"We were going to dinner." Kenneth Carson shook his head as Pallioti shepherded him to a chair. "With the consul and his wife," he said. "Or at least we were supposed to. I mean, I did."

He took the cup Enzo handed him, tasted the coffee, and made a face. Then he drank it down. The winter sunlight falling through the suite's window was unkind. Kenneth Carson's skin looked gray. A night's growth of whiskers bristled his cheeks.

"Annie insisted on going running. She does that." Kenneth Carson shrugged. "She's, well, obsessed. Like a lot of these runners. That's how we met, actually." He glanced up and smiled. "I operated on her knee."

Enzo remembered the magazine article and nodded.

"Or actually, I didn't," Kenneth Carson said. "Not really. I went in and did the minimal then oversaw her physio. I can't do that with most of my patients, or I'd be out of business." He put the cup down. "It worked for Anna, though. She qualified for Boston this year. You know, the marathon. It's a big deal, that's why she went out yesterday."

"To go running?"

It was Enzo who asked. Kenneth Carson took a moment to nod, and Enzo wondered again how many pills he'd popped.

"She didn't even want to come, I mean on this trip." Kenneth Carson looked down at the cup and saucer and seemed mildly surprised to find himself holding them. "I only convinced her," he said, "finally, because it's Kris's birthday. And because it was only eight days. She said she couldn't leave, she has a couple of big jobs on at the moment—" He glanced at Pallioti. "She consults on web design. Builds pages and stuff for corporations. Although that was bullshit," he added abruptly. "About the jobs. She didn't want to come because of Boston. The marathon. Training. Distance runs. All that shit. I promised her I wouldn't bug her about it—she could run where and whenever the hell she wanted. Jesus!" He started suddenly. "What if she's been hit by a car? What if—"

"There's no record of her being admitted," Pallioti said. "But we're checking the hospitals again, to be certain. She wore an ID?"

"Yeah. One of those wristband things. And, yeah, she had it

on. It's missing." Kenneth Carson leaned back in his chair and sighed. "I don't know if that's worse or not. About the hospital. To be honest, she was so mad at Kristin. And at me, because of Kristin. And just because. We haven't been getting along that well," he said, "for a while. So I thought she might have just gone back to the States. But her passport and her purse—everything's here."

"Would that have been like her?" Pallioti leaned forward. "To leave without telling you?"

Kenneth Carson shook his head. "No. Not really." He made a face. "Anna's nothing if not responsible. Even when she's mad."

"But you argued? About Kristin?"

Enzo remembered the way Anna Carson had sat at the meeting in the consulate, studying her hands, barely whispering. He'd thought then that she was just tired.

"Yeah, we argued. Sure we argued." Kenneth Carson made an attempt to smile. "We're married. And like I said, we've been going through sort of a rough patch. Couples do. But Annie's had it rough with Kristin. Kris never gave her a break, not one. Her patience is pretty much worn out. She didn't want me to pay for this year thing to start with, at least not here, in Italy. God knows why. There was another program she thought Kristin ought to go to, in Paris. Or she thought we should send her to a crammer, you know, for her grades, to get the credits. Then this went and happened, Kris taking off—again." He shrugged. "So, yeah, we argued about it, so when she didn't show up—I mean, I wasn't that surprised."

"When your wife didn't show up?" Pallioti had unbuttoned his overcoat. He leaned forward on the stiff brocade chair. "When your wife didn't show up where, Dr. Carson?"

"At the restaurant. Some fancy place in town where we were supposed to be meeting Edward, the American consul, you know, and his wife. They thought it would make us feel better.

It was nice of them. Anyway, Annie didn't go out running until late, and I knew she was going a long way—she does these distance things, and I was mad at her because I thought she did it on purpose—go out late so she could miss the dinner. She said if she wasn't back that I should go ahead, apologize for her, and she'd meet us there. Come on over as soon as she could."

"But she didn't?"

"No. No—" Kenneth Carson shook his head. He reached up and tugged at the collar of his shirt as if it was making him hot. "No," he said. "She called me. At about seven, said she'd just gotten in. She'd slipped on some steps somewhere and she was afraid she'd twisted her knee. She was going to put ice on it, put it up, and stay off it, so she wouldn't be coming." He glanced from Pallioti to Enzo. "I wasn't really surprised," he said again. "She doesn't like the consul, Edward, much. And, like I said, we'd been arguing."

"So you thought she was lying, about her knee?"

Kenneth Carson opened his mouth and closed it. He appeared to have been about to snap at Pallioti, rise like a fish to the bait of defending his wife, then decided against it.

"No," he said. "No, not exactly. I mean, not necessarily. It might have been true," he added finally. "I mean, I know how much running Boston means to her, if—" His voice fizzled out. "I went to the bar," he added a moment later. "Here in the hotel, when I got back from dinner. I drank—I don't know how much. Too much. A lot. When I finally got up here, the bedroom doors were closed and the sofa bed was made up. Annie'd left a note. On the pillow. She said her knee was OK, but she needed the sleep. She'd taken a pill and didn't want to be disturbed. She'd see me in the morning."

"Do you still have it, the note?"

Kenneth Carson nodded wearily and pulled a folded piece of paper out of his pocket.

"You're getting quite a collection of those," he sa'
watched Pallioti read it. "Do you have any idea where sin
might be?"

"I'm sure we'll find her." Pallioti glanced up. Someone who
didn't know him might have found his smile reassuring.

As Pallioti began asking Kenneth Carson about his wife's
background, trying to feel out what, if anything, he actually
knew about the woman he was married to, Enzo stood up and
slipped through the double doors into the suite's bedroom. A
bottle of Ativan, the prescription made out to Anna Carson by
Dr. K. Carson, sat on the side of the sink in the bathroom beyond. Good, Enzo thought. They'd relax him, but they shouldn't
make him dopey. Or worse, irrational or weepy.

Back in the bedroom, he gathered up Anna Carson's handbag. Kenneth Carson had opened the safe. He had already told
them there was nothing missing from it, and Enzo found nothing in it except their passports and some jewelry—a double
string of pearls, a couple of bracelets. The rings he'd noticed—
Anna Carson's wedding band, the diamond, and the large
emerald—were nestled in a velvet box. Only the small gold
locket she'd been toying with was missing. He'd get a description out on the database, in case it turned up in one of the
city's less reputable antique shops. Or as a marker on a corpse.
Enzo took another quick look around, noticing that her running shoes were gone, and decided there was nothing else the
room could tell him.

A moment later, as he let himself out of the suite, Enzo heard
Kenneth Carson describing his wife. And came to the conclu-
sion that the poor man had no more idea who he was married
to than he and Pallioti did. He wondered if the US Federal Marshals, who were notoriously tight, would ever care to share that
information with any of them. Or if they'd all die wondering.

Riding down in the elevator, Enzo was neither surprised nor reassured to see that Anna Carson had left her credit cards and
driver's license in her wallet. Wherever she was, and wherever
she was going, she didn't intend to be Anna Carson. He made
a mental note to keep an eye open for the ID wristband, but
doubted it would turn up.

On reaching the lobby, he pushed through the revolving door
and spoke for a moment with the doorman. Then he set off to
the larger banks within a couple of blocks of the hotel. On seeing his identification, the managers, who might otherwise have
found it odd that he was carrying a woman's handbag, thought
better of saying anything. At the third bank he visited, Enzo
found what he was looking for. Shortly after nine a.m. yesterday
morning, Anna Carson had used the card registered to her business to withdraw a total of two thousand euros in cash. There
had been no sign of it in the suite. The money and her Black-
Berry had gone with her.

The spare keys to Kristin's apartment, however, had not.
When he got to the building in San Frediano, Enzo found them
in the mailbox, thoughtfully wrapped in a flyer from the Laundromat across the street.

Standing in the doorway of Kristin Carson's room, Enzo Saenz
saw immediately what had happened. And knew he was to
blame for it. After he had tipped her off, set her running by
ham-fistedly sidling up to her in the hotel lobby like some sleazy
private eye out of a bad novel, Anna Carson had come here and
rifled Kristin's things. Cherry-picked a disguise so she would not
waste precious cash, or leave a credit card trail by buying clothes
the way her less-experienced stepdaughter had.

The wardrobe door was still open. There was a hanger on the bed, and an indent on the spread where a bag or small suitcase had obviously been placed. Enzo stepped forward carefully, as if wary of disturbing the chilly, stale air.

A gap in the clothes hanging every which way on the wardrobe rail suggested that something large had been in the space. He closed his eyes, summoning the pictures stored in his head, and thought it might be a jacket, a bulky winter thing in a dark color, possibly blue or green. The missing cowboy boots were easier, he remembered because he'd tipped them up and checked inside them. A quick look through Kristin's drawers showed gaps there, too. He fished the Alitalia tag that had not been there yesterday morning out of the wastepaper basket. There was a small red duffel bag at the very back of the wardrobe. They knew Kristin had taken the matching suitcase, but there had been something else with it. A backpack, also red, part of a set, now gone.

Enzo ducked into the bathroom. The cabinet that was obviously Kristin's was emptier than before. Sitting on the smeared glass shelf, dead center, was the wristband, its metal bar with her name, age, and telephone number inscribed on it. Anna Carson might as well be standing in the doorway raising her middle finger at him.

"Fuck you, too," he muttered.

Tamping down a flash of rage, Enzo fished a plastic evidence bag out of his pocket and swept the contents of the shelf into it. Then he returned to the bedroom. Crossing the floor in two quick strides, he slid the desk aside and got out his penknife. The shoe box was exactly where he had left it, which might mean that Anna didn't know about it, or that she knew about it and didn't care. Slipping on a pair of gloves, he tagged, dated, and took it, this time not bothering to replace the grate.

Enzo was so angry that it was not until he was leaving the

room that he realized what was wrong. The pillow on Kristin's bed was empty. He stopped and stood staring at the indent where the little white bear had sat.

~

The church was dark, lit only by dull electric orbs that were supposed to look like censers and the tall candles that guttered on either side of the altar. Which was why Anna had chosen it. Evening mass could be counted on for shadows. Shadows and women.

She'd lingered outside first, sitting on a bench across the street for the better part of an hour. Forgetting to search for mittens or gloves in Kristin's apartment had been a mistake. Anna'd kept her hands in her pockets, flexing her fingers back and forth, although it hadn't done much good, and had been wondering what she would do if her luck failed—how long she could last sleeping rough in this cold—when she saw the woman.

Dark, with shoulder-length hair, athletic, probably in her early forties, she'd walked quickly along the opposite pavement, passing directly under the streetlight opposite Anna's bench, then hurried up the steps to the church. Like a prayer answered, Anna thought, a kiss blown by her guardian angel. She'd have to ask someone if angels still looked out for you when you no longer believed in heaven.

Light sliced the steps as the woman slipped through the church doors. After they closed, Anna counted three times to sixty with a breath in between—long enough to make sure the woman was not coming out again. Then she stood up and crossed the street.

As soon as she stepped inside, the smell came rushing back, darting up and touching her like a child playing tag. Burnt offerings. Incense and myrrh. Smoke, and the mossy undertone of damp stone. Her eyes were already adjusted to the dark from sitting outside, but even so she blinked, feeling the past shimmer around her. When she finally stepped forward, her feet were hesitant, as if she was testing black ice.

It took her a moment to spot the woman, pick her out from the handful of hunched shoulders and bowed heads. She was in the third pew from the back, which was probably where she always sat. People who came to evening mass rarely came on a whim. Almost all of them would be regulars, professionals, or late-shift workers of some kind or another who, thanks to the demands of kids or husbands, couldn't get their daily obeisance in in the morning, so stopped on their way home, doing their duty to God along with the evening shopping.

From her bench across the street, Anna had noted that some of them carried grocery bags from the supermarket two blocks away. The dark-haired woman had one, and a white box from the bakery two doors down. She'd been juggling them with her fashionable short-handled purse. Two more kisses from the guardian angel. Anna slipped the backpack off her shoulder, moved quietly up the aisle, and slid into the same pew.

Having propped the grocery bag at her feet and placed the purse and the white box beside her, the woman had leaned forward, burying her face in her hands to pray. Anna arranged the pack to take up as much space as possible, discouraging anyone else from joining them. Then she folded her own hands and bent her knees, peering through her laced fingers. The little yellow lights over the confessional boxes were lit up, announcing that the priest behind his curtain was ready and waiting to take away the sins of the world.

Watching them, Anna felt time falling in on itself like a badly built house of cards. Living in the brave new world of New England, where everything began promptly in 1776 and moved forward in relentless and orderly progression, she had forgotten what it was like to feel not just years, but centuries all jumbled up and sidewiping each other like cars in an accident. Super-markets tucked into palazzos. Sodium lamps burning in brackets made for torches. Time, life, buildings—all slithered to-gether. Years and purposes playing Pig Pile.

Ten minutes before mass was due to begin, the woman lifted herself back onto the pew. Anna waited a moment, then did the same. The woman looked at her, question in her eyes, asking silently if Anna would watch her things while she went and did her bargaining with God. Anna nodded. The woman smiled her appreciation, then slid to the far end of the pew. The high heels of her boots clicked on the ochre tiles as she approached the confessional.

Anna watched her kneel. The yellow light went out. The black beetle toes of the priest's shoes shifted slightly as the woman be-gan to whisper. Without taking her eyes off them, Anna reached out and folded her fingers over the shiny tortoiseshell handle of the purse.

Expensive leather whispered across the pew. The zip made almost no noise. The woman's head was bent even closer now to the confessional's curtain. Anna slid her hand into the purse, groping past the familiar shapes of a lipstick, a compact, a phone, and set of keys. The wallet was at the bottom. She re-sisted the temptation to look at it as she lifted it out and slipped it into the deep inner pocket of the parka.

Closing the purse Anna stood up, shouldered Kristin's back-pack, and walked quietly to the doors. Outside wind smacked her in the face. Eyes tearing, she picked her way down the church steps, then ducked her head and walked slowly down the pave-ment, every fiber in her body resisting the temptation to run.

                            ᵔ

Now, almost three hours later, she leaned against the padded headboard of the hotel's double bed and unwrapped a sandwich. Prosciutto and pecorino, the original ham and cheese. Just smelling it made her realize she was hungry. The Catholic Church in Italy might not have moved with the times, but retail had. Both the supermarket and the big drugstore next to it had been open until nine p.m. Anna had bought the sandwich, then gone next door for scissors, comb, tweezers, and hair dye. It wasn't the woman's money she'd been after, it was her face.

Graziella Farelli's identity card lay on the bedside table. Anna had studied the photo carefully, forcing herself to stand in the mouth of an alley under a streetlight before she'd done her shopping. In the ID picture Graziella was a little fairer than she'd looked in the church. It had taken some time, but Anna thought she'd made the color match pretty well. She put the sandwich down, hopped off the bed, scooped up the card, and padded into the bathroom. Several of the hotel towels were ruined, but her eyebrows were about the right shape and color and her hair looked good. She studied the photo for a moment, then indulged in a few more minutes of careful snipping.

When she was done, reddish brown curls lapped her forehead and hung to her shoulders. She'd left the length deliberately because when the police came looking for her they'd look for a woman with short, dark hair. The opposite of long and blond.

Don't do the opposite, it's too predictable.

Always sidestep, never turn.

The litany came back, popping into her head as if it had never left. As if thirty years had never happened.

Ciao, Carina. Da quando non ci si vede.

⁂

"Before she was Anna, she was Angela."

"Angela." Enzo turned the name over, fingering it like a coin.

Pallioti nodded and glanced up, his eyes uncharacteristically owlish over the tops of his reading glasses. "They keep the names as close as possible," he said. "Try not to change the initials. Or so I'm told."

Enzo knew better than to ask how he had come by this information. Rome. A ministry. A friend. Someone who knows someone who knows someone. All reasons why it had been both more efficient and faster to turn the riddle of Anna Carson's identity—or rather, Enzo thought sourly, the lack of it— over to his boss. Lorenzo had not only been the most elegant of the de' Medici. He had been the most powerful.

Pallioti laid his hands on the open pages of the thick file that had appeared, as if by magic—not to mention in record time— on his otherwise bare desk.

"Angela Vari," he said. "Born, Ferrara, May 11, 1958."

Enzo looked up. Pallioti nodded.

"Yes," he said. "She's Italian. Or at least, she was."

That explained James MacCready's question, which he'd thought so odd at the time. Enzo wondered again about what lay below the good ole boy manners and silly speech. Pallioti was watching him.

"We need to find her," he said quietly. "If we find her, the chances are good that we find the girl."

Enzo nodded. It still was possible, of course—there was a minute outside chance—that either Anna Carson's disappearance had nothing to do with her stepdaughter running off with a member of the Red Brigades, or that in some bizarre way this was all benignly connected. But neither he nor Pallioti believed it. They were dealing with a kidnapping. Kristin had been lured, and taken, and with every hour that passed, her chances of survival lessened—it was the golden rule in abduction cases. The one that came right after the golden rule that said family members were number one suspects.

"So," Pallioti asked, "do we have any idea where Anna Carson is?"

It was just after nine p.m. Looking out at the city lights, Enzo realized that since returning from Kristin's apartment he had all but lost track of time. Most of the rooms in the new police building had no windows. This was supposedly a gesture toward security—designed to thwart snipers and bomb throwers, and, more commonly, the more ambitious members of the press who had actually been known to perch on rooftops brandishing binoculars and telephoto lenses in order to get a look at evidence and suspects. It sounded good, but Enzo suspected the lack of windows really had more to do with the Black Arts. Architectural design in the service of police efficiency. Deprived of dawn and dusk, humans could stay awake and immersed in whatever they were doing for days. You could work an investigative team to death and they wouldn't even be aware of it.

He, for instance, had no idea how long he had spent with the photo technician. They had agreed about the clothes Anna Carson was likely to be wearing, and thanks to the samples from Kristin's bathroom, how she might have made herself up. But they had argued about her hair, the tech insisting that Anna's hair would now be short and black. Enzo had given in at first, then realized it was a mistake and made her change it. In the end they had compromised and produced several composites, all different.

Enzo had them dispatched to the bus station, and the train stations, and at the same time had requested the tapes from all of their CCTV cameras. He'd done the same at the airport and car rental companies, but with considerably less optimism since using them required photo ID. The tech could think what she liked, but he'd learned his lesson. Instinct told him that unless Anna Carson already had one ready and waiting for her somewhere—in which case they were screwed—she'd get well clear of the city before dealing with the problem of a new identity.

With that in mind, he'd posted an urgent notice concerning pickpocketing and purse snatching on the nationwide database. The victim would be between thirty and sixty, likely female, but possibly a clean-shaven male, and would definitely be Caucasian, no more than five feet seven inches tall, and probably of lithe, athletic build. He or she might or might not be Italian, would probably not be blond, and would have had identity documents stolen within the last twenty-eight hours while in a public space where he or she might have noticed someone carrying a red backpack.

Like the description of Antonio Tomaselli's car, it was vague, and broad enough to be essentially useless. But combined with the composites, it might be enough for them to get lucky. Not that Enzo was optimistic. He had a bad feeling about Anna Carson. Or Angela Vari. Or whoever the hell she was now. Maybe, he thought ruefully, that was what had alerted him, what he had recognized in her. The chameleon gene. The blank space of a fellow shape-changer.

"No." He leaned back on the appallingly uncomfortable but very stylish black leather sofa that had come as part of Pallioti's new office. "No," he said again. "We have no idea where she is." Enzo felt his sneakered foot begin to tap, and looked out of the window. "She could be anywhere."

Pallioti watched him. "Well," he said finally, "you're right, of course. She could be. Angela Vari could indeed, be anywhere. But officially she's dead."

Pallioti leafed through several of the file's pages until he found the one he wanted. He held it up. "She died in an accident. In prison. A fall down stairs, I believe. In December 1980." He peered at the paper. "Yes, that's right. While being escorted from the physical recreation area in the isolation block on Tuesday, December the ninth. It says here that she slipped."

"How very convenient."

Pallioti smiled. The expression was not full of warmth. "Oh, yes," he agreed. "Very. So much so, in fact, that other than the guard who was with her, there were no witnesses."

"Really?"

"Absolutely. And by that time Angela Vari had no family either. Her mother died when she was born. Her father, who raised her, was gone. No aunts, uncles, and cousins to speak of. So there wasn't exactly an outcry. A brief piece appeared in the papers and the body was cremated."

"Convenient again."

"*Cèrto.*"

Pallioti took his glasses off, picked up his pen, and tapped it on the edge of his blotter.

"They probably called it Operation Lazarus," he said. "Or something like that. It's expensive," he added a second later. "That kind of magic trick. But I gather that in this case, enough of the right people thought it necessary. Have the fingerprints come back?"

Enzo shook his head. They had dusted all the makeup samples and sent a team to the apartment. Pallioti shrugged.

"They will. The only thing that might be interesting is if anyone else was there."

"They weren't."

"No," Pallioti said. "I don't think so, either."

He stood up and walked to the window. He had rolled up his shirtsleeves. With bare forearms and without his cuff links, he looked strangely naked. The thin gold face of the watch his sister had given to him glinted on his wrist. Pallioti complained frequently that it was finicky and Swiss and hard to read, but Enzo had never seen him without it.

"Angela Vari's mother was an American. She worked here, in repatriation, for the Red Cross, after the war. Fell in love, got married, stayed. It was enough, apparently, to convince the

Americans to take Angela—the fact that her mother was a citizen. And they owed us some favors."

Pallioti spoke without turning around, still staring down at the piazza.

"Angela spoke fluent English. Her father kept it going at home after her mother died and she studied it in school. So that made it easier." He glanced over his shoulder. "Our friend at the consulate was right. After she was cremated in December 1980, she was enrolled in the US Federal Witness Protection Program. She arrived in the United States in January, 1981. So, voilà!"

He turned around.

"Her accent is brushed up, a few years are peeled off her age, and Angela Vari becomes Anna Vanetti. They gave her an Italian family background, got her a place in a college in Boston, and, well—" Pallioti spread his elegant hands. "Really, she never looked back. I suppose you could say, death became her. Arguably better than her previous life." He smiled at his own little joke.

"Anna Vanetti was an excellent student," he went on. "She got a scholarship to graduate school, worked for a consultancy in small business development, and eventually started her own company. AV Design. Which became AVC design when she married Dr. Kenneth Carson in June 2001. First marriage for her, second for him. No natural children, one stepdaughter, Kristin. Like all protected witnesses, Anna has an emergency number. She's never called it, not once in thirty years. In fact," he added, leaning against the window ledge and crossing his ankles, "I'm almost surprised she's still on their radar. But that's one of the strengths of their program." He regarded his shoes for a moment. "It's one of the reasons the Americans are so successful with this. The rules are draconian, but once you agree to go into the Witness Protection Program, they agree to protect you. Forever. In Anna Vanetti's case it hasn't been necessary. She never put a foot wrong." He looked at Enzo. "Until now. Or not," he added. "As the case may be."

"You haven't told me why," Enzo said. "Why they went to all that trouble, all that expense. To make Angela Vari disappear. Why was she so important?"

Pallioti smiled one of his non-smiles.

"She was a high-value witness," he said. "It was 1980."

Enzo felt the unpleasant prickling again, as if someone was rubbing sandpaper down his arm, and realized he knew the answer. He wondered if he'd known it the second Pallioti had told him who Antonio Tomaselli was. Wondered if that was who he had really been asking Giulia about last night—not Tomaselli at all, but the woman he had faced, touched, stood so close to that he had seen the flecks in her eyes and smelled, under sweat, the faint woody scent of her perfume.

You won't recognize them, his mother had said. And she had been right.

"That was the thing that was so difficult about the Red Brigades." Pallioti pushed himself off the window ledge and returned to his chair. "You have to understand this, because it's important. And because we didn't, at the time. You see, the BR weren't like the other left-wing groups. They weren't a personality cult like the Baader-Meinhofs, or some bunch of tatty students living in squats and occasionally killing people. They were disciplined. And their security was very, very good. Excellent. They were extremely professional." He shook his head. "If we'd really understood that, if we'd really known—"

Pallioti took his glasses off and pinched the bridge of his nose. He'd been junior, only beginning his career in the police. Even so the weight was personal. Enzo could see it. And hear the unspoken words that hung in room. *If we had really understood that, if we'd really known how good they were, taken them more seriously, Aldo Moro might still be alive.*

"So this wasn't some long-haired bunch of left-wing junkies." Pallioti picked up his pen, stared at it, and put it down again. "They understood keeping cover. They knew how to fit in and how important it was to do it. They weren't on an ego trip. They looked completely ordinary, even boring, and they behaved completely normally—no fireworks, no showing off—and, yes, some of them did have girlfriends, boyfriends, lovers, whatever, who had no idea what the hell they were doing. It's the perfect cover. Nobody was hanging around boasting in bars. They even published a manual, with instructions, detailed ones, on how to keep their houses, and how to leave for work at eight, and come back at five, how to keep their cars registered, and not throw parties, and be sure to obey traffic rules and stop for red lights. They worked in cells," he added. "Strictly on a need-to-know basis. It was one of the reasons they were virtually impossible to infiltrate." Pallioti shrugged. "It's so simple and so few people actually have the discipline to do it. If you never tell—"

It was one of acknowledged wonders of policing that most people—virtually all of them, in fact—simply had to spill, sooner or later, to someone. Forget forensics and clues and evidence, the human ego needed to talk. Blab. Confess. It was yet another universal truth the Catholic Church had cottoned onto a long time ago. The rare ones who had the discipline not to do it were almost impossible to crack.

"There was one effort, early on," Pallioti said, "at infiltrating them. It was marginally successful, but only marginally, and it never happened again. They learned the lesson and got even tighter and after that, the security services got nowhere. They could never put anyone inside the Brigate Rosse. That," he said, looking at Enzo, "was what made Angela Vari so valuable."

"She was an informant?"

"Not quite. Although some people did think she was a hero.

Others thought she was nothing but a duplicitous liar, playing the system when it was most vulnerable."

"Why?"

"Because she didn't come forward until after Moro was dead. And—" Pallioti stopped talking and stared out of the window. Light spangled the dark glass. "Well," Pallioti said finally, "the upside was, that when she did, come forward, she gave them Tomaselli. Without Angela Vari, they wouldn't have got him. When they did, that led to others. And to the apartment where they'd kept Moro, the People's Prison. The whole thing. It all unraveled very fast after that."

Enzo knew what he'd just heard, but he asked the question anyway, if only to hear the words out loud. "You are saying that she knew Antonio Tomaselli, and that she was inside the Moro kidnapping?"

Pallioti nodded.

Enzo gave a low whistle. This really was manna from heaven. No wonder they'd gone all-out to protect her. An informant like that would be, literally, worth her weight in gold. "So I don't get it," he asked. "What was the downside?"

Even as he said it, Enzo felt the prickle again and realized it didn't matter, because he already knew the answer.

Pallioti turned to him. "Angela claimed she wasn't one of them. She claimed she didn't know, had no idea, to begin with anyway, what Tomaselli was doing. What, or who, he was. But—"

He swung back toward the window. The pen beat a sharp little tattoo on the sill then stopped.

"But?"

"But some people just didn't buy it, because what made Angela Vari so valuable also made her suspect. She was Tomaselli's girlfriend. More than that." Pallioti looked back at Enzo. "They were living together," he said. "They were lovers. They had been for a long time. I gather since they were very young. She was, I suppose you might say, the Juliet to his Romeo."

Or, Enzo thought, *the Lady to his Macbeth.* He stood up.

"So has she gone to look for him? Or to join him?"

Pallioti shook his head. "I don't know. Until we know why Tomaselli's taken the girl, we won't know. We've isolated Dr. Carson, by the way, MacCready's babysitting him, and we have a team in the suite and in the hotel in case either Tomaselli or Angela Vari make contact, which one of them will—unless Tomaselli goes directly to the media, in which case—"

Neither of them wanted to think about the "in which case," about the shit storm that would descend if it hit the news that Red Brigades were not only not dead, but up and running again.

"If Tomaselli has already made contact with Angela, which he probably has"—they both thought of the missing BlackBerry—"then she's either gone to join him, meaning this was all preplanned, or she's acting on her own to get Kristin back. Why she'd do that, I have no idea. What I do know," Pallioti said, "is that, either way, she's the only lead we have, so you are going to find her. And find her quietly and fast, while we still have a hope in hell of controlling this. I don't need to tell you that if it goes public, the stakes go up, and everyone loses."

Enzo did not need to ask if the arrangement was only between the two of them.

"How you do it, and what you think about it," Pallioti said, "is up to you." His smile twitched. "Call me a cynic," he added, "but, personally, I find it hard to believe that out of all the teenagers in America, Antonio Tomaselli happened to pick Angela Vari's stepdaughter by coincidence."

Enzo was already on his feet. Pallioti placed his hands on the pile of papers that covered his desk as if he could stop the past leaking back into the present.

"One more thing," he said. "There were people, back then,

who blamed her, Angela, personally, for Moro's death. Intelligent people, who never trusted her—magistrates, police, even some of the psychiatrists, who were sure she was playing a double hand. Who thought she was that good."

He held Enzo's eye for a moment, then began squaring the papers. "So not prosecuting her was controversial," he said. "But the doubters lost the argument. They needed her. Then the Red Brigades starting killing witnesses, and even the jails weren't safe, so they made Angela Vari disappear. They had a code name for her," he added. "They called her the Butcher's Daughter. I don't know why. I haven't had time to read this, but I'm assured it's all here. Everything. Her past. This," Pallioti said, sliding the file toward Enzo, "is how you'll find her."

Part II

Ferrara, 1965

THE FIRST TIME ANGELA saw Antonio she was seven years old and thought he was a leopard.

"Are you hiding?"

His voice comes out of nowhere, like the Cheshire Cat's. Angela opens her eyes. He is standing above her, the long grass coming almost to his knees, almost to the bottom of the short trousers all the little boys wear in the summer.

She knows, of course, who he is. Ferrara is a small place, so everyone knows who everyone is. And Antonio is new, which makes him an object of special interest. So Angela knows that he is two years older than she is, and that he has a brother who is two years older than that, and that his family has moved from the country so his father can work in one of the new factories. She knows, too, that they live in one of the buildings that have been put up specially for people like them on the far side of the Darsena, the old port where the Po used to run before it changed its mind and meandered away like a senile relative.

Those buildings are taller than any in the old city, except for the bell tower, and even though they're not supposed to, Angela and her friends have gone to see them. They've stood clutching each other's sleeves and giggling because they're forbidden to wander outside their neighborhood, much less outside the city walls, and because the buildings are ugly. Gray and made of dirty-colored concrete and glass, the apartments in them are stacked one above the other like shoe boxes. Each has a tiny balcony where laundry loops from metal railings and flaps in the wind.

Angela blinks at the memory. She can feel spots of sun and shade on her face, and the prickle of grass through the thin material of her summer dress.

"No," she replies. Although it isn't true, because of course she's hiding.

It's a Sunday, one of the last August afternoons before school starts and autumn brings the first whisper of winter—foggy mornings and sharp nights and early reports of frost in the hills—and they've come out to the orchard, a group of children and an assortment of aunts and uncles and fathers and mothers and someone's grandfather in the back of Signor Pirotti's truck, to help with the picking. Trestle tables have been set up between the avenues of trees and all the other girls have gone off to pick flowers to make into necklaces, or hold under your chin to see if you like butter.

Angela thinks that's stupid. Everyone knows it's just a smudge of yellow and has nothing to do with butter. So she's rambled off and lain down in the shade. Closed her eyes and listened to the shouts of the boys' ball game, and the rise and fall of the adults' voices as they unpack the food. She's half asleep, drifting on the smell of the fruit trees and the low throb of Signor Pirotti's bees that live in the hives by the gate, when she hears his voice.

"What's your name?" Antonio asks.

His eyes are dark as wet stones. He looks at her like she's something he's found—a forked stick for slingshots, or a squished garter snake. Leopard light falls through the leaves and into his black hair.

"Angela," Angela says, and he nods.

"You're the butcher's daughter."

Since it really isn't a question, Angela doesn't answer. Although she does wonder what he's heard, because it's strange to have only a father and have your mother be dead. It hangs around you like a smell, and there is always the suspicion you might pass it on, like the flu, and make other mothers die. Angela knows some of her friends whisper. They say her mother touched her going out of the world as she came into it and left a thumbprint in some private place. She's heard there are bets. About lifting up her dress.

But Antonio doesn't ask to look, or lean down and grab at her hem. Instead he says, "The butcher's daughter," again, as if he likes the sound of it. Then he whips his hand from behind his back and gives her an apple.

It's not a big one. In fact, it's tiny and there's something wrong with it because it's fallen off the tree too soon and has little black spots on it, and Angela knows if she bites it, it will feel like chalk on her teeth. But she keeps it anyway. It rides home in her pocket, jumping against her thigh, and when she gets to her bedroom, she puts it on the windowsill.

At night the apple changes. It catches the light from the street lamp and the dark spots vanish and it seems to grow. To swell until, from where she lies in bed, Angela thinks it looks not like an apple at all but like something from one of the fairy stories her father sometimes reads her. Rocking on the edge of dreams, she half expects its skin to split and release a tiny winged person. Or a jewel. Or at the very least, a wish.

When, after three weeks, the apple begins to grow soft and wizen and look like the face of the old man who sells newspapers in the kiosk by the cathedral, Angela refuses to throw it away. It spawns a halo of fruit flies, and still she won't get rid of it. Her father indulges her. But not Nonna Franchi, who is not really her grandmother at all, but the old lady who comes to clean the apartment, to sweep the floors and bang the rugs and polish the heavy brown furniture with beeswax and linseed oil. Nonna Franchi survived the Nazis. The apple doesn't have a chance.

So Angela is not surprised when she comes home from school one day and finds the sill empty.

Even so she stands for a moment, looking at the spot where it sat, where the stickiness has been rubbed away, and feels a kind of hollow in her stomach. Then she closes her eyes, and under the sharp tang of the vinegar and lemon juice Nonna Franchi uses to clean the windows, she can smell the memory of August.

The apartment where Angela lives with her father has five rooms and is on the second floor of a house in the Via Vittoria, which is in the ghetto and only a few steps from the Spanish Synagogue that was built for the Jews when Duke Ercole d'Este, who was good and kind, invited them to come to Ferrara after they had been expelled from Spain by King Ferdinand and Queen Isabella, who were not good and kind.

Angela knows this because she learns about it in school. Where she also learns how the Nazis ruined the synagogue. How everyone was too afraid of them to say anything to stop them, so they smashed everything inside and put chains across the door. This story makes her worry about the Jews. Sometimes, putting her key in her own door, she looks over her shoulder at the padlock on the synagogue's door and at its shuttered windows, and thinks that the ghosts of the Jews are locked out and have nowhere to go. Other times she's sure she sees them. Gathered at the corner, or walking just ahead as she comes down the street, the soles of their shoes shuffling on the cobbles.

One day her teacher—who is new that year, and young and blond and pretty—reads, as part of a lesson, the Sh'ma Yisrael, the most important Jewish prayer. "Hear, Oh Israel. The Lord is Our God. The Lord is One." She recites standing in front of the class in her blue skirt and white blouse. Then she explains that it is said first thing in the morning and the last thing said at night. And that it is the prayer of beseeching, and of martyrs. And that it is always on the lips of the dying.

Angela is only vaguely aware of martyrs, and has no idea what beseeching is. But she remembers the words, and wonders if they were on her mother's lips when she died. If she said them before, or after, or at the same time that she whispered, "Angela." And from then on, the prayer echoes in her head like bells.

The words call her at sunset, and again at dawn. Sometimes she hears them in the rustling of the birds in the eaves, or in the clack and rattle of shutters opening and closing down the street, or in the low muttering of the wind as it kicks lost paper along the pavements.

"Papa, are we Jewish?"

Angela asks this one night, knowing full well the answer is no, but still half hoping it will be yes, although she is not quite sure why. Perhaps because they never go to mass. She is taken sometimes by the Ravallis downstairs, or by Nonna Franchi, who fears for her soul. But she does not go with her father. They never lean duck-toed, clutching a rosary, or have their foreheads smudged with ashes. So at least if they were Jewish, it would explain why, and mean they are something.

But as she knows he will, her father shakes his head. Confirming their nothingness, he runs his hand across the top of her hair the way he always does, and says, "No, Kitten."

"Then why do we have this apartment?"

From where she lies on the knobbly carpet, a book open in front of her, her father looks huge. Sitting in his armchair, he looks like a giant in a story.

"Why do we live in the ghetto?"

Angela knows that for some reason she shouldn't persist with this, but she does anyway, and for a moment she thinks her father's answering smile, which takes longer than usual to come, is sad. Which is strange because her father never looks sad.

"Because lots of people live in the ghetto now, Kitten," he says, finally. "Not just Jews. This apartment belonged to your grandpa."

"But why? If we're not Jewish?"

Her father regards her for a moment.

"It was the war," he says finally. "People needed places to live. They just needed a place to live."

Angela nods. This seems reasonable enough. But in some way she does not quite understand, it doesn't answer her question.

Her father got the apartment with the brown furniture and the knobbly rugs and the blue brocade sofa no one ever sits on after her grandparents died and before she was born and at the same time he inherited the butcher's shop on Via Carlo Mayr. Angela knows all about it. And knows, too, that he and her mother never intended to stay. Because they had big plans.

After they got married, Angela's mother, Annabeth Who Was Good with Numbers, kept the books and started setting aside money to open a second butcher's shop, one with what she called a deli counter, for sandwiches and cheeses and salamis. Then, after they had taken Ferrara by storm, conquered it with American-style corned beef and pastrami, her parents planned to open a third, and even a fourth shop in other towns. And after that, they would have so much money that they would rent out the apartment in the ghetto and move beyond the city walls, or up to one of the newer houses near the Angels' Gate where the streets are wide and have trees.

Angela's mother missed trees. As he tucked Angela in, plumping the pillow with his chapped hands and squaring the edge of the blanket, her father told her that on the street where her mother was born, the trees were huge. They grew high as houses, and spread like giant umbrellas, and in the autumn their leaves turned as red as rubies.

Angela didn't really believe him, at least about the rubies. But as she grew older and was allowed to go on errands alone, she found herself drawn toward the Angels' Gate. Like all children in Ferrara, she knew that it was one of five gates in the city walls, and the only one whose doors were always closed, and that they had been that way for almost three hundred years. Because when the last Este dukes were banished by the pope, when their carriage—windows curtained so they could look no more upon their city—had trundled down Corso d'Este for the last time, the doors of the Angels' Gate had swung shut behind it. And the townspeople had locked them. And sealed them with tears. And vowed never to open them again, because their dukes were gone.

Walking toward the gate, Angela felt herself growing smaller and smaller. The noise of the ghetto and the crowds in the piazzas fell away as she left the Castello behind her, and passed the Questura, and the palazzo opposite where the little fat boys sat holding the portico on their shoulders, their dimpled legs dancing in the air. Beyond the Diamante with its strange triangular stones, and the Parco Massari where adults rubbed the nose of Verdi's statue and children were not supposed to run, the silence deepened until finally all she could hear was the slap and click of her shoes on the pavement that had begun to buckle and become slippery with leaves because of the trees.

The Angels' Gate itself was crumbling, but the houses below it looked new. Or at least new compared to the houses in the ghetto. Some sat in gardens ringed by fences. If no one was around—and it seemed no one ever was—Angela would cross the road and peer through the iron railings and tell herself that her mother lived there, and that if she looked closely enough or waited long enough, she would see her. Coming down the steps with a handbag on her arm. Or moving like a shadow behind the glass of an upstairs window.

She understood, of course, that this was not really possible. That it was not, in the way adults meant it, likely to happen. Because, like the old Jewish men in their soft leather shoes, her mother was dead. Angela knew that. And knew that what was left of her, if anything at all, was not behind a newly painted door or a silvery pane of glass, but lying under the feet of the stone angel in the cemetery where once a year she and her father left a bouquet of flowers. Not that it mattered. Because she could no more stop herself from walking up the Corso d'Este and looking through the railings than she could stop herself hearing the prayer in the rustle of birds' wings and the run and clack of the shutters.

Neither of which she ever told anyone about. Not Nonna Franchi, nor Signora Ravalli from downstairs who sometimes braided her hair. Not even her father, who was a big man who wore a cap and whistled tunelessly and whose face always seemed on the edge of smiling and whose plans grew less and less ambitious, until by the time Angela was twelve and went to what she thought of as the grown-up school, he could barely bring himself to open the shop on Saturdays, much less imagine an empire built on corned beef and prosciutto.

⁓

It was more than six years before Angela spoke to Antonio again. She saw him, though, from time to time. Once, she spotted him in a group of boys who hung about the Piazza Trieste on weekends, loitering near the record store, trying to look dangerous and failing because they were too young and too skinny and everyone knew who they were. Another time she found herself standing almost next to him waiting to cross the street, but was too afraid to catch his eye or say anything. And one Saturday afternoon, as she walked home with her father after he had closed the butcher's shop, Antonio appeared ahead of them in the Via delle Volte.

It was winter and very cold. White ice stippled the eaves of the buildings and lined the brackets of the streetlights. Antonio came out of nowhere like a ghost, pushing a bicycle with one hand and carrying a sack of groceries with the other, and Angela noticed that he was wearing only sneakers and not boots like everyone else, and that his coat hung from his shoulders.

She didn't dare call his name, but she wanted him to look back and see her, to reach into the shopping bag and hand her an apple. He didn't. Head bent, he seemed intent on the spinning wheel of his bike. It had a loose fender, and when he turned off into an alley, she heard the click and rattle as he crossed the broken cobblestones.

Listening to the sound grow smaller and smaller, Angela remembered the apartments that looked like so many shoe boxes, all stacked one on top of the other. And the long, low shops below them that were fronted with plate glass. As they passed it, she stared into the blackened mouth of the alley that had swallowed him and was so narrow you could stretch your arms and almost touch both sides, and felt again the wide, empty street beyond the Darsena where she and her friends had been nothing but little boats drifting on an open sea. Angela reached for her father's hand, which was warm and broad as a bear's paw. As they walked on, she scuffed the toes of her new boots and felt sad for Antonio, wheeling his bike out beyond the walls into what the TV called "The New Italy," with its crosshatching of railroad tracks and highways, depots and factories that popped up overnight like mushrooms.

It is almost a year after that, late one afternoon in early October, when she sees him again. Summer has stayed too long. It makes the air thick and turns the sky mauve and everyone knows it will leave any day now and all at once, like an embarrassed party guest. So while it is still warm, Angela dawdles.

She has already made one loop around the castle on her way

home. Now she stops to stare down into the moat and wonder if Lucrezia Borgia—whom her class is studying—was really as beautiful as everyone said or if she was gap-toothed and had bad breath, and what will happen if she drops her school bag into the still green water, if it will sink or float. She's lifting it up, resting it on the warm stone of the balustrade and toying with the idea in a way that is tempting but guarantees she'll never do it, when she hears someone call her name. Well, not exactly her name.

"Butcher's Daughter."

The words are like a hand on the back of her neck. Angela looks around. A man walks by, head bent, following his dog, which strains at its leash. A police car rumbles over the cobbles and disappears around the corner into Via Frizzi. She pulls the bag back, snagging the skirt of her uniform on the wall, and begins to think she imagined the voice, when he appears beside her.

At sixteen Antonio is almost as tall as her father. His black hair is still curly, but wilder. If Nonna Franchi saw it she would come after him with scissors the way she came after Angela when she was little, stalking her through the apartment brandishing the blades that glinted, bright and sharp as the knives that hung along the back wall of the butcher's shop.

"What are you doing?"

Angela shrugs. A dark fuzz shadows Antonio's chin and cheeks, but his eyes and smile are exactly the same, and she's suddenly flustered by the idea that he can look straight in and read her mind. See every thought as if it's written down, just as he had the day she was hiding in the orchard, and that he knows perfectly well she was thinking of dropping her books into the moat.

"Nothing."

Antonio looks at the sky. Then he looks back at her.

"I got a place," he says, "at the Liceo Classico."

Angela notices he is wearing smart clothes. A pair of dark trousers, leather shoes, a long-sleeved white shirt. Nothing like the canvas sneakers and thin coat she saw him in last winter. The exams for the Liceo are difficult. Already the threat of them sits like a big ugly bird perched on the windowsill of her class. It caws when the teacher's back is turned. It cackles and whispers that the weak and the stupid will be sacrificed, plucked off the path that leads to university and everything that goes with it. Job. Car. House with trees. When the bird looks at Angela, she sees in its yellow eye the scrubbed counters of the butcher's shop and feels the meaty breath of the cold room.

"I didn't thank you," she says suddenly, pushing the bird away. "I never thanked you. For the apple."

For a moment Antonio looks confused. Then he laughs.

"Come on," he says. "I'll walk you home." And he reaches out and takes her bag and slings it over his shoulder.

Although Angela has been told how her mother chose her name before she was born because she already knew Angela would be her beautiful angel, and although her father assures her she is prettier than any princess in a book, she knows it isn't true. She knows that she will never look like the girls on television or in films or on the fronts of magazines. But she is not too tall, or too fat, or scrawny either. Nor is she loud, or stupid. Her greatest achievement, in fact, is that she isn't anything. She understands when to be quiet and when to laugh and how to get along without drawing much attention to herself the same way a chameleon understands when to turn brown or green.

This shell of ordinariness has been a project. A quiet little vocation she has worked on the way Signora Ravalli works on the ugly decoupage trays she sells in the market, adding layer after layer of lacquer to cover the talk of devil's thumbprints and dead mothers. But now, walking next to Antonio, who is carrying her bag, and who has remembered, if not exactly her name, at least who she is, and who is actually talking to her—telling her about the Liceo and his friends and the football club he's joined—Angela feels her shell melting. It's perilous and terrifying, and part of her wants to turn and run. The part of her that does not feel him burning around her like a halo.

They turn toward the Duomo. Pink-gray light feathers the roofs and chimneys of the old town. One by one the windows of the municipal offices turn yellow. As they drift across the wide lozenge of the Piazza Trieste, Antonio tells her that he has an exception that waives some of his book fees, but that it won't be renewed if he fails to live up to his promise.

"It's hard," he says.

They pause before the brightly lit window of a shop, and Angela notices that his cheeks are thin. His nose is sharper than she remembered.

"But do you like it?"

Antonio shrugs, as if liking it or not liking it has little to do with anything, and Angela's suddenly afraid the question was so dumb that he'll give her bag back and walk away.

"My father thinks it's stupid," he says. Antonio's studying a jacket in the window. "He says I'll end up in the factory anyway. So what's the point? He says I'm trying to be too good for what I am. Not like him and my brother. My mother's happy." He stops studying the jacket and looks down at Angela. "You don't have a mother," he says.

She shakes her head.

"Do you like your father?"

Angela nods. Although *like* does not seem to be a possible word when it comes to her father. *Like* is a small word, and everything about her father is too big for it.

"You're lucky," Antonio says. Then he adds, "I'm going to university. I don't care what my father says. I'm not going into the factory. I'm not going to be him. Or my brother. Work like that, so you can lose everything. Like my nonno's farm. I'm not doing that. I'm going to university."

The words are a challenge, clipped and angry, and before she can stop herself Angela reaches out and touches the back of his hand.

"Me, too."

She has never said this before, not even to herself, but the minute she does, she knows it's true. She's not going to be plucked off by the bird. Antonio looks down at her fingers. Then he twines his own in hers. She doesn't know how she expects his skin to feel, but she isn't surprised that it's as smooth and cool as the skin of the apple.

They turn away from the shop and wander into Via Mazzini. As they get closer to Angela's apartment, the streets narrow. Huddled shoulder to shoulder, houses slice the purple sky. Streetlights smudge dirty walls. The smell of cooking and the tinny voice of a television or a radio waft from open window to open window. Snatches of conversation snag and tangle in lines of drying laundry.

Antonio stops outside her door. Their light is broken. In the shadows he looks different. The past has padded itself back onto his cheeks and softened the sharp line of his nose, making him a leopard again—nine years old and standing in long grass. His fingers leave Angela's. He hands her the bag of books. Then he reaches out and brushes the fringe of curls off her forehead.

"It's pretty," he says. "Your hair."

❧

It was not long after that—after the night when Angela, watching the street lamps pick out Antonio's white shirt, stood on the step for so long with her hand raised to her face that Signora Ravalli finally poked her head out her kitchen window and asked if she had lost her key again—that she was adopted by Barbara Barelli.

She thought of it that way because Barbara's choice of her as a friend seemed as arbitrary as picking out a stray cat or dog from the animal shelter. And because the dedication Barbara applied seemed, even to Angela at the time, more suited to something like a new pet or a cause than a friendship.

Barbara was a year older. Her family had moved to Ferrara at the end of the summer because her father was teaching at the university. She was tall for her age and slightly snaggle-toothed and very good at sports. Which, Angela thought, made the fact that she was Barbara's chosen friend even more unlikely.

Still, Barbara began to wait for her between classes and at lunchtime. At the end of the day, she sought Angela out from the throng that poured through the school gates into the freedom of the afternoons. Crossing the Corso Giovecca and meandering down toward Via Mazzini, the two girls window-shopped, keeping up a running commentary on the clothes they would buy or not buy—a fantasy significantly less real for Angela than for Barbara, who with two older sisters, one already working in Milan, and a professor for a father and a mother teaching at the music conservatory, lived in a house with three floors that looked onto the Parco Pareschi.

By the time winter arrived, Angela was used to finding Barbara leaning against the wall of the Spanish Synagogue in the mornings, as often as not holding a bag from the bakery on the corner, jam melting through the thin paper onto her gloves, powdered sugar sprinkling the cuff of her coat. They ate the pastries on the way to school, talking between mouthfuls, brushing crumbs from one another's sleeves and chins like monkeys picking lice.

In the evenings, after they finished their homework, Barbara wheedled Angela off to the Corso Martiri. Striding past the lit walls of the castle and statue of Savonarola that Angela had been afraid of when she was little, Barbara would push open the door of a café and herd Angela before her into the fog of cigarette smoke. They always sat in the same corner, on spindly chairs, and sipped hot chocolate bought with Barbara's pocket money while Barbara dispensed beauty advice, giving Angela tips on what she should wear and how she should do her hair.

The secrets they shared as they ate, and ogled clothes, and lay across each other's beds on Sunday afternoons, were mainly Barbara's. Things her sisters had done, or that she had overheard them saying. Rows her parents had. And graphic descriptions of the rustles and small cries that emanated from their bedroom afterward.

Angela did tell about being chased at nursery school, and about the bets that were made concerning exactly what was under her skirt, and even about the time she saw her father standing under the streetlight kissing Signora Ravalli. But she never told Barbara about the ghosts. Or about the fact that she still sometimes heard the Sh'ma Yisrael in the autumn rains. She never told about walking up the Corso d'Este to peer through iron railings. Although she did once mention something about trees with ruby leaves, and was pleased when Barbara's father, who had recently lectured in America, confirmed that this was, in fact, true. But she said nothing about being her mother's angel. Or about the apple. And she never once mentioned Antonio.

For a while, after the night he walked her home and carried her bag and lifted her hair from her forehead leaving behind nothing but the brush of his fingertips, she had thought he would come back. She'd looked for him on the street and in crowds at the market. Had scanned the faces of the boys who hung around Piazza Trieste on Saturday afternoons. From time to time, when she could slip away from Barbara, Angela had even gone home exactly the same way, and at the same time, as she had on the day he had appeared beside her. When she did that, she would be sure to stand in exactly the same place, and look over the wall and down into the moat, and to ask herself exactly the same questions, about Lucrezia Borgia and the books.

It became a ritual, like staring through the railings of the houses on Corso D'Este. A sort of prayer. As if, in holding faith with that afternoon, she could wind back time. Re-create chance. Summon Antonio from the ordinary evening air the way an alchemist summoned gold from lead.

But he never materialized. And finally all she could think of was to wander along the city walls on Sunday afternoons while Barbara was at one of her mother's recitals or having lunch with her family. Then Angela would stand in the line of trees that topped the ramparts and listen to the raucous shouts of the boys and the shrill burst of the umpire's whistle, and search the bobbing heads until she picked Antonio's out from the group racing up and down the ragged pitch beyond the Angels' Gate.

Summer came and went. The football games stopped. Barbara's family rented a villa on the coast below Rimini for the month of August. Angela was invited for a week, and found it hot and sandy and rather boring, and was more glad than she would have guessed when it was time for her to return to Ferrara, where she helped her father in the evenings as he scrubbed the marble tops of the counters in the butcher's shop and washed the floor and sprinkled it with sawdust. On Sundays she sometimes went with him to his cousin's farm where the veal calves were raised, driving in the butcher's van, her father's big hand beating time to the radio, dry wind blowing through the open windows of the cab that had nothing as fancy or expensive as air conditioning.

In September Angela started at a new school where, increasingly, she found herself wandering happily, and then lost, in lines of equations. Angles and spheres and cubes floated through her dreams. She marked the anniversary of the night Antonio had walked her home by slipping out after supper and walking up to the Castello, as if her presence could summon him. The weather was colder and the big square empty. When she stopped in the Via Mazzini to stare in the window of the same shop, she thought for a moment that she saw him in the reflection, hovering at her shoulder. But when she spun around, it was not Antonio at all, just some other boy with curly hair and bad acne who stared at her, then smirked and slunk away.

Christmas arrived. On New Year's bells rang and fireworks exploded. Angela had forced herself to stop going to watch the football games. She had told herself it didn't matter if she ever saw Antonio again or not. And mostly she believed it. Mostly he felt like a dream. Or sometimes a ghost. But occasionally something would tug at her sleeve. She would remember the warm indolent smell of August. Or see a smattering of speckled light. Or spot someone in the street, walking just ahead of her, who might be him. Then she would climb up onto the city walls and stand in the lines of the trees and allow herself a guilty look down onto the football pitch, just to prove that he was real.

It is on a Sunday like this, in February, that, without quite meaning to, Angela takes Barbara with her. The fog of the previous week has finally given way to a limpid blue sky. It is still very cold. Even with the sun out, frost coats the branches and silvers the tiniest twigs. Dead thickets glitter in the old Hebrew cemetery. Ice makes a thin bright skin across the mud-churned puddles.

At Christmas Barbara's parents increased her pocket money and opened a bank account for her, because she has to get used to independence. Barbara's parents talk a lot about independence and rarely ask where the girls are going or what they are doing, so Barbara telephones and suggests they take the train to Bologna and go to a film. But Angela is feeling a tug in her stomach, the sort of thing she imagines stitches straining over a wound must feel like. The night before she dreamed of Antonio. Woke up in the dark with a hot-hand feeling on the back of her neck, sure his fingers were lifting the hair off her forehead. So when Barbara reels off a list of what's playing, Angela says nothing. Finally she mutters something about taking a walk to get some exercise, and to her surprise, after a small silence, Barbara agrees. She announces that the films are all meant to be stupid anyway, and that Angela is right. They should go for a walk. Angela puts the phone down feeling as if she's been shoved from behind in a crowd.

When she arrives at the Barellis' house and rings the bell, Barbara is waiting.

"Come on." Before Angela can even step inside, Barbara grabs her by the arm and spins her around, barely giving her time to hear the rising voices that are coming from the dining room. "Let's go," Barbara hisses. "Let's get out of here."

She runs them down the steps.

"They're arguing," Barbara says, as they reach the pavement. "Papa and all his friends. It's supposed to be a lunch party, but all they ever do is argue. Every weekend. I can't stand it. Talk. Talk. Talk." Barbara's hair, which is pulled back in a long dark braid, swings like a pendulum. "All they ever do is talk about politics. They don't do anything, just talk. They never shut up."

It's a conversation Angela and Barbara have had before. More than once. Well, not really a conversation, Angela thinks, since she doesn't say much. Barbara's father teaches politics and economics, and since the oil crisis of the autumn before and the general strikes that followed, the Barelli house seems, especially on Sunday afternoons, to be full of cigarette smoke and shouting.

As a result it's not uncommon for Barbara to seek sanctuary at the apartment, where the girls work at the kitchen table or watch television undisturbed because Angela's father does not care about politics and is often out on Sundays in any case.

Since the supermarket opened down by the train station, he has been forced to keep the butcher's shop open on Saturdays, which means he now spends Sunday afternoons getting ready for the week ahead, doing the books and working in the cold store. Running the meat grinder. Invoking the recipes his father taught him as if they are a magic shield that will protect against Styrofoam-backed shrink-wrapped chops and pellucid watery chicken breasts.

"I can't wait to get out of here."

Barbara pulls her new jacket tighter around her as they turn the corner and pass the high dark walls of the Casa Romei. "I hate it," she says suddenly. She stops in the street and turns on Angela. "Don't you?" Barbara's cheeks are pinched with cold and unhappiness. "Hate this town? It's like a prison. It's even got walls like a prison. I can't wait until we go to university."

Barbara shakes her head and starts walking again.

"We had a fight about it," she says. "Papa wants me to go here. But I'm not going to. I won't. I told Mama. I swear. Laura didn't, and I don't have to." Laura is Barbara's middle sister. She left in September to begin the university in Padua. "He's only picking on me," Barbara adds, "because I'm the last one left. Because there isn't anyone else he can boss around."

Angela nods. She might suggest that perhaps Professor Barelli wants Barbara to stay because he will be lonely with no daughters in the house. But she isn't sure if this is true, or even if it is, if there is any point in saying it, or in doing anything but nodding, which is probably all Barbara wants her to do. Certainly she does not want Angela to say that she could not imagine leaving her own father. Or, for that matter, Ferrara. That to her the walls are not a prison, but an embrace. Angela remembers how sad she felt for Antonio that winter night when she thought of him living outside them. Her father's newspapers, the ones he falls asleep reading in his chair, skitter through her mind. The pictures of striking workers, and of the men who were kidnapped in Milan, their faces staring out after they'd had their heads shaved and their photos taken and been left chained to the rails of the Fiat factory with placards hanging around their necks because the Red Brigades said they were fascists. She thinks of the photos of people throwing stones. And knows she does not want to go out there. Ever.

They pass the wire-topped walls of the hospital, cross the traffic circle, which is quiet on a Sunday afternoon, and climb up the steep bank onto the ramparts.

"Come on." Barbara bangs her hands together as they reach the packed gravel path. "I'll race you."

These races take place frequently and are pointless. Barbara runs on the girls' team at school, and is taller and faster, and stride for stride can beat not only Angela, but almost anyone else. Angela laughs and chases her anyway. Through white huffs of breath, she sees her friend's long gangly body transformed as her black braid flies out behind her, catching the halfhearted sun.

As they reach the section above the football pitch, Angela slows. Shouts, cut by the blade of a whistle, rise in the chilly air. A group of parents and girlfriends stand at the top of the bank, stamping their feet, digging their hands in their pockets, calling encouragement and clapping. As Barbara runs on down the avenue of trees, her figure growing smaller and smaller, Angela stops, hovering at the edge of the supporters, and scans the game. But she doesn't see Antonio.

Something in her chest deflates as she watches the pack of boys hurtle down the muddy pitch. Damp rises through the soles of her shoes. Then the ball flies, and a clump of arms and legs and jerseys tangle and collapse. The referee shouts and waves his arms. The players line up for a penalty kick, jostling and pushing, and suddenly there he is. Antonio is standing in the wall, in front of the goal. After the kick comes, and is successfully fended off, he runs up the field with his arms above his head.

"Who is he?"

It's not until Barbara speaks that Angela realizes she has come back and is standing so close, her chest rising and falling, her face flushed and eyes bright, that Angela can feel the hot huff of her breath.

"Who's who?"

Even as she says it, Angela feels the telltale pink flush burning up her neck and into her cheeks. Barbara grins, watching her as if this is the single most interesting thing Angela has ever done. Then she looks back at the pitch, shoves her mittened hands into her pockets, and says, "He comes from the factories, doesn't he?"

Angela shrugs.

"What's his name?"

"I don't know."

Angela turns and begins to walk away. She's making for the path that cuts down toward the Certosa, suddenly anxious to be off the walls. "Come on," she calls. "I'm cold."

But Barbara doesn't move. Instead she stands looking down onto the football pitch, leaning forward and frowning, her hands dug into her pockets, her braid hanging over her shoulder. Angela watches. And for a moment she thinks Barbara looks exactly the same way she does when she's spotted something in a shop window, but can't quite make out what's written on the price tag.

It is exactly two months to the day after that, on April 18, 1974, when The Red Brigades kidnap Mario Sossi.

❧

Angela saw it first on the television news. It was an hour or two after supper, which had been spring lamb, chunks so pale they were almost white, braised with peas, tiny and bright green.

After eating Angela and her father had stood side by side at the deep white sink, passing dishes, forks, knives, from hand to hand, washing and drying. Angela would never have told Barbara, or anyone else for that matter, but it was her favorite time of the day—these few minutes she and her father spent moving around the stove and sink and table, clearing away, wiping, scrubbing and drying, no words necessary between them, the warm smell of the meal they had just shared still hanging in the room.

When they finished her father placed his hand on her head, as he had done every night since she could remember. Then he sighed, a smile lighting his broad, round face, and ambled into the sitting room, where he turned on the television and picked up his paper and sank into his sagging brown chair with the pages spread across his knees.

Angela knew it would not be long before he fell asleep. And sure enough not a half hour later, from the kitchen table where she sat, her exercise books spread across the scarred wooden surface, she heard the muffled grunts and little gasps that meant she could turn off the television. Cut dead the aimless mumble about strikes and weather reports.

The nights had grown warmer. Before dinner she had opened the window. Now she got up and closed it, fastening the latch, then went across the hall to the sitting room. From where she stood in the doorway, Angela saw her father's mouth open, his head lolled back, resting against the worn cushion. It occurred to her that his hair, although still abundant, was almost white, and she found herself wondering when that had happened, and why she hadn't noticed it before.

His blue eyes were closed, the lashes dark against his cheeks, which had bright red patches on them. Her father's hand twitched, fingers jumping on the newspaper as if he was trying to point something out. Angela turned toward the TV. She was about to switch it off, when the picture shifted abruptly to a street, then to an ordinary-looking house. The announcer said it was in Genoa. A picture of a man in the white-and-black outfit of a prosecutor appeared and was rapidly replaced by a policeman, who announced that someone called Mario Sossi had been kidnapped. Witnesses saw him shoved into a van. Five thousand police and carabinieri had been called to the city. The picture switched to a line of traffic. Carabinieri officers moved from car to car, opening trunks and doors. Some carried submachine guns cradled in their arms like babies.

Angela stood staring. She had never been to Genoa. She had never been anywhere larger than Bologna. She leaned down and switched the television off, driving the pictures away, sending them back where they belonged, outside the walls.

But Mario Sossi was not banished so easily.

By the next morning his face stared from the racks of the corner shops that sold magazines, and gazed from the rumpled pages of newspapers being read in cafés. In the electrical shop it filled every screen of a whole row of television sets.

Then a new photo was released. In this one Assistant Prosecutor Sossi no longer wore his black robes and milk-white collar. Instead he sat with his hands folded between his knees and looked small and sad and unimportant. Hardly someone worth kidnapping. Shoving into a van. Calling an "Enemy of the People." A banner hung behind him. On it were printed the words *Brigate Rosse*. Below them was a five-pointed star.

The star bothered Angela. The two bottom points were longer than the others, so it looked as if it was leaning backward, like something propped unevenly against a wall. Its angles, she thought, were not correct. It wouldn't be possible to work out an equation for that star, and if you did, the sums would not come out the right way. Looking at it made her feel queasy, the way the glasses of wine Barbara's parents sometimes pressed on her made her feel.

"*Sossi Sparito nel Nullo.*" "Sossi Disappears into Thin Air" the newspaper headlines cried. But it wasn't true. Because no matter what the newspapers or the politicians or the Carabinieri said, Mario Sossi was everywhere. Even Ferrara's walls and ramparts couldn't keep him out.

As the days passed and Mario Sossi's family—his wife and his children—begged and pleaded for his safe return, Angela began to dream of him. He slithered under the rusted iron footings and wriggled through the padlocks on the Angels' Gate. He slid like rain through the alleys of the ghetto, but the shadow he threw as he passed under the street lamps was not his own. It was not even human. Instead it was a long, sharp shape scratched against the dark walls and closed shutters. A five-pointed star that swayed in time to Mario Sossi's footsteps as they whispered across the cobbles like a prayer.

"My father says he's a political prisoner."

Barbara announces this as they are walking home from school seventeen days after Assistant Prosecutor Sossi has vanished into nothingness and become everywhere at once.

She lifts her braid and drops it, puffing her cheeks like a blowfish. Summer has arrived abruptly, rushing the trees into leaf and turning the mud on the paths that run along the top of the walls to dust. The cafés have doubled their outdoor tables and the old men walking their dogs have shed their scarves and jackets and unbuttoned the tops of their collars. Stretching their wattled necks, they look this way and that as they amble along the pavements blinking like ancient tortoises. In less than a week Angela will be sixteen.

She starts to reply that it is not Barbara's father at all who has said that Mario Sossi is a political prisoner but the Red Brigades themselves, who have just sent another of their communiqués to the newspapers. In this one they have announced that Mario Sossi is being put on trial for his crimes against the workers, and that after that, because he is a political prisoner, he can be exchanged. For four terrorists he was prosecuting, whom the Red Brigades would like flown to Cuba or Algeria. Or possibly North Korea.

"Criminals!" Angela's father had shouted at the television the night before. "Anarchist scum!" He had even thrown one of his slippers.

But Angela can't be bothered to point any of this out. It's too hot and she wants to get out of her school clothes and Barbara won't pay any attention anyway.

"They got in a big fight about it last night." Barbara slides her eyes sideways like a cartoon cat.

"My mother and father," she says, in case Angela thinks she is talking about someone else. "My mother says they're nothing but spoiled children, the Red Brigades. My father says they're fighting capitalism. I think they should get divorced," she adds, presumably referring to her parents, not the Red Brigades, although Angela thinks the country divorcing them might be a great idea, especially if they'd shut up. "They don't do anything anymore but fight," Barbara says. "My mother says she's taking me on holiday alone this year. She doesn't want my father to come."

Angela looks at her. Barbara is watching her feet now, concentrating on them as they fall one after the other onto the pavement.

"We're going to Positano." Barbara shakes her head and tugs her braid. "To stay with my aunt. Her new husband has a villa. And a boat."

"But do you want to?"

As far as Angela knows, for the last few years it has been Barbara and her mother who do nothing but fight. Signora Barelli is neat and very precise, like a pile of papers squared at the edges.

She has long-fingered hands that she flexes and rubs cream into, and is, in Angela's opinion, rather mean. She calls Angela "Barbara's little friend." As if she's a hamster. Or a mouse that talks.

Professor Barelli, on the other hand, is large and unruly, like a sheepdog. He sometimes pulls Barbara's braid when she walks by, a sort of yank of recognition, as if he's just remembered who she is. His hair falls in his eyes and Angela is always afraid he is going to set it on fire when he smokes. Last year he won some sort of award for teaching, a fact Angela finds hard to understand because his suits don't seem to fit properly and he shuffles as if his shoes are about to fall off. On the rare occasions when she eats at the Barellis', he makes loud pronouncements, then huffs and laughs like a broken vacuum cleaner.

Angela stops. Behind them a woman on a bicycle swerves and rings her bell. The girls step into the shadows at the entrance to the theater. Barbara shrugs.

"My cousins are OK," she says.

Angela has no idea if this is true, or if it is wishful thinking, since until that moment she has never heard Barbara mention her cousins.

"I've never met the husband," Barbara adds. "Neither has my mother. My aunt only married him last month." Barbara fingers the edge of her book bag. "We're leaving right after school." Her cheeks color. "Mama's already bought the tickets."

She does not need to add that there will be no invitation for Angela this summer. Unlike Rimini, Positano is too far away. And there are the cousins, and the new husband, and the boat.

"But what about your father?"

The idea of Professor Barelli rambling through the house alone, smoking his cigarettes in an empty sitting room and cooking his meals in the big fancy kitchen while he makes pronouncements to himself and laughs at nothing, seems impossible to Angela. Barbara shrugs again.

"He's teaching at a summer school in America." She smiles and drops her braid. "I might get to go visit him," she adds. "In August. Come on." She grabs Angela's arm and steps out of the shadows. "Let's go get something to eat. Let's eat lots."

They have hamburgers. And French fries, and gelato, and by the time they part on the corner of Via Mazzini, Angela feels sick. As she turns into her street, she looks at her watch. It's just before six, but her father won't be home yet. He keeps the shop open until seven on weeknights, although he grumbles frequently that there isn't much point because more and more people go to the supermarket, where they can buy everything at once. It's only the old ladies, her father says, who come to peer through the glass of the display case and ask questions about the cut of the fillets and how long the beef has been hung. And they always come in the morning, early and dressed in black. So what is the point of leaving the doors open until seven so he can stand behind the counter all by himself?

Angela doesn't know what to say to that. She doesn't know the equation that would make the supermarket go away. As much as she would like to, she doesn't know how to reduce it to zero—cancel it out with involtini, and veal piccata, and the soft, fat manicotti her father still makes sometimes on Saturday night.

She goes to her room and lies down on her bed and closes her eyes and tries not to see the summer stretching out ahead of her like a long, hot, empty road. Or her father standing by himself in the shop. Or the picture on the front of the day's newspaper, which, for once, had been not of Mario Sossi, but of his wife, who had tears running down her face because she did not want to go away from her husband to Positano or any-where else, but wanted him back. And who, when she was not allowed to go on television anymore, had written letters to the pope, and to the president. Pleading with them to somehow do what five thousand police and carabinieri have so far failed to do—reach down and fish Mario Sossi out of the nothingness he has vanished into.

For Angela's sixteenth birthday, Barbara gives her a silver bracelet. Her father gives her a record player and a locket with the letter *A* engraved on it that once stood for Annabeth, because it was her mother's, but now it stands for Angela because it's hers.

He puts the gold chain around her neck, but his fingers are too big and too callused to fasten the tiny clasp, so Angela does it herself. Then she hugs him, and feels his arms around her and breathes in the smell of him—the carbolic soap he uses to scrub down the counters of the shop, and the detergent from the Laundromat that lingers in his shirts, and the sweet woodiness of the cheap cigars he buys with his newspaper every morning and thinks Angela does not know about because he smokes them after work while he helps Signor Pirotti, the two of them side by side puffing like steam engines as they pull the metal gates down across the front of the Pirottis' fruit stall and then the butcher's shop and fasten them with the same padlocks their fathers used.

A week later, on May 18, the Red Brigades announce that they have decided to execute Mario Sossi. They say he has been tried in a revolutionary court and found guilty. They say that he is an enemy of the people—a cohort of the fascists and the capitalists who keep the proletariat enslaved, and that therefore he must die. Then they change their minds and free him. On the thirty-fifth day Mario Sossi comes back from nowhere.

Then, once he is free, once everyone knows where he is—home again with his wife and children—he vanishes again. He disappears from the television and the magazines and the front pages of the newspaper as if he had never been. And after that school ends, and Barbara leaves for Positano, and Angela goes to work in the butcher's shop.

At first her father argued. He did not, he said, spend his days up to his elbows in sausage meat so his beautiful daughter, who is so clever at math and English and is going to be the first person in their family to go to university, could learn to pull the guts out of chickens. If her mother knew, he insisted, she would reach up from the grave, grab him by the shirttails, and pull him down and slam the lid.

Angela, however, pointed out that she intended to work for someone, not only because she had nothing better to do, but also because she wanted to make some money of her own, so it might as well be him. She also pointed out that it would only be for the summer, and then suggested that if he did not want her slicing liver and arranging beef tongues, he could at least let her run the cash register and keep the books, which was, after all, what her mother had done after they married and while she had been planning their business empire based on prosciutto and American corned beef, whatever that was.

Faced with this, her father agreed. Grudgingly. So as the days grew hotter and the nights grew shorter, Angela began to walk in the footsteps of her parents and grandparents. Every morning she threaded her way down the Via Vittoria and along the Via Ragno and into the Via Carbone, which had once been the haunt of the charcoal sellers. She passed under the dark, cool arches of the Via delle Volte, where she had seen Antonio that night and where before the war the prostitutes had lingered like stray cats, and stepped finally into Via Mayr with its traffic and potholed pavement and brick-fronted buildings rimed with soot.

The butcher's shop was on the corner. A few years earlier, before the new supermarket had opened, her father had, in a fit of optimism, invested in a new sign and a new front window. Their name, Vari, marched across the plate glass, which was kept spotless. But the red and black letters that hovered above, spelling out MACELLERÌA, had been made grubby with winter rain and the exhaust fumes from the trucks that rattled by on their way to the Ripagrande.

Angela didn't know if the white coat she put on every morning had actually been her mother's, but she liked to imagine it was. After buttoning up, she braided her hair and stuffed it under a cap. Then she sat behind the cash register and tried to imagine that in this white-walled room surrounded by knives and lumps of flesh, it would be possible not only to fall in love, but to build dreams—of a house with trees that had spreading branches and leaves made of rubies. Tried. And failed.

She did not do much better with the books. The long and the short of it was, her father was in debt. Several years earlier he had borrowed to pay for the new sign and the window and the butcher's van. All of which had probably seemed reasonable at the time, when the choice people had was which butcher to use rather than whether to use one at all. Now all that had changed.

As she watched him, his large hands unexpectedly graceful as he teased out gristle or brought a cleaver down, she understood why he had not wanted her to see the accounts. The more he fell behind, the greater risk the bank considered him, and the higher they raised his rates. Month by month the amount of capital his repayments covered grew smaller and smaller while the share that went to interest grew bigger and bigger. It was like a silly nursery rhyme about running around and around in circles. Or worse, like the mushroom clouds they were shown in movies at school. Sometimes Angela feared the debt would blossom and spread forever, the interest growing and growing, until it turned the sky black and blotted out the sun.

In the quiet of the afternoons while he worked in the cold room after the morning rush—when there was one—Angela took to easing open the cash register. Holding her hand over the bell so he wouldn't hear it ping, she slid half the lire notes he paid her back into their little black plastic slots.

It's a Sunday at the end of July when she decides to wash the sign. Her father has taken the van and gone with Signor Pirotti, whose own van has broken down, to collect an order of cherries from somewhere near Imola. They rattle off just as the bells start ringing for mass. Standing in the street, Angela waves. Then she takes the keys to the storeroom in the alley that they share with the fruit stall and fetches the ladder and a bucket and sponges and a bottle of the detergent they use to mop the floors.

The ladder is old and very long and heavier than she thought it would be and it takes her some time to maneuver it out the narrow side door. Then she has to drag it around the corner and into Via Mayr, bumping the ends over the curb. She's relieved the street's empty, closed up tight for Sunday, so there's no one to witness her first ham-fisted attempt at getting it up against the front of the shop. Afraid of resting it on the glass, she finally props it against the grimy brick.

But when she puts her foot on it and begins to climb, it feels flimsier than its weight suggests. A rung is broken, and the bucket is heavier and more unwieldy than she thought. There's a hook at the top, but hanging the bucket makes the ladder tilt, which frightens her. Down feels like a long way. Finally she's reduced to leaving the bucket on the pavement, soaking the sponge, going back up the ladder, and leaning over to swipe inefficiently at the M and the A and eventually the edge of the C. The E is out of reach.

Sweat mingles with the dirty, soapy water on her hands and arms. It dribbles down her side, until the thin cotton shirt she's wearing clings like a second skin. Angela rubs the hair from her eyes with the back of her arm, and wonders how she's going to clean the Ls and the E and R in the middle. She feels the sun beating on her back and on the top of her head and thinks suddenly of Barbara on her uncle's boat in Positano. Which makes her think of Barbara's mother, of her smiling her smile that is not a smile at all, and saying, "Now, what about you and your little friend?" or "Would your little friend like to stay for lunch?" and how she wanted to turn and shout, "My name is Angela!" but never had, and never would. She thinks about that, and about the columns of numbers in her father's books that get larger and larger in the wrong way. Then she begins to cry.

The M and A and C are dripping down onto what was the clean plate glass window her father polished every morning. The ladder has given her a splinter that catches and rips at her thumb. The pig and the cow painted on the shop tiles laugh at her. She decides she hates them, and has no idea how long she has been standing there, crying and sniffing and feeling the damp squelch in her shoes, when she hears his voice.

"That looks better," Antonio says.

"No, it doesn't."

Angela doesn't even turn around to look at him. She shakes her head, suddenly beyond caring about anything—what she looks like, or what Barbara's mother thinks, or even about the fact that Antonio has appeared like magic and is standing not two feet away and speaking to her while her nose is running and her cheeks are turning red.

"It's a mess. It's just a huge, big mess."

Antonio steps in front of her. He is wearing jeans and a white shirt and carrying a gym bag. A pair of football shoes are tied by their laces and dangle from the handle. He looks at her for a moment. Then he looks back at the sign.

"I can't reach." Angela wipes her nose on the back of her hand and knows she's sounding like a baby, but she can't help it. "I wanted to surprise Papa." Her voice is perilously close to a wail. "And now I've gone and messed up the window, too."

Antonio laughs. Then his face sobers.

"Hey," he says. He reaches out and touches her cheek with the tip of his finger. "It's only soap and water."

He steps into the shop doorway and puts the gym bag down, and before she realizes what he's doing, he's taken the ladder and jiggled it around, releasing a latch she hadn't even noticed and somehow opening the rungs so the top feet will reach well above the sign. He steadies it against the wall.

"You hold it." He turns to her. "Like this."

Antonio grabs the ladder and braces his foot against the bottom rung. Angela stares at him.

"What are you doing?"

He cocks his head and smiles at her, rolling up the sleeves of his shirt.

"I'm washing the sign, Butcher's Daughter."

Before she can say anything—protest that he will be late for wherever he's going, football practice, obviously, or that he will get wet—Antonio takes the bucket, throws the sponge into it, and starts to climb. Angela darts forward, grabbing the ladder, bracing her foot as he'd shown her, feeling his weight as he moves upward as if she's holding him in her hands.

"I'm going," he says a moment later, without looking down at her.

Angela has no idea what he's talking about. Balancing, he holds the bucket with one hand and wrings out the sponge with the other. Water plops and foams, splatting beside her shoes.

"To the university, at Padua." He begins to clean the middle E she had not been able to reach.

"Remember?"

She nods. Of course she remembers. The old wooden ladder is digging another splinter into the heel of her hand, but she doesn't feel it. Instead she feels the strong, hard bones of Antonio's fingers. She feels his skin, smooth and tight as an apple's. He switches the bucket, washing the first, then the second L.

"Philosophy." He shakes his head, making the ladder wobble.

Laughter bounces down to her. "In a few weeks. I can't really be-lieve it."

"Is your father still angry?"

Antonio shrugs. He leans out to clean the second E, then starts climbing back down. The long stretch of his leg is above her. Then the small of his back. When his foot hits the pavement, she lets go of the ladder. His arms brush hers as he turns around. He smiles, hands her the bucket, and grabs the rails, shifting the ladder sideways.

"Yes," he says. "But not as much as he pretends to be." He takes the bucket and starts to climb again. "They've been out on strike," he adds without looking down. "So he has plenty of time to sit at home and tell me that nothing but a day's hard, honest work will get me anywhere in this world. Needless to say," he adds, "he doesn't consider studying a day's hard, hon-est work."

Antonio laughs again as he says this, but this time it doesn't sound as though he thinks anything is funny. Suds stream across the black and red letters and down onto the window. The smil-ing pig vanishes behind a cloud of foam. The pavement is hot. The soapy water slides onto it, and begins to steam, rising like breath around Angela's ankles.

"*Miserabilismo,*" Antonio says. "It's stupid. They strike and strike, but they don't even ask for anything. Just enough to sur-vive. Bread. Lousy little scraps, as if they work all their lives and that's all they deserve. Me"—he glances down at her and smiles—"I told my brother, I told Piero, he deserves more than bread. He deserves roses, too."

Bread and roses. Angela sees a round loaf beside blooms, swollen and warm in the sun.

"Piero wants me to go," Antonio is saying. "He can't tell Papa, but he wishes he'd gone. Or at least tried. I keep telling him it's not too late, but he won't listen. What about you?" Antonio asks, and although he is not looking at her now but back at the letter he is washing, Angela nods.

"Here," she says, telling him what she cannot tell Barbara. "I want to get a place here."

"Why?" He glances down at her over his shoulder. "There's the whole world."

Angela starts to say, *Because I can't leave my father. Because I'm worried about the books and the cloud. Because without me, he would vanish into nothingness.* But Antonio's concentrating on the sign again. As he finishes the last block of shiny black beyond the A and begins to back down the ladder, she says instead, "I've been watching you. I mean," she adds quickly, "playing football. I've seen you."

Antonio jumps down the last rung. He stands facing her, so close she can see where he's nicked himself shaving above his upper lip. It's everything she can do not to reach out and touch the tiny cut.

"I know," he says. "I've seen you."

The air is hot and close and his eyes on her face are like fingers on her skin. Angela realizes she is holding her breath. Antonio smiles. He puts the bucket down. His hand reaches out. The pad of his thumb presses her chin.

"We should change the water," he says. "Or it will just make the window dirty."

Later, when Angela looks back on that day, it feels like it's trapped in glass. Preserved. Perfect and sparkling, like something hidden in the back of a drawer.

Antonio helped her wash the big front window. They changed the water, and again she held the ladder while he finished the top. Then they stood, side by side, swiping the bottom half of the glass with the dripping sponges, their arms waving back and forth like seaweed.

While they did this, Antonio talked about his father. And

about his brother, Piero. He talked about their jobs in the factory, and about the lives they had that he did not want. He was going to be a professor, he said as they wiped the last slow slides of suds.

Then, while they rinsed the sponges, he told her about the farm north of Ravenna where he had been born and that his grandparents and their parents and their parents before them had owned. He talked about living there before his nonno died and it had been lost and his father moved them to Ferrara. He told her about the flatness of the fields and the herons that stood in the irrigation ditches, still and white as flags on a windless day. And about his grandfather's dog that slept by the well, its yellow coat fluffed with heat, its paws scrabbling a dream his nonno said was of rabbits because all dogs dream of rabbits, although this dog had rarely seen one and was used only for hunting ducks. He told her about the wind at night. And about how he and Piero had lain in their room at the top of the house listening as it snickered through the reed grass.

The words unspooled like threads kept in the dark because they are too fragile to bear the light of day. Angela rode the rhythm of his voice and said nothing, because what flowed out of him was not something you would interrupt or reply to any more than you would interrupt or reply to music.

"Some people think it's ugly." Antonio had shrugged as he emptied the dirty water into the gutter. "They say it's empty. That there's nothing out there anymore. But I think it's the most beautiful place in the world." He'd taken Angela's sponge from her, dropped it into the empty bucket. "It's not far from Pomposa," he'd added. "You could see the tower from my nonno's farm. Hear the bells. There were still monks there, then. They'd give us things. Honey, sometimes. Teas they made. Herb stuff. Have you ever been?" he'd asked. "To Pomposa?"

Angela had shaken her head. She had almost been there once, to the great abbey that sat on the edge of the marshes, a place of pilgrimage hung between land and sea. The school trip had been scheduled, then canceled because of snow.

"So," Antonio had said a minute later as he'd collapsed the ladder. "I'll take you."

He'd helped her put the things away, carrying the ladder around the corner one-handed and propping it against the wall of the storeroom. Then he'd stepped back into Via Mayr, and picked up his gym bag, which was spattered with drips, and slung it over his shoulder.

"To Pomposa," he'd said. "I'll take you someday. It's beautiful."

After he'd walked away, Angela stood outside the shop. She watched the wet prints of his shoes on the pavement as they dried in the sun and the last plume of the soap as it caught in the drain, the bubbles popping one by one. Then, finally, she went inside and sat at her place behind the cash register, and unlocked the big drawer, and took out the accounts and order books she was supposed to be working on. But the numbers made no sense. They kept shifting, rearranging themselves into pictures of Antonio's face. And of the span of his back under the white shirt. Of his arms, brown below the rolled-up sleeves. His foot on the rung of the ladder.

The street was almost empty because it was a Sunday in midsummer, but every time a car went by the roll of the tires sounded like his voice. *I'll take you to Pomposa.* And she wished, more than anything, wished with a desire so deep it made her stomach hurt, that she had run after him. That she had grabbed his arm, and made him tell her, *When?*

It's barely two weeks later, on Ferragósto, when she sees him again.

The holiday falls on a Thursday. By Wednesday afternoon there's barely a car on Via Mayr. Everyone who is leaving town has left, and everyone else has already stocked up for the weekend. The shop has done better than expected. For once they were so busy that Angela had to serve behind the counter, lifting out the soft round lumps of roasts, feeling their cool dead weight in her hands. She has selected slivers of veal, and plump pimpled legs of chickens. Cutting waxed paper off the big rolls, she's laid them out, these dead parts, and sprigged them with parsley before wrapping them up and sealing the ends, tying the packages with snow-white string and a bow of ribbon so they look like presents. At two o'clock, when her father decides to close the shop for the weekend, he takes an envelope out of his pocket and hands it to her.

"Here, Kitten," he says. "For all your hard work." He reaches out and tousles her hair, his big hand resting, momentarily heavy, on the top of her head. "Buy yourself something pretty. For Saturday night."

On Saturday night there will be fireworks at the castle and a dance in the piazza. A band from Bologna is playing, and flyers plastered over the city promise there will be a street fair. No one knows exactly what this means, since Ferrara has never had one, at least in living memory, but there's a general air of excitement.

Even so, as her father shoves the envelope toward her, Angela begins to protest. With Barbara gone, she has no one to go with. Some of the other girls from school will be there, of course. But that isn't the same. She starts to hand the envelope back, but her father presses it into her hand.

"Buy yourself a dress," he says. "Go dancing. Have some fun." He closes her fingers over the cheap paper. "There's not much point." He nods at the interior of the store, at the scrubbed marble and newly mopped and sawdust-sprinkled floor. "There's not much point in all this, if I can't buy my daughter a dress."

The dress is blue and green, and blotched with huge flowers. Angela spends half the money on it and puts the other half in her savings account, and even then she almost doesn't go to the dance.

Standing in front of her mirror on Saturday night, her dark hair corkscrewing in the heat, the material already sticking to the backs of her legs, she feels a burst of shame. The dress is a halter top. In the store it looked pretty. Alluring, even. Now her small breasts feel like they barely fill the cups. Even with a cardigan on, which makes her look like an old lady, she feels scrawny and exposed at the same time, as if she's about to go out in her underwear.

She'd take the thing off, put it back in the box, and slide like a snail back into the shell of her jeans and old flowered blouse, spend the night curled up with her book, except for the fact that her father is in the sitting room pretending not to, but waiting for her all the same. Waiting to see her step out of her bedroom door—not his slightly bedraggled, pale-skinned "Kitten"—but a princess. A Cinderella transformed by a wad of lire. By an envelope of notes worn soft as chamois, each earned with the chop and slice of a butcher's knife.

She picks up the pink lipstick she's bought and rims the edge of her lips. Then she fills in the space with gloss, rolling it back and forth across the faintly chapped skin the way Barbara has showed her. They read an article about it, about how to achieve what the writer called "That Just Bitten Look." Bitten by what? Angela had asked, and Barbara had rolled her eyes. She puts the cap back on the gloss, which smells strongly of peaches, like something you pour on ice cream. Through the open window she hears footsteps on the street, and the sound of laughter.

The music started at eight, a high-amped blast of bad imitation Doors. According to the school friends Angela met up with, the band was known for its repertoire of American hits.

Every Saturday night at a cavernous club in downtown Bologna they pumped out Jefferson Starship and mispronounced covers of Janis Joplin and Jimi Hendrix. Now the statue of Savonarola in Corso Libertà raised its hands in horror as Jim Morrison set the night on fire. Or possibly in approval. In the swirl of lights, it was hard to tell. A troupe of mimes performed in front of the Duomo. Crowds milled around them, eating food from the stalls on the Piazza Trieste while pigeons fluffed their wings and stamped up and down along the ledges.

After an hour of watching the swing of the colored lights and giggling at the couples brave enough to dance, Angela grew tired of the group she'd met up with. Looking at them, with their huge hoop earrings and colored plastic bangles, she had the strange thought that they had always been there. That underneath their long dresses and bright eye shadow, they were not young at all, but ancient and decaying—a gathering of medieval court ladies in outlandish costumes who had been dead for years. She turned away, haunted by the possibility that the past might smear into the present until the two were indistinguishable. That the silent mimes and howling band were no different from the jesters and freaks, the monkeys and misshapen dwarves that had always been kept for amusement and still haunted the dark corners of the Castello.

A crafts market has been set up in the courtyard of the Palazzo Ducale. All the women keeping the stalls have long hair and headbands and gypsy dresses. The men wear leather jerkins. Peace medallions wink from tangles of chest hair. Someone has hung a banner that says NO TO NATO on the Municìpio stairs. Angela glances at her watch. She is not particularly interested in crafts, but it's barely half past nine. Her father is having supper with the Ravallis. If she comes in now he'll hear, and worry that her dress wasn't expensive enough, or that she's not popular and no one wanted to dance with her. One more hour, she thinks, and the men will go to the taverna. Get to their feet, hiking up their trousers, and wander out in jovial packs, puffing cigars while their wives and sisters—and in some cases still, mothers—watch them leave with a mixture of hurt and relief before congregating in the Ravallis' kitchen to boast and complain about them. Then Angela will be able to slip through the door. Swim under the current of gossip and clatter of dishes, and make her way upstairs and into to the apartment without anyone noticing. Now she has time to waste.

The crafts stalls are made up mainly of wooden toys, horses and trains on wheels, and of ceramic bowls the color of mud, and incense burners shaped like Indian goddesses. Some feature purses and belts made of what look like leftover strips of leather. She wanders, picking things up and putting them down, measuring her steps like a man on a mechanical clock.

The air is heavy with the smell of grilling sausages and patchouli oil. Angela sneezes and stops for a string of people who dance by waving their arms and shouting "Where have all the flowers gone?," the English rolling awkwardly off their tongues. Out by the Castello the band begins to play "Stairway to Heaven."

"Are you hiding?"

She is standing beside a jewelry stall, fingering a blue-beaded bracelet, when she hears his voice. This time, she laughs.

"Good," Antonio says. "So am I."

He is wearing the same white shirt, the same jeans. His sleeves are even rolled up again. He nods at the bracelet.

"That's pretty," he says, and before Angela realizes what he's doing, he digs into his pocket, pulls out some notes, and hands them to the thin girl who sits behind her display of chokers and earrings threading beads onto fishing line. A baby lies at her feet in what looks like an old dresser drawer. It squirms, lets out a red-faced cry, and lapses into silence as Antonio takes the bracelet out of Angela's hand and slips it onto her wrist.

"Happy birthday," he says.

"It's not my birthday."

Angela closes her free hand over the beads as if she's afraid that, once he knows this, he'll take them back.

"Well, you have a birthday don't you?"

He's smiling at her as she nods and wonders why, exactly, she's finding it so difficult to speak.

"In May," she manages, finally.

"May what?" He reaches out and touches her hair as if he's touching a leaf or a petal.

"May eleventh."

"So how old are you, now?"

"Sixteen."

In the last hour the light has faded and the crowd has thickened. Antonio takes her arm. They dodge a juggler and another line of dancers whose shadows twist and writhe. One of them staggers, then falls in slow motion and lies laughing on the flood-lit cobbles.

"I'm going to the university," he says. "To Padua. Tomorrow, on the nine o'clock bus. So you have to dance with me." Angela is aware of his fingers kneading her arm through the cheap nylon of the cardigan. She shakes her head.

"I'm a terrible dancer."

"So what?" Antonio grins. "I helped you wash your window. You have to. That's the price."

Her tongue is cottony, reluctant to make words, so instead she nods. He guides her across the piazza. As they reach the mouth of Via Garibaldi, a figure jumps in front of them. As tall as Antonio, his hair is wild. Crimson face paint streaks his cheeks.

"Surrender!" he shouts. "Surrender the princess!"

Angela starts backward, but Antonio laughs. He lets go of her arm and punches the boy in the shoulder.

"Shut up, you drunk!"

For a moment they wrestle, their arms twining around each

other, heads butting. Then they stop. Antonio grabs the boy's ear, and still laughing orders, "Apologize to the lady."

To her surprise, the boy does. He makes a low, swishing bow.

"At your service," he says, still grinning.

"Angela," Antonio supplies.

"At your service. Angela."

The boy takes her hand and kisses it.

"Don't be an ass."

Antonio cuffs him around the head, then they both start to laugh and suddenly, seeing them side by side, with the same wild hair, same black eyes and sharp noses, Angela realizes who this is.

"Piero." Antonio puts his arm around his brother's shoulder. "You'll have to forgive him," he says. "This is my stupid older brother, Piero."

"And this," Piero says, "is my clever little twerp, Antoni-on-io."

They stand there, in front of her, so alike they might be reflections of each other. Piero's face paint has smudged the arm of Antonio's white shirt. The lines on his cheeks are smeared from wrestling. They look at each other and laugh. Then Piero reaches into his back pocket and pulls out a silver hip flask. He hands it to Antonio and punches him on the arm.

"Have fun, little brother," he says, as he bows again to Angela, and spins away, whirling into a stream of people who are running around the corner toward the castle.

"Sorry." Antonio looks faintly sheepish, but the grin doesn't leave his face. "So that's my brother." He takes her arm again, laughing and shaking his head, and Angela realizes she is laughing, too, and that she had expected Piero to be older. Older and stern and worn down by working in the factory instead of a lithe, clownish boy with face paint and espadrilles.

"I love him," Antonio says suddenly. "More than anyone in the world. I wish I could take him with me. I wish he wasn't staying here."

They are standing below the arch that leads to Via Garibaldi. A group runs past them. Squeals of laughter snag the music. When Antonio kisses her, Angela is surprised at how warm his skin is, how his lips move over hers as if they belong there. His tongue runs along her teeth, then slips into her open mouth. He has one hand on the small of her back. The other cradles her head. She reaches for his shoulders and thinks he tastes of something. Grappa. Cherries. When he stops and looks at her, his fingers are laced through her hair.

"Butcher's Daughter," he says. Then he traces his thumb down her forehead, and across the tip of her nose. "Come with me, to the Montagnola."

Behind them, the people in the street bark laughter, stumble, and clutch each other, their silhouettes lit by shop windows. The Montagnola is on the ramparts, at the far corner of the walls, beyond the Angels' Gate. Grass-sloped and furred with undergrowth, it looks down over the Certosa and the darkness of the cemetery. Angela has heard the joke that is probably not really a joke, has heard Signora Ravalli say more than once that half the babies born in Ferrara are conceived there. Antonio runs his thumb down to her chin. He leans forward, his lips dabbing the gloss that smells of peaches. She tastes him again, then kisses the soft hollow of his neck, amazed by the softness and the slight pulse she can feel under her lips.

"Don't you?" he whispers. "Don't you want to come with me?"

"Yes." The word comes out as barely more than a breath, barely more than a single beat of her heart. Angela lifts her head away and looks at him. "Yes," she says, louder this time. "Yes, I want to come with you."

Later her mind would keep skittering back to the bicycle. To the way its wheels bumped over the cobbles. To how its fender rattled as he pedaled across the bridge and down Corso d'Este, leaving the castle and the lights and the dancers and music behind them.

Angela sat on the crossbar, holding her dress up so it wouldn't get caught in the spokes. Dust stirred and rode on the hot air, the faint grit of the summer night brushed her cheeks. The palazzos were pale and still. No lights burned in their windows and there were no street lamps. In the soft blackness ahead Angela could sense the shapes of the trees, and the house with the glossy front door where she looked for the memory of her mother.

The cobbles eddied into broken pavement. The Angels' Gate loomed, and for a split second she wanted to let go of the crossbar and stretch out her arms and give the huge doors a mighty shove. She wanted to break the rusted chains and push them open so she and Antonio could ride like this forever, into the emptiness beyond.

The bike judders on the grass tufts between the patches of rubble, and Angela jumps down. She wobbles on her sandals. Antonio laughs, and catches her, and offers her the flask. The grappa does taste of cherries. It makes her cough. He pats her on the back, then slips his arm around her and guides her up the track onto the ramparts where a wide path runs through the avenue of trees that leads to the Montagnola.

When they get there, he hides the bike in a thicket. As they climb the steep path, twigs snatch at Angela's dress and reach for strands of her hair. She slips and trips on a root, but Antonio has her arm. When they reach the top, he pushes a bush aside, and guides her down the slope a few steps until they are standing on a patch of grass.

They are up so high that, over the feathered tops of the trees, Angela can see the square tower of the Certosa guarding its field of the dead. Colored lights shimmer above the Castello a mile away. The noise of the band, a tune she can't quite make out, floats on distant beams of pink and green. Antonio's lips brush her ear. His arms are around her waist.

"You don't have to," he whispers. "You don't have to, if you don't want to."

She can feel his hips. The heat of his chest against her back.

"I want to."

She turns around and looks at him, as sure of this as she has ever been of anything. Antonio reaches into his pocket. He hands her the flask. This time she takes less. He takes a swallow of his own, then lays it on the grass and reaches up and pushes her cardigan off her shoulders.

Afterward, Antonio's leg is heavy across her. He slithers down, his lips fastening, teeth smooth against her breast. When he raises himself on his elbow, she can feel his eyes, and follows his fingers, as they walk the pale contours of her body.

"Was it?" he asks. "Was it your first time?" His hand moves across her belly, the jut of her hip. "It was," he says. "Wasn't it?"

Antonio traces a slippery pattern on the inside of her thigh. Angela nods and closes her eyes. In this new place where there is nothing except the feel of him, she loses track of time. Her fingers lace through his hair. She cradles his head, back arching, while his mouth feathers her stomach. She folds her legs around him, and feels her breath leave her body as he lifts her up and moves inside her.

"Do something for me," he murmurs, and turns her over.

Antonio pushes her hair up. She feels his lips on the back of her neck. He kneels between her legs, runs his hands down her back. A moment later, Angela's mouth flies open. Her eyes tear. She bites down and tastes dirt. Earth under grass. Her hand clutches at the rolled ball of her cardigan. At a stone. At Antonio, as he reaches for her, and their fingers twine, and lock.

"Ti possiedo," "I own you," he whispers. *"Ora, tu sei mia. Per sempre."* "Now you're mine. Forever."

The next morning when she wakes up, Angela is dizzy. It takes her a moment to realize where she is. Not on the Montagnola, but in her room. Turning her head on the pillow, she sees slats of sun coming through the shutters. Bright bars wobble and tilt. The room feels unbearably hot. And close, as if the walls are inching in and will crush her. She moves her legs gingerly. Pain rolls up her in waves.

A faint greasy slick meets the tip of her tongue when she runs it across her lips. Saltiness and the taste of copper mixed with the sweet aftertaste of the grappa rises in her throat. Her head spins. She rolls sideways, closing her eyes. Breathing in the familiar smell of her sheets and pillow, Angela slides her hand between her legs and fingers the bruised, swollen skin and realizes that she's crying. That tears are seeping under her lids and clotting her eyelashes and wetting the pillowcase—not because it hurt, or because it still hurts. But because she's just remembered that it's tomorrow and he's gone.

Barbara came back a week later.

The heat hadn't budged. It pressed down like a hard bullying hand, threatening to melt the stones and ramparts back into the marshy delta they had risen from. With no rain and almost no dew at night, the pavements and cobbles were dull in the morning sun. The smell of garbage hung in the air.

Around the city the fields spread away, flat and green. Nothing moved on them in the daytime. The harvest workers, pickers who migrated south to north with the crop and slept in barns and tents, started before dawn and stopped just after sunrise, their tiny figures vanishing like mirages. Standing on the Montagnola, Angela could smell the sour stink of the irrigation ditches on the evening wind and the drying mud of the Po as it lay withering in its banks.

She went almost every day. Walked at sunset like a pilgrim along the path, then climbed the mound and slithered down to the spot where they had lain. At first she thought she could still see an imprint in the scraggy grass. But little by little it faded, and after that she found no sign of Antonio. No hint that he had ever brought her there. If it hadn't been for the soreness, for the raw skin and the spots of blood, she might have thought she'd imagined the whole thing.

At first she was sure he'd write, or maybe even telephone. Ask her to come and visit him in Padua, which was hardly far away. Or come home. Show up outside her door on a Sunday morning with a bouquet of flowers. But after the second week, then finally the third, she knew he wouldn't. By the time she started school again, Angela felt an emptiness so large it became a weight. A leaden nothingness she dragged behind her.

She would not hear from him because he did not love her. Or even want to remember her. Having her had been the same as getting drunk or fulfilling a dare. She tortured herself by wondering if he had thought of it already when he stopped to help her clean the shop sign. If he had planned it that far back, or if it was just an impulse on the night. If it had been his idea, or Piero's—*Have fun, little brother*—for no more than the price of a bracelet.

When, right on time, she got her period, she slid the blue beads off her wrist and buried them in the bottom of a drawer.

"What's the matter with you?"

Barbara peers at her through a veil of cigarette smoke. They have finished classes and are sitting at a table outside a dingy café near the market that Barbara has chosen because she says her mother, who would have a fit if she saw her smoking, never comes to this side of town.

Smoking is Barbara's new thing. She picked it up while she was visiting the college campus where her father teaches summer school in America where, she told Angela, everyone smokes. Everyone, apparently, also drinks beer and listens to Neil Young and a band called The Grateful Dead.

Sitting below the open window of Angela's room so Barbara can blow smoke straight outside and not enrage Nonna Franchi, they have played Barbara's new *Harvest* album over and over. And listened again and again to Carole King singing "You've Got a Friend." And to The Dead—as Barbara reminds her sternly they must be called—singing "Casey Jones." The stack of records Barbara brought back with her also includes James Taylor. But Angela's banned him. She's insisted that he's a sop and she hates him. But the truth is, she can't bear to hear "Fire and Rain."

Now she looks at her friend through the haze that always seems to surround her. Barbara prefers American cigarettes. Marlboros, if she can get them. The smell makes Angela queasy. The taste of the smoke Barbara breathes out through her nose like a dragon makes her mouth dry. It gets in her clothes and in her hair. She can't believe that even Barbara's mother is so indifferent that she doesn't catch on. But Barbara insists it's the case, and Angela doesn't have the energy to argue. She doesn't have the energy for anything anymore. She feels like she hasn't been alive since Antonio dropped her off at the top of her street that Sunday morning, smoothed her stained dress, and handed her her ruined cardigan. Lifted her hair and kissed her on the forehead, then rode away as the first light snaked across the August sky.

"Nothing," she says, shaking her head. "Nothing's wrong with me, I'm just tired."

When she first knew Barbara, Angela hadn't told her about Antonio because she'd wanted to hoard him, to keep him like a treat she was too selfish to share. Now she doesn't tell her because she's ashamed.

Barbara reaches across the small rickety table and touches her hand. She had her hair cut in America, too. Her long braid is gone. Barbara's new bangs fall in her eyes. Sometimes Angela has the disturbing feeling she's someone else.

"Angie." The tips of her fingers press the back of Angela's hand. "Angie, come on," she says. "Tell me. I'm your friend. Remember? What is it?" Barbara leans forward. "Is it your father?"

Angela shakes her head again. Then she can't stop shaking it. She goes on and on, as if she can rattle loose the memories that have latched on to her and are sucking her dry, slurping her blood and even her tears like vampires.

Suds billowing and streaking on glass. Antonio's arms below the rolled-up white of his sleeves. His wet footsteps, and the bounce and jolt of his bicycle. The soft dark and the looming shape of the Angels' Gate. The thwap of bushes. And distant music. And lights. And Antonio's hands as they untie the knot behind her neck, and rock her backward, and push her dress up, wadding the slithery nylon into a belt around her naked waist.

Grass. Her legs. The taste of his skin.

Tears streak the eyeliner she is not supposed to wear to school. They pool in the cleft of her chin and drip onto her hands and her lap.

"It's him, isn't it?" Barbara's fingers wind around hers. "It's the factory boy? It's what's-his-name? Antonio?"

Barbara gets up, leaving her cigarette burning in the colored tinfoil ashtray. Somehow she circles the rickety table without either tipping it over or letting go of Angela's hand. She puts her arm around her shoulder.

"That bastard!" she says. "That fucking bastard."

Barbara squeezes, and Angela feels the silky expensive cotton of her blouse. She smells the sandalwood oil Barbara has taken to rubbing behind her ears and into the hollows of her collarbones.

"Are you pregnant?" Barbara whispers. "Is that it?"

Angela shakes her head.

"Are you sure? Because if you are, my sisters can, there's—"

Angela shakes her head again, vicious and hard this time, her forehead knocking against Barbara's jaw.

"Well, thank God for that!"

Barbara wraps both arms around her and Angela presses her face into her friend's shoulder. She doesn't care that people walking past are looking at them, or turning away and deliberately not looking at them. She grabs and holds on as if Barbara's a raft and she's in danger of slipping off. Of going under and being swept away, drowned in all the pictures she can't get out of her head.

Barbara's mother is away teaching a master class in Vicenza. Her father is not coming home from the university these days until well after dark, and sometimes not even then.

"They sleep in different rooms," Barbara hisses. "Like it's a hotel."

Guiding Angela up the stairs and across the landing as if she's an invalid, Barbara pushes open the door to her bedroom, which is pale blue and white and three times as big as Angela's, and looks over at the park across the street. She goes and makes tea and brings it back in two white mugs. Then, curled on the bed and clutching a plush velour cat, one of Barbara's huge collection of stuffed animals, Angela takes the tissues Barbara hands her. Balling them up and dropping them onto the floor until they make a sodden snowy drift, she tells Barbara everything. Every single moment she can remember since the first time she ever saw Antonio. Angela talks until her throat is hoarse. She even tells about the apple.

When she's finally done, Barbara, who is sitting beside her on the bed, leans forward and brushes the hair off Angela's forehead. Angela would like to tell her not to do that because that's what Antonio did, but she doesn't. Silence eddies around them.

"He's scum," Barbara whispers. "I don't care how handsome they are. Or how well they play football. They're scum."

She stands up and walks across the room, her bare feet silent on the white shag rug.

"You'll feel better," she announces a minute later. She looks at Angela and nods. "Now that you've said it all. It's catharsis. It's what psychiatrists make you do. Get it all out. You'll feel better."

Angela isn't sure she believes this. She'd like to, she really would. But she doubts it. It's like people saying you'll feel better if you throw up. You do, for a while. Until you feel sick again.

Standing beside her dressing table, Barbara is toying with her lipsticks. Angela watches in the mirror as her hair falls in her eyes. Barbara brought back a bunch of makeup from America. The best is a whole set of lipsticks packed in a little pink case, each one named for a flower. Peony. Iris. Desert Rose.

"Did it hurt?"

Barbara's voice drops to a whisper. She meets Angela's eyes in the mirror. "You know," she says, "when he did it—"

Angela nods. Outside the two tall windows the sun has dipped, leaving behind a deep hazy gold. She feels herself nod again as she watches the honey light drip across the sill and pool on the white fluffy rug.

"Yes," she says. "It hurt."

But what she doesn't say is that she hadn't cared. That she had wanted him to go on hurting, and that in the days after he left, she had wanted the hurt to stay. That she wants it even now. That what is worse is that it faded, like his footsteps on the pavement. Because at least the hurt meant that for those few hours, he'd been there. And now it's gone, and she has nothing left of him.

⁓

It was about a week later that Barbara gave Angela her first pair of running shoes. They were white with blue stripes on the sides, and when Angela opened the box she actually burst out laughing. Or did the closest she'd come to it in the last six weeks.

"Well," Barbara said, "at least I made you smile."

She sat back on her haunches and blew a thin stream of smoke out Angela's window. It was a Saturday afternoon. Angela's record player clicked, dropping a new record, and Neil Young went off mining for a heart of gold.

"But I don't run," Angela protested. "I don't know how."

Barbara snorted.

"Yes, you do," she said. "Everyone runs. Everyone knows how. Besides, I'll show you. I even got you the right kind of socks." She pulled the plastic shopping bag she had brought with her across the floor, reached into it, and threw two pairs of ugly thick cotton socks toward Angela. "And sweat pants." A baggy pair of gray pants followed.

"We'll have to go in the morning, before school." Barbara stood up, stubbed her cigarette out on the sole of her shoe, and tossed the butt out the window. "That's it," she said. She looked at Angela and grinned. "That's my last one."

"What?"

Barbara nodded. "I'm giving them up. For the track scholarship."

This was Barbara's latest plan. She had decided that even Rome, or Milan, or Torino were not far enough away. She wanted to go to university in America. Her parents weren't thrilled by the idea. Her father said America was a sinkhole of capitalist, militarist corruption. Her mother said there were perfectly good universities right here in Italy. For once they agreed. They were not going to pay for her to go to America even if she got into the Ivy League, whatever that was.

Barbara, being Barbara, had retorted that she'd pay for herself. She'd get a scholarship. There were millions. Her sister in Milan was sending her information. The easiest to get were in athletics, even for women. Especially for women. According to Barbara, American universities were practically giving athletic scholarships away. Since something called Title IX, and since Joan Benoit had won the first women's marathon at the Los Angeles Olympics, all the American universities were falling over themselves to have women's track teams. The only problem was to decide where you wanted to go.

Angela couldn't help doubting this. But if Barbara was willing to give up cigarettes, she thought she should do her part by pretending to be enthusiastic. Or at least interested. She'd put the shoes and the ugly baggy pants on and go running, once or twice. Play along until Barbara got tired of the whole thing. Or until someone gave her a new pack of Marlboros, or it simply got too cold.

At first it was hard, hot, panting work that made her head swim and her legs ache. Then, little by little, as the weather grew chillier and November slid into December, the runs Angela shared with Barbara grew easier. Eventually they even became pleasant. As January came on, alternating days of low freezing fog with cold hard sunshine, the two girls ran side by side, saying nothing, their feet falling in time. Breath matching breath.

Then came a weekend when Barbara went with her mother to Padua to visit her sister at the university and, somewhat to her surprise, Angela found she wanted to run by herself. As her father's snores growled behind his bedroom door, she laced up her shoes feeling both guilty and excited, the same way she had felt when she was little and had slipped without his knowledge beyond the confines of the neighborhood.

The city streets were still with Sunday morning. The first sun caught the shards of glass on top of the walls of the old military barracks, making them glitter like white-tipped fangs. Crossing in front of the Corpus Domini and the Annunziata and the great patterned face of the Schifonoia, her running shoes silent on the cobbles, Angela felt herself fading into the city. Becoming transparent—just another ghost rubbing shoulders with the old men in their black coats, and with the d'Este, and with La Borgia herself. All of them mingling like smoke.

At the Punta della Giovecca she climbed onto the ramparts. Beyond the walls the fields were washed in mist. She could hear, but not see, a car. Standing suspended between earth and air, Angela felt as if she was on the edge of precipice. Tension thrummed her arms and legs and back. For a second, she had the impulse to turn around. To stop, because what she was doing—coming here to run alone—was a betrayal of Barbara. An infidelity, as surely as the nights Barbara's father had taken to spending with his students were infidelities. Then she gave herself a little shake.

Her first step cracked ice in a puddle. The next left a footprint in frost. Her breath bloomed and trembled on the chilly air as heat began to throb into her mittened hands. Above her, the white sky was traced with naked trees. Below her, her feet fell—one chasing another, faster and faster, until she almost believed she was no longer touching the ground.

When Barbara came around that night, to report on the hotel where she and her mother had stayed, and on what they had had for lunch, and on the fight her mother and sister had had over her sister's new boyfriend, which made her mother so angry she'd almost driven off the road on the way home—to say all of that, but mostly to say that she had not only not seen Antonio, but hadn't even thought of looking for him—Angela listened.

When Barbara finally stopped talking and remembered to ask her what she had done with her weekend, she shrugged and said that on Saturday she had worked in the shop, as she now did every Saturday, and that afterward she had studied for the exams that were looming in front of them. She told Barbara she had gone to the Laundromat, then done some ironing while she watched TV, and said nothing about running. Nothing about the black lace of branches, or puffs of breath, or how with every step she had sensed a piece of herself flaking away—anxiety and pain, disappointment, even happiness, all shedding like scales. She kept it instead to herself. Hoarded it, the way she had once hoarded Antonio.

She thought of him. She knew she wasn't supposed to, that Barbara would say it wasn't good for her. But she couldn't help it. Sometimes she opened her bottom drawer and rummaged under the old sweaters until she found the blue beads. Then she would crouch, her hand folded over them, eyes closed, rolling each one between finger and thumb. Other times her hand slid between her legs and conjured him, summoned him the way she imagined a gypsy at a fair summoned spirits when she rubbed a crystal ball.

As the winter deepened, Angela fell into an easy pattern of deception. And was surprised by how much she enjoyed it. She lied mainly by omission. By silence and stealth. And grew increasingly certain that lying made her feet turn faster, made her feel as if she was nothing but a shadow, flying across the frozen ground like the shadows of the crows that dipped and fell above the empty ramparts.

On the mornings she didn't run with Barbara, she went by herself, very early. Other times she went at dusk. She took to saying she had to work for her father, then changing in the back room of the shop and slipping down the alley past the storeroom and into Piazza Travaglio where she climbed up the path beside the Porta Paola. From there she would run along the top of the walls—past the flat white roofs of the hospital, past the line of trees above the football pitch, past the Montagnola, past each memory and year as if she was running through her life, outpacing herself until she reached the Angels' Gate.

There, chest heaving as her heart slowed, she would come down and pause behind the iron railings of the houses at the top of Corso d'Este and watch the curtained windows. When she turned away, she would see the castle all lit up in the distance, burning in the heart of the city. Sometimes it looked like a fire at the end of a tunnel. Or like the sparkling lure that teases a fish. Other times she imagined its lights must look like the lights birds see when they gaze down from the night sky, silver pinpricks far below where they hover in cold and silence.

On evenings like that, the walk back along the Corso made Angela feel as if she was drifting back down to earth. Or being reeled in. Every step making her more solid, more prone to the rules of gravity and memory. Until, by the time she got to Via Mazzini, passing the spot where the gates of the ghetto had once been, she would be worrying about her exams, or her father's books, or being late for school or dinner.

Her father still did most of the cooking, but Angela helped him. Sometimes she did it all herself. And she was thinking about jointing a chicken—about the quick, firm whack of the cleaver, and the clean split of bone, and cut of skin—and about whether she had remembered to buy enough carrots, and if they might be out of oil, when on the first Thursday in February she came around the corner into Via Vittoria and mounted the steps and put her key in the lock and smelled burning.

Her immediate thought was that something had spilled on the stove and rolled into the gas flame, or been forgotten in the oven. That her father must have turned it on, then gone downstairs to the Ravallis' to borrow salt or butter or the onions she had forgotten to buy and that any second he would reappear, swearing, as if the oven itself was the miscreant.

She ran up the stairs and pushed open the door to the apartment. A haze shimmered in the kitchen. Whatever it had been was surely blackened by now.

"Oh, Papa."

He had grown more forgetful, preoccupied by the shop and by his diatribes against the supermarket, and—she knew, although they never mentioned it—by the mushroom cloud of debt that refused to shrink no matter how much of her savings account, which admittedly wasn't much to start with, she squirreled back into the cash trays.

Angela darted through the doorway, eyes fixed on the pan that sat smoking on the stove. She turned the burner off and, pulling her sweatshirt sleeve over her mittened hand, grabbed the handle and tipped it into the sink where it sizzled and hissed like a devil in the Purgatorio. The burning oil made her eyes tear, so it was not until she had shoved open the window and was trying to fan the sheet of cold air that she turned and saw her father.

He lay on the far side of the old scarred table. The chopping board he had been working on had tipped and fallen beside him. Red chunks of tomatoes—the first from Sicily, sold out of a van on Corso Porto Mare—oozed on the tiles. His face was contorted. His mouth open, as if someone had punched him suddenly in the stomach. Flung over his head, his hand still held the coring knife.

"He's not dead. He's not dead."

Everyone tells her this. The ambulance people who bring a chaos of bleating sirens and flashing lights. Signora Ravalli who rides with her in a police car to the hospital. The doctor who comes, trying not to look as if he is in a hurry, to tell her that something is very wrong with her father's heart and that they will do the best they can. Even Signor and Signora Pirotti, who have left their supper and come to sit with her in the waiting room.

"He's not dead," they say, and clutch her hands as if it is supposed to bring some comfort. Which it does. Even if Angela is not sure what it means. Not really. Because even though everyone tells her that her quick thinking has saved his life—that he had a massive heart attack, and that if she had not returned and found him and called the ambulance, well, things would be very different. Even though everyone tells her this, she is not sure what she is supposed to think about it.

Because he looked dead to her. He felt dead, when she touched him. And he feels dead now, lost somewhere behind those doors she cannot go through where they are cracking open his chest and reaching in to grasp his heart the way she has seen him crack open the chest and reach in to grasp the heart of a lamb or a cow. Angela closes her eyes and wishes that she did not know what those organs look like. Liver, kidneys, the round and oozing heart. But she does.

Sitting in the hard molded-plastic chair, she reaches into the neck of her sweatshirt and feels for her necklace. The gold is warm from the heat of her body, and as she rubs it she imagines that she is rubbing off the A for Annabeth. That she is freeing it. And that it is breaking apart—swirling into a million tiny pieces that rise and finger their way through the closed doors and fly down the labyrinth halls of this hospital where her mother left the world and she came into it, until they find her father and settle themselves. Nest like birds on his cracked open heart. And form an A. For Annabeth and Angela.

It is almost midnight when the Pirottis take her home. Her father is doing as well as can be expected. She can't see him, can't even glimpse him through a glass window until tomorrow, at visiting hours in the afternoon, and perhaps not even then. So there is no point in her sitting there. The nurse says she should have something to eat. That she should get some sleep. She is a nice woman with gray curling hair that escapes from her cap in little horns. When she brings out a pile of forms and asks Angela if she is old enough to sign them, to be legally responsible for decisions about her father's care, the lie skips out like a heartbeat.

Deception, Angela thinks, is truly second nature to her now. She swears and signs on the line.

If they notice, which they almost certainly do, the Pirottis say nothing. When they were young, girls her age got married. During the war they picked up guns and shot and got shot at. For the poor, at least for those who labor with their hands, childhood is a modern invention. Like birth control pills and divorce and feminism, it's made up to get you out of doing what everyone really knows you have to do. Besides, they've all heard what happens if someone like her father doesn't have a daughter, or a wife, or a son. He could be moved anywhere. Shuffled and forgotten like a pack of worn-out cards. This, after all, is what families are for, to grab your hand in the crowd. There is, of course, her father's cousin who raises the vealers. He passes through Angela's mind like a shadow. And vanishes just as fast. She hasn't even called him. She can't imagine what she would say.

When they reach her building, the Pirottis want to come inside. Signora Pirotti offers to spend the night. But Angela shakes her head. After all, she's hardly on her own. In the ghetto no one is on their own. The Ravallis are downstairs. Nonna Franchi is around the corner. Barbara lives five minutes away. She's surrounded. But all she wants is to go back to the apartment. Alone. She can't stand the idea of sympathy, or crying, or anyone else's food.

Behind the closed door and freed of the burden of other people's eyes, Angela wonders if she had not gone running, if she had been here, could she have changed this? The doctor said no. More or less. Not that she asked him directly, begged for his absolution as if he was some kind of priest. But he called her father's heart a ticking time bomb. Said that the only miracle, other than the fact that he had not died instantly, was that this had not happened years ago.

Angela thinks of that now and wonders if her father knew. If when he held a pig's or an ox's heart in his hand, he understood that there was something wrong with his own—felt it, reluctant in his chest like a clock that has to be coaxed into running.

If he did that, if he urged his heart on day after day, pushing it to one more beat, Angela knows he did it for her. She knows this just as she knows that, if he is holding on now, if he is clinging to the fragile web that stops him from joining her mother, he is also doing it for her. The knowledge makes her stop. She stands on the stairs as if his love has turned her to stone.

Unable to tolerate the box of her own room, she sleeps on the sofa. She wraps herself in the old maroon blanket that usually lies folded across the foot of her parents' bed and puts her father's slippers on her stockinged feet. During the night they fall off and flap onto the floor as if they're trying to walk back to their place beside his chair.

When Angela wakes up, it's dark. Stiff from propping her head on the uncomfortable armrest, she smells the stale woody scent of cigars and thinks, just for a second, that she has fallen asleep in front of the TV and had a bad dream and that she can hear her father snoring, the grunts and snuffles jumping like puppies at the door of his bedroom down the hall. Then she smells the charcoaly beef smell and the greasy residue of burned oil and sits up, her clothes tight with sweat, her arms and neck aching.

The strip of sky above the roofs is the dirty black of winter dawn. The stars, if there were any, will be fading. Angela looks at her watch. It's half past five. She wonders if her father is still on this earth, or if he's gone, if while she was sleeping he slipped away to join her mother, and realizes with a pang that a part of him has probably wanted to do just that for a very long time. She saw him kissing Signora Ravalli once, years ago. But other than that, as far as she knows, he's never glanced at another woman. He's gone to his shop, and sharpened his knives, and driven out to see the veal calves, and mixed sausage meat, and worked in the cold room without feeling the warm, slick rub of another naked body. The band of someone's arms around him. He's locked the shop and smoked his cigars and walked home to cook dinner, for her. So he could read her a story, lay his hand on the top of her head. Pass her a crumpled envelope and tell her to buy a dress.

Angela sits on the edge of the sofa and knows what she has to do.

It's chilly in the bathroom, even when she turns on both bars of the heater. But she takes a shower anyway, and dries her hair. She braids it, tight, watching her face in the mirror, the elastic held between her teeth. She gets dressed and makes herself strong coffee, skirting that piece of the floor. She cuts bread from the loaf and eats it standing up because she doesn't want to sit at the table, or see the stain from the tomatoes that has sunk into the wide-grained wood and will have to be scrubbed away and even then will probably not vanish altogether, but linger like the handprint of an unwanted guest. When she starts to wash her cup, she stops. She can't turn on the faucet. The burned pan is still in the sink, blackened lumps of beef curled in it like dead mice.

In the hallway she pulls on boots, a hat, and her coat. When she realizes she will have to reach into the pocket of her father's coat for his keys, her throat tightens, the silence of the apartment washing around her, the stillness behind her father's bedroom door booming in her head. She takes a deep breath as her fingers finally reach out and meet the soft, worn wool. She has to close her eyes and bite her lip.

When she finally steps outside, the cold is like a slap. Angela's glad. She turns away from the Duomo and the university and school. As she goes down Via Vittoria and into Via Carbone, she hears the prayer in the rustling of the pigeons and in the click of the street lamp as it switches off. Then, under the familiar whispered words, she hears something else—the high, tuneless, notes of her father's whistle, scattering before her like pebbles.

⌒

"I don't get it," Barbara says. "I mean, I just don't get it. What the fuck are you doing?"

It's the night before Valentine's Day, exactly a week since Angela's father had his heart attack and she started opening the shop by herself. Barbara runs her hands through her hair, digging her fingers into her scalp and pulling at the ends to show that Angela's making her crazy.

"It's like you're quitting."

Her voice rises to something close to a shriek. If the shop was still open, Angela would tell her to calm down. But it isn't, so she doesn't bother.

"It's like you've just decided to be a fucking quitter," Barbara announces. "Shit!" She bangs her fist on the cash register, making it ping. "It's like you're giving up fucking everything!"

In place of smoking, Barbara has taken up swearing. *Fuck* is now her favorite word, although she knows lots of others, too. Angela's not sure where she's learned them all. From the bathrooms in the bus station? From her sisters? She has no idea, but she supposes she's lucky not to be called something worse than a fucking quitter. A syphilitic cunt, perhaps? A witch's tit? Those are two of Barbara's current favorites, along with various anatomical references to Jesus, whom she's decided she no longer believes in.

"I mean." Barbara takes a deep breath and lowers her voice, trying another tack. "I mean"—she says—"I understand, Angie. I do. Really. I do. Shit. But your dad's OK. I mean, he's going to be OK? Right? And you're still telling me you're not coming back to school?"

Angela does not point out that legally she could have left school a year ago. That lots of people do. People who have to do boring things, like working in a factory, or taking care of their parents and paying bills and putting bread on the table. People who do not have, for instance, white shag rugs. Or cases of lipsticks named after flowers. Nor does she point out that her "dad," whom she has never called Dad in her life, is anything but OK. That he's OK only if you count being alive, and sitting up once, and being able to mumble for a few seconds at a time because you can't talk, much less feed yourself or walk or go to the bathroom as OK. She doesn't say it. Any of it. Any more than she actually says she isn't going back to school.

Because she doesn't have to. At least not to Barbara, who knows it already because she has always had the disturbing ability to know Angela—better it seems sometimes, than Angela knows herself. Which is why they are such good friends. Which is why Angela does not mind her swearing any more than she really minded her smoking. Because Barbara is Barbara, and the luxury of not having to explain to her, or even talk, feels like leaning back in a hot, perfumed bath. Feels like closing her eyes and letting her limbs float while the water creeps up to her neck, and chin, and mouth.

For a brief second, Angela remembers the day they watched Antonio playing football. She remembers how Barbara knew instinctively who she was watching, which exact person, and what it meant. And how, instinctively, she also knew what had happened when she came back from America. How she knew it all, just as she knows now, even before Angela really does herself, that Angela has no intention of going back to school this year. Or of taking her exams. Or of having any chance of going to university. At this particular moment in time, in fact, she's really only interested in arranging sausages on trays.

Tomorrow is Friday but since she can barely stand the sight of beef, sausages are now Friday's special of the day. Given the occasion, the fact that it is also Valentine's Day, she wonders if she should have done something with hearts. Ox. Lamb. Human? Barbara watches as she crimps the white doily she's used to edge the display and carries it into the cold room.

Before she switches out the light, Angela looks around at the cold room's empty shelves. It's lucky the shop isn't very busy because she's used up almost all the inventory. There are only a few more chops. Some shoulder of mutton and rag-end necks. Some ground meat. A side of beef is due to be delivered tomorrow, but the truth is, she has no idea what to do with it. The pigs and lambs, thank God, come in pieces. As for the sausages, she stayed up half last night battling with the meat grinder, and with the peppercorns and fennel seeds that look like mouse turds, and the slimy casings that feel like exactly what they are.

She closes the heavy white door, fastens the latch, and washes her hands in the big sink, feeling the chalky scrape of the soap that is already toughening her skin, making it red and hard. Then she reaches for the books that are kept below the register so she can close out the day.

"You can't do this."

Barbara's voice is resigned even as she says it, but Angela loves her for trying. For the fact that she won't quit. This is the third night in a row Barbara has turned up at the shop. She has gone to the hospital with Angela, too. Bought displays of dyed carnations and spiky gladiolas and written cards that say things like "Get Well Soon!" Now she's perched on the spare stool beside the register wearing her running clothes—a new set of dark blue sweatpants and a matching sweatshirt with the logo of some American university in bright yellow on the front. She reaches out and puts her hand over Angela's, stops the pencil that is about to move across columns and will add up to nothing more than the growing shadow of the mushroom cloud.

"Your dad wouldn't want you to." Barbara looks at her. "You know that, Angie," she says. "He's so proud of you. He wants you to go to university. He doesn't want you to do this." Barbara studies Angela's face. Then her fingers grip Angela's. "You haven't told him, have you?"

Angela doesn't look at her.

"You haven't told him." Barbara nods. She almost smiles. "He thinks the shop is closed. He thinks you're still going to school." She's like a stonemason who's finally got his chisel in the crack, and she's leaning hard. Determined to cleave this rock away. Split it from the mother cliff.

Angela can feel Barbara's eyes on her face, but she doesn't say anything. Because there is nothing to say. The truth is, she has no idea what her father thinks. She's not even sure he knows it's her who comes and sits beside him every evening, who watches while the nurse spoons mush into his mouth that opens the way a baby bird's or a kitten's mouth opens. Still, as usual, Barbara's right. Just in case, on the off chance that he does know who she is, she hasn't said a thing.

She's sworn the Pirottis and the Ravallis and Nonna Franchi to silence, too. And for now at least they'll do what she wants because they feel sorry for her, and for her father. And because they agree. They're not convinced that the university is a suitor who lives up to his word. Look at all the children who go, who take up the promise of the New Italy all bright-eyed, and come away with a paper that says they know Philosophy or Economics or all the Great English Novels and still can't get a job because there are no jobs. What good is that? Besides, unlike Barbara, they know about families. They know what they're for. They understand that until her father comes back, she must keep the door open, and the lights on, and the blades sharpened—and make sure there is something to cut.

Which is why she has accepted the offer—the one made by

the cousin who rears the vealers. He called yesterday to say he has heard about her father, and that he wants to help. That he'll come in twice a week to do the butchering. For a fee. Which Angela can't afford, but will pay. Because otherwise there will be nothing for her father to come back to.

The cousin's name is Ubaldo, which Angela thinks is both appropriate and unfortunate, because although he isn't that old—a good ten years younger than her father at least—he's losing his hair. It's slid back from his forehead and now hangs, caught like a glasses strap behind his ears.

She has, of course, known Ubaldo all her life. But not well. More like you know a building or a tree you walk past from time to time. She can't, for instance, remember a conversation she's had with him. If Ubaldo has conversations. Which, frankly, she doubts. And she hasn't been to the farm for years. Back when she did occasionally go with her father, they didn't stay long. Her father only lingered to play cards and drink Ubaldo's bad wine and worse grappa when he went on his own, when he craved, she supposes, unadulterated male company. Which he certainly got. Ubaldo lives alone with three dogs, rib-thin yellow things, and with his herd of dairy cattle, and the vealers—leggy boy calves with sweet wide eyes who suckle and graze and are teased for a few months with the possibility of a future.

It seems cruel, that dangling promise of summer days. But who is Angela to talk? She wears leather. She eats veal. And the calves run and buck on sharp, salty grass and are killed at home, which everyone says is better, and Ubaldo doesn't seem like a cruel man. Rotund, he's the same shape as her father, if not quite as tall. They might even look alike, if Ubaldo had her father's mane of hair, and his smile, and if there wasn't something wrong with one of his eyes, which wanders, making him appear—admittedly through no fault of his own—both sly and feckless at the same time.

Not that it affects his touch with the knives. Watching him the first evening, Angela has to admit, he's good. Fast at slicing muscle and cracking bone. They have agreed that he'll come twice a week, in the evenings after he's finished on the farm. He'll make up enough cuts to stock the cold room, and cut roasts for any special orders, not that they get many these days.

This arrangement makes Ubaldo happy because he says he loves her father like a brother. And besides, he can use the extra money. And it gives him an excuse to come into town. Get off the farm, stretch his legs. He winks at Angela as he says this, his eye veering wildly sideways. She makes a point of not understanding. And of hovering at the cash register. When she has to go to the storeroom, leaving him alone in the shop, she locks the cash register, turning the key surreptitiously and slipping it into her pocket.

And she watches him. More closely than he knows. It occurs to her that she's been rather stupid, to get herself into this position, to become dependent like this, and that it's because she never really watched her father. So she has resolved that on the evenings when Ubaldo is here, while she sits at the register, the books open in front of her, or wipes the empty glass cases and mops the floor and sprinkles sawdust like powdered sugar, she'll watch what he's doing. Take note of how he separates the rib bones, prying them apart slowly, almost tenderly, before he raises his arm and brings the cleaver down. Of how he lifts a loin and runs his hand over it, feeling for the grain of the meat. Or trims the fat in one neat long cut from a pork belly.

⁂

By the end of the first month, Angela's not surprised her father almost died. It's exhausting. All this serving and smiling and watching, it's much more tiring than she would have guessed. And not in the same way that wrestling with equations and proofs, or even running, is. It doesn't leave her with a virtuous ache. It just leaves her feeling as if she's been drained. In fact, recently she's felt more than once that someone's pulled the plug on her life. That everything that was previously Angela has whirled away.

One night, after visiting her father—who was asleep, propped up like a giant doll, his head lolling, tubes running in and out of his arm—she finds she doesn't have the energy to eat. She's tried to keep her strength up, she knows it's important, but she can't be bothered to cook the sausages she brought home. Even slicing bread seems too much. She blinks. The blade of the bread knife ripples. She gives up and drops it on the kitchen table, abandons the loaf on the cutting board, and opens a can of soup and drinks it sitting on the sofa, out of the pan.

The soup tastes like nothing at all, which is oddly comforting, as if flavor might require too much effort. As Angela spoons it toward her mouth, she watches the television with one eye. When she's finished, Angela takes the pan back to the kitchen and dumps it in the sink beside the other pans and the selection of dishes that seem to have found their way there. Then she goes back into the sitting room and puts on her father's slippers and rolls herself in the maroon blanket. The news has started. It shows a picture of what looks at first to be a castle or a barracks, but turns itself into a prison. Monteferrato in Turin, where they are holding Renato Curcio, one of the leaders of Brigate Rosse—they of the five-pointed star—who kidnapped the prosecutor Mario Sossi. Made him disappear into thin air back in what seems like another lifetime but was, Angela realizes with something of a shock, not even two years ago.

Or rather, the prison at Monteferrato where they were holding Renato Curcio. Until four o'clock this afternoon when a woman arrived for visitors' day with a parcel that turned out to be a gun. She is believed, the TV newsreader says excitedly, to be Renato

Curcio's wife, another founder of Brigate Rosse, another kidnapper. Margherita Cagol.

A picture flashes on the screen as the newsreader says this. Margherita Cagol is pretty and has dark hair that falls to her shoulders. The photo is black and white, but the newsreader assures the nation that her eyes are green. She doesn't look all that much older than Angela, or very different from anyone else you'd see in the street. She could walk into the shop and Angela would sell her a pork chop without even thinking about it. But the newsreader insists that would be a mistake. That the public should be vigilant. And that anyone who sees her should call the Carabinieri. Immediately. At a special number where operators are standing by. Because Mara, as she prefers to be called, is very dangerous.

Angela feels her eyes closing. The photo on the TV screen wavers as if it's underwater. First Mario Sossi, she thinks, now Mara's own husband. No wonder they're worried. Walls can't stop her. Jails won't keep her out. Mara Cagol makes men disappear like smoke.

Urban guerrilla warfare plays a decisive role in the task of achieving political disorientation of the state. It strikes directly against the enemy and clears the way for the resistance movement. Armed propaganda achieved by means of guerrilla operations is a phase of the class war, the statement in the newspaper says. Then, a bit farther down it adds: *The Christian Democratic Party must be liquidated, destroyed, and dispersed. The Christian Democrats are not just a political party, but the black soul of a regime that for thirty years has oppressed the masses and workers of the country.*

These are the latest communiqués from the Red Brigades who, since Mara—as the press now obligingly call her—staged her prison break, have not, as Nonna Franchi would say, let the grass grow under their feet. They haven't buttoned their lips, either. Apparently no one ever told them to be seen and not heard. Or if they did, they weren't listening.

Because these days the Brigate Rosse seem to feel the need to announce to the nation their innermost thoughts and desires on a regular basis. When they're not shooting people in the legs. Or kidnapping them. Or both. Last month, a Christian Democrat Party leader was gagged and chained to his desk, along with six office workers. He was tried then and there, found guilty, and *gambezzati*-ed, shot in the knees. The latest kidnap victim is an industrialist called Vittorio Gancia. No one knows if he's been *gambezzati*-ed or tried. No one knows anything at all, because last week he disappeared like smoke.

Sparito nel nullo!

It sounds like a toast. And feels like a rerun of a movie. Or, Angela thinks, a sickness that flares up. A fit of epilepsy. An infection that won't die. Someone vanishes. There's a police hunt. One thousand, two thousand, four thousand carabinieri are mobilized—antibiotics battling a virus in the national blood. Cars are stopped. Doors are kicked. People cry on television.

This time it's coming from Milan, not Genoa. Not that it makes much difference to Angela. She looks at Vittorio Gancia's picture, half expecting him to be Mario Sossi, then blinks as the words swim across the newspaper. As the letters dance down the page, jigging in time to the snicker and huff of her father's snoring. It's comforting, that sound. If she closes her eyes, just for a minute, she can almost believe she's at home, working at the kitchen table or sprawled on the knobbly rug, and that he's asleep in his chair. But, of course, he isn't. And neither is she.

The infection started the day before. Or two, or three days ago. It's a little bit like the Red Brigades, nobody knows for sure. What they do know is that it, too, has announced its intentions.

Her father has been moved back from the recovery ward—where he did exercises squeezing tennis balls and was rolled around in a wheelchair to look at fish tanks and out of the window—to a ward with private rooms where all the nurses and doctors wear gloves. All the time. And sometimes even face masks. Angela has to put one on when she comes close to him. Her lips can only brush his skin through paper. Her hand takes his through a film of plastic. His eyes look up at her, and she is not sure who he is seeing. She wonders if she looks enough like her mother. When she bends down to kiss his forehead it smells clammy, like a steak that's been left a little too long in the cold room.

The doctor has reassured Angela that it's not so uncommon with heart patients, for them to get infections. Especially heart patients who are made weak with recovering, who are worn down. Those are the words they use, over and over. *Worn down*, as if her father's a step on a staircase, or one of his own blades. A strip of steel ghosted to the edge of nothingness from too many years of slicing flesh and being stropped on a whetstone. That's how he looks, too. Not exactly thinner, but smaller, as if he's retreating inside himself, walking backward out of the world.

Angela thought dying would be dramatic. She's seen those movies, where everybody stands around and holds hands and cries while the person who's doing the dying smiles weakly and gives them advice. Folds words of wisdom into little parcels they can take away and keep forever.

She knows it's naïve. Still she thought it might be at least a little like that. But it isn't at all. It's just this walking backward. Or in her father's case, shuffling. It's just the inside of him getting smaller and smaller, until in one moment that she will not quite be able to put her finger on, he won't be there anymore and she'll realize she is alone in the room, and that his carcass is nothing more than that. Just a carcass, like a million she's seen before. An old frame of bones. Some worn flesh inside pallid skin. Too much fat. A mane of white hair. Twisted hands, chapped and red from a lifetime in a butcher's shop.

The newspaper slips to the floor. She opens her eyes and

looks out of the window. Spring was very late this year. On the ramparts, the fingertips of trees turned green but refused to unfurl. Shoots thrust through the muddy earth that edged the paths, then thought better of it and retreated. Haze hung over the fields, an unfulfilled promise of growth shimmering in the evening sun.

Then, all at once, about a month ago, everything unfroze and smelled as if it was rotting. Her birthday came. Barbara gave her a suitcase with her initials on it, which she insists Angela will use for university after she takes her exams next year, which will, when all's said and done, leave her not too far behind. Will be little more than a pause quickly forgotten. That in ten years, five years even, when they have their new jobs and new lives, no one will even think about it, much less remember.

Neither of them say that this will be possible only if her father dies. And Angela knows it won't happen even then. She takes the suitcase, though. She hugs Barbara, holds her close and smells the sandalwood oil she's still rubbing on her collarbones, and makes a joke about the new braces her mother has insisted she have on her front teeth. Afterward they drink a whole bottle of wine by themselves.

It's Wednesday, the fourth of June, when Angela's father finally dies and she isn't even there. She's in the shop watching Cousin Ubaldo feather slices of veal, which is not as easy to do as it looks, to make them thin as pieces of pink paper. In the moment he leaves the world, she's staring, hypnotized by the silver blade. She sorts this out in her head—exactly where she was standing, what she was doing—when she gets to the hospital later that night and finds his bed empty.

The hospital staff—the nurses, who have taken off their paper masks and plastic gloves, unveiling themselves like brides—are very kind. They sit with her. They explain about how his heart stopped. How the infection crept through him, skirting the barriers set up by the antibiotics, jumping the walls, stealing into his blood, his lungs, his heart. They tell her that he was in no pain, that he fell asleep and his dreams carried him away.

Angela thinks about that. With the nurses gathered around her, with one of them holding her hand, she imagines her father wandering down halls. Sees him getting smaller and smaller as he pushes open doors, until finally he finds the one her mother stands behind. Angela imagines his voice hushed with anticipation. She hears him whisper, *"Annabeth?"* And sees her mother, turning around and smiling. Reaching for his hand as he takes hers and the years blow away like fallen leaves.

His body has already gone to the morgue. When they ask if she would like an autopsy, Angela's throat tightens. For a second, she thinks she will be sick, then she shakes her head. When they ask if she would like to see him—to say good-bye, or to be certain, presumably, that they are not making this up—her heart stops. Quite suddenly, she feels light-headed, as if her body is no longer subject to the rules of gravity, as if it's left the ground and is rising, like a balloon that might go too high and pop.

She must look strange, because a nurse puts her head between her knees, then brings a glass of water. They stand around her in a semicircle, and finally it's all Angela can do to ask them to call the Barellis. She can't face the Pirottis' tears, or the mewling sound she knows Signora Ravelli will make. She can't even face Nonna Franchi. As someone hurries away to make the call, she sits there, frozen in the plastic chair, and realizes that she doesn't even care if Barbara's mother comes, or her father with his disorganized smile and smell of cigarettes. At least, she thinks, they'll be quiet. At least they won't cry or wail or clutch at her. Which is important because she has the feeling that something has happened to her insides. That suddenly she has a thin inner lining made of glass that even the slightest noise or wrong word might shatter.

"Angie?"

Barbara's face swims in front of her. She is squatting, one of her hands on each of Angela's knees, and Angela wonders if she has been asleep because she didn't hear Barbara arrive, wasn't even aware of her until she spoke. She blinks, pushing away the maze of hallways she has seen her father wandering down.

"Angie? They told me. I came right away."

Barbara's brown velvet eyes are liquid with tears. One escapes. She lets go of Angela's knee for a second and teeters as she wipes her cheek with the back of her hand.

"Do you want to go home?" she asks. "Or you can come to our house. Mama's away but—" Barbara nods. "We'll get a taxi."

"No."

Angela's own voice surprises her. It sounds as if it belongs to someone else. Someone angry. She shakes her head and tries to smile so Barbara won't think she's angry with her.

"No taxi," she says. Because she knows absolutely that she cannot be inside anything as small as a car.

"I want to walk," Angela says, but that is not quite true. What she wants to do is run. Climb up onto the ramparts and run around and around and around the city walls. Circle Ferrara so fast she turns back time—swirls her whole life, all her past, and her father, and her mother into a safe pocket of stone, trapping them there, so they can never escape and she will always know where to find them.

"Come on," Barbara says. "Come on, let's get out of here."

She helps Angela to her feet. Angela lets her. She doesn't resist as Barbara walks her down the long hallways, past door after closed door.

Outside the night feels almost chilly, freshly washed and still damp, as if there's been rain. Angela realizes she has no idea what time it is. The light was falling down when she arrived, sometime just after seven. She looks at her watch as they pass under one of the street lamps in the hospital parking lot. It's nearly ten p.m. She has no idea what she has been doing for the last three hours.

"Are you sure you want to walk?" Barbara stops and looks at her, her face creased with concern. "I can get a taxi," she says again. "I can—"

Angela shakes her head. "I want to walk," she says.

She tries to smile. Barbara nods and reaches for her hand, and together they step out onto the Corso Giovecca.

They take the long way, turning away from the main thoroughfare and winding toward the heart of the old city. Silence seeps in and thickens as the sound of traffic fades. They are dwarfed as they pass the Schifanoia, where for a second Angela stops, thinking of the murals of the months—of the dancing women and flying animals. Of the flowers and stars that rest inside its great stone shell like hidden pearls. She has read that the faces in the paintings are the faces of the d'Este mistresses and court ladies, that all the goddesses were modeled on the dead, and she wonders if from now on she will see her father's face. If he will look down at her from carved lintels. Stare out from the ornate frames of paintings. Barbara waits and says nothing. Then they walk on, their footsteps tapping time, measuring the beginning of this new life as they pass Santa Maria in Vado and the blank-faced wall of the Annunziata.

They continue like this, not speaking, holding hands, feeling the layers of the city close around them, until suddenly Angela is aware of something other than their footsteps. A voice, muffled and crackling. It sounds like a radio that's been turned up so far up it distorts, or a huge television set that's been left on.

"What's that?"

She stops, unnerved. Barbara shrugs.

"Probably the vigil."

"What vigil?"

For an insane moment Angela wonders if the city somehow knows that her father is dead, and if all the old black-dressed ladies, and the fruit sellers, and the women from the bakery and the laundry and the man from the kiosk where her father bought his cigars have turned out to make speeches and light candles for him.

"What vigil?" she asks again, and Barbara looks at her.

"For Mara."

"Mara?" Angela frowns.

"Oh," Barbara says, as if something has suddenly occurred to her, "you don't know? I mean, you didn't see the TV tonight?"

Angela shakes her head. Of course she has not seen the TV. She has not seen anything except halls and doorways and her own shoes when the nurse shoved her head between her feet. She has no idea what Barbara is talking about.

"They killed Mara Cagol."

For a second Angela doesn't know who Mara Cagol is. Or was. Then she remembers. The five-pointed star that looks like it's leaning backward. The men who disappear like smoke.

Before she can ask anything, Barbara says, "This afternoon. They were doing house to house searches. You know, looking for that guy, the rich guy who got kidnapped. Gancia. Anyway." She shrugs and starts walking again. Angela falls in beside her.

"Yeah," Barbara says. "They were doing house-to-house searches. I don't know, somewhere outside Milan. And all of a sudden there was a lot of shooting. At least that's what they say. At this one house. Two carabinieri were killed. And so was Mara. She was inside." Barbara shrugs. Her eyes slide sideways, finding Angela's. "My dad says she was murdered. He heard, when they found the body, that she'd been shot in the back. Other people are saying she was wounded and trying to crawl away and they just shot her. You know, like an animal."

They have reached the small piazza in front of the Palazzo Paradiso. The noise is coming from a man standing on the steps speaking through a megaphone. It makes his voice so muzzy that Angela can't really make out what he's saying to the two, or maybe three, hundred people, mostly students, who drift and eddy below him. She looks around. Flyers have been pasted on the walls of the surrounding houses. LOTTA ARMATA PER IL COMUNISMO, Armed Fight for Communism, the headline reads. The same photograph, the one on the television, stares out from all of them. Over and over, everywhere you turn, there is the pretty dark-haired girl with the five-pointed star leaning backward behind her. Underneath, the words *Mara, il tuo assassìnio non restera impunito*—Mara, your assassination will not go unpunished—appear again and again.

Someone is handing out candles. One is thrust into Angela's hand, and before she even knows what she is doing she is holding a flame, raising it above her head. It flickers, then glows—one of dozens, hundreds, that fill the tiny piazza, turning it into a sea of stars. All fallen to earth and burning for the memory of Mara Cagol.

Angela's father is buried five days later, his body laid at the foot of the stone angel beside Annabeth's. She has been waiting for him, Angela thinks, for a long time. A lifetime. Hers. Seventeen years, four weeks, and one day.

Bending to place the white roses she has brought, Angela feels the locket inside her black dress, tapping against her chest like a finger tapping some last tiny message from her parents. She presses her hand against it, wondering if she should have given it back, sent it to be with her father the way she sent his best suit and blue tie and the black shoes Nonna Franchi had come to the house to polish specially.

Leaning in the kitchen doorway, Barbara had watched the old lady, and commented afterward that it was creepy, the way she had rubbed and polished. Spat on the toes, her creased lips puckering a kiss to bring up the shine. But Angela didn't think so. If anything she wished that there was more—a few favors, a few small kindnesses that could be done for the dead.

The best she had been able to think of was cleaning the apartment. Especially the kitchen. After the funeral, after the lunch the Ravallis insist on hosting—the Pirottis and Nonna Franchi and Angela and Barbara and even Cousin Ubaldo, clustered around their table—it still smells like bleach. Acrid and eye stinging. Barbara opens the window and stands in front of it, eating a cucumber from the dish on the counter, cutting it into wedges, salting it, and chewing it methodically. Angela sits at the table watching her. Outside there are footsteps, and the sound of a Vespa. Angela lays her head on her arm and closes her eyes, breathing in the sharp smell and letting her hand wander across the scrubbed wood, reading the map of its scars.

Later, despite the heat, she wraps herself in the maroon blanket and lies on the couch, her father's slippers on her feet. At dark Barbara makes a nest of cushions and bed pillows on the floor beside her. When, in the early hours of the morning, Angela's hand drifts to the floor, she feels the silk of Barbara's hair, then the answering pressure of her fingers. A few moments later Barbara unwinds the blanket and slips beneath it. Her body is hard and soft at the same time. Her long thighs and muscled back as warm and smooth as sun-touched marble.

⸰

"Here," Barbara says. "Try one of these. They're orange. You like orange."

Angela opens her mouth and closes it. She was going to say that she does not like orange, at least not in particular, not any more than she likes any other kind of fruit flavor. But she doesn't have the energy. Since the funeral her mind has been heavy and lumbering, like an overweight animal. And Barbara is only trying to help. She is sitting on the stool beside the cash register in the butcher's shop with a box of chocolates on her lap insisting they will make Angela feel better.

The box is huge and made of quilted satin, like the inside of a coffin. It's a gift from Barbara's parents, to congratulate her because she has actually won a scholarship to one of the American universities. She heard the day before yesterday. She had been on a waiting list, and now someone has decided to go somewhere else so Barbara will be able to go in her place. To somewhere called Ohio, which means nothing to Angela because she knows nothing about America.

Barbara insists—when she isn't touting the beneficial effects of the chocolates—that Ohio is beautiful. From the way she says it—her voice high and fast, as if her insisting can make it be true—Angela doubts this. She doubts, in fact, that Barbara knows anything about Ohio. In fact, she doubts Barbara can even remember which of the seemingly hundreds of applications she filled out belonged to this particular university. She suspects Barbara will arrive expecting to be somewhere else. But that doesn't matter, because Barbara is happy, and for once both her parents are proud of her, and she is going to escape them. So she has brought the chocolates to share with Angela, who isn't the least bit interested in them.

She doesn't like their shape, the small glossy brown lumps. And the smell of them—the bitter cocoa-ness and sweet ooze of the cream centers—is making her feel sick. Angela glances at the box. Its quilted sides bulge like a dead animal that's rotting. The nests of paper rattle as Barbara selects one and bites into it, her teeth flat and shiny now that the braces have been removed.

"Ubaldo's in love with you," she announces.

Angela shakes her head.

"Don't be stupid."

They have had this conversation before, several times since the funeral. It is true that Ubaldo comes to the shop more often now, that once or twice he has even appeared on the weekends, carrying his rolled-up newspaper that he picks horses out of to bet on, and wearing what looks like a new cap. But Angela thinks this is just because he feels sorry for her. The idea of anything else makes her even queasier than the chocolates.

She pushes the cash register, which opens with a ping. There is more than usual in the black plastic trays, but she does not find that especially reassuring. She knows it is only because, like Ubaldo, everyone feels sorry for her. So they are coming to buy ground meat and roasts and chops in the same way that Signora Ravalli has taken to leaving her soup—pots of saffroned yellow broth slick with egg yolks and shredded chicken that she finds almost nightly on the landing. Angela pours them down the sink where the celery and sinews stick in the drain and have lately begun to smell.

Soon, she thinks, Signora Ravalli will stop. And so will everyone else. They will all forget her father is dead, just as Barbara is forgetting it. Then they will stop feeling sorry and go on vacation because it will be August. And when they come back, sun shriveled and short tempered, they will return to the supermarket where everything is cheaper and wrapped in colored plastic.

Barbara nods, not because she is reading Angela's mind and agreeing, but because she is still going on about Ubaldo.

"He is," she says. "You'll see. I bet he asks you to marry him. You can be Signora Ubaldo."

The words hit Angela in a puff of violet cream. Her stomach drops. She has to cover her mouth. Her eyes water as she looks up, not sure what she's looking for, and comes face to face with the grinning pig painted on the wall.

"Angie?" Barbara's hand is on her arm. "Angie?" she says. "I was only kidding."

"I'm fine." Angela pushes her hand away. "I'm fine," she mumbles. And before she knows what she is doing, she has grabbed one of the chocolates, and stuffed it in to her mouth, and swallowed.

Barbara leaves on the twelfth of August. She is going to stay with her father while he finishes his summer teaching job, then he will take her to Ohio. Before that she goes with her mother to Milan to shop for her new life. When she comes back, Angela goes after work to the Barellis'. She sits on Barbara's bed surrounded by the stuffed animals and watches as Barbara shows off her new clothes, then helps her to pack them in her new suitcase, which is pink and has flowers on the side. They talk— make promises, bring food from the Barellis' kitchen, and eat it sitting cross-legged, picking crumbs out of the white shag rug. But for all of that, their conversations aren't the same. This leaving has built a wall between them. Or rather, Angela thinks, a window. A plate-glass window just like the one at the shop. They can see each other through it. They can read each other's lips. Even tell what is behind each other's eyes. But there is no press of flesh. They can stand hand to hand, but they can no longer touch.

On the actual day, Angela arranges for Ubaldo to be at the shop and goes with Barbara's mother and sister to the train station. When the train comes, she hugs Barbara. She can smell the sandalwood oil, feel the familiar brush of her hair, but it's like holding a doll. Something inside of her is already gone. Angela is almost relieved when she finally climbs into the carriage and opens the window and leans out and waves. Angela waves back. As the train begins to move, she keeps waving. She doesn't stop until it has grown as small as a toy.

Angela leaves the platform with Barbara's mother and her sister, who has finished university in Padua and is home for a visit before going back again to live with the boyfriend everyone hates. When they reach the front of the station they look at her like she's something they've found and don't know what to do with. Finally Barbara's mother asks if Angela would like a ride home. Angela shakes her head and thanks them, then stands and watches as they walk quickly away not looking back, as if they're afraid it might encourage her to follow. After they have driven off, she goes down the steps and turns in the other direction.

It is very hot, and most of the town is already closed for Ferragósto, but the supermarket is open. In all these years Angela has never once been inside it, and only rarely walked past—and then fast and with her head turned, as if whatever's in there might jump out and grab her. Now she stands looking at the big bright green sign, and at the posters advertising soap powder and discounts on pasta. The rubber mat makes a pinging sound as she pushes open the door. Inside the air is as cold and damp as winter fog.

Angela goes up every aisle, examining the toothpaste and the shampoo, the plastic bags of oranges and grapefruit, and all the boxes of cereals and different kinds of tea before she comes to the meat counter. Which isn't really a counter because there are no display cases. Instead the meat is all piled in a kind of trough. Frost spangles its back, as if the chops and bacon and legs of chicken are guests of an ice queen.

Each cut sits on a little Styrofoam tray—pink for pork, blue for lamb, yellow for chicken, and green for beef—and is wrapped in layers of see-through film. Angela pokes a chicken thigh. She expects it to be hard, at least partially frozen, but it's oddly springy, as if it's made of rubber, not flesh. The indent lasts a moment, then oozes away. Two women pushing silver carts come around the corner. Angela watches as they stop and pick up packages and put them down again and finally don't choose anything. When she leaves she sees them standing in the checkout line with frozen pizzas. She bought one herself. It's pepperoni with double cheese, and when she gets home she puts it in the oven, then eats the whole thing standing at the kitchen window looking down on the Spanish Synagogue, whose doors are still padlocked, and still peeling, and that someone really ought to paint.

On Ferragósto she doesn't go out. Instead for the first time in a long time she goes into her room and sits on the floor and pulls out the bottom drawer of her bureau. For an awful moment, she can't find the blue beads. At first she tells herself she doesn't care. Then she realizes she's crying. Her fingers scrabble through a layer of sweaters. She pulls out a handful of old socks and a pair of moth-eaten mittens, then finally, there they are.

They're bluer than Angela remembers. She pushes back the shutter and holds them up to the evening light. Faint strains of music are coming from the Castello. She doesn't know what the band is this year, or if they'll play "Stairway to Heaven." Closing her eyes, she lets her hand slip between her legs. That night when she lies down on the couch she keeps the bracelet on her wrist.

Eighteen days later, on the first of September, the factory explodes.

If she hadn't heard it, Angela might not have been aware of it, at least not right away. She isn't aware of much these days, except the shop. Anywhere else—in the apartment, walking home—she can barely move. But there, she can't stop. She's taken to cleaning the meat grinder using an old toothbrush, and to polishing the window. She arrives every morning while the sky is still the color of pearls and the only sound is the high swooping cheep of the swallows. In the storeroom she mixes up lemon juice and vinegar in a preserving jar the way Nonna Franchi used to. Then she stands on the street making circle after circle, tighter and tighter, with wadded up handfuls of newspaper. At night she spends extra time washing the floor before sprinkling the sawdust, watching it fall through her fingers like honey-colored snow.

Angela had just finished serving a customer, and had resumed her scrubbing, when the explosion happened at eleven o'clock in the morning. It was a Wednesday and summer was officially over, so all the shops were open and everyone was back from vacation and having coffee or eating granita at the pavement bars, or wandering between the fruit sellers' stalls in the Palazzo Municipale.

Later, during the official inquiries and trials that followed, they would read in the newspaper about how the factory's management, in an effort to streamline and increase efficiency, had, with the consent of the union, cut its maintenance routine. So when a spark flew into an unemptied bin of papers, the resulting fire—which had not been very big or seemed very serious at first—rapidly became both, because the extinguisher the foreman grabbed did not work. After that, they would read, it was a matter of seconds before the flames found the pocket of gas that had built up during the holiday due to a leak in the pipe and poor ventilation.

Not that the shoppers and strollers and coffee-drinkers of Ferrara were aware of any of that at the time. They were not aware of much at eleven o'clock that morning, except perhaps that the day was already very hot and that there was a shortage of cucumbers and melons due to the late spring. Until they heard the noise.

It was a combination of a crack and a boom—the sort of

thing that might have heralded the end of the world in a low-budget disaster film—and was followed by a shudder. By a physical rocking of the air. People walking on the walls said they felt them quaver. Glass rattled. Bicycles tipped over. At the Duomo a pigeon fell straight down onto the steps. Then, as people turned and looked upward—wondering if, despite the flawless sky, they had heard summer thunder—they saw a second sun.

Some described it as a giant fist—a hammer of God that opened its fingers and hung for one perfect moment like a vast blessing hand. Then snapped closed with a roar. And was swallowed by a shimmering blackness that rose and spread and undulated to the sudden yowl of sirens.

Like everyone else, Angela ran into the street. She stood beside the Pirottis and the man who owned the leather repair shop and the ladies from the laundry, all of them staring upward, mouths open, hands slack, until someone ran shouting from Via delle Volte toward Porta Paola. Others followed seconds later, thundering like a buffalo herd toward the noise.

Antonio. Antonio's building. The words ran through Angela's head, stopping her brain until someone else shouted that it was one of the factories—a fire, an explosion, an attack—and Signora Pirotti, whose bad knee stopped her from running anywhere, pushed Angela onto the pavement because fire engines and ambulances were already screaming up Via Mayr.

By afternoon, the word goes around that, because all the ambulances are busy, bodies are being laid out in the Sacra Famiglia—that the dead are waiting in the house of God. Few of the factory workers shopped inside the walls—as a rule, they preferred the newer stores, purpose-built for the apartment buildings—but still the shop shutters come down. All along the street, Angela hears them rattling like trains on broken tracks.

It takes her fifteen minutes to walk to the church. It is said that, a thousand years ago, Sacra Famiglia was the sight of Ferrara's first cathedral, although Angela has always wondered how anyone knows for sure. If it's true, nothing is left of the cathedral now, although the present church is old enough. Angela has always considered it sad, like a lost dog. Because when the river changed its course and the city moved with it, Sacra Famiglia was left behind, stranded beyond the Darsena, outside the safety of the walls.

The blades of helicopters whump-whump as they land on the parking lot, then rise like giant carrion birds, ferrying their bloodied cargo to hospitals bigger and better equipped than Ferrara's. Cars and ambulances come and go. Firemen and carabinieri and first-aid crews scurry back and forth from a makeshift tent where those who were most severely burned wait to be airlifted. The tent has been put out here, Angela hears someone say, because it was necessary to get as far away from the factory as possible since it is still burning and there have already been a couple of smaller explosions. No one knows how many more pockets of gas the flames might find.

She is by no means alone. Other people have come, too. Women mostly. Some old, some young. Wives and sisters and mothers. Some run back and forth, darting from a fireman to a policeman, grabbing sleeves, shouting, begging. Others stand in small knots, blank looks on their faces. One girl, not much older than Angela and heavily pregnant, waddles like a penguin along the pavement, tears streaming down her reddened cheeks. No one notices, or if they do they don't care, when Angela eases open the huge door of Sacra Famiglia and slips inside.

What hit her first was the smell. It always did, on the rare occasions when she went into churches—the strong, sweet, cloying scent of the incense, dense and heavy, like a spice cake on the edge of burning. She breathed the familiar odor of damp stone, the smell of centuries she had grown up with, cold marble, and the faint mildew of plaster mingling with the smoke from the votive candles. This time, though, there was something else. Something animal, both familiar and different from the smell of the butcher's shop—blood and flesh, mixed with feces. Human shit. Angela balked like a calf at the door of an abattoir, blinking as her eyes adjusted to the light.

When she finally stepped inside, she felt the high empty flight of the roof above her. It was quiet, and very still. So much so that it took her a moment to pick out a faint, low, continuous murmuring, and to understand that it was coming from two priests as they moved in concert, up and down, bending over the dark shapes of what had, until a few hours ago, been men, reciting the prayers for the dead.

There were other people in the church, too. Several nuns, one of whom had a clipboard and seemed to be trying to identify bodies, and a handful of women doing exactly what she was doing. Moving from corpse to corpse. Slowly, silently, methodically, looking for a familiar face.

Afterward, she did not understand how she knew he would be there. But she did. She had known it when she left the shop, padlocked the shutter, and instead of turning toward the city and the apartment, had gone down across Piazza Travaglio and passed through the walls at Porta Paola, following the route Antonio had taken a thousand times, the way he had been going that winter night when she saw him all those years ago.

Now she stood looking down at the face that was the reflection of his. A little thinner, the nose not quite as sharp, nor the mouth as generous. The eyes would be the same, if he opened them—black as river stones. But Piero would never open his eyes again.

Angela dropped to her knees, aware too late that she was in a slick of blood. Piero's heart had not been pumping or they would not have brought him here. It was just the last shadow of his life she knelt in. His hair was still wild, half of it. The other half was matted. Her hand came away, sticky and dark, when she smoothed the curls off his forehead. *Face paint,* she thought, *it's face paint,* and she saw again the low, sweeping bow, the idiotic half-drunken grin, the way he and Antonio had wrestled, their bodies twining like young, limber snakes. And then Antonio was standing on the ladder above her, looking down, smiling. *I told my brother, I told Piero, he deserves more than bread. He deserves roses, too.*

Angela reached down and touched Piero's forehead, his eyes, his lips.

"Bread and roses," she whispered, her fingers resting on his skin. "For you, bread. And roses."

It is two days before she opens the shop again, and even then more than half of Via Mayr is still locked down. Angela weighs the keys in her hand. She's afraid of stock spoiling, and besides, she has spent two days in the apartment with its dirty dishes and piles of clothes in the sitting room and sounds of the Ravallis snuffling below. She bends to undo the padlock. The sky is milky, and there's still a strange smell in the air. The street is so quiet it might be Sunday. She notices a thin black dusting on the pavement. The remains of lives. It's fallen all over the city, wormed its way into the cracks and smeared the windowpanes.

The shop reveals itself little by little as she pushes the shutter up, like a picture developing. First the empty display cases, then the register and the meat grinder on its stand, finally the grinning pig and laughing cow. She steps inside and feels the coolness and the silence. Her father's white coat still hangs on its peg. The collar is frayed, one pocket ripped and restitched. She touches it, her fingers resting on the worn cloth.

"*Buongiorno,* Papa," she says, just like she does every morning.

By ten a.m. there have barely been any customers and there is nothing left to clean or polish, so she opens the books. Barely a week after her father died, Angela had a visit from a man at the bank. He had been only a little taller than she was, and had worn a gray suit made of a fabric that hissed when he reached out to shake her hand.

"Signor Carossi," he had said, and smiled, revealing pink gums. Then he had offered his condolences for her father's death, and asked what she planned to do.

Angela had stared at him, not understanding the question, until finally he had chewed his lower lip and assured her that he understood that this was a difficult time, and that the bank, presumably in the person of himself, was eager to help in any way it could. When she had not replied, he had chewed his lip some more, then said perhaps it would be better if he came back in a few weeks so they could have another chat. Finally he had turned to leave, but had stopped again, lingering in the doorway, allowing warm dusty air from the street to blow in. There was something, he said, that she ought to know. That he felt he ought to tell her. The supermarket had expressed an interest in buying the butcher's shop. The bank man had tried to smile as he said this, then added that he hesitated to mention it just now, and he was sorry if he had upset her. But he thought it might help her to know she had options.

A week later she had received a letter informing her that the interest rate on the loan had been increased due to the bank's enhanced risk as a result of the death of the proprietor and subsequent unavoidable changes.

Now, with the books spread in front of her, all she can see are clouds. Mostly the mushroom cloud, which seems, like the smoke that rose from the factory, to have grown darker and thicker. To quiver and turn to dust and stick all over her. She closes her eyes, but that is no better. Piero bows and laughs, crimson running down his face. There is a tap on the glass.

Angela starts and looks up. Ubaldo is standing on the pavement. He grins at her and waves, his bad eye veering so he appears to be looking two ways at once. He pushes through the door, his newspaper tucked under his arm.

"Ciao."

Ubaldo drops the paper on the counter beside the cash register. The front page is still covered in pictures of the fire—of the ruins of the factory, and of men with blackened faces, and of what appear to be pieces of twisted metal.

Ubaldo whistles and puts his apron on. Then he crosses the shop, flips the paper open, and runs one of his big hands down the page which lists the day's races.

"There," he says lovingly. "There she is. Our fame and fortune."

His finger with its chipped nail rests under the name of a horse called Delilah. But Angela is not looking at that. Her eyes have slid to the facing page where there is a picture of men in dark suits, union officials coming down the steps of a building in Rome, their faces grim. The caption says it is the headquarters of the Christian Democrat Party, where they have been holding meetings to ensure the ongoing protection of workers' rights. Below, in black-lined columns, are the names of the dead.

Ubaldo is saying something—about this horse, and how much he has bet on it, and what they can do with the money when it wins. Angela blinks. She sees her finger reaching out, touching the name, reading it like braille.

Piero Giovanni Tomaselli, twenty-four, of Ferrara.

She closes her eyes and hears them laugh. She sees Antonio. She feels his hand on the small of her back. But it isn't Antonio's. It's Ubaldo's.

"Carina," he is saying. "Carina—"

Warmth seeps from his huge body, as if he's one of his own cows with their pale wet mouths and soupy eyes. The hot damp of him presses through the thin cotton of Angela's smock, and through her blouse, and onto her skin. She can feel the bulge of his stomach. She can feel his belt buckle, and the hardness below.

"You're tired," Ubaldo murmurs. "You work too hard, you should let me—"

Angela jumps backward. The stool flies sideways. Pinned against the marble counter, she spins, reaches up, and grabs.

"Don't!" The blade of the filleting knife flashes. "Don't ever touch me again!"

For a moment both of them stand frozen. They watch as the bright line of blood runs down Ubaldo's arm, as it opens in a stream and begins to dribble through the dark hairs on the back of his hand. A drop lands and blossoms on his apron, poppy-red against the washed-out stains from cows and pigs and sheep.

Ubaldo stares. For once both his eyes are on the same thing. His mouth opens and closes, like a fish gasping for air. Then he turns and crashes into the stool. Like a terrified animal, he scrabbles over it, and around the counter, slipping on the sawdust as he grabs for the door, which crashes open.

The last time Angela ever sees him, he is bolting down the pavement, holding his arm with his free hand, lurching and slipping like a terrified horse.

She goes to see the man in the bank three days later. They agree that she will keep the butcher's shop open until she has used up all the inventory in the cold room, sold the chops and bacon and roasts Ubaldo had prepared. She does it fast. She puts up a SALE poster like the one in the supermarket. And then it's over. On the last day, the day when Signor Carossi comes in his hissing suit and she gives him the keys, he asks her if there is anything she would like to keep. She looks around. What would she do with the meat grinder or the cash register? How would she get the grinning pig or the cow off the wall? Finally she chooses several knives. She wraps them in her father's apron. Then, at the last moment, she takes his white coat, too.

It wasn't difficult for Angela to find work. The Pirottis were more than happy to pay her to do their books, and their son-in-law was a carpenter and he paid her, too. She insisted on doing them at home because she did not want to walk down Via Mayr. If she had to go to Via Ripagrande or to Via Settembre, she skirted the blocks near the butcher's shop. She slipped up only once, when it was unavoidable, when a woman who had a tailor's shop near Piazza Verdi wanted to hire her. Even then she waited until sunset, as if somehow that would help, before scurrying, trying to keep her head bent although it was a clear evening and wasn't raining or even very windy. It didn't work. Forced to stop when she crossed the street, she'd looked up and seen the shop front, the plate-glass window and even the macellerìa sign, boarded over. The sheets of plywood were pale, almost white in the dusk. Already they had been covered with posters. Green ones, advertising laundry soap and roasting chickens and discounted cooking oil.

Christmas came and went. Angela spent it with the Ravallis. Barbara did not come home, but wrote to say her father was taking her to San Francisco, where they would meet her sisters and then go skiing. She sent Angela a tracksuit from her university, and asked how the studying for her exams was going and when she was going to take them?

The answer was never. By December Angela had five or six small shops she did the books for, and in January a pizza parlor up near the Piazza Ariostea hired her to come in three afternoons a week. The owner had a bakery, and bar, too, and had fired his last accountant for stealing. He paid her under the table, in cash. On her birthday they gave her a party, and told her she was still *una piccola bambina,* a little kid, at twenty, which was especially true since she was only eighteen. After that first night at the hospital, she had found it too complicated to stop lying about her age. So she didn't.

The day she was dreading was June 4. She watched it inch closer and closer on the calendar, as if it would mean something, this mere fact that her father had been dead for a year. Barbara had telephoned on her birthday. The university in Ohio didn't finish until the end of the first week in June, or else, Barbara said, she would have come home. Instead she suggested that Angela should come to America in August, for a holiday. Barbara would send her a ticket. She was going to buy a car and they could drive to Yellowstone Park, or maybe even all the way to California. Angela said that sounded nice, but she knew from the sound of Barbara's voice, from how fast she was talking and the high insistent pitch of her words, that it would never happen. That her father would send her on a trip, or her mother would rent a house somewhere, far away and very expensive, where there was no room for Angela.

During the last week of May, it suddenly became very hot. The grass in the center of Piazza Ariostea turned bright green and the low hedges sprouted faster than they could be clipped. Nasturtiums and pansies tangled out of the windowboxes she passed on her way to the pizza parlor. The tubs of little plants, African violets and miniature cyclamen, the florist next door set out on the pavement had to be watered almost every hour, and finally brought in under the canopy.

The second of June was a holiday, but Angela went to the pizzeria anyway. The owner was considering enlarging the place, putting a bigger restaurant room out in the back, and had asked her to look at the numbers. Besides, she did not want to stay home. For the last three nights she had lain awake on the sofa, watching the shadows from the street move across the sitting room ceiling, certain she could hear her father snoring down the hall.

The pizza parlor had nothing as fancy as air conditioning, so after letting herself in she turned on the fan and got a chair and propped the street door open, hoping there might be a breeze, or at least a slight shifting of the hot muggy blanket that had draped itself over the city. The office was behind the bar. She jammed its door open, too. Just before noon, she heard someone come in.

"We're closed," she called, wondering if she should hang the sign over the back of a chair where it could be seen from the street. There was no reply. Probably it was the owner, come back for something he'd forgotten last night. When no one appeared in the office doorway, she finally got to her feet and went out into the main room.

He was standing with his back to her among the wiped tables with their upturned chairs, his hands in his pockets, sleeves rolled up. His arms were brown, as if summer had imprinted itself forever on his skin. Sunlight from the open doorway caught his hair.

"Ciao, Carina," he said, turning around. *"Da quando non ci si vede."*

Part III

Florence, 2010
Sunday, February 7

Enzo Saenz was giving up and going home. The last two days had been an almost total waste of time. He had watched hours of security tape from the cameras at the airport, and the bus stop, and the train station and seen—precisely nothing. At least nothing that even vaguely resembled Anna Carson, in or out of disguise.

It was true that there had been several moments of excitement, two at the bus station and one at the airport, when individuals of medium height wearing jackets and carrying red backpacks had come into view. But all of them had turned out to be duds. That had been the high point of the weekend. For all intents and purposes, Anna Carson, like her stepdaughter, had vanished.

The databases were showing precisely nothing, either. There was no further information on the black BMW. The crime-scene techs had lifted fingerprints from all over Kristin's apartment that matched Anna Carson's, whose did, in fact, match Angela Vari's. But so what? She'd been there with her husband the day after she arrived, and left her ID bracelet in plain sight, for Christ's sake.

Despite the high-level hand-holding—James MacCready and even the consul were also doing their part—Dr. Carson was just barely being persuaded not to go public. Not to rush to the nearest television studio or newspaper office. The thought made the back of Enzo's neck cold. National honor, not to mention departmental rank-pulling and a tidal wave of machismo, would result in bringing in the flying squad. TV-style SWAT teams would look tame in comparison. He could close his eyes and see bullet-proof vests and helicopters and machine guns. If that happened then no one, not Enzo, nor James MacCready, nor Pallioti nor His Dickheadness, the consul, nor God Himself could put any money on which way it would come out for Kristin, or Anna, Carson. The idea was enough to keep Kenneth Carson quiet. For now.

Enzo took a breath and wondered if he'd been wrong. Yet again he saw Anna Carson's eyes widen as she stared at the tiny screen on the phone, and saw her glare as she denied what she had seen. There was no question that she'd been angry. But some niggling part of him now wondered if the anger had come, not from belligerence—a vestigial Brigate Rosse instinct telling her that all and any policemen should go fuck themselves—but from fear. If he had reached out, been less aggressive—if, for instance, he had bothered to find out who she was before he had ambushed her—perhaps he might have been able to talk her out of running. Or at least make an educated guess as to where, and why, she had.

He sighed, wondering, too, why he couldn't accept that he knew the answer to that one. Leopards didn't change their spots. As far as he could see, Angela Vari had been Brigate Rosse. And a turncoat with it. When it got too hot, she'd gotten scared, gone running to the police, and offered them the one thing she had—Antonio. In short, she'd shopped her lover to save her own neck. Charming. He just wished he could figure out what the hell she was up to now. And why she'd bothered to take the kid's teddy bear.

Enzo slammed the drawer of his desk shut. It was past five on

Sunday evening, and the building was unusually quiet. Pallioti had gone to his sister's. For the briefest moment, Enzo allowed himself to dwell on Seraphina. On her smile, and her voice, and her beautiful house. And beautiful son. And charming husband. Whom she loved. Then he pushed her out of his mind. Or, more realistically, put her back in the shadowed corner where he kept his cache of safe, unattainable longings.

Tommaso, her little boy, had just turned four, and although no one would ever have dared say so, it was common knowledge that Pallioti was entirely besotted by his nephew. Just the week before Guillermo had caught him perching the child on his desk and showing him how to call the mayor on the emergency line. *"Pronto, pronto,"* the child had lisped. Not that the mayor would have noticed. The telephone seemed to confuse him at the best of times. Still it was a known fact that if Pallioti was in a particularly foul temper on a Monday morning it was probably because he had not had his weekend Tommaso fix. Enzo wondered if he felt the same way about his cat, and thought, though he might not want to admit it, that he probably did. She had been neglected for the last several days, and was in a reasonably foul temper herself.

He stood up and looked at the USB drive that had been dropped on his desk an hour earlier. It held the logs he had requested from across the country—every identity card that had been reported stolen since Thursday by anyone, male or female, who might conceivably bear any physical resemblance to Anna Carson. There had been daily updates, but so far, like everything else, they'd led nowhere. He picked it up and shoved it into his jacket pocket.

Thirty minutes later when he opened the door to his apartment, the cat switched her tail and gave him the evil eye.

"There's no point in looking like that," he said. "I'm sorry. I brought you a treat."

She glanced in the other direction, as if he might conceivably be talking to some other cat, then hopped down off the sofa and sauntered into the kitchen. Feeling like a supplicant, Enzo picked up her bowl and opened the bag without even taking his jacket off. He told himself he'd only stopped at the supermarket because he fancied something that wasn't out of a can, it had nothing to do with the cat.

"Ciao to you, too," he muttered as he put the bowl on the floor. Then he took off his shoes, shrugged out of his jacket, and went to stand under a hot shower.

Dinner was a fat, speckled river trout. A glass of wine. Buttery yellow potatoes barely bigger than his thumb that were already coming up from the south. When he'd finished, donating the bones to the cat bowl, Enzo poured himself a second glass, and felt more human. He hit the button that raised the shade and stood for a moment, swishing the deep, almost purple wine in the globe of the glass and staring out at the city.

The sleet of the last few days had finally been driven away by a sharp, biting wind that tore down from the mountains, rattling the empty branches of the trees and chasing the last dead leaves from the gutters. It had rippled the water of the Arno until the customary brown was spittled with whitecaps, then whipped into the piazzas, snatching at newspapers and bus schedules and discarded paper cups before leaving behind a night sky spangled with stars.

Enzo felt the cat brush his legs, as close as she ever got to thanks, then heard her patter away and make a soft whump as she jumped back onto the sofa. He thought of his grandparents, and wondered if the old man had his telescope out—if he was taking advantage of this clear night to climb up onto the roof terrace in his overcoat and trace Orion's belt. Pick out the bear, and the twins, and the bull. He wondered about his mother, if she was in her studio, lost in her strange world of colors. Or if she had gone out to walk her property as she sometimes did on winter nights, moving through the pale twisted trunks of the olive trees.

He should stop, he thought suddenly. He knew too many policemen who had spent too long walking the boundary of what was decent, what was bearable to humankind. Pallioti was the exception. He had somehow safeguarded his soul, every romantic last drop of it, but he was rare. Many more reached forty, then fifty, with something dead behind their eyes. It wasn't too late to have a family—a wife, children, something more than fantasies and a cat to come home to. Medical school was probably out of the question by now, but he wasn't stupid, and there were plenty of other jobs he could do. He rolled the glass in his hand, raised it, and let the wine slide across his tongue. Then he turned and looked at the USB drive that sat on the counter. Five minutes later he'd booted up the computer and was scrolling through the entries.

Enzo's first instinct had been to ignore the South, then he thought he'd better not ignore anywhere. Still he bet on Rome. That had been Angela Vari's last stomping ground, the place in Italy that would be freshest in her mind, even if it was thirty years ago. If she still had contacts, they were likely to be there.

After forty minutes of sifting through reports of stolen purses, pickpocketed wallets, and mysteriously vanished passports and identity cards that by their numbers suggested they should litter the streets of the capital, he felt his certainty ebb. A few cases were remotely likely, but nothing stood out. He moved on to Milan. There he noted two names, both of them young men. It was possible, but difficult, and on the whole he didn't see why she'd take the hardest option. He made a note of the names to follow up in the morning nonetheless. Then found himself yawning, and was contemplating finishing the bottle and taking up the task over breakfast, when he saw that it had been an unusually quiet weekend in Reggio. Parma, Modena, and Bologna between them had only a handful of missing cards. He glanced at his watch. It wasn't exactly late. He might as well finish the province before he called it a night. Five minutes later Enzo Saenz sat up suddenly. Then he leaned forward and squinted at the computer screen.

~

"The description fits, and it's Bologna. Close to Ferrara."

Pallioti felt himself smile, out of nostalgia as much as anything else. He recognized the edge in Enzo's voice for what it was—the desperation that passed for hope in policemen. The need to believe you'd found something, anything, that might crack a case gone dead. Which, let's face it, this one had. He'd spent the afternoon at his sister's playing with his nephew, watching his pager for notice from the team at the Excelsior that someone had made contact, knowing somehow that it wouldn't come, and thinking of nothing else.

"So you think she's going to Ferrara?"

"I didn't, but I do now. Don't you?"

Pallioti nodded. He supposed he did. Whether it is good for us or not, we go back to what we know. A thin snow had begun to fall. He had parked his car, tipped the garage attendant, lingered to discuss the likelihood of Italy retaining her World Cup title, and was walking home. Light slanted through closed shutters, picking up shreds of snow and ice, making them fluorescent against the dark.

"In any case." Enzo sounded testy now, not unlike his nephew when he stayed up too late. "I've spoken to Bologna. They're going to try to get this woman, the one whose wallet was lifted, to come in tomorrow morning. So I'll be leaving early. I just wanted to let you know."

Pallioti murmured something about being in touch, then the

phone went dead and the only sound in the street was his footsteps. His fingers tapped the smooth metal case. He did it without being aware of it, the way some people pulled their ears or fiddled with their tie. Morse code, more than one person had told him it sounded like. His private little SOS. Or, in this case, Angela Vari's name. He turned the corner, heard a bell begin to toll from across the river, a faint hollow sound, and stopped and fished in another pocket for his keys.

The past had been with him all day. Now it had followed him, like a waif tugging at his sleeve. Almost twenty years ago, during the blood-letting commonly known as the Second Mafia War, he had been seconded to Palermo to work on a kidnapping. That time the victim had been a twelve-year-old boy, snatched on his way home from a riding stable to teach his father, who had decided to make a deal with prosecutors, a lesson. The family, certain they could deal with the problem themselves, refused to cooperate. As a result the police were one step behind for the almost eleven months that the child was moved, and held, and moved again like an increasingly pathetic chess piece. In the end the animals who had taken him got bored and strangled him, dissolved his body in lime, and sowed the bones in some god-forsaken field.

Enzo's voice made the waif bolder. Pallioti had been to Ferrara only once, quite a long time ago. Flat as a pancake and very windy, it was reputed to be beautiful, but he had found it rather sinister—a time warp enclosed by walls, the great brooding castle with its moats and dungeons looming over the center of town, looking down on abandoned cannons and a statue of the screaming Savonarola. The waif trotted after him across the empty lobby of his building. It hung about as he waited for the elevator. Pallioti didn't like flat places. All the shadows were wrong.

"Alessandro. How good of you to call."

The voice was exactly as Pallioti remembered it—thin, smooth, and cold. Like surgical thread that had been stored in a freezer, which made it all the more incongruous that its owner was so large. All fat men were expected to sound like Santa Claus.

"I'm sorry I didn't have the time earlier. I wanted to thank you. For your help."

"Not at all. I take it you got what you needed."

"Yes." Pallioti thought of the dog-eared files he had handed Enzo Saenz two days ago. "Thank you," he added. "I'm sure your help—expedited things."

There was a sound on the end of the phone that was something between a chuckle and a humph—a general acknowledgment of the man's importance. Pallioti smiled. It wasn't something his friend had ever been exactly shy about, even in the old days, when they had first known each other. When the man on the end of the phone had taken Pallioti under his wing, offered him his patronage, much as Pallioti now gave his to Enzo. Not that he would ever be as important, so, sadly, Enzo would probably never find him as useful.

Pallioti swirled the grappa he had poured. He'd thought twice about making this call at all. Asking for a little help in getting a sensitive file sent quickly was one thing. What he was about to ask for now, on the other hand—dirt, intuition, the squishy viscera at the heart of history—was something else altogether. It was also why he had decided to use his own landline, and to call the man at home. Cell phones were inherently insecure, and everyone knew the ministry lines were bugged. He wondered if the sleek phone thing that sat on his sleek black desk in his overdesigned office was tapped, too. Probably. Probably there was some poor drone sitting hunched in a basement somewhere listening to endless loops of the mayor shouting *"Pronto!"* Pallioti pushed the thought aside and wondered how best to get what he wanted. Flattery usually worked.

"I'd been meaning to say—" Pallioti examined the neatly clipped edges of his nails as he spoke. "I want to congratulate you, truly, on the latest initiative. With the Americans," he added. "Deeply impressive. I was going to write. But, well." He coughed self-deprecatingly, suggesting he knew that the quality of his letter paper, never mind the words written on it, could never really come up to snuff. "In any case," he oiled on, "it's very good of you. And on a Sunday night, to take the time to talk. I appreciate it. Deeply. I wouldn't impose unless it was important. I know I can count on your—discretion."

What a load of garbage. Hogwash of the first water. Since being elevated to his present great height, the fat man was known to spend most of his time farting around on golf courses. And as for the new Transatlantic Intelligence Sharing Initiative, anyone with half a brain knew it was gobbledygook. Sharing intelligence, or for that matter anything else, with Uncle Sam—if it wasn't an oxymoron in the first place—only went one way. Not yours. And if by any chance anything remotely impressive had been done, with the Americans or anyone else, it had been done, not by the man himself, but by his minions. Who would then have been banished, sent scurrying away with their tails between their legs and their lips buttoned so their master could step up and take the credit.

The only bit of what he'd said so far that was true was the last bit. Or rather last two bits. He suspected what he was asking for really was important. Crucial, in fact. And the fat man was discreet. At a price. He'll make me pay for this, Pallioti thought. He'll make me pay. Extravagantly, and at the time and place of his choosing. And if I'm lucky, just through the nose.

The silence on the other end of the line caused him to wonder if he'd gone too far—slathered it on with too big a paddle, if such a thing was possible. But apparently not.

"Of course," his friend said finally. "Anything at all. What can I do for you, Alessandro?"

"Tell me about Angela Vari."

There was a pause.

"Angela Vari?"

Pallioti rolled his eyes. They hadn't actually spoken when he'd asked for help obtaining the file; he'd gone through one of the minions. But surely the fat man had known what, or rather who, was in the papers he'd had rushed from Rome.

"Angela Vari." This time her name was followed by a faint humming sound.

"Yes," Pallioti said. "That's right, Angela Vari."

"Hhhmm."

Pallioti, whose patience was limited at the best of times, sipped his grappa and resisted the impulse to snap, *Oh, for God's sake, just tell me what you know, you silly fat fool! Before someone gets killed!* The humming stopped.

"She was the girl," the fat man said slowly. "In the apartment, where they held Aldo Moro."

No, that was Brigitte Bardot's younger sister.

"At the risk of being impertinent, may I ask, Alessandro, why you're suddenly so interested in her?"

Because she climbed through my bedroom window last night and I'm begging her to have my children.

Pallioti was tempted to lie, then he remembered the old saying about never bullshitting a bullshitter. He took a breath, started to speak, then stopped when the humming started again.

"She was a strange girl," the fat man said finally. "I do remember that. I wasn't certain, you know. Even at the time."

So his friend had been one of the doubters. Pallioti didn't know if this surprised him or not. He put his glass down.

"You weren't certain?" he asked. "That what she was telling you was good?"

"No." The word was drawn out. "No. Not so much that. No," his friend said again. "The information she gave us was good." He laughed. This time it was a tight, sour little sound. Miles away Pallioti heard ice clink in a glass. "The proof was in the pudding, so to speak." There was a splash of liquid, the tap of a bottle being put down. Single malt, if Pallioti remembered correctly. He'd always thought it an affectation, and vaguely un-patriotic. Something no real Italian could actually like.

"We'd never have got Tomaselli, it wouldn't have happened," the fat man said. "At least not for a long time, probably, without her. So, no. It wasn't that."

There was another pause. Pallioti could see him, sniffing his drink as if it was food that might have gone off—which, frankly, given what the stuff smelled like was about right—and weighing what he would tell. And what he wouldn't. A slurping followed, and finally a sigh.

"It was just," his friend said. "Well, Moro, really. Did you ever meet him?"

"Aldo Moro?"

Pallioti shook his head. He refrained from pointing out that Aldo Moro had been dead for over thirty years, and that while he, Pallioti, had always been fast-tracked, often thanks to this man's efforts, he had hardly been enough of a star child to be called to Rome to discuss nuclear capability, or the ins and outs of NATO enlargement with the prime minister, or the foreign minister, either of which Aldo Moro might have been at any given time.

"No," he said, "I never met him." And left it at that.

"Well, I liked him. A lot of people didn't. Found him a cold fish. Inscrutable and all that. He was very private. People say they respect it, but actually they resent that sort of thing. It reminds them that at heart we're all Peeping Toms. And he was bright, of course," his friend added. There was another slurp and clink. "Moro. Very bright. People resent that, too. They say they don't, but they do. He was a quiet man as well, and, well, something more than that. It made people uncomfortable."

"Something more than the fact that he was intelligent and modest about it?"

It was a feeble attempt at humor, but his friend was right. Lots of people, certain types of men especially, were more comfortable with a good old dose of braying and backslapping.

His friend had the good grace to laugh. Then he said, "Well, yes. Actually. It was more than that. There was something, well, unearthly about him."

"Unearthly?" This was such an uncharacteristic statement that Pallioti wondered how much whiskey, exactly, had been consumed down in Rome. "Something 'unearthly' about Aldo Moro?"

"Yes. And not down. Up. You know what I mean? There are certain people, well—you wouldn't be surprised if they grew wings."

Pallioti felt himself go still. He had heard plenty of politicians described as Satan's henchmen, or even the Big Guy himself. But the other—and coming from this source—was a first. He remembered the posters after the body was found, Moro's soft, sad face. What else was his friend going to suggest? he wondered. That during his fifty-five days in purgatory Aldo Moro got holes in his feet and in the palms of his hands?

"She was the same," his friend added.

"Angela Vari?"

Pallioti reached for his grappa bottle.

"Yes. She was a very strange girl."

"Strange how?"

"Well." Pallioti heard his friend take a sip of his drink. "A born martyr. Kept sticking her hand in the flames, for a start. Went on and on about some smashed synagogue and how silence was as deadly as bullets. That kind of stuff. You know, she said she killed him—Moro—at first."

"Aldo Moro? Angela Vari said she killed him?" Pallioti sat up. This was news. And would kick things into a whole different league. "Was it true?"

"Well, who knows what was true. He was all but riddled with bullets, and we couldn't exactly pinpoint the time of death. But my instinct? No. I thought it was garbage. What evidence we could find said so, too. But as I said, Angie was a strange girl." Pallioti could almost hear the fat man shrug. "Perhaps that's why they liked each other."

"Liked each other?"

"Yes. Alessandro, are you having trouble hearing? Is that why you keep repeating everything I say?" His friend chuckled. "Moro and the Vari girl. Yes. They were, apparently, well, according to her anyway—we didn't exactly have a chance to ask him—friends. They used to talk."

"Talk?"

"Yes, Alessandro. Talk. So she said. Whisper, actually, if you want to be pedantic—" He had the good grace not to add, "Which you apparently do." "About, well, things," he added. "Philosophy. Religion. Love. Good. Evil. You do remember? It's called a conversation."

Pallioti didn't know which unnerved him more, the idea that he might appear to have forgotten what it was to indulge in abstract discourse with another human being, or the idea that the blond American doctor's wife who had been sitting across a conference table from him less than a week ago had discussed love, religion, and evil with Italy's most famous murdered politician. And might have grown wings to boot. Perhaps she'd flown away. Perhaps that was why they couldn't find her.

"How very Mary Magdalene," he murmured.

A bark of laughter issued from the phone.

"Well, I wouldn't go that far. But somewhere along those lines, in her version anyway. She said he reminded her of her father."

"Her father? Aldo Moro?"

The sad-faced, elegant man who had once turned up for a photo-op on the beach in a black suit and tie? Of course, Pallioti had never actually seen a picture of Angela Vari's father, but from what little he knew—

"I know. I know," his friend said. "Her father was a butcher from Ferrara. The resemblance wasn't immediately obvious to me, either. But she wasn't making it up, Angela. She meant it. I believed her. I think Moro became a sort of surrogate papa to her. During all those days in that ghastly little cell. A sort of reverse Stockholm syndrome, or something. She cooked for him, you know. That was her job. Nourishing him. Body and soul."

"You don't mean?"

The grappa choked on the back of his tongue. But then again, why not? Since they were banging this particular drum. You never knew. The rumor had always been that, starved of seeing each other for months if not years, couples had managed to have sex in the cages in the courtroom during the Red Brigades trials. It was probably utter nonsense, of course. There was almost as much rubbish written about the BR as there was about Mary Magdalene. On the other hand, if he'd been locked in a tiny room for days and days and suspected he was about to be killed and a young girl had—

"No, no!" his friend, who had obviously been thinking along the same lines, barked. "No. No. No, there was none of that. This was a purely platonic affair. Angela and Aldo. A meeting of minds. I'm quite sure of it."

Both of them were silent for a moment. Chastened as schoolboys.

"Not so surprising, I suppose," his friend added a moment later. "The meeting of minds, I mean. They were idealists after all, the Brigate Rosse. And so was Moro, in his way. No," he said. "That was all it was. I'm sure. Certain, in fact. She was Tomaselli's body, if, in the final analysis, apparently not soul. Moro might have won that round." The ice clinked again. "Some of her money was used, you know," he added, "to buy the apartment, the one they kept him in, on Via Montalcini. Angela always claimed she didn't know. That she handed it over to Tomaselli and believed him when he said he'd put it in the bank for her."

Pallioti could see his friend's head shaking, either because the girl had been so incredibly naïve, or because the lie was so preposterous.

"Blind love, literally. If you believe in it. Or her," his friend said. "But she did care for Moro. I do believe that. Loved him even, I think."

"So." Pallioti stared at the clear liquid in his own glass. He could feel himself frowning, furrowing the little troughs between his eyes that he sometimes thought got deeper with every passing day. "I don't understand," he said. "If she, if Angela Vari, cared so much for Aldo Moro. If he reminded her so much of her beloved father—I assume he was beloved?"

"Oh yes. Yes, as far as I know. Very beloved. She was apparently devastated when he died."

"Well." Pallioti hesitated. "If that was the case then. If—"

"If she loved Aldo Moro, why did she wait until the day of his funeral? Why didn't Angela Vari save his life? Why didn't she come to us before he was killed?"

There was a silence.

"Yes," his friend said a moment later. "That's the problem. My question, too. That was what I never understood about the Butcher's Daughter."

"Did you ask her?"

"Of course. We all asked her."

"And you never got an answer?"

There was a hesitation, and for a moment Pallioti thought he might lie. Might not be able to resist the temptation to play the know-it-all, provide the answers even if he didn't have them, just to make himself look good. But he didn't. When he spoke again, for the first time his friend sounded old. Old and tired. Too worn out to even think of picking up a golf club.

"No. Not really. Tomaselli promised her it wouldn't happen and she believed him. Love. That great catch-all. She said she believed him, in part anyway, because they didn't kill Mario Sossi. I don't know. Of course," he added, "some people thought they did get an answer out of her. Or, rather, some people—quite a few, if you want the truth—thought they knew."

"Knew?"

"That she was a bald-faced liar. As guilty as the rest of them. Worse really, since she used Moro's memory. Made up stories about how much she cared for him. How much he reminded her of her father. Blah, blah, blah. At least the others didn't stoop to that." He sighed. "There were plenty of people, Alessandro, who thought she might as well have pulled the trigger. Or, despite evidence to the contrary, that she did. At least once. There were ten shots fired into him, after all. Plenty to go around."

Silence throbbed down the phone as they both remembered the photograph that had been splashed across front pages around the world. Aldo Moro wrapped in a blanket and curled like a baby in the boot of a car, one white hand cupped to his chest.

"And you?" Pallioti asked finally.

"I don't know."

Pallioti could see his friend running his hand over his eyes that had once been bright and hard and perhaps still were, but now had sacks under them like a bloodhound's.

"I honestly don't know," he said. "I never did. And yes, I asked. But no, my friend, I never did get the answer. Perhaps you will. I take it that's what all this is about. That she's come back."

It wasn't really a question so Pallioti didn't answer. There was another sigh from the end of the phone.

"I confess, I'm not surprised," his friend said. "I wondered, when they let Tomaselli out of jail, if she'd turn up. He went to her funeral, you know."

"Tomaselli?" That did surprise Pallioti. From what he remembered of the time, no one was going out of their way to do favors for the BR. "Antonio Tomaselli?" he said again. "You let him out for Angela Vari's funeral?"

He was answered by a chuckle.

"I'll send you the photos. You can see for yourself. Come on, Sandro," his friend said a few seconds later. "Don't sound quite so surprised. We're not completely inhuman. He went in a prison van, had armed guards with him, and stayed all of fifteen minutes. Just long enough to be convinced she was dead."

"Even so. If the BR had gotten wind of it, they might have tried—"

"Another of their famous Brigate Rosse stunts? Like Mara Cagol busting her husband out of jail? Yes, the thought crossed our minds, too. We didn't exactly send out invitations, but—" He let the words linger. Then added, "Sadly nothing happened. The place was as quiet as a grave. So to speak."

Unease that had lingered like stale smoke began to solidify in Pallioti's mind, shift into discernible shapes. All of them ugly.

"Are you saying?"

"Come, come, Sandro," the fat man said quickly. "I'm not saying anything."

No, Pallioti thought. But he had heard it. Loud and clear. They had staked Tomaselli like a goat. Dangled him beside Angela Vari's empty tomb hoping the bait might draw and/or provide the opportunity for a little mopping-up operation. A little vengeance on the hoof. Pallioti could hear it now. *Tut Tut, terrible tragedy, but if dangerous criminals will try to make a run for it, if their outlaw compatriots will go about shooting at the police, trying to free terrorist prisoners—well, really, what can you expect?*

"Alas," his friend murmured, "as I said. It was a nonevent. Little Angela was buried and everyone went safely home to prison. Do you have any idea," he asked abruptly, "by the way, why she's come back? I mean specifically?"

From the dead, or to Italy? Pallioti was tempted to ask. He thought about adding something about them being one and the same, but the joke went dry in his mouth.

"Not really," he lied, and knew as he said it that it sounded like what it was.

"Hhmm," his friend said. "Interesting." And then added, "Well, lovely to hear from you, Alessandro." His voice became almost jovial. "I'll get you those photos. Just to prove we do have a heart." He laughed. "But, old friend—" he added suddenly.

"I'm listening."

There was a pause. Pallioti heard a wheeze of breath.

"There were people who never believed her," the fat man said quietly. "Intelligent people. Remember that. And there were those who believed her and never forgave her. Didn't really feel, as our American cousins say, like letting bygones be bygones. So it's worth remembering that the fact is—no matter what Angela Vari's reasons for staying quiet were—she knew where Aldo Moro was being held. She knew what was happening to him. And she did nothing." Pallioti heard the clink of ice. "When the deal was done with the Americans it was suggested to *piccola* Signorina Vari—possibly even by me—that she make her departure and not return."

"I see," Pallioti said slowly, wondering if he did.

"All I'm saying, Sandro, is that if by any chance little Angela has happened to grace our shores again, well—if it were me, I'd keep an eye on her. And on Tomaselli. In fact especially on To-maselli. It might be awkward if they attracted, how shall we say, the wrong kind of attention? I don't need to tell you about long memories in certain quarters. And, well, salt in the wound, that kind of thing. It can get nasty."

Pallioti felt the hair rise on the back of his neck.

"Call it what you want," his friend said quietly. "Some people might use the word *justice*."

It was almost midnight. Anna Carson stood in one of the tunnels in the Via delle Volte, her back against a damp stone wall, and watched snow fall between the arches. Flakes drifted down, lan-guid as feathers, and melted on the dark cobbles. There were a handful of new restaurants in the street, all of them closed now, lights still glowing over their brightly painted signs. TRATTO-RIA MARIA AND ENRIQUE, whoever they were. BISTRO-BAR BUZZ— LIVE MUSIC EVERY FRIDAY! THURSDAY IS MARTINI NIGHT! The ef-fort at gentrification had gone only so far, though. The arches were still as dank and sinister and smelling of piss as they'd al-ways been.

These days the Via delle Volte was apparently touted as a local highlight. *The Middle Ages come to life!* the tourist brochure she'd seen had said. Although why, exactly, anyone thought that might be a good thing was always slightly mysterious to her. Rats, plague, shit, darkness, and fleas. The flyer had been selec-tive describing the street's history, too. Until the war Via delle Volte had belonged to the prostitutes. When the Fascists came to power they'd turned a blind eye until they hadn't, then it had be-come a tunnel of running footsteps punctuated by the occasional shot and scream. By the time she'd walked home at night with her father—by the time she'd stood hanging on his hand watch-ing Antonio in his canvas shoes, pushing his bicycle on a night not unlike this—it had been nothing more than a dark alley. A boundary between the ghetto and the Via Mayr, the strange little bridge houses spanning it like tired hands. Probably those had been gentrified now, too. At least on the inside. From the outside their windows were still tiny and multipaned, their doors as narrow and dark as the doors children should not pass through in fairy tales.

Anna looked at the vault above her, at the pitted stone, the cracks, and white rimes of lime, and was not sure why it hadn't collapsed. Why all the rooms hadn't fallen down into the street—lace curtains, pots and pans and toothbrushes. She rolled her shoulders, flexed her hands to stop them from freezing, and shifted the pack at her feet and the two shopping bags piled on top of it. She was cold and tired, spoiled by the last three nights she'd spent in the relative comfort of hotels.

On Thursday she'd taken the first train north. Jumped on as soon as she'd reached Santa Maria Novella, not picky about the destination as long as she got clear of Florence. She'd ended up in Reggio, which had been all she'd wanted—a medium-large town with a fair selection of hotels. The one she'd chosen, just behind the inevitable Duomo, had been a bit down at heels, with a full dining room, and family run. Which virtually guaranteed not enough staff at dinnertime when she'd made sure to ask for a room. She shouldn't have been able to check in without an identity card or passport. But when the harried girl behind the desk had asked for it, she'd fussed with the backpack, pulling half the contents out, strewing them across the lobby floor until she was handed a set of keys and told to bring her ID down later. On Friday morning she'd made sure someone else was on duty, then paid in cash and vanished during the breakfast rush.

Thanks to Graziella Farelli, no such antics had been necessary in Bologna. Anna had stayed there two nights and left early this morning, hoping that the reports to whatever database kept the details of where everyone stayed and when wouldn't be updated until Monday. She was betting that bureaucracy still shut down for the weekend.

Now, however, things were different. Using Graziella's identity card to register at another hotel would be too risky. She had dodged and weaved, changed her appearance as best she could, but tomorrow was Monday. It would be only a matter of time. If Graziella Farelli had not realized already, she would surely understand by tomorrow morning that her wallet really was missing rather than just misplaced. Then, if she had not already done so, she would report the loss of her ID card and wallet first thing. By which time a description of Anna Carson would also be turning up on whatever databases descriptions of missing women turned up on.

Despite the fact that they had been basically on the verge of splitting up, arguing more or less nonstop—about Kristin and everything else—Anna had no doubt that Ken would have reported her missing, and sooner rather than later. She suspected, in fact, that he had gone demented. It would be a matter of control, she thought acidly, as much as passion. She'd found that comforting once. The God complex, so well documented in doctors, and especially surgeons, had made her feel secure. Then it just drove her crazy. They'd almost split, she couldn't count how many times. At the eleventh hour he'd always talked her into staying, not because he loved her, but because he needed to win. And over and over again, she'd given in, although she wasn't sure why. Habit? Inertia? She smiled bitterly. The irony was, up to a few years ago, she'd stayed for Kristin. Told herself that no matter how much the kid acted out, she'd lost one mother and couldn't lose another. She'd told herself Kristin needed her.

It was the last refuge of the weak, Anna thought. The rallying cry of the martyred and the spineless. Not to mention the egocentric. *He needs me! She needs me!* The sick joke was, if she had actually gotten it together to leave, packed her things and walked out the door, vanished from their lives the way she'd vanished from others before, Kristin wouldn't need her. She'd be sitting in a nice apartment, or in a college dorm in Boston, or New York, or wherever, happily going about her usual business of making someone else's life hell, instead of—

Anna didn't want to think about *instead of.* She reached into her pocket and felt the scratchy, balding head of the little white bear. Her finger pressed his bright black eye.

A bell began to toll. Seconds later it was joined by another. Midnight. The witching hour. Time for the dead, and the un-dead, to walk. Anna picked up the pack and fitted it onto her shoulders. Then she took a shopping bag in each hand. She looked both ways. No windows were lit and no one was moving. A streetlamp glowed at the mouth of Via Carbone, highlighting the black skeleton of a bicycle, blue plastic shopping bag tied over its seat. She stepped out from under the arch, Kristin's boots leaving dark footsteps in the snow.

She had arrived in Ferrara just after noon, and been immedi-ately struck by how ordinary and how surreal it felt at the same time. Like one of those dreams when you meet yourself as a child. The castle had seemed, not smaller, as memory required, but bigger and uglier. Cannons had been placed at the entrance, cannonballs stacked beside them, as if the town expected to be attacked. The moat was fetid and green and laced with ice. The row of shops cowered in the opposite buildings.

Anna had turned away, heading automatically for Corso d'Este, where the gray faces of the palazzos still faced each other, tears of damp running from their shutter latches. The fat legs of the little boys still dangled from the portico of the Prosperi Sacrati. A winter fog, so cold it felt splintered with ice, drifted across the afternoon. It was thick enough that, as she neared the end of the street, she had not been able to see the Angels'

Gate, and had the panicked thought that it might not be there. Or worse, might have been restored. Made glossy and new. Or been removed altogether, replaced by some sleek architectural statement. Then, all at once, it had loomed in front of her, the crumbling pillars and great wooden panels with the giant padlock still sealing in the past.

Laughter had come from the top of the walls as a bicycle rattled down the path, the boy standing up and pedaling hard, his girlfriend on the seat behind him, clutching his waist. Anna had watched them disappear. Then she'd turned around. The line of houses were still behind their iron railings. The doors had been repainted, and the gravel of a few of the driveways replaced by fancy herringbone pavement. Winter branches still laced above the frost-white lawns. Stone steps still led to the front doors.

The cemetery had not changed much, either. She'd been half afraid, as she wove her way between the crypts that stood like tiny houses, her fingers brushing the monuments as if she was blind, that her parents' grave might have disappeared. Or been moved to make room for the more recently departed, or those who at least had someone left to remember them. But the stone angel still stood near the wall of the little courtyard, hanging back as if she was shy, her wings half spread, one hand raised.

Anna hadn't understood as a child that her father probably hadn't been able to afford the statue. That part of the mushroom cloud that had haunted her and helped to kill him had probably begun with its pitted marble cheek and folded gown. The angel had looked so exactly the same, down to the chip on her sandaled foot and the wilting bouquet that lay on her pedestal, that at first Anna hadn't even noticed the new line of engraving that had been added below her parents'.

Angela Vari, Daughter, 1958–1980.

When she finally caught her breath, she'd asked herself what she'd expected. Then wondered if she'd had a funeral, and if so, if anyone had bothered to come.

The bouquet had answered at least part of the question. The flowers were real, not plastic or fabric, like some she'd seen, the livid blues and reds where the dye had leaked off spackling the gravel. Curious, she'd lifted the fresh blooms. A card was stuffed down in the stems. *Annabeth, Marco, Angela—Forever in my prayers, Renata.*

The smell of chicken soup. The sound of kitchen shutters banging open, a voice scolding. The warmth of a hand slipping her a coin for the collection at Easter mass. The sight of her father, one drunken summer night, holding a woman in his arms, kissing her in the shadowed halo of a street lamp. Renata Ravalli, who all these years later kept them in her prayers.

Anna found herself grateful. But the fact that the Ravallis, or at least one of them, were obviously still alive and might still live in Via Vittoria made her wary. After leaving the cemetery, she'd taken her time, circling like a hungry cur dog. It had been more than an hour before she crossed Corso Giovecca and slipped into the ghetto, then sidled like a thief into Via Mayr.

What she'd found made her stop in her tracks. Although she didn't know what she'd expected. A minimart? The delicatessen of her mother's dreams? A bijou little slow food shop selling cold cuts and pickles all wrapped in fancy paper with names like *Nonna's,* and made in China or New Jersey by Kraft or Nestlé? She'd braced herself for that. Or simply for a hole in the wall. Or a new line of glossy shops. Possibly even a fast-food place, or a pricey trattoria with faux scarred tables, paper napkins, tripe on the menu, and six stickers on the door announcing it had been recommended by travel websites. Anything but what she saw.

There was a hole in the sign. MACEL ÌA it read, the letters chipped and barely legible above sheets of plywood that had been nailed across the front of her father's shop. *Fuck Berlusconi!*

someone had spray painted. Three *Avatar* posters were pasted below, suggesting the prime minister might be bright blue and have a tail.

Anna was not sure, but she thought a small squeak escaped her, a twinge of outrage from the Angela who still dwelled inside her. "Fuckers," she had found herself muttering. Then she had darted across the street like her younger self, dodging between a rattling gray van and a new Mercedes whose driver had honked and raised his fist.

Glancing down the block she'd seen that the Pirottis had somehow survived and were still open. Mindful that if Renata Ravalli was still alive, Signor and Signora Pirotti might be, too, Anna had ducked around the corner where a van that looked suspiciously like their old one was parked, and seen the door to the storeroom.

The lock had been damaged, part of the hinge pulled away, either deliberately or by mistake. She'd eased it open, telling herself she only wanted to look. Inside, leaves and bits of newspaper littered the floor. Rust marked the old porcelain sink. A workbench along the far wall where the buckets had once been stacked was piled with crates and what looked to be bits of a vacuum cleaner. A big ladder, possibly the same one she and Antonio had used, hung in cobwebbed brackets on the wall, half its rungs missing. The place was obviously abandoned. Then, under the grime, she'd noticed the outline of the hatch—the little door her mother had insisted on putting in to hand buckets and sponges and soap and bags of sawdust through.

Now she stood holding the fruits of her afternoon shopping spree, and felt her stomach sink. There was just enough light from the street lamp on the corner to see that someone had come along and closed the storeroom door. Anna hesitated, then put the bags down, pulled off the mittens she had bought, and felt along the rotting sill. Relief flooded through her. It wasn't locked.

It had just been pushed, or had blown shut, and was jammed. She got her fingers in a crack and pulled.

Inside it was pitch dark. Anna closed the door and dug in one of the bags for the flashlight she'd bought. It was a big one, a Maglite, the same kind the police carried at home in the States, useful equally for lighting dark corners and bashing people over the head. The bright white beam made the little room seem even smaller. She ferried her bags to the far wall beyond the ladder, then took the pack off, rested it at her feet, and began to feel with her free hand around the edge of the hatch.

The hatch's wooden panel didn't budge. Anna huffed in frustration. Then her fingers found the little slip lock. She tried to pull it back, but it stuck. She put the flashlight between her feet, pointing up at the cobwebby roof, and used both hands. It still wouldn't move. She was beginning to wonder if it had been super-glued, when finally, she picked up the Maglite and put it to its other intended use. One good whack and the lock gave. The hinges on the little door creaked as she pushed. She hoped they hadn't rusted out, wouldn't snap so the whole thing came off in her hand. Whining, the hatch finally swung back. Anna took a deep breath, then shined the Maglite through the opening.

The first thing it caught was the marble counter, thick with dust, then beyond, darkness, and a weird shine—the window made black by the boards nailed over it. Threads of light zigged and zagged in a silver spider's web, a black hole at its heart where someone had thrown a rock at the glass. The name, Vari, was gone, replaced by two lines of red lettering: *Carne Rapido!* Anna read backward. *Sette Giorni per la Settimana! Sette à Sette!* Meat fast! Seven days a week! Seven to seven!

So the supermarket hadn't let it go derelict after all. They'd merely tried to beat her at her own game. And failed. The ghost of Angela felt a spurt of satisfaction. She swung the light up and caught white tiles, half expecting to see them cracked, too, attacked out of sheer spite. But, no. The pig and the cow still grinned and laughed.

Anna set the flashlight down, reached for the pack, and shoved it through the hatch. Next she lowered each of the shopping bags, trying not to tip them over, or at least not to break anything. Then she dropped the Maglite through the hatch. The beam canted wildly as it hit one of the paper sacks. Finally she took a deep breath, put both hands on the ledge, and hoisted herself up.

Monday, February 8

The first thing Pallioti saw when he walked into his office was the package sitting in the center of his desk. He stood with his overcoat on his shoulders, staring at it. His friend had been as good as his promise.

Enzo had already called in, reporting that he'd arrived in Bologna at the crack of dawn and spoken to one Graziella Farelli, who'd had her bag rifled in church, and who did bear a passing resemblance to Anna Carson, if Anna Carson cut and dyed her hair. But so did a lot of people. Tallish, good-looking-ish, and dark-ish wasn't exactly unusual. So far that was the sum total of their progress. Pallioti sighed, took his coat off, and hung it in his closet, smoothing the arm and flicking a speck of icy grit from the cuff.

Turning around, he rather hoped the package might have vanished. But it was still on his desk. Some poor lunatic on a motorcycle had probably raced through the night from Rome, risking life and limbs, his and others, to deliver it. He snorted and reached for the silver letter opener he kept in his top drawer. The thing was almost a foot long and sharp as a shiv. As handy for opening throats as letters, it had been given to him by a woman he had once, very briefly and a long time ago, thought he might marry. Apart from a vague memory of her voice—which had been low and almost obscenely beautiful—it was the only relic of the affair. Which seemed fitting. Weighing it in his hand, seeing his initials engraved on the blade, he thought it was actually a far more appropriate gift than it had seemed at the time. He wondered if he'd given her the obligatory coin for it. Probably not, otherwise they'd have been married happily and he'd be bouncing grandchildren on his knee. Not sure what the point of looking at photographs of Angela Vari's funeral would actually be, he slit the packing tape in one clean cut.

The photographs were eight by tens, black and white, glossy and slightly cracked and old-fashioned looking. Pallioti spread them on his desk, wondering when it was that things created in his own lifetime had begun to feel like antiques. There was no note, no billet-doux, from his friend trapped in the fat man's body. Yellowing paper tabs were taped to the bottom of each shot, giving the names of the unwitting subjects. High-tech for the time.

Surveillance photos always gave Pallioti the creeps, partly because he found them so interesting. There was something horribly irresistible about gazing on people who did not know they were being watched, a nasty little jolt every bit as satisfying as a grappa. If God was sitting up in his heaven, gazing down on the faithless had to be his favorite pastime.

His friend had sent fifteen photos in all. Which meant there were almost certainly more where these came from. Jesus, Pallioti thought, fanning them across his blotter, didn't they have anything better to do than document the burying of an urn filled with sand? He wondered how many photographers had been crouched behind monuments and lurking in mausoleums. Tomaselli himself appeared, on first glance anyway, to be completely unaware of his starring role. He wasn't in chains, either.

Nor were there a cadre of minders—only two that Pallioti could pick out, standing respectfully far back. His estimation of the prison services went up a few notches. The fat man hadn't been joking after all. They did have hearts. He pulled out his glasses and slipped them on.

Even through a telephoto lens, even in black and white and over the space of three decades, it was obvious that chains were hardly necessary. And would have been obscene. Because Antonio Tomaselli was devastated. His handsome face appeared empty and slightly crumpled, like a piece of paper that had been screwed up and only partially smoothed out. He stared at a hole at the foot of a stone angel as if he wished he might somehow be sucked into it. In one photograph, he stood with his hand over his mouth, his shoulders hunched in grief.

He had loved her.

Pallioti straightened up, ashamed of himself for being surprised. He drummed his fingers on the edge of his desk. Then he leaned down and examined the prints more closely.

Almost all the shots showed a priest and five mourners. The death had been reported in the papers. That was the point after all, for everyone—or at least certain people—to know Angela Vari was dead. But the piece had run only after the fake interment. So the mourners here would have been those who had been previously notified, her equivalent of family.

Three of them were clearly older. The fat man had said Angela Vari didn't have any immediate family, so probably they were friends of her parents', or very distant relatives of some kind. They stood together in their baggy black coats. The elderly man wore an old-fashioned black hat of the type Pallioti remembered their gardener wearing to his mother's funeral. The two women wore headscarves and no gloves. Wound in their pale fingers, he could make out what looked like lengths of string. Rosary beads. Heads bent, they intoned their prayers for the dead. Pallioti could almost hear the words, smell the faint sickening waft of incense drifting down the years.

As if by mutual agreement, Antonio Tomaselli and the second younger mourner stood on the other side of the grave. Tomaselli wore no overcoat, just a dark suit and tie. The prison service, or someone, had been generous. The clothes appeared to fit. They even made him look a halfway suitable partner for the woman who stood beside him. She was tall. Her dark hair was pulled back, accentuating the strong bones of her face. She appeared to be about Antonio's age, but something in the way she stood suggested that she was at least twice the man he was. Possibly twice the man any man was. She wore a black overcoat, not unlike Pallioti's own, black heels, black gloves. Even from thirty years away, Pallioti could tell they were expensive. She reminded him of those statues of Pallas Athena he'd seen in picture books. He wouldn't have been the least bit surprised if in the next photo she'd been holding a spear, or had an owl emerging from her forehead.

No such luck, although one of the photographers did catch her putting her hand on Antonio Tomaselli's shoulder, speaking to him much the way a parent would speak to a distressed child. In another picture, she had stepped to the background and was holding her arms out, fending off the two police minders, her mouth open, obviously telling them to leave Antonio alone as he stood in tears, his hand on the outstretched arm of the angel.

Pallioti straightened up and frowned. If this woman was part of the prison service, all he could say was that it had sure gone to hell in the last thirty years. He squinted down at the faded little yellow strips of paper. The old people were named as Alda Pirotti, Tommaso Pirotti, and Renata Ravalli. Antonio Tomaselli was Antonio Tomaselli. The woman, unsurprisingly, was not Pallas Athena. Her name was Barbara Barelli.

The train left right on time. It was old and dented and unglamorous, but prompt. Anna lifted the bike she had stolen into the luggage van. There had been at least two dozen pig-piled outside the library in Piazza Paradiso, some shoved close enough to be chained to the metal rack, others chained to other bikes, or to themselves—back wheel to front, hobbled like cowboys' horses.

She had lurked around, searching for one that wasn't locked, and had almost been undone by a pair of old ladies who had walked by slowly as turtles, exchanging snatches of gossip. They hadn't seemed to notice her, but Anna knew better. Nonna Franchi had had eyes not just in the back, but probably in the sides and top, of her head as well. Seeing them she had missed Nonna with a pang so sudden it felt like a cramp—a vicious little stab of loss. When she was sure they'd turned the corner, she'd grabbed the handlebars and hefted a bike she'd spotted out of the tangle. Moments later she was pedaling through Piazza Trieste, telling herself that the fact the thing had gears at all made up, almost, for the spectacularly uncomfortable seat.

Now she climbed into the carriage, which was all but empty, and settled herself by the window, watching as Ferrara slipped into a wasteland of railway yards and industrial estates. Silver fencing topped with razor wire guarded the business parks that had expanded like inkblots, sprawling into the flat featureless countryside. There was no sign anymore of the factory that had exploded. It would have been pulled down years ago. Somewhere there would be a plaque, an obligatory listing of the names of the dead. Beside an entrance door, or in a lobby. Next to a dribbling fountain whose bottom was lined with pennies and waterlogged cigarette butts.

Anna leaned back in the seat and drew her new jacket around her. She'd replaced her whole wardrobe yesterday, with cheaper and certainly less fashionable substitutes. Now she wondered if she shouldn't have gone whole hog and dyed her hair again as well. Or cut it shorter. She'd considered it, but wasn't really sure what she could do. Going back to blond would make her look too much like Anna Carson, American Housewife, and darkening it and chopping it off wouldn't really make that much difference. Besides, it was so obvious they were probably looking for it. In the end she'd bought a bunch of hair elastics, pulled it back tight, and decided to keep it up under the decidedly unflattering knitted watch cap she'd purchased. With any luck and no makeup—she'd pitched all of Kristin's Goth eyeliner and mascara and the horrid lilac lipstick with no regret at all—she might be mistaken for a guy.

She'd been sorely tempted to keep Kristin's beautiful, and very warm, down jacket to layer under her new sleeping bag—even with a pad, the shelf of the cold room left a lot to be desired—then had told herself not to be stupid. So it had gone, along with everything else—the pack that was so obvious she might as well be waving a flag, and, of course, Graziella's wallet. She couldn't use the ID card again. Although she still had well over a thousand euros of her own left, she'd taken what cash there was, then zipped the wallet into the deep inner pocket of Kristin's coat, and pushed the whole lot through the panel of the Caritas box. Graziella Farelli had looked like a nice person and it was a nice wallet. Maybe when the Good Samaritans, or the Brothers of St. Francis, or whoever they were, found it, they'd mail it back to her.

The train jerked and slowed. Anna had been standing between carriages for the last ten minutes, worried the station was so small and would be so empty that she would not have time to jump out and get the bike from the luggage van. If that happened, she would have to walk, and that would take a very long time.

She bent and peered through the grimy window, watching as the platform slunk into view. It was nothing but a concrete terrace and a shelter sided with Plexiglas like a bus stop, two slat benches inside and a sign hanging above. There wasn't a house in sight, or even another building. The stop was just a stop, barely even a place. In the middle of nowhere.

A guard stuck his head out of one of the forward carriages, watching as she ran back to the luggage van. The moment she'd lifted the bike down, he raised his hand. The train was moving again by the time she slammed the door. Its gray rump rattled past, then grew smaller and smaller until, finally, it shrank to nothing, swallowed by the empty stretches of the fields. Anna turned around. There was only one road. A blast of wind, smelling of mud, hit her in the face, making her eyes tear as she got on the bike and began to pedal.

After forty minutes, her calves burned. She stopped, bent and massaged her legs, fingers easing the knotted muscles. It was not true that you could flip from one sport to another. That legs could run, pump, and kick equally happily. At least not at her age. Not anymore. She hadn't been on a bike in years and the seat of this one was so fiendish she found it more comfortable to stand up. Anna licked her lips and tasted salt. She'd stopped once to consult the map she'd bought yesterday. It had been reassuring, a check on her nerves, but the truth was, it hadn't been necessary. The sea marshes couldn't be more than five or six miles away now, as the crow flew. She knew exactly where she was.

Tucked into the passenger seat of Antonio's tiny rattling Fiat, her hand on his thigh, her elbow hitting his as he searched for the gears that were so loose it was hard to tell first from third, she'd felt her hair blown back in the draft from the open window as she'd watched the fields and the rows of the orchards, green and dense with summer.

"I've never brought anyone here before," he'd said suddenly. He'd smiled, not taking his eyes off the thin grayed strip of road.

"To the abbey?"

She'd turned to him as she asked, and found herself still amazed that he was here. Or that she was here with him. Or both. Although, in the week since he had walked into the pizzeria, they had barely been out of each other's sight.

Angela had taken him home, to her den of memories and piles of clothes and dirty dishes. They had climbed the stairs and closed the door and fumbled, barely speaking, into the sitting room, to the sofa, to the worn rug, for—she wasn't even sure how long for. The rest of the day. The night. The next day. She had called and told the pizza man she was sick, forgotten several of the small jobs she was supposed to do, and hadn't cared. Lying in the dark, and then in the shuttered half-light, and then in the dark again, running her hands across Antonio's body, feeling the slick sweat of his arms, his thighs, his stomach, tangling her hands in his hair, she hadn't cared about anything. She hadn't even asked where he'd gotten the car, or why he wasn't going back to the university at Padua, or what he was going to do in Rome, which was where he said he was going. He could tell her, or not. All she had cared about was that she could touch him. Smell him. Taste him. Feel him inside her like the beating of her own heart.

He shook his head.

"Not the abbey," he'd said. "Not Pomposa. We'll go there after. We're going to the farm. My grandpa's farm. I told you, remember?"

And she had nodded, because of course she remembered. She remembered every word he'd ever said to her. Every time she'd ever glimpsed him. She'd squeezed his thigh then, run her hand up, and leaned back, watching his face as the summer rippled away beyond the open window. They had stopped a few minutes later. Clambering out of the little Fiat, and climbing the embankment. Falling into the grass on the other side, they'd pushed clothes up, pulled them down, not caring if a car or a fruit truck or even someone on a bicycle came by and saw the flash of naked skin.

When you're young, you think sex is love, Anna thought. And maybe you're right. Or as right as you'll ever be. It's the brain that lies, not the body. Not the skin, the blood. Cells, for Christ's sake. Viscera—liver, heart, gut. She wiped her eyes with the back of her hand. The fields around her were as flat and featureless as the sea. For all she knew, this was the very spot where the junky little car had stopped. The past ought to have markers. Way signs. A pile of rocks, or a forked stick. Something to at least tell you how far you had to go. And let you know when you arrived.

Forty minutes later she finally saw the pillars, rising out of nowhere, two abandoned columns fronting the ghostly outline of a track. Fog was creeping in from the sea, hazing the already weak afternoon sun. It was colder. By tomorrow morning the whole world would be sugared in frost.

Anna got off the bicycle. She was aware of her heart hammering, suddenly frantic, as if it didn't want to be here and was trying to escape—scrabble through her breastbone and take flight. Or run. Bound ahead on its own.

Ciao, Carina. Long time. Where are you?" she'd demanded, standing in the breakfast room at the Excelsior, and he'd laughed.

Where do you think? he'd asked, and if she'd allowed herself to, she could have felt his breath seeping through the tiny phone she'd held clamped to her ear.

Now she almost thought she heard his voice, hanging in the still, chilly air.

Where do you think I am, Carina? he'd asked again. And then, *Last time, I came and found you. Now it's your turn.*

Anna half expected the ground to give way as she stepped through the pillars. Or to find that, like something out of a children's book, she'd stepped through a slit in time. That all around her the fields would billow and roll into green, and she would look up and see the Fiat parked on the pale packed gravel. See Antonio leaning against the door. Hear him say, "This is where I grew up. This is my nonno's farm."

She hadn't been able to see the house and barns then, and she couldn't see them now. The fields looked to be flat. But like an animal playing possum, the landscape was not as empty or as dead as it appeared. The track, rutted and frozen and all but impassable, ran on for some way before it fell down into the slight dip, almost a hollow, the buildings nestled in. She propped the bike against the crumbling brick pillar and felt in her pocket for the knife.

It was a filleting blade, mid-length. She'd found it last night in the butcher's shop. Or rather it had found her. Backing out of the cold room, she had felt something finger her hair, almost giving her a heart attack. A shine with the Maglite caught some old utensils, abandoned on a cobwebbed hanging rack. The knife had not been as sharp as she would have liked and, lacking a whetstone, she'd used the underside of the marble counter to sharpen it. Then she'd wrapped the blade in a sock. Not surprisingly the point had stuck through, jabbing her in the thigh as she'd pedaled.

Despite the chill, sweat rolled down her chest. Her hands were itchy in the cheap wool mittens. She followed the track, watching it disappear over the edge of the world. When she reached the lip of the hill, she stopped and let her eyes roam down the shallow slope. Then she began to run.

But even as she did, even as she pulled her hands from her pockets, flailing, tripping on a tuft of weeds and regaining her balance, Anna knew she wasn't wrong. She had come to the right place. She recognized the little pond. And the stand of poplar trees. And, as she got closer, the well in what had been the front yard where Antonio had been so happy to find the bucket still attached to the winch even if it leaked and the water was brackish. Gathering speed, she hit loose gravel, scrambled, and let out a cry, not caring who saw or heard her—and knowing at the same time that there was no one to see or hear.

The fire must have happened years ago, because earth had blown and packed over the rubble. Spikes of dead grass poked up, furring the yard like whiskers on an old man's cheek. Anna climbed over the shattered sill of the foundation. The house had been derelict, but still standing, still with all its doors and windows, when Antonio had brought her here. He'd gone around the back, and pushed open the kitchen door. Led her into the stone-floored room. Showed her where the table had stood, and where his mother and grandmother had cut notches on the inside of the pantry wall, marking each birthday he and Piero had passed.

Anna had realized at once, as soon as she saw him in the pizzeria, that Antonio had changed. He was leaner than he had been a year before, his features sharper, as if Piero's death had stripped a layer off him. Pared him down, exposing a new hardness in his face and in the set of his shoulders. She had not had to ask to know that he no longer believed in bread and roses. That afternoon, standing in the farmhouse kitchen, she'd watched as he pressed his finger into the last shallow indent that had marked the top of his brother's head. She'd seen him push against it. Lean hard, as if he could make the wood splinter and somehow release Piero's ghost. Finally he had wiped his eyes with the back of his arm. Then he'd taken her hand, and they'd climbed the stairs, stepping on every creaking board.

Standing in the room under the eaves, Antonio had put his arms around her. He'd whispered in her ear. Then he'd leaned down, and with the elbow of his shirt made a circle on the dusty pane so she could see what he had seen every morning from the bed he shared with his brother—the sea of fields that spread around them, lapping the island of his grandfather's farm.

A shard of glass glinted in the weakening sun. Faint char marks were still visible on some of the pale square stones. Anna wondered how it had started. If someone had been living here and had been careless, left the stove on or let an electrical box short out. Then she thought of the boarded-up front of her father's shop, the spider's web in the plate glass, and wondered if that was what had happened here, too. If they had come to avenge Aldo Moro, cresting the hill with torches, moving down the slope bearing gasoline cans and rags the way centuries before they had sacked the houses of traitors and burned the hovels of witches.

If so they hadn't got to the barn. It was still standing on the far side of the yard. The roof had fallen in, taking half the walls with it, but for a crazed moment Anna had the idea that she might not be wrong after all—that Antonio had set up some kind of camp in the ruins, and that any second now he would appear, or she would spot the bumper of a car under a tarpaulin or pile of brush. She skirted the crumbling building and peered through one of the busted-out windows. There was nothing inside but the sagging skeleton of a tractor.

Her tears welled and burned in the cold. She had been so sure, so absolutely certain when he said *find me*, that this was where he meant. Where he would have gone. Anna turned around. He had to be watching. From somewhere inside the broken shadows. Or up on the hill.

"Antonio!"

She cupped her hands to her mouth and bellowed, then jumped as an egret exploded through the bulrushes at the edge of the pond and flapped toward the sun.

"Antonio," Anna whispered to the empty space.

Then she screamed it so loud her lungs scorched.

Enzo Saenz watched the blurry figure hurry through the tunnel that connected the platforms of the Bologna train station. It scuttled out of one security camera's range and into the field of the next, dodging passengers coming in the other direction, the pack making it hunchbacked. At the top of platform three it came up the steps and stood, disoriented for a moment in the daylight. Then it turned abruptly, walked toward a bench, and stopped to study a vending machine. Enzo leaned forward as it reached into a pocket and found a coin.

Come on, he thought, come on.

Slowly a pale, ungloved hand reached out and pushed a button.

"Bingo," he said out loud, and froze the tape.

The junior detective who had been sent to the Bologna train station and returned with the trophy of the CCTV tapes grinned, trying to suppress the excitement—the thrill of being part of what was obviously a major investigation, even if he didn't know what it was. Scuttlebutt in the cafeteria said the woman they were looking for had murdered her husband, who was a mafioso who had abused her for years, and was now on the run, and possibly in possession of a series of secret bank numbers leading to accounts in the Cayman Islands that she planned to use as bargaining chips. A rival story circulating through the gym showers said she was a courier for a trafficking ring based in Bari who'd gone rogue. In the course of the last few hours, Enzo had heard each told in increasingly elaborate detail and had done nothing to refute either. Instead he'd stood by the coffee machine, tearing open sugar packets and nodding in a way he hoped might suggest both were true.

He glanced at his watch. It was past two o'clock in the afternoon. They'd been at it all day, and were still running Graziella Farelli's name through the database that covered hotel stays. Now that they'd spotted the figure from the Sunday morning tape, he was sure they'd get a hit, and probably sooner rather than later.

Probably from somewhere large, business-oriented, and not more than a few blocks from the station. If they could get to the room before the cleaning crews—and let's face it, probably after them, too—they'd almost definitely pull some fingerprints. Maybe they'd get a visual ID from the desk or a room service guy and could put together a more accurate photo fit. Find out if she was using an accent, or pretending she didn't speak Italian, or had been overheard talking on the phone. Anything would be helpful. He started the CCTV tape from the station again and watched as the blurry person peeled a wrapper off something, then wandered away and vanished behind a pillar. It was her. He could feel it right down in the bottom of his gut.

"Gotcha," he muttered to himself.

Then he turned around and asked the junior assigned to help him if they could get a team to the station, preferably yesterday. If they could seal the vending machine, see if they could lift a print from a button that matched Angela Vari's. They should try the garbage, too, if the bins hadn't been emptied. She'd thrown the wrapper away. If they could pick up Angela Vari's prints they would know they were following Anna Carson, not just some dark-haired woman carrying a red backpack who might be her. That wasn't a wild-goose chase he had time to go on.

Everybody who'd worked at the station yesterday morning would need to be questioned, too. Thanks to Graziella Farelli they had a photo fit and a sketch. Someone—a conductor, a ticket salesman, a platform guard—would remember something. Sunday mornings were quiet, and cherry red was a memorable color.

The young man was already running out of the room.

Enzo Saenz shook his head, wondering if she'd ever get smart enough to throw that damn backpack away. Then he wound the tape back, slowed it down, and watched the figure again. The feeling that a block of ice was cracking inside him grew. He held out his hand. Someone slapped a train schedule into his palm. Enzo ran his eye down the lines of tiny print, and resisted the temptation to yip.

The date/time stamp from the CCTV picture in front of him read "Sunday, February 7, 10:14 AM." The next train on platform three had been the 10:20 to Ferrara.

~

Not fifteen miles from where Enzo was sitting, Pallioti slumped in the front seat of an unmarked police car and wondered if he was losing his mind. The thought occurred to him with increasing frequency these days. Sometimes he felt he no longer knew himself. As a rule people got more sensible as they got older. He had the distinct impression that he'd been getting rapidly crazier.

Right this second, for instance, he was supposed to be having lunch with the mayor, then having yet another meeting with Kenneth Carson, during which he was supposed to reassure the poor man, yet again, that the entire force of the Italian state was working on his behalf, and to hint, without saying anything at all, that there was every reason to expect the happy family would be reunited, possibly within hours. He was supposed, in short, to be doing his job—sitting behind his desk like some po-faced coot, keeping his hand firmly on the tiller. Steering the Good Ship Law Enforcement through waters deep and turbulent.

Instead he was running around behind Enzo's back behaving like he was some sort of half-baked psychic receiving messages from old photographs. Next he'd probably start demanding pieces of Kristin Carson's clothes, closing his eyes and making whirring sounds and talking in broken sentences about auras and bodies of dark water. It was sad, but it couldn't be helped. Barbara Barelli had stuck to him like a burr.

He'd put the photographs away finally. Turned his attention to other matters—Kristin Carson wasn't the only mess they had on their hands. People were still busily stuffing carved giraffes with heroin, laundering money through a chain of hair salons in the Oltrarno, and counterfeiting fashion labels in the basement of a Chinese supermarket out beyond the Fortezza da Basso. In other words, life in Bella Firenze was going on as usual, and all its busy little bees had to be attended to. He had chaired a meeting finalizing the details of a raid on a sweatshop and come back and told Guillermo to get him everything he could find on the Barelli woman. Her name was familiar. He thought it was from something he'd seen recently. He wished to hell he could remember what. He read too much. He was getting old. His brain wasn't what it used to be. Possibly it never had been.

An hour later Pallioti had listened in silence to what his secretary had to say. Then he'd ordered a car from the garage and set off for this fancy private neighborhood in a suburb of Bologna, where he now lurked like a deranged stalker outside the office-*cum*-home of Avvocatessa Barbara Barelli. Any second she would probably call the police and he would get arrested for harassment, or inappropriate parking, or just being a man in a dark overcoat. Because if what Guillermo had told him was remotely accurate—and Guillermo being Guillermo, it inevitably was—Dottoressa Barelli was not shy about asserting her rights, or those of her clients.

She had begun her career as a lawyer representing sports stars, all women, a number of whom had fought and successfully won the right to be reinstated to National Teams after accusing an extremely prominent track coach of harassment. Pretty much a straight case of *Sleep with me and get a berth on the team, or don't and stay home. Your choice.* The settlements had been large, the publicity embarrassing, and the coach in question had left to spend more time with his family before moving on to greener pastures in South Africa when his wife threw him out.

The case had made Barbara Barelli's name, but she hadn't rested on her laurels. According to Guillermo, she developed a specialty in women's rights. Female factory workers whose overtime pay was half of men's, a consortium of prostitutes challenging the law that insisted brothels were illegal and thus forced them onto the streets, a lesbian couple who wanted to adopt. All of them and more had found their way to Avvocatessa Barelli's office. Over the course of the last two decades she'd won some cases, and lost some, and become something of an icon in the process. So, given her long history of challenging the paternalistic establishment, it might not have been much of a surprise that she had acted on behalf of one of the more notorious members of the BR.

Except that it was. Because not only did Barbara Barelli not deal with criminal cases—much less terrorism charges, which were a specialty in themselves—she didn't represent men.

Guillermo had pulled a long interview off the Internet in which she expounded at some length on the thesis that men had more than enough representation in society and that she therefore felt it her duty to devote what small talent she had to equalizing the balance on behalf of the repressed, that is, the millions of women who labored daily under an iron fist. A footnote said the talk had been given at a number of professional women's associations across Europe, where it was invariably met with thunderous applause. Which had left Pallioti both disturbed— the idea of wittingly, or arguably worse, unwittingly, being an iron-fisted oppressor, didn't sit that well—and puzzled. Because whatever else Antonio Tomaselli might or might not be, he was definitely a man.

Barbara Barelli had first begun representing him shortly after she qualified to practice law, some few years after the photographs had been taken at Angela Vari's funeral, and had stuck with him ever since. He was not only one of her very rare male clients—if not her only one—his was her only criminal case. It didn't make sense. Tomaselli would almost certainly have been far better off with one of the handful of lawyers who represented the other Brigate Rosse members. Who, indeed, had made careers out of it. But he had apparently chosen, and stayed with, Barbara Barelli, right up to last year, when she had handled the final negotiations for his release.

Pallioti wanted to know why.

And preferably sooner rather than later. He had initially thought Anna Carson was their best lead when it came to finding Kristin. Now he realized that surely, if anyone knew where Tomaselli was, or how to contact him, it would be his lawyer? A woman who, if the pictures were anything to go by, had known him for a good three decades and must therefore also be a close friend.

Impatience prickled him. Pallioti glanced at his watch. It had taken just over an hour to drive up from Florence. Guillermo had checked and found that Barbara was not due to be appearing in court in either Milan or Bologna today. Of course she might be in Rome, or Naples, or anywhere else where the sisterhood was being oppressed by iron fists like his, but Pallioti didn't think so. There were two identical dark blue Mercedes parked on the paved forecourt. One was registered to a Hedwige Aarlheissen, who was listed as living at the same address as Dottoressa Barelli. The other was registered to the *avvocatessa* herself.

Pallioti knew this because Guillermo had told him, and because he had seen her drive in thirty minutes ago, get out of it, and walk into the house. Being a great believer in the advantage of surprise, he hadn't called ahead, but had stayed in the highly recognizable unmarked police car for the last half hour in the hope that Hedwige would decide to go shopping, or to the gym, or somewhere. He didn't know what the relationship between the two women was, but he thought Dottoressa Barelli might be more forthcoming if he spoke to her alone.

⌒

"Bar, he's still there."

Hedwige stood by the window, far enough back so she couldn't be seen, and pointed across the street. Barbara looked up from the kitchen island where she was chopping cherry tomatoes. As usual the blade was flashing so fast Hedwige was convinced Barbara would, one of these days, amputate at least one, if not several, of her own fingers. Still she watched, fascinated. When she was a child her parents had taken her to a Japanese steak house in New York where everything flamed, sizzled, and was slashed. It had been every bit as good as a horror movie and was one of her favorite memories. Her parents, on either side of her, had drunk mai tais and laughed and caught bits of steak thrown through the air, snapping at them like circus dogs. Perhaps Barbara could have a new career as a chef in a place like that, if she ever gave up being a lawyer. Which she wouldn't.

"What man?" Barbara said, without looking up.

"The one in the car who's been sitting across the street for the last hour."

"What?" Barbara frowned.

They were having guests for dinner, some magistrate and a singer she'd taken up with who, for whatever reason, Barbara was hell-bent on impressing. Hedwige had no idea why, and she wasn't jealous—they'd been living together for fifteen years, the green goddess had gone to ground long ago—but she was annoyed. Because when Bar got like this she was like a terrier after a rat. This particular rat was some kind of fancy marinated concoction involving many small vegetables and things in shells. Obsessive Behavior 101. It made Barbara a demon on a case, but it was a pain in the ass to live with. Multitasking was not, on the other hand, a mystery to Hedwige. Back in the day, she'd been a heptathlete. Barbara had been a sprinter. Big surprise.

"The man," she said. "Who I told you about when you came in. He's been sitting across the street, in a car, for the last hour."

"What does he look like?"

Hedwige shrugged.

"He's in a car. I don't know. Dark hair. Dark coat."

Barbara finally put the knife down and walked to the window. Unlike Hedwige, she went straight up to the glass.

"Son of a bitch!" she swore, turning toward the front hall.

"What?"

"It's a cop, for Christ's sake. In an unmarked car. You can tell those things a mile away."

A blast of cold air hit Hedwige in the face as Barbara yanked the door open. Whoever the policeman was, Hedwige felt sorry for him.

"Dottoressa."

Pallioti had gotten out of the car as soon as he saw the front door open. In her early fifties, Barbara Barelli was, if anything, more impressive in person now than the photographs suggested she had been thirty years ago. He had been right. She did look like Pallas Athena. A very angry Pallas Athena in designer jeans and a red silk blouse.

"What the hell do you think you're doing?" she demanded, and he found himself putting his hands up, like a cow rustler in an old western.

"I have told you," Barbara Barelli said. "I have told you, and I have told them. I will not put up with this kind of shit. And I mean it. If you think you can intimidate me just because—"

"Dottoressa, please."

Pallioti began to reach into the inside pocket of his overcoat, then paused, wondering if he should tell her what he was doing in case she shot him. Then he realized she didn't have anywhere to hide a gun and proceeded gingerly. He held out his credentials, hoping his hand wasn't shaking. Barbara Barelli took them. Her hands, he noticed, were long fingered and fine, tipped with perfectly manicured pink nails. She frowned, lines almost as deep as his own cutting under her dark, swept-back hair.

"Florence?" She looked at him as if she thought he might disagree. "What are you doing here? Who are you?" she said. "I don't understand."

Pallioti refrained from pointing out that that might be because she hadn't asked.

"Alessandro Pallioti." He extended his hand, and was a little surprised when she took it.

Her grip was as firm as his own.

"So I see." She dropped his hand and returned his credentials. Then she cocked her head and asked, "So what can I do for you, dottore?"

"I have to ask, you are Avvocatessa Barbara Barelli?"

She smiled, either at the idiocy of the question or because he obviously felt so stupid asking it, and for a split second Pallioti saw a very different woman. Then the avenging goddess was back. She folded her arms and nodded.

"I am," she replied. "Should I say it out loud? The whole title? Are we being taped?"

Pallioti smiled and put his credentials away. He liked Barbara Barelli.

"No." He shook his head, then looked toward the house. "I just didn't want to make more of an ass of myself than I already have."

"I'll forgive you," she said. "I still don't understand what you want."

"I want to talk to you about Antonio Tomaselli."

Looking back on it later, Pallioti thought he might as well have said, "I want you to have wild sex with me in the back of the car." Or "I want your help kidnapping eight-year-olds and starting a prostitution ring." Either would have evoked the same distaste. And swift but clear judgment that he was out of his mind.

Avvocatessa Barelli's face closed as if a steel shutter had been pulled over it. Her black eyes turned as hard and cold as ice on stones. Without another word, she turned on her heel and began to walk back to the house.

"Dottoressa!" Pallioti called. "He's missing. He has a seventeen-year-old girl with him. We believe he's abducted her."

She stopped dead, standing in the middle of the road. The heavy silk of her shirt rippled across her back, caught in the breeze that huffed off the mountains he had just driven through. It occurred to him that she must be cold.

"She's seventeen," he said again. "Well, actually eighteen, just. Her birthday was on Friday. She's a student. An American. Her name is Kristin Carson."

Barbara Barelli shivered. She turned around.

"What did you say?"

"The girl is a student. In Florence. An American. Her name is Kristin Carson."

Pallioti stepped forward. He pulled a copy of the photograph of Kristin from his coat pocket and held it out. "She's from a town called Concord," he said. "In Massachusetts. She's taking a year on a program with an American school. To study art history. Then she wants to go to college."

Barbara Barelli reached out and took the photo. She studied it, frowning.

"We think he contacted her first on Facebook."

The frown deepened.

"When?" she asked finally.

"As far as we know, for the first time, about nine months ago."

She glanced up. "Just after he was released."

"Yes." Pallioti nodded. "As far as we know. It might have begun even earlier. He suggested that she come to Florence, for the year abroad. He even did the research. Sent her the information. Said it was a way for them to be together."

"You're saying he stalked her on the Internet, groomed her, lured her here—and now he's abducted her?"

Pallioti nodded.

"She was last seen ten days ago, getting into his car."

At that Barbara Barelli closed her eyes. Then she opened them and asked, "Her parents?"

"They're here. They came over from the States, for her eighteenth birthday. Last week. They were throwing a party for her. Fancy. A lot of her friends. That's what makes us think she may be being held against her will. Otherwise we might be inclined to think she was just off on a lost weekend. She was seeing Tomaselli. Going out with him. Apparently she was smitten."

Barbara smiled. There was no warmth in it at all.

"Oh yes," she said. "She would be. He can be very charming."

"Apparently. But Kristin was looking forward to her party. She was, by all accounts, excited about it. Had bought a dress. Been fussy about the food. The cake. She'd invited Tomaselli as her date. As I said, we know she went off with him on Wednesday the twenty-seventh. She hasn't come back. Do you have any idea at all where he might be? Or how we could contact him?"

She shook her head. "No," she said. "No, I don't—" Barbara Barelli looked down at the photo in her hand again. "And you say no one's heard from her? Not at all?"

"As far as we know, no."

She caught the qualification and raised an eyebrow. Pallioti did not elaborate. He thought it best to leave Anna Carson, and who she might or might not have spoken to, out of it for now.

"Messages have been left on her phone," he said. "By us, her friends. Her parents. As far as we know, none of them have been answered."

Barbara Barelli swallowed. She handed him the photograph.

"It's cold out here," she said. "Perhaps you'd like to come in."

The house was large and new and very fancy. Not unlike the matching Mercedes that sat outside, the automotive equivalent of stone lions flanking front doors, or griffons perched on gateposts. Barbara Barelli may have devoted her working life to championing admirable causes, but she'd clearly been well paid for it.

"This is Hedwige, my partner."

The tiled entryway opened onto what Pallioti believed was known in America as a family room, a large airy space containing a number of sofas and armchairs and a glass-topped dining table and vast flat screen television, which in turn opened onto a kitchen area—a sort of corral of polished granite interspersed with vicious-looking stainless steel machines. The woman who was doing something with one of them looked up at Pallioti and smiled. She was as fair as Barbara was dark, and as tall, and, obviously, even under a sweatshirt and running pants, as well toned and muscled. The two of them reminded Pallioti of a pair of very fit horses. But where Barbara's dark eyes were still and flinty, this woman's were as round and dewy as a doe's. When he shook her hand he half expected her to nicker.

"I'm making a smoothie," she said. "Do you want one?"

Pallioti had no idea if she was talking to him or to Barbara Barelli. He had no idea what a smoothie was, either. In certain circumstance it might have sounded obscene. He was not reassured by the stainless steel machine or by the pile of vegetation that lay beside it.

Barbara Barelli rescued him.

"I think we need something stronger."

She opened a refrigerator that was as large as most people's wardrobes. Pallioti watched as she lifted out a bottle of white wine. He shook his head as she reached for a couple of glasses, then wished he hadn't. Eating or drinking anything offered— even smoothies—pretty much guaranteed that you'd get thrown out later rather than sooner. No matter how much they wanted you to go, most people wouldn't show you the door while you had a glass or a plate in your hand. Hedwige had stopped what she was doing and was watching Barbara.

"Perhaps I'll change my mind," Pallioti murmured, but Barbara didn't seem to hear him.

"That son of a bitch," she said suddenly. "That fucking son of a bitch. I trusted him."

Her hand shook, slopping wine onto the counter. Hedwige took a towel from a rail by the stove and mopped it up.

"Have a seat." Barbara waved vaguely toward the sofas and chairs. Then she said, "Oh, sorry," and poured Pallioti's wine.

This time it went in the glass. He took it, sipped, and put it down and thanked her. She nodded, but she wasn't paying attention to him. Her eyes narrowed as she stared toward the television, which was turned off. Finally she looked at Pallioti again.

"The parents," she said. "The girl's parents?" As if she had forgotten what he told her in the street. Perhaps, she had. The news that a client she had worked to get released might have abducted a teenager was likely to be as startling as it was unwelcome. Pallioti had the feeling that Dottoressa Barelli did not like being surprised and did not take well to being wrong. And given her attachment to women's causes, this would be something of a double, if not triple, blow.

"I never liked him," she said suddenly. "Not from day one. The first time I saw him. Son of a bitch."

Pallioti waited. When she said nothing more, he frowned.

"Then, dottoressa, if I may ask—"

"Oh, ask away." She put her glass down and he noticed it was almost empty. "I did it because I believe that even if you don't agree with what someone's done—even if you think they're despicable—it's my job. I did it for the system, because otherwise it cannot function and we're all screwed." She threw back her head and laughed. "There. That's the high-minded explanation. The good law school answer. The truth?" She reached for her glass and looked at Pallioti. "I did it," she said, "for a friend. Love." She shrugged. "It's why we make all the biggest mistakes in our lives, isn't it? I even tried to like him. I did. I tried to like him because—" She waved her hand again and let the words go. "The parents," Barbara Barelli asked, looking at him. "I'm sorry. You were saying?"

Actually Pallioti had not been saying. He slid his own glass, almost untouched, a little farther away.

"They're in Florence. They're very worried. Naturally. I have to ask you, dottoressa, and I understand it puts you in an awkward position—" Barbara Barelli made a huffing sound, as if there was nothing he could tell her about awkward positions. "Once more, given the circumstances, you'll understand why I have to ask—if you've heard from Antonio Tomaselli? Or have any idea, any idea at all, where he might be?"

At that, Barbara smiled.

"And once more, I have to tell you—privilege, dottore. I may have just said I don't care for him, and I don't. But I am Antonio's lawyer."

Pallioti nodded. He had not really expected more, but he realized he had hoped for it. He was aware of Hedwige, silently watching both of them.

"For the record," Barbara added, "and in the spirit of goodwill, given the circumstances—I will say that the last time I saw him was, I don't know? Three months ago." She waved a hand. An obviously expensive watch caught the light and glittered. Pallioti wondered if there was a matching one on Hedwige's wrist.

"Do you have any idea where he is?" Barbara Barelli asked.

Pallioti shook his head.

"We've checked known addresses," he said. "Known associates. Of course."

"Which led you to me?"

"More or less." He thought of the pictures.

"But nothing?"

She didn't sound surprised. But then again, Pallioti thought, why would she be? Why should any of them be? Tomaselli'd been Brigate Rosse. And that's what they did. Went underground. Disappeared. Melted away like smoke. A few gunshots and, *Poof!* Now you see them. Now you don't.

"I was hoping I might ask you—" Pallioti paused, then pressed on. "Is there any family property, for instance? Anything, any place, from his childhood perhaps, that he might have mentioned?"

She shook her head.

"No. Not that I know of. Of course, he was in prison almost thirty years. So—" She shrugged as if this explained anything.

"Think, dottoressa." Pallioti watched her closely. In his experience prison gave people more time to remember than to forget. "It could be very important. If he has this girl—"

Barbara looked at him sharply.

"And you really believe he does? Honestly? You aren't just fastening on him because he used to be BR?"

Pallioti looked at her for a moment.

"We can't prove it," he said finally. "But, yes, I believe that she is with Antonio Tomaselli and whether or not it began that way, or he intended it from the start, I believe that he is now holding her against her will."

"Why? Why would he do that? Has there been a ransom demand?"

Pallioti shook his head.

"No. As I said—"

"Then why?" Barbara cut him off. "Why would Antonio abduct or kidnap, or whatever you want to call it, a seventeen-year-old American? I can't see what's in it for him."

It was the lawyer's question—and Pallioti had no intention of answering it. Not that he had the answer, but he thought he saw a glimmer of it. Revenge? Love—as Barbara had just said herself—the most warped and powerful motivator of all? To punish the woman who'd betrayed him? Or to reel her back in? Or both? Hook her, using her stepdaughter like a bright lure dangled in front of a wary fish? He looked at Barbara Barelli. And reminded himself that whether he liked her or not, there was no question of trusting her. Or showing his hand. She was playing for the other side.

"Kristin was last seen by anyone," he said carefully, "getting into Antonio Tomaselli's car. Since then she's vanished. No, I know it's not proof. And you're right, there's been no ransom demand. Nothing like that. In point of fact there's been nothing at all. But, yes, we do believe he has her. As I said, I do."

Barbara crossed her arms and nodded.

"So I ask again," she said. "Why?"

"Why do fucked-up creeps take girls?"

It was Hedwige who spoke. Pallioti had almost forgotten she was in the room. She pushed herself off the counter where she'd been leaning.

"It's what sickos do," she said, her tone of voice suggesting strongly that she'd evidenced this opinion of Antonio Tomaselli before. More than once. "He fucking killed Aldo Moro, or—" Hedwige looked at Barbara and shrugged. "OK. OK. Or he stood there while somebody else did it. Who knows? And frankly, who cares? What's the fucking difference? You're part of it, you own it."

Barbara sighed. "Hedwige—"

"No." Hedwige glared at her. "No. I mean, what the fuck do you expect from a guy like that? That he's going to change? Jesus Christ, Bar. In your dreams. The Red Brigades ran around shooting people in the legs. And that's when they were being nice. They weren't fucking heroes. They weren't anything but self-righteous little killers. And don't give me why," she snapped. "You know why isn't worth shit when you start shooting people."

Hedwige's chest was actually heaving. The argument had clearly raged between them before, and more than once. But as interesting as it might be to hear its ins and outs for the umpteen-hundredth time—like most people of a certain age in Italy, Pallioti had had this discussion himself—he didn't feel inclined just now. Hedwige's words chilled him, and amplified the tiny voice inside him that he had half thought he had managed to stifle, but had driven him here in any case. She was right. And they all knew it. Antonio Tomaselli—like everyone else who had been involved, everyone else who had done nothing to stop it— was nothing but a cold-blooded killer.

Pallioti glanced at his watch, and thought again of Kristin Carson. And of her increasingly distraught father, who held his phone like a man with his finger on the trigger. That genie could not be kept in the bottle forever. Sooner or later Dr. Carson would stop listening to them and start making calls. To friends in Washington. To television stations. To newspapers and bloggers and God knows whom.

And if they could do nothing, couldn't find hide nor hair of his missing child, why should they blame him? Wouldn't Pallioti himself do the same? Wouldn't any parent? Yes. Even if all hell broke loose. Which it would. Armed searches and SWAT teams, and roadblocks and bullets. Lots of bullets.

Given his conversation of last night, even the faintest prospect of an armed publicity-hyped hostage rescue was enough to make Pallioti cold to the bone. Killed by the abductors, or killed by the rescuers—how much difference did it make? Dead was dead. He had visited that field in Sicily, had picked up a clod of that earth and kept it for some months in his overcoat pocket, until it had melted away to dust. He took a card from his wallet and laid it on the counter.

"If you think of anything—" He found he was looking from Hedwige to Barbara, and then back to Hedwige again. "Anything," he said again, "at all that might help us. Please call me. It's confidential," he added. "No one ever needs to know."

Barbara Barelli followed him into the entryway.

"It wasn't all garbage, you know. What I said earlier, about why I do this."

Pallioti smiled as he buttoned his coat. "I know."

"We both have our jobs." She held out her hand. "I'm sorry I couldn't be of more help to you. But I take mine as seriously as you take yours. I also don't lie," she added. "I haven't seen Antonio in the last three months."

Her grip was as firm as her gaze, and again Pallioti realized he liked her. You could do worse, he thought, much worse, than have this woman stand up in court for you.

"You should know," he said, groping for the words. "You should know that Antonio Tomaselli has—" He tried again, then failed, and shrugged. It sounded so ridiculously melodramatic.

"Enemies?" Barbara finished the sentence for him, still holding his hand. Again the not very nice smile played over her face. "People who'd like him dead?" she said. "Who find the fact that he's out of prison an affront, and would use any excuse to correct the little problem of his being alive?" She cocked her head, her dark eyes reading his face. "You don't want to believe that, do you?" she said. "You couldn't survive if you really thought that the state—that your beloved *polizìa* even—might go around eliminating those they find inconvenient. Or just plain don't like. That they might do a little correcting when they think the courts have gotten it wrong? No," she said. "I've heard of you. I've read about you. You couldn't do it. Because if you did, you wouldn't be one of the angels, and that's what keeps men like you going. You have to believe in the difference, between you and them." She shrugged. "Or else you're just two sides of the same coin. Both judges. Both executioners."

Pallioti looked at her for a moment. Barbara dropped his hand.

"Well," she said. "To answer your question. Yes, I have told Antonio. Believe me, I have told him."

"And did he believe you?"

Barbara crossed her arms, hugging the red silk blouse.

"To be honest?" she said. "I have no idea. I wasn't lying about that, either. Yes, I've represented him a long time. But I don't know Antonio all that well. I doubt anyone does. Perhaps even Antonio. On the other hand, he's not stupid. And I doubt anyone in jail ever forgot about Ulrike Meinhof."

In May 1976 Ulrike Meinhof, the cofounder of Germany's Red Army Faction, otherwise known as the Baader-Meinhof Gang, had been found hanging in her maximum security cell. Her death had raised a certain number of uncomfortable questions, such as how someone whose possessions were monitored and who was kept under twenty-four-hour observation managed to rig a noose and hang herself.

"That was Germany," Pallioti said, and stepped out onto the gravel.

"Of course," Barbara Barelli said. "You're right. That was Germany."

She followed him, standing on the top step. The weak sun caught her blouse, and the band of her expensive watch.

"I saw it, you know."

Pallioti turned. He was aware of the cold, and of the fact that it was late in the day.

"Saw what, dottoressa?"

Barbara Barelli blinked, her arms folded her tight across her chest.

"Mara Cagol's autopsy report."

He frowned.

"Not the one that was released to the press," she said. "There are always two. But surely you know that? I saw the real one."

Barbara Barelli looked at him for a moment.

"Mara was shot in the back," she said. Then she swung the door closed, and left him standing alone in the drive.

◦

Blood dribbled down the door panel. It welled in a ridge of the molding, then spilled and trickled, leaving a thin red trail on the cracked gray paint.

"Let me out!"

Kristin's voice was hoarse. She pounded on the door, ignoring the cut on the pad of her palm, the soft fleshy place where the nail hammered halfway up had caught and ripped open a flap of skin. It might have hurt, if she'd thought about it.

"Let me out! Of. Here!"

She uncurled her hand and sucked. When had she last had a tetanus shot? If she got gangrene or lockjaw, if she started to foam at the mouth, would he take her to a hospital? Or just dump her by the side of the road with a tag around her neck? Or let her die here?

The skin, thin and papery, caught her tongue. Her blood tasted like pennies. She'd swallowed one once when she was a kid. As a dare. And lain awake the whole night afterward, wondering if she'd die.

"You have no right, you miserable fucker. You have no right to keep me here."

It came out as a mutter, almost an afterthought. And it was wrong anyway. *Might makes right.*

The words echoed in her head, rattling in a child's high, snotty voice.

She was hearing that a lot since he'd locked her in here— a kid, screaming—as if she'd come back to haunt herself. Kristin licked her lips—pennies again—and slid down onto the floor, watching the blood on the cracked gray paint, staring at it as if it might form itself into letters and feeling a tremor of satisfaction that at least she'd damaged the décor. Such as it was.

The room was mostly bare. Tiled floor. Mattress in the corner. Two blankets. A plastic garden chair. Bars on the window. A plastic bucket and roll of toilet paper—for emergencies. There was a toilet down the hall. A rust-stained sink where she brushed her teeth. Cold water only. He stood over her, but looked away when she pulled her pants down, trying not to sit on the cracked toilet seat. Kristin almost laughed. So much for the love nest of her dreams. So much for the hundred-dollar scraps of lace she'd bought, and all her fantasies of who might bite what off whom.

At first she'd assumed this had to be some kind of game. Maybe some kind of S and M thing he was into—wild sex in bare rooms. A little *Last Tango in Paris* that would surely be followed by champagne and caviar. She looked down at her dirty black pants. The new boots, all scuffed up. The cashmere sweater that probably smelled under the armpits. At least he'd let her change her underwear, twice so far. And looked away while she'd done it. Virtually covered his eyes. A gentleman to the core, since the moment they arrived—stepped out of the car after a five-hour drive to God knows where on roads that seemed to grow darker and darker. He hadn't shown one whit, not the tiniest bit of interest in the curve of her belly. Or the pale creaseless skin. Or the pink blush that rose around her nipples hardened with cold.

At first that had hurt most—that he no longer wanted her. Would barely even speak to her. That instead of love, instead of destiny, something else flickered in his eyes. Something beyond distaste. Something close to revulsion. At first, that had made her cry. Then it made her angry. Finally, on the second or maybe the third day, when she heard him coming, heard his footsteps tapping on the stairs like Morse code, the echo ricocheting through the empty house, she'd taken her clothes off and lain down on the mattress. She'd arranged herself, hair fanned across the blankets, like a gift. Determined to make him want her, to understand whatever game he was playing. To make him see her again. Look at her the way he used to look at her. She wanted him to lick his lips. Take her hand. Call her *Carina*.

"I want you," she'd said, making her voice warm, imagining she was purring as he opened the door. "Please, baby." Despite her best efforts a tremble had come into the words, a pleading. "Please," she'd said. "Please."

She'd reached a hand toward him—a hand he'd kissed, how many times? And for a moment he'd smiled and she'd felt something—a warmth, a flare of hope?

Then he'd said, "You shouldn't catch cold. Get dressed."

And she'd realized the smile was because he was laughing, at her, which was when she'd screamed.

"My dad!" Kristin had jumped up. "My dad will come for you! You can't get away with this!"

She'd slapped him, just once, before he caught her hand, and dragged her down the stairs, and locked her in the basement.

There were no windows. No Ping-Pong table. Or green shag rug like the one in her parents' house, the one Karen said she'd chosen because it looked like grass. Karen had painted flowers on the wall, too. Big sunflowers, with yellow and brown petals that matched the plaid on the sofa. There were twenty-three of them. Kristin knew because she'd counted.

After she'd heard her mother's car start, she'd counted the flowers, sure Karen would remember and come back for her before she got to the end of the row. She'd eaten a cookie from the pack Karen had given her for every flower. When she got to the end, she'd started counting again. She hadn't started to cry until the cookies ran out. She hadn't climbed the steps and knocked on the door, Mr. Ted gripped in her free hand, until she'd counted the flowers six, seven, eight times.

"Mommy?" she'd whispered it at first, as if Karen might be right on the other side, her ear pressed to the keyhole, waiting to hear.

In his basement, his Seventh Circle of Hell—when had she thought that was a joke?—the floor was packed earth. The walls were made of stone and wept with damp, and there was no light. With nothing but a blanket wrapped around her, Kristin hadn't tried to count anything. Even if there had been anything to count, she wouldn't have been able to, because of the thing that crept up and wrapped itself around her. Clung to her skin. Sealed itself over her ears and nose and mouth. When she choked on it, her eyes streaming, the taste of cookies rose on the back of her tongue and made her gag. Then, before she knew it, she'd screamed. She'd bent double and bellowed the single word. "Mommy!"

Which was when she knew he'd won.

After that she'd reached for her waist. There was nothing to use, only her nails. But she could feel them. The scar tissue ridged, like lips. Sealed, not a word coming out. The belt that held her in. *Mom, Me, Mom, Me.* Kristin walked her fingers across her belly, bumping in time. *Mom, Me.* And didn't need to count.

She knew how many cuts there were. Twenty-three. One for every flower.

A day later when he let her out, she'd clutched the blanket around her, covered herself up, and hadn't looked at him.

That had been three, maybe four or even five days ago. She'd tried to keep track. There was a pile of dead leaves in the empty fireplace. Every morning, she took one and put it under the mattress.

She'd thought at first that the rustling they made had been mice. She'd even climbed up on the chair. Then, gradually, she'd realized it was just a draft. Now the noise seemed almost friendly, a comfortable little muttering. She wondered if she was going crazy. If making friends with inanimate objects was what happened. Would she start talking to the mattress next? The bucket?

She'd assumed the leaves had blown down the chimney and the thought had given her a little hiccup of hope. But when she'd crawled to the back of the hearth and looked up, she hadn't been able to see light. She realized they must have blown in through the window the last time it was opened. Whenever that was. The locks were welded closed. Sticking her hand through the bars, she could reach them, could finger the cold, hard metal. But she couldn't make them budge. Or break the glass. She'd thought of that first. Had picked up the chair and tried ramming a leg through. But the bars were too close together. And now she wasn't sure what good it would do her anyway, even if she could smash the window. It wasn't like she'd be able to squeeze through the bars and climb out. And even if by some miracle she did, there was no overhang, no porch roof, not even a drainpipe to climb out onto.

The house was a cube. A cube plonked down in the middle of nowhere. Which was why he didn't bother to close the shutters. There was no point. There was nothing beyond. Just a sea of dead grass. Frozen gray, swaying on the wind. Its furred top mottled to gold in the rare moments when the sun split the clouds.

"Ispettóre Saenz?"

Enzo jumped. He'd finally left Bologna an hour earlier— they'd found the hotel, and a box of hair dye and a bunch of ruined towels in a laundry chute, and most important, lifted a fingerprint off the vending machine. Then he'd driven like a bat out of hell to Ferrara, half high on the idea that he might even find Anna Carson tonight and get home in time to sleep in his own bed.

"I am Carla Rossetti," the woman said.

Her outstretched hand and gray tailored suit made him suddenly aware that not only had he not shaved, but after two frantic drives and a long day in the Bologna police station, he looked, and possibly smelled, like a tramp. His habitual uniform of jeans, running shoes, and leather jacket felt as if he'd slept in them. His shirt was rumpled. He had no luggage. The fact that he outranked Ispettóre Rossetti by some considerable distance did nothing to mitigate the fact that if she had not been standing beside him, the receptionist at the unexpectedly chic Ferrara hotel where Guillermo had booked him a room just in case would undoubtedly have taken one look at him and thrown him out. As it was the young man behind the desk contented himself with raising an eyebrow.

Guillermo, who had spoken with the Ferrara police, had given Enzo the name of his contact. Too late, Enzo realized, he had assumed—for no particularly good reason, and probably quite a few bad ones—that Ispettóre Rossetti was a man, not the mahogany-haired Amazon he was facing.

"Shall we?" She gestured toward the tables and chairs scattered around the lobby. "I have what you asked for. Or would you rather" —she hesitated and smiled—"unpack? I'm happy to wait," she added.

For a bald-faced liar, she wasn't bad. Enzo wondered what it was—kid, lover, husband? All of the above? A cold splash of loneliness hit him, so real he almost shook himself like a dog. He had nothing to unpack, and never a reason not to wait. And still held out the hope that he would not need the room at all and would be heading back over the Apennines in a matter of hours dragging Anna Carson like some bounty hunter's prize so he could go sleep alone with his cat. It must have shown on his face, because Carla Rossetti looked sympathetic.

"I'm afraid the news isn't very good," she said. "Perhaps we ought to order a coffee." She was nice enough not to say that he looked like he needed one, just waved to a waiter hovering by the bar and headed for a table.

A double espresso later, Enzo was forced to agree. The news was not very good. He didn't know what story Guillermo had cooked up when he'd called Ferrara and asked for their help, but it didn't really matter. The net result was the same. "Graziella Farelli" had not checked into a hotel, or a B and B, or a guest house, or rented a tourist apartment. Not last night, or the night before, or anytime in the last week.

"I ran it backward a few days, just to be certain," Ispettóre Rossetti explained.

Enzo took the printout she handed him, refrained from telling her that she'd wasted her time, and thanked her instead. He made a mental note to write a citation and make sure it got to the right person. More women needed to be promoted and she had been nothing if not thorough. She'd even checked the city's homeless shelter.

But not only had "Graziella Farelli" apparently not slept anywhere in the city, she hadn't booked any kind of transportation, train, bus, or boat—there was a tour company that ran down the river even in this frigid weather, bird watchers mostly, according to the ispettóre—in order to try to leave it.

Nor had she rented a car. Or bicycle. Ferrara apparently, had a higher density of bicycles per capita than any other town in Europe, except for someplace in Belgium. Carla Rosetti informed him of this with no small measure of pride. Enzo was tempted to ask if she'd checked Rollerblades and skateboards, too, but decided against it.

The second sheet of paper Ispettóre Rossetti pulled out of her briefcase did not make him any happier than the first. Only two handbags and one man's wallet had been reported missing or stolen in Ferrara during the last forty-eight hours. One belonged to a sixty-year-old day laborer who weighed two hundred pounds and was bald. One to a student with blue eyes and blond hair who stood five foot two, and the last to a seventy-five-year-old who was in a wheelchair in an old folks' home. When she asked if she ought to check any of these out in person, Enzo told her not to bother. Anna Carson was too smart to pull the same trick twice. No red backpacks or green quilted down jackets from somewhere called Barneys had turned up at checked luggage in the bus or train stations, either. And no cars had been stolen. The long and the short of it was, if Kristin's stepmother was in Ferrara, she was either sleeping rough or staying with someone.

Or she had led them a very pretty dance. Been even cleverer than he'd given her credit for—a mistake he vowed then and there not to repeat, even if he had to write Brigate Rosse one hundred times on the pad in the hotel room where he was now certain he'd be staying.

Realizing they would trace her to Bologna, he thought, and to the wallet and hotel, Anna Carson could have bought herself some time to do he didn't even want to think what by making certain she was seen getting on the Ferrara train—which was, after all, where they would expect her to go—and then either getting off before she got here, or immediately catching another train to God knows where. Or she'd arrived, trotted to the bus station, and paid cash on a local puddle jumper. Or she'd ducked off the station in Bologna, somehow avoiding the cameras, and never left at all. The possibilities were virtually endless.

Enzo knew Guillermo had not told Ferrara any more about the mystery woman they were searching for than he had told Bologna. The same stories would circulate here soon enough, maybe even better ones. Although, he thought, it would be hard to come up with something much better than the truth—that Brigate Rosse, now in their fifties, were back. And still winning. He groaned inwardly. Or perhaps he only thought it was inwardly, because Carla Rossetti was looking at him with something like concern on her face.

He thanked her, then he told her what he needed. She listened without taking notes and said she would go herself, immediately, to the train station. She would send someone else to the bus station. They would get the CCTV tapes for him and set up at the Questura. She showed him where it was on a little green-and-red tourist map and told him a room would be at his disposal for as long as he needed it beginning with all night tonight.

If he could not spot Anna Carson getting off a train or onto a bus in Ferrara, Enzo would have to go back to Bologna and pick up the trail where it had gone cold. The thought made him sick with frustration. He thanked Carla Rosetti again and waited until she left. Then he went to the front desk and asked the clerk where he could find a store that sold underwear and socks.

It was past seven p.m. when, showered, shaved, and re-dressed, he left the hotel. Coin, God bless it, had not only been open and willing and able to supply socks, underwear, and shirts, but had even stretched to a new pair of jeans, two very warm rolled-neck sweaters, and gloves, which Enzo usually disdained. Not tonight. There was a damp chill hanging in the air that threatened to turn his very breath to ice. Before it left his lungs. Ferrara was not only flat, it was freezing. A fact the locals obviously knew how to deal with. The animal rights people would have a fit—or a field day, depending on how you looked at it. Enzo had never seen so much fur in his life. Walking out into the piazza was like walking into a convention of bears. They stood chatting in groups, walked arm in arm, and rode by on rickety bicycles, mink whispering, tatty plastic shopping bags dangling from the handles. Even the men wore long fur coats. He imagined Moscow was something like this. But with vodka. And more snow.

Before venturing out, Enzo had taken time not only to call his grandmother and ask her to feed the cat, but also to feed himself, and to go back over his file on Angela Vari while he ate. After finishing with room service, he had taken a pen and marked up the tourist map Carla Rossetti had given him. Made little Xs on the old Spanish Synagogue, and on the corner of Via Mayr where her father had had his shop. He doubted, frankly, that she'd do anything that obvious—and since she was supposed to be dead he could hardly go knocking on doors and asking if anyone had seen her. But there was no harm in looking. He figured the detour would take him only a few minutes before being locked up all night watching CCTV tapes.

Enzo walked along the walls of the Castello and passed under the arch that led out to Corso Libertà. The Duomo shimmered under the gaze of its floodlights. People thronged in front of it, their shadows dancing on the piazza. The market stalls were still open and doing brisk business. The scene looked almost medieval. It was the silence, as much as anything else, Enzo realized, that gave the town it's slightly unreal air. As it was closed to traffic, the only noises that echoed off the buildings of the old city were human—laughter and snatches of conversation or arguments, punctuated by the whirr and rattle of bicycles and the sharp ding of their bells as they coasted over the cobbles.

There was no way to tell anymore where the Ghetto had begun. No plaque or statue marked the place where the giant gates had once swung shut, locking away half the inhabitants from dusk to dawn. Enzo stopped in front of the newer synagogue where Bassani had worshipped, and where, in *The Garden of the Finzi-Continis*—which he had been disappointed to read in the hotel brochure didn't actually exist—Micol had sat in blond splendor looking down on all the broken-hearted young men. There was a plaque by the door listing name after name, entire families who had been swept up during the German Occupation and shipped in cattle cars, east, toward sunrise and death. The street where Angela Vari had lived was opposite. Enzo turned down it and felt the past close around him.

The houses were not that tall, most of them three stories. Jammed together, they blocked out what light there was, reducing the sky to nothing but a darkened strip. He felt as if he was walking into a canyon. There weren't many streetlights. As a result, he missed the Spanish Synagogue, got to the end of the street before he realized his mistake, and doubled back. When he finally found it, he discovered that the door of the mangy brick building was padlocked, and the paint peeling. There was a plaque here, too. Something about the d'Este dukes, and then—*Distrutta nel 1944 per mano dei Nazifacisti.* Destroyed in 1944 at the hands of Nazifascists. He could barely make out the words. Someone passed on a bicycle, nothing more than a dark shape teetering down toward the corner. A pigeon rustled its feathers against the cold. A block away footsteps and laughter rose and died. Enzo turned and looked across the street.

The house where Angela Vari had grown up was no different from the others. If anything, it was a little smaller. Narrow, brick, and only two stories high. There was a lamp over the front door, which looked to be newly painted. Four windows looked out from each floor, shutters closed over all of them. Light snuck through the slats in the lower ones. The second story was dark. Enzo knew that during the war displaced families had sometimes moved into the ghettos and taken over whole houses and apartments. Furniture, clothing, pots, and pans. After the Jews had been rounded up and taken away, others had simply stepped into their lives. Sometimes, literally, into their shoes.

He wondered if that had happened here. If that was how Angela Vari's family had come to call this place home. Standing in the street, looking at the house, Enzo thought of the girl whose father had died, who had labored on here alone in what must have been her own kind of hell, a void of loneliness, and wondered where she was now. Had she survived all these years only to find the past repeating itself? Had she come back and found someone living her old life? Or had she found no one, and moved in herself, a ghost reclaiming its safe haven?

For a moment, the idea gripped him, and he became convinced that that was exactly what she had done. That somehow she had gotten inside, found a key, gone up the stairs, and was there now, in the dark behind those closed shutters. So close that if he called her name she'd hear him.

Enzo felt himself start to cross the street. Then he heard a phone. A young couple carrying grocery bags emerged out of the dark. He watched as in the light from the door lamp the woman dug her cell phone out of her pocket with her free hand, shifting a bulging bag to the other. The man laughed and fished in the other pocket of her jacket as she talked, pulling out a set of keys. They smiled at Enzo as they went up the steps to Angela Vari's house. She was still talking as the door closed behind them. A minute later the upstairs lights went on. Enzo Saenz turned and walked away.

The Questura was in the opposite direction. It was cold and felt like it might snow and he needed to watch what would probably be dozens of hours of CCTV tapes. But he didn't care. He

found what he was sure had to be Via Ragno, and then a damp
tunnel lit by a few neon bistro signs that was the supposedly famous Via delle Volte. A shorter tunnel took him to Via Mayr. A
line of cars moved slowly down it. He jerked to a halt as abruptly
as if he had come to the banks of a river and stood watching as
their lights caught the shuttered fronts of shops. Then he saw the
one on the corner that was boarded up, felt the familiar prickle,
and walked down the opposite pavement, resisting the urge to
hurry.

When he stopped and looked up, he saw that the sign above
the graffitied boards had been vandalized. Half of the letters were
missing. But there was no question about it. It had once read MA-
CELLERÌA. *Butcher*. Beside it, the narrow mouth of an alley opened
into darkness.

Enzo stood very still, watching the front of the deserted shop
for perhaps five minutes. Then he slipped across the street and
into the alley. Pausing to let his eyes adjust to the dark, he
saw a van pulled toward the back, taking up almost the entire
space. From the way it listed he could tell that it had at least
one flat tire, if not a missing wheel. Either way it hadn't moved
recently and wasn't going anywhere soon. He edged forward,
feeling down the wall, until he found it. The door was sodden,
half rotten, and unlocked.

Barbara Barelli leaned back in the driver's seat of the Mercedes
and indulged in the luxury of pure rage. She had parked on the
road and called Antonio, realizing almost as soon as she'd done
it that it was pointless. At least she'd had the wit not to leave
him a message, tick him off like some outraged schoolmarm. As
if that would do any good. Finally she'd decided to walk in. Sniff
the lay of the land. Light was falling out of the sky fast. By the
time she got halfway down the drive and saw the buildings they

looked black and white, as if not only life, but color, had leached out of them.

Standing there she'd remembered everything Antonio had told her. Every heartrending detail. About his grandparents. And his childhood. And how much the countryside meant to him. He'd been good, she had to hand him that. He'd sensed the dregs of sympathy and guilt, the legacy of her nice, liberal, middle-class upbringing. The vague, uneasy suspicion that people like her—and her parents, and the state, and possibly all of Italy—had not only been responsible for what the BR had done, but in some dark place had willed them to it. Had sent them out to rob and kidnap, kneecap and murder, by proxy. And then, of course, there was Angela. The stiffening corpse of love and obligation they'd stepped around so carefully for almost thirty years.

Barbara closed her eyes and heard herself laugh. She supposed, really, she had to hand it to him. Antonio had played her, well and truly. And she hadn't even seen it coming. Not until it was way too late. Until he had her right where he wanted her. Ironic that in the end she and Angie should have that in common.

There'd been no sign of life at the so-called farm, but that didn't mean anything. He'd hardly hang out a WELCOME sign. The car was probably behind the house, or in the barn, which sat to the left and was long and low and made of stone. Barbara remembered it from the property description. *Outbuilding—possible use for conversion as vacation cottage.* In some other universe, maybe. Vacationing here defied imagination. Just before she'd turned away, she'd thought she might have seen something, a movement in an upstairs window. But when she'd looked again, she'd realized it had been a mistake. Nothing but the last reflection of daylight playing on the glass. And yet, for all that, she was sure he was there. She could smell him, huddling in the dark. Waiting like a spider beside his baited web. Barbara was not given to histrionics, but as she'd walked back to the car she'd felt the hair stand up on the back of her neck.

After that she'd driven away, found a ratty little tourist bar on the road to Pomposa, and gone inside and sat at a table nursing a coffee and grappa—watching the sun set, such as it was, and wondering what the hell she should do. Her first instinct had been to wait until morning. The cops always did things at dawn, usually around four a.m., when the mind and body were least present, floating happily between life and the ether, and thus unlikely to respond well to loud bangs and lights and screaming and guns.

Barbara'd always considered that a bit cowardly, to be honest. Sort of cheating. All those big men with their combat gear eking out the last little advantage of surprise, doing everything they could to stack the odds. Not that she was necessarily averse to a little odds stacking. A win was a win, and she could certainly eke out twelve hours.

She'd about decided to do that, take a page out of their book and wait at least until first light before she confronted him, when she'd thought of the girl. Barely eighteen. Blond. Missing ten days. He'd known her name. He'd tracked her and stalked her on Facebook.

"Fucker," Barbara had said out loud, causing the bartender to jerk awake. Then she'd stood, paid the bill, gone out and gotten in the car and driven back.

Now she hovered at the head of the drive, engine purring, foot on the brake. The car's headlights spread into the dark, then wavered and gave up when they found nothing to hang onto. Night had dropped over this nowhere Antonio had chosen. Barbara flexed her fingers on the leather steering wheel. She thought of the card nestled in her pocket. Sitting in the bar, she'd taken it out, run her finger over its sharp edges and the discreet raised letters of its engraving. Alessandro Pallioti. The idea was deeply tempting—to call the number and shove all this into his elegant lap. Lean back like a fainting heroine and let him catch her. It was his job after all, and he was reputed to be good at it. She'd even liked him. But she couldn't do it. It wasn't her style. Besides, there was more to it than that. You reap what you sow. She took her foot off the brake.

The big Mercedes bounced in the deep ruts of the drive. If she got stuck or messed up the undercarriage, Hedwige would frigging kill her. She loved these cars like they were babies. Rounding the curve, Barbara saw a faint glow in the lower windows of the house—in what must be the kitchen and sitting room. She reached the yard and swung around so she was facing outward, then opened the door. Wind swept in, blowing salt, chasing a handful of dead leaves and corralling them between the single bent tree and a broken stone trough.

When she finally got out of the car, she heard the distant echo of a bell and realized it had to be coming from Pomposa. It would be an electric carillon now, or maybe even a recording, tolling the memory of the faithful. Barbara closed the car door and took a breath. A feeling she didn't want to name skittered up her back.

"Don't be a baby," she muttered.

She'd done things that were harder. Lots of them. In prisons. And courtrooms. And police stations. So what was the big deal? All she had to do was walk up and knock on the door.

⁂

Hearing Antonio's name fade to nothingness, Anna had nearly given up. It had crossed her mind that she had to be insane. That all of this—stealing Kristin's clothes and that poor woman's wallet, dyeing her hair, coming here—all of it, was crazy. She should have taken the police child's offer. Let him help her. Talked to him. Told him who she was. And what she knew.

Walking back up the hill and along the track, getting on the bicycle, and beginning the long ride back to the train station, she'd decided. She'd even stopped and turned on her phone. She'd turned it on twice a day, at seven a.m. and again at seven p.m., exactly as Antonio had told her, but there had been nothing from him—no text or email. Only a series of calls from Ken. Out here, there was not even a signal. But still her mind was made up. As soon as she was back on the train and could pick up a signal, she would call Ken. When she got back to Ferrara she would go straight to the Questura. This time she would tell everyone everything.

Then, standing on the little platform as the light bled from the sky, waiting for the thin gray line of the train to come slowly into sight, Anna had remembered Antonio's voice. Remembered exactly what he'd said as she stood there in the Excelsior, the perfectly ordinary sounds of people eating breakfast clattering around her. *This is between you and me, Carina. No one else. Just us. Do you understand? Do you believe me?* And she had thanked God that there had been no signal, no possibility of a call. No police station to walk into.

It was dark by the time the train pulled into Ferrara. Anna abandoned the bicycle at the station, left it in one of the racks outside the ticket office. Its owner, if he or she cared, would find it soon enough. Unchained bikes had been pilfered for rides to the train even in her day. She walked back to town on aching legs, cold rippling through her. The bells tolled eight as she reached Piazza Trieste.

Crowds were wandering through the night market, milling around the outside heaters and gathering under the porticos of the tiny shops that huddled below the southern wall of the Duomo. The smell of food made her almost desperate. Anna bought a sausage in a roll, and then another with cheese melting across it and bitter greens, chalky on her teeth. She ate them walking among stalls, watching the vendors who stood wrapped in sweaters and scarves and overcoats drinking from steaming paper cups, thumping their hands to stay warm and calling back and forth from their stands, which were as gaudy as the stands on any carnival midway. Lettuces and peppers were piled with livid orange carrots. There were pyramids of tomatoes and swollen bulbs of eggplant, their skins purple and glistening. For a moment she felt as if she had not seen color, or tasted food, for thirty years.

She bought a coffee and sat on the steps of the Palazzo Municipale, watching people drift back and forth under the arch, and thought of nothing. As exhaustion washed over her, she felt the same odd, familiar sense she had sometimes had as a child—that time had slipped away. That past and present were mingling like the water of muddy streams. Drifting, she let go. And felt herself spinning and turning. Any moment she might thud up against a bank, and climb out, and walk home to find her father waiting for her. See Nonna Franchi sweeping the steps. Signora Ravalli gossiping at the corner. Hear Barbara on the phone, shouting about schoolwork.

She started, spilling the dregs of the coffee. Cold bit into her. Getting up, Anna crumpled the cup and threw it away. Then, after using the bathroom in the bus station, holding the broken door of the stall, smelling the acrid stench of ammonia and piss that didn't seem to have changed at all since she was girl, she threaded her way through the shadows, crept down the alley, and slipped like a stray cat through the broken door of the storeroom.

She'd left the Maglite under a bucket. Anna felt for it in the dark, then flipped it on, realizing as she did that she was so tired she could barely stand up. It didn't matter if she was sleeping in a down bag with nothing but a hardware store two-bar heater for warmth, bed was all she wanted.

For a second, as she shone the flashlight at it, the far wall of the storeroom seemed to waver in front of her. The hatch was ajar. She thought she'd closed it this morning, but obviously she hadn't. Careless. Although she doubted anyone ever came in here to notice. Still, as she pushed it open, putting the light in her pocket before she hoisted herself up and slipped through, she told herself she ought to be more careful.

Her feet hit the floor of the butcher's shop with a soft thud. She was reaching back to pull the hatch shut when a hand closed over her mouth.

⁓

Anna Carson was stronger than she looked. She bucked, bit, kicked, and tried to elbow him in the stomach. Enzo gave her an A for effort, but he was better, faster, and twenty years younger. He had her facedown on the floor with her hands cuffed behind her back in considerably less than a minute. He'd have had no problem doing it in the dark, but the flashlight helped. Especially when he found the blade stuffed in her pocket. It was damn near nine inches, and sharp.

He set it on the counter along with the light and wondered why he didn't feel more triumphant. Or at least pleased with himself. He'd done it. Tracked her and run her to ground. Cornered her like an animal. But here in the weird shadowed light of a derelict butcher's shop it hardly seemed like a big victory—more the tawdry end to a shabby little story of revenge and betrayal that he didn't even understand. It was hard to look down on this woman and think of her as an enemy of the state. But maybe that had always been the advantage people like this had—the fact that they looked so ordinary. Just like one of us.

She didn't swear or call him names or threaten to sue him, which surprised him a little, especially since she was American. She didn't spit at him, either, which was virtually de rigueur.

Instead she just lay there like a dead fish. His own very small penlight had given him just the briefest glimpse of the den she'd made for herself—the sleeping bag, the camping lantern, the tins of food, the opener and single spoon and bottle of water. The tiny little heater. The bucket and pack of wipes. It might have been the enviable nest of any homeless person, or even a particularly destitute student. Or more likely, an illegal immigrant who'd struggled from God knows what hellhole in Africa or Asia, come halfway around the world to find a so-called job working for nothing and living like an animal in The Glory That Was Europe. Nothing but the little white bear had given her away. He'd found it tucked on a shelf under the counter in the cold room in what had obviously been an effort to at least conceal, if not hide it, and for some reason he hadn't been able to put it back. Instead he'd sat it on her sleeping bag, then gone into the main shop and switched out his light and stood so still beside the hatch that he might have been dead himself while he waited for her.

"Angela Vari, also known as Anna Carson, I'm arresting you for theft and trespass and conspiracy to kidnap. I will be transporting you back to Florence, in custody, where you will be questioned in the presence of personnel from the US Consulate."

The announcement was as much courtesy as anything else, and drew no response at all. In fact Anna Carson didn't make a sound until he took out his phone. Then she found her voice.

"What are you doing?"

The question was so bizarre that Enzo actually paused. What did she think he was doing? Phoning for Chinese food? He smiled. It wasn't particularly pleasant.

"I'm calling for backup. From the police. To get us out of here because I don't think you'll get through that hole with your hands cuffed and I want to get back to Florence before dawn."

"Don't."

She had twisted around and was staring up at him.

"What?"

"Don't," Anna Carson said. "Please. Please, whatever you do, don't call the police."

He had addressed her in English, but when she spoke it was in fluent Italian, and sounded so panicked that Enzo crouched down beside her. Her eyes were wide, enough of the whites showing that he was afraid they were about to roll back in her head. It was probably the influence of the place, but Enzo couldn't help thinking of an animal, just before it was about to be slaughtered. An uncomfortable feeling ran through him.

"Why don't you let me help you get up? You'll be more comfortable." He started to apologize in case he'd hurt her, then brought himself up short. She had after all been about to knife him. "Here." He took her arms and helped her to her feet, conscious of trying to be gentle. Or at least not rough.

"Don't," she said again, as soon as she was standing up. "Don't. Please. Please don't call the police."

"I am the police."

Enzo looked at her. Had she forgotten who he was? Had she lost it completely? Regressed in some weird way? Or did she think she was going to get tortured? Beaten up? After thirty years of college and living in the States and watching the news on TV every night, presumably reading a newspaper—was she still really convinced that those kind of things happened in European police stations? The expression on her face certainly seemed to suggest it. The woman was terrified.

"I won't let anything happen to you, Signora Carson," he said. "You're safe. I promise you."

"No." She shook her head, panic rising in her voice. "No. No. No!" she wailed. "You don't understand."

"What don't I understand?"

Enzo, who had taken his phone out again, lowered it.

"It isn't me. It's Kristin. He'll kill her."

Even in the weird low light he could see that her face was white. That high red patches had blossomed on her cheeks, making her look as if she had a fever.

"He'll kill her," Anna Carson said again. "Antonio will kill her. He will. He promised me."

Enzo tried to keep the urgency—the desire to grab her and shake her—out of his voice.

"You've spoken to him?"

She nodded.

"Since he took Kristin?"

She nodded again.

"When? How recently? How many times?"

"Once. I called her phone. That day, after I saw him in that picture the girl took. I left a message on Kristin's phone and he called me back. He told me that if I told anyone—that it was just between us—that I had to come for her, find him, and that if I told anyone anything, or went to the police, he'd kill her."

The words came out so fast she was panting. Enzo looked at the phone in his hand.

"You have to believe me," she said. "You have to. I know him. I promise you, I know him. He isn't lying. He's done it before."

Enzo had turned the phone off. It had been against his better judgment, but he'd done it. The ghost of Aldo Moro was alive and well. He'd been all of two, but he was as haunted by the failure to save Moro as every other policeman in Italy.

After that they'd stood for a good minute or two in the butcher's shop, he and Angela Vari, or Anna Carson, or whatever he was supposed to call the woman who now sat across from him on the opposite bed in his hotel room. Finally she'd said, "At least, please. Please, let me explain."

Enzo hadn't answered.

"You said once, you said in the hotel that day," she'd added.

"You saw. You knew that I'd recognized him—and you said if I talked to you, you'd help me."

He had said that. It was true. He just wasn't sure exactly what he was supposed to do about it now. Or actually he was. He knew perfectly well he was supposed to call, if not Carla Rossetti—who would have come and dismantled the plywood and brought cars and blue lights, and seen Anna Carson, and presumably wondered who she was and what the hell was really going on—then Pallioti. He was supposed to report in to Florence, lay this all in the lap of Lorenzo, who would pat him on the back and tell him what a good job he'd done, before—before, what?

"Please," she said. She'd been watching him, reading his mind. "Please just let me at least talk to you. Just let me do that. Then, if you don't believe me, you can do whatever you want." She shook her head. "It's not like I can stop you. But just hear me out first. Please. Do it for Kristin."

So he had.

He'd gathered up all the knives, the ones hanging above them, and the one she'd had in her pocket, and tossed them through the hatch. Then he'd refastened the handcuffs in front of her so she could climb through. When he'd told her that if she tried anything, anything at all, not only was the deal off, but he'd hogtie her and call every cop in Ferrara, she'd nodded. Then at the last moment she'd said, "Wait!" And gone back into the cold room and picked up the little white bear, holding it out in front of her, awkward in the cuffs. Enzo took it from her and tucked it in his jacket. Then he'd helped her climb back into the storeroom.

In the alley he'd taken off his jacket, draping it around her shoulders, holding her close as they started down Via Mayr, hopefully looking more like a courting couple than a guy with a woman in handcuffs. Force of habit dictated that he'd already checked out the side entrance to the hotel lobby, which was fortunate. Enzo brought her in that way, avoiding the desk, counting on the fact that the drinkers in the bar would be too absorbed in their own conversations to notice the man and woman huddled with cold and lust who scuttled toward the elevators and promptly disappeared.

Now they sat facing each other on the matching queen-size beds, Anna Carson with her hands cuffed in front of her and Enzo looking at his watch and thinking he'd give her exactly one hour. One hour he'd be able to explain, if he had to.

He glanced up. Even in the softly lit room, she looked ragged. The sleek blond woman he had met a week ago was gone. Grubby and exhausted, her cheeks were white and blotched an unhealthy red. Enzo stood up and undid the cuffs. A voice in his head reminded him that she was still Angela Vari, that he could still end up writing Brigate Rosse a hundred times on the pad. He gave it a nod. He was twenty years younger and a cop and he had no intention of letting her out of his sight. She rubbed her wrists and tried to smile.

"Thanks."

"Are you hungry?"

She shook her head, diffident, almost shy, like a child trying to behave. Enzo felt a pang of shame, then told himself not to be stupid. He was just doing his job. Or rather, he wasn't. And it wasn't too late to correct that. One call to Carla Rosetti would have Anna Carson safely in a holding cell, a second would have Pallioti on the way.

"Bathroom?"

She shook her head, then said, "Well, yes, actually. I'd kill to wash my hands and face, with soap. And if you had a towel."

He helped her take her jacket off. She moved stiffly, like someone who'd been beat up. Or had been sleeping on a metal shelf. Enzo gestured toward the bathroom, then followed, stood in the door and watched her. The crest of her back, her shoulders as she bent over the sink, were narrow, fragile even, under the heavy, cheap sweater she was wearing. He couldn't help noticing that the dyed hair, which was probably closer to her natural color, was actually more flattering than the fake blond. Even dirty, a few stray curls caught the back of her neck. When she looked up into the mirror after drying her face, he realized again that her eyes were green, not brown. They met his in the glass and he looked away, suddenly embarrassed that he was standing here.

"OK," she said and tried to smile again. "Thank you."

They went back into the room. Anna sat on the opposite bed again. She picked up the little white bear, then put him down, propping him against the pillow. Enzo retrieved a bottle of fizzy water from the minibar and poured them both a glass. She took hers, sipped it, and nodded.

"I don't know how to explain to you." She looked at him. "I don't know."

She ran a hand over her eyes. Enzo noticed the ringless fingers and remembered the boxes in the safe. He'd thought then that she'd abandoned them because she didn't want to be recognized. Now he realized it wasn't that at all. Stripping them off her fingers had been her way of reentering the past.

"You see," she said, "it all goes back."

Her voice was so tired it was wavering. Watching her, Enzo wondered what it must have been like, how exhausting it must have been to shove aside one self and grow accustomed to another—to put lives on as if they were layers of clothing, then be condemned to wear them forever.

"It's as if it never stopped." She looked up and gave a half-hearted smile, as if she'd been able to hear what he'd just been thinking. "Not really," she said. "I mean, I tried to fool myself sometimes that it was gone. But it wasn't. It never is. It just gets put aside for a while, and now it's happening all over again."

"What is?"

The beds were so close their knees were almost touching. Enzo shook his head. A minute ticked by then another. If she wouldn't, or couldn't, talk to him, there was no point. He was about to say that this was a bad idea, that he had changed his mind and was taking her back to Florence, now, when she said, "Rome."

"Rome?"

Anna Carson nodded.

"Rome. Rome is happening all over again."

Enzo reached out and took her hand. It was cold. He held it for a moment in both of his. Then he said, "Tell me."

Part IV

Rome, 1978

THE MAN SAT ON the narrow bed, elbows resting on his knees. He wore a white shirt with the sleeves rolled up and the collar open, and suit trousers of a navy blue so dark it might have been black. The matching vest and jacket were hung neatly over the back of the chair in the corner which, other than the bed and a desk made of two sawhorses and a piece of plywood, was the only piece of furniture in the room. The bulb of the overhead light buzzed like a trapped fly. There were no windows.

Angela stood, staring. She could feel Antonio behind her, standing just outside the open door with his back turned, like a sentinel. The plate was warm in her hands. Manicotti, a recipe of her father's. She had made it this morning and carried it here on the bus, changing three times, lugging the basket like Little Red Riding Hood.

"Ah. You've brought me lunch."

The man's face was long and creased. His features, the wide mouth and rounded nose, were soft and sagged slightly, as if he might be melting. Which was certainly possible. The room was tiny—no more than a big utility closet tucked between the kitchen and bathroom—and very hot.

"Thank you," he said, and smiled.

Angela started and stepped back, clutching the plate as if he'd growled. She'd been told he was angry, that she had to come because perhaps he would take food from her, since he wouldn't take it from anyone else. The description had made him sound like an enraged animal. So the smile threw her off.

She took a breath and put the plate down on the plywood desk beside a pad and a pen, then opened her mouth, started to say, "I hope you like it," before she remembered she wasn't supposed to talk to him. Or acknowledge him. Or even look at him any more than she had to. Mostly she wasn't supposed to tell him her name. All she was supposed to do was feed him and pretend he wasn't there.

She pulled the plastic knife and fork out of her pocket, laid them beside the plate, and backed out the door.

⁓

Later they would ask her, and ask her, and ask her, how she hadn't known. And she would tell them, and tell them, and tell them again, all the while knowing that most of them did not believe it, and finally wondering if somewhere, deep down in the well of herself, she did not believe it either.

Sometimes, when they accused her of lying, she was tempted to agree with them—to say that she had lied as surely as Antonio had lied when he told her that he was enrolled at the university in Rome. When he left their tiny apartment every morning at eight, and came back every evening at six, and talked about his classes and his friends and what he had done during the day. That it was no different at all, except that the lies she had told had been to herself.

Then she would almost agree. Would be tempted to say that of course she had known—from the start. From the moment Antonio walked into the pizzeria. From the moment he turned around. That all through that long hot summer, every time he held her in his arms, or kissed her, or moved inside of her, she had known.

She'd been tempted to say it not only because it was what so many of them—the police and the magistrates and prosecutors and even psychiatrists—already believed. And because it would make them happy, and would be easier, and also because it would be reassuring. Much more so than the truth. Which was so simple, and so terrifying. That she had had no idea at all. That she had slept, and lived, and eaten, and made love, under the shadow of that sickening tilted five-pointed star, and never even known it was there.

Because she loved him. Because when he told her something, she believed him. Because it is not normal to look into the face of the human being you expect to spend your life with and suspect that they are living another life. That every time they walk out the door, or around the corner, or are away from you, even for a minute, they become someone you do not know.

It was a myth, that love encompassed everything. In fact, she had finally understood, it encompassed very little. And only what you wanted it to. Only what protected it. Like everything struggling to survive, love was selfish, and narrow, and fanatical. That was why it made so many people kill for it.

So, no. When Antonio had finally suggested, after they had been in Rome for several months, after they had sat on the scratchy old sofa in the apartment in Trastevere and watched on television as the body of the German industrialist Hans Martin Schleyer had been removed from the trunk of the car where the Red Army Faction had deposited it after kidnapping and eventually shooting him, when about a week after that, he had suggested one evening that perhaps she should sell the apartment in Ferrara to the Ravallis after all, since surely they would never be going back there, she had not thought much of it. Certainly she had not suspected any connection between the two things. Any more than she had suspected, after the sale, that he had not put the money in the bank. Locked it, as he promised, into a savings account for their future. For the apartment they would one day buy. For the children they would one day have. Certainly she hadn't looked at him across their rickety little table, her bare foot resting on his as they drank coffee in the mornings, and thought it was being used to construct a box, a windowless cell, a cage to keep a man in, in a utility room on Via Montalcini. That that was what he spent his days doing. That while she was keeping the books at a trattoria down the street and at the dry cleaners around the corner, Antonio was not taking classes at all, but building a People's Prison.

To look into his eyes and think that would have been crazy. As crazy as, she was later told, looking into his eyes and not seeing it had been.

Love was just love, she had snapped at them then. It didn't come with a crystal ball. And it didn't promise not to lie.

He had finally told her on March 20, four days after the kidnapping. And even then he had not really told her. Or she had not really heard. It was hard, later, to remember which.

What she does remember is that it was a Monday, and that the trattoria was closed so she had been able to work in peace all afternoon and with the television in the stuffy little office turned off. Which was a blessed relief, because by then she is sick, sick to death, of hearing about the kidnapping of Aldo Moro. And even more than that, she is sick of the Red Brigades.

She cannot read, or hear, one of their stupid long-winded communiqués without being back in the hospital. Without feeling the hard molded plastic of the chair and the newspaper as it slips from her hands. Without hearing the labored wheezing breaths of her father's dying. She doesn't blame the BR for his death, exactly. But she can't separate them from it, either. The same way you cannot separate the taste of the food that is in your mouth from the moment when someone tells you they no longer love you, or the song that is playing on the radio when they raise their hand and hit you.

So she is happy to have the television off. And when she walks home, carrying the bunch of tulips she has bought and thinking that soon she will be able to wear sandals again, she looks away from the newspaper kiosk that is still displaying the picture from two days ago, the one Brigate Rosse released of their latest prisoner, the most recent "enemy of the people" to *sparito nel nullo*. Aldo Moro, the sweet-looking, sad-faced man, who smiles quizzically from under a five-pointed star.

Being one of the people herself, Angela finds it hard to feel much enmity for him. She doesn't see why she should, but mainly she doesn't care. What she cares about is that the owner of the trattoria is going to give her more hours after Easter, which will mean more money, which may mean they can begin to think about moving to a slightly bigger apartment. Antonio does not want to touch the proceeds of the sale of Via Vittoria—he says that should be a lockbox for their children, and she agrees. But it would be nice to rent something where the kitchen was not a closet and where the bathroom was separated from the bedroom by more than a curtain.

Not that she doesn't love where they live. She does. The building is on the side of a small piazza. There are mews where the carriage horses that work up in the tourist sites are stabled on the other side. She likes the smell of them, and the sound of their hooves on the cobbles when they leave in the early morning, and the soft shuffling they make as they settle themselves at night. It is warm enough now to leave the window open, so she can hear them and imagine that they reach Antonio in his dreams and take him back to his nonno's farm, and the dogs that slept by the well, and the warmth of his brother, Piero, huddled against his back on a winter night.

She keeps a mint in her pocket and gives it to one of the older horses that is looking out over the stable door before she goes into the building and runs up the stairs and is surprised to find Antonio, home early and sitting on the sofa, waiting for her.

When she bends to kiss him, he pulls her down, but she waves the tulips at him, and laughs and skips toward the little kitchen where the window faces west and is open, spilling sunlight into the scratched porcelain sink. She runs the water in a vase she bought out of a car trunk on the corner a few weeks earlier and feels his hand on her back.

"What are you cooking tonight?" he asks.

Angela shrugs. She takes a knife and begins to strip the leaves and cut the stems of the tulips.

"Can you make manicotti? The kind your father used to."

A pile of greenery is building up in the sink. She wonders if she can take it down and feed it to the horses and thinks she better not in case it's poisonous.

"I don't have what we need. I'd have to go to the shop and—"

"I bought it."

She turns around and looks at him. Antonio is never picky about food. If anything, he doesn't care. And although he makes the bed and even, occasionally, washes things, she has never known him to buy groceries. Not even an apple. If the milk goes sour it sits in the fridge until she notices. He is watching her carefully.

"Can you?" he asks, and Angela feels something inside of her. A tiny glitter of cold. As if she has swallowed an ice chip.

She picks up the vase of tulips, edges past him, and places it on the table.

"It's not for me," Antonio says. "It's for someone special. He has low blood pressure. He isn't eating."

For a second, they stand there looking at each other, with the table and the tulips, which are yellow, between them.

Then Angela says, "Someone special?"

She can feel herself frowning. Can this be a professor at the university? The parent of a friend? He brought two boys back once, said they had something to do with printing things. They sat at the table and drank beer and then went out to a bar. Does one of their fathers have low blood pressure? Even before Antonio shakes his head, she knows. Deep inside her, somewhere in that well, she knows. So maybe they were right—all those people who would later accuse her of lying. Maybe they were right all along.

After he tells her, she sits down, hard. The wobbly chair creaks.

"You?"

She can't finish the question, but he shakes his head anyway. He is leaning against the little kitchen counter now, the sun catching his hair.

"I didn't have anything to do with that," he says. "With Via Fani. I don't even know the people who did. Our job is just to run the prison. That's how we do it," he adds. "We don't tell. Only what people need to know. That way it's safer for everyone. I don't even know their real names and they don't know mine. That's why I didn't tell you. To keep you safe."

And to keep you safe, she will think later. But she doesn't think it now. Now she just stares at him. Her stomach is doing something strange. It's falling, in slow motion. Sinking like a sack of kittens through dark water. She reaches out and grabs the edge of the table, as if it will hold her up.

"How long?" she asks finally. She is trying to remember. Something happened in Padua, something bad. But when? Before he went to the university? After? And then she realizes. That isn't it. That doesn't matter. This isn't about that. This is about the hand of God that opened in the sky. The unions, and cost cutting, and maintenance. And Piero. This is about bread and roses.

Antonio nods.

"Someone has to do something," he says. "We can't just do nothing. The communists won't do it, they've sold out. The unions won't do it. The Christian Democrats are rotten. They're all rotten. No one stands up. No one fights."

Angela doesn't say anything. She closes her eyes and sees a field of flickering stars. She feels hot wax on her hand, and the warm stickiness on her fingers as she touches Piero's forehead, his eyelids, his lips.

"We're going to put him on trial," Antonio says. "We're going to make him answer for what's happened. We're finally going to make them listen."

Angela thinks of Mario Sossi, of his white collar and prosecutor's robes. She remembers his wife. The letters to the pope. The letters to the president. Aldo Moro was going to be president, all the papers agreed. She has not seen his wife. She doesn't know if Signora Moro, too, is pleading and crying. But she has seen the police. The newspapers, the TV. The radio says there are fifty thousand police, carabinieri, army. There are roadblocks all around Rome. They are stopping cars on the highways. They are opening trunks, pointing machine guns. It is the biggest manhunt in Italy's history. Maybe in Europe's history.

She opens her eyes and meets Antonio's. Black as wet stones.

"The police," she whispers.

He shrugs.

"If no one says anything, they won't find him." He pulls out the other chair and sits down. "If someone does say anything, they'll kill us. All of us. We know that. They'll shoot us the way they shot Mara."

Angela remembers this, how the night her father died, Barbara said something. Something about Professor Barelli insisting Mara Cagol had been shot in the back, like an animal, as she tried to crawl away after being wounded. *Mara, il tuo assassinio non restera impunito.* She looks at Antonio and shudders. She has just seen him covered in blood.

In the next moment, he has his arms around her.

"I'll be all right," he says. "We'll all be all right. This will make things better. They'll have to listen now. They'll have to change. You'll see. For the future. For our children's future." She pushes her face into his shoulder, into the warm, familiar soap smell of his shirt.

"I need your help, Angie." He strokes her hair. He rests his chin on the top of her head. "It will all be all right. Nothing is going to happen to me. No one is going to talk. But I need your help. We don't want to hurt him. We just want him to own up, admit what he's done, and make them change. But if he won't eat, if we can't get him to eat, we can't take care of him. Do you see? Will you help me?"

Angela nods. She keeps her eyes closed. But she nods.

The manicotti lasts two days, during which the trial of fifteen Brigate Rosse members begins in Turin. One of them is Renato Curcio, the husband of Mara Cagol. Now that she is gone, Angela thinks, he has no chance of disappearing. There is no one to arrive on visitor's day with a box full of guns. If he is even allowed visitors, which she doubts. No matter what Antonio says, the police are not stupid.

Angela considers this as she cooks a chicken. Her father's knives, along with some of his clothes, his cap and his slippers, his white coat with its frayed collar, and the old maroon blanket from the end of her parents' bed, and a few other things—one of his cigar boxes she hides in the back of a cupboard and stores lire in, and a music box that is broken but belonged to her mother—have come with them to Trastevere.

Angela sharpens the knives herself, but only when Antonio is not there because he can't stand the sound, the chalky scrape of the blade on the whetstone. He doesn't like the points, either. He turns his face away when she tests the tips, bouncing them on the pad of her thumb. He winces when she runs the blade against her finger to make sure the cut will come clean.

It's strange in him, she thinks, this squeamishness, this distaste for blood. Because it bothers her not at all. Angela brings the cleaver down with a cool smack, relieving the chicken of first one leg, then the next before she splits the breast wide open.

Antonio said no bones in the chicken. Angela doesn't know if this is a precaution against choking, or in case one might be secreted away. Sharpened in the dark after they turn out the light in the little room, then used as a weapon.

She finds it hard to imagine. How many people could you stab with a chicken bone? And surely they have guns? At least the rest of them—not Antonio, he hates the things. Not that she would know what the others have or don't have because so far she has been to the apartment on Via Montalcini only once and she didn't see anyone. Except Antonio, and him. But she knew the others were there. She heard them, in another room, scuffling like mice while she lifted the baking dish out of the basket.

Angela has always been a quick learner, so she understands this already. She would have even if Antonio hadn't told her. It isn't exactly, as the Americans say, rocket science. But it is crucial. The key, you might say. The most important of what she already thinks of as the BR's—she doesn't like to use their whole name, even to herself—litany. Of the prayers from their private little Book of Hours.

Each shall see and hear according only to his need.
You cannot betray,
Or be betrayed,
By what you do not know.

The words cackle like a witch in a rhyme as she throws the tiny dice of green pepper and chunks of tomato into the burning oil.

⁓

This time he stands and makes a little bow as she comes in.

He's been working at his desk. The pad is open. He flips it closed, but not before she sees the words running across the page. *My Darling, I think of you. Kiss the children for me.* There's a book, too. Something about Marx. He picks it up and places it on the bed.

"My homework," he says, smiling at her. And then, "Thank you for this. The last was delicious. Your mother taught you well."

"Father."

The word is out before she even realizes she's said it. Angela feels the horrid familiar flush creeping up her neck and into her cheeks. She glances over her shoulder. Antonio is outside the door again, but she can't see him because this time, without thinking, she pulled it halfway closed behind her.

"Your father?" His voice is a whisper. He's watching her as she puts the plate on the desk. "Your father taught you to cook?"

Angela nods. Without meaning to, her hand feels for the locket where there is now a tiny photo of him opposite her mother's. She drops it, then takes the plastic fork and spoon rolled in a paper napkin out of her pocket.

"I have daughters." The words are not much more than a breath. "I love them very much."

Angela feels her hand hesitate. She places the implements beside the plate.

"I hope you enjoy the food," she murmurs, then she turns and leaves.

Outside Antonio locks the door and drives the bolt home.

"What did he say to you?" he asks.

Angela shakes her head. She even manages to smile.

"That he liked my food."

She brushes past him and picks up the basket, mutters something about not wanting to miss the bus. She has come by herself and is leaving alone this time. Antonio kisses her and smiles at her and lets her out of the apartment. She rides down in the elevator and walks across the lobby. When she gets to the street, she can't stop shaking.

"Ciao, Carina," he says when he comes home a few hours later.

Angela smiles.

"Da quando non ci si vede," she replies.

Hey, Sweetheart, long time, no see. They sound like a bad American movie. The one they saw last month. Or maybe the month before that. Both of them love movies. They love sitting in the back, in the dark, watching the story loom over them. Antonio puts his arms around her, he pushes her toward the little kitchen. She's wearing a skirt. When he lifts her onto the counter, she wraps her legs around him.

"I need you to do something," he says. He runs his finger across her lips and down to the top button of her blouse. "I need you because I know I can trust you." He reaches for his belt buckle. Then he asks her to deliver the first letter.

The envelope is absolutely plain. There is nothing written on it at all. But it feels as if it's made of lead, as if it's going to fall through the bottom of her handbag.

You get off the bus. You walk three blocks. There's a phone booth, on the corner. Go into it, but not until ten o'clock. Don't be early, don't be late. Lift up the receiver, look like you're making a call. Then hang up and leave the envelope on the top of the telephone. Come out and walk away. Don't look back.

Antonio's voice throbs in her head. He's with her while she rides the bus and gets off and walks alone through the dark streets.

When she sees the phone booth, she feels a pang of relief. She's been here almost seven months now, but Rome is huge. She only knows her own little pockets of it, and although she followed his instructions exactly, she was afraid she might have made a mistake—got on the wrong bus, walked the wrong way without realizing it. Antonio has never been angry with her. Not once. He's never even raised his voice. All he's ever shown her is love. But there is a part of her, some tiny sliver, that knows what his anger would taste like. Earth on her tongue.

The door of the phone booth is cold to the touch. Inside it smells of mold and old leaves. Angela lifts the receiver and feels the damp, slightly sticky plastic, the memory of other people's words. She pretends to drop a token in and dial a number, her old one in Ferrara with two digits wrong, then waits and looks out the scratched Plexiglas window. There's no one walking on the street, which is wide and quiet. Lights shine from the houses and apartment buildings. There are trees, not as big as the ones by the Angels' Gate, and not with ruby leaves, but nice enough. This is an expensive neighborhood.

She finishes her make-believe call and puts the receiver back. Then she reaches into her bag and takes out the envelope and places it on top of the phone, making sure it is tucked in the little crack where the casing is bolted to the wall so it won't fall onto the dirty floor. She spends a few moments on this, because it feels important.

Then she leaves and closes the door carefully. She can see the envelope quite clearly, an oblong of white, and for a second she's gripped by panic. Antonio didn't say anything about that, about whether she should try to hide it. But in a phone booth, where? Her watch says three minutes past ten. Angela looks at the letter one last time, then turns away and starts up the pavement, her footsteps sounding too loud as she passes under a streetlight. Half a block later, she checks her watch again. Four minutes past. Then, for a reason she can't explain, she stops.

There's a cluster of trees just here, and a gate pillar, and the edge of a wall. Angela steps into their shadow, then turns and looks back. The phone booth hangs on the edge of the street lamp's halo. They will have put it there deliberately, she thinks, to make everyone feel safe. Her hands are cold. She shoves them into her pockets, and is suddenly aware of the hard pattering race of her heart. The wall is rough and snags her coat and hair. She has no idea why she is doing this. She knows she should go, should keep walking, do as she's told. She knows Antonio would be angry, even furious, if he knew. She feels his breath on the back of her neck. *Ti possiedo, per sempre. I own you, forever.* Still she can't help herself. She waits.

The woman comes from the opposite direction, her shape emerging out of the dark. Angela is too far away to see her face, but from the way she walks, from her build, she guesses they're about the same age. Angela can tell, too, that she's trying to walk slowly—trying to look normal, whatever normal is supposed to look like when your father has been made to disappear like smoke. She stops on the curb opposite the phone booth. Silhouetted in the streetlight, Angela sees the bulge of her stomach as she turns sideways and realizes she is pregnant. Unconsciously her hand goes to her own belly, which is flat and hard. There is no traffic. The girl looks both ways anyway before she crosses the street.

Her first steps are tentative. Then she can't keep herself from running. Like an animal that's broken loose, she dashes. Her dark coat and green scarf catch the light as she almost falls against the phone booth door, shoving it open with both hands. Even from this distance Angela can see her arm reaching out through the blur of the Plexiglas, snatching for her father's letter, for the words he has sent from nowhere.

It's very late when Angela finally gets home, almost midnight, and Antonio is waiting for her. He puts his arms around her. Runs his warm hands under her sweater and up her back.

"Did you deliver it?" he asks.

"Yes," she says. She lays her head against his chest. "Yes."

Later she lies in his arms and feels him holding her down, anchoring her into the world. On the way home on the bus, it had started to rain. In their cramped little bedroom, Angela closes her eyes and feels herself rocked on the muffled noise from the streets below. On the whoosh of tires and the stamp of the horses. And finally on the slow huff of Antonio's sleeping breath and her waking one as they mingle, and rise, and fall.

I have daughters.

I have daughters.

I have daughters.

Aldo Moro's interrogation has begun.

Its purpose is to clarify the imperialist and antiproletarian politics of the Christian Democratic Party and to ascertain the direct responsibility of Aldo Moro

The communiqué, which had been sent to newspapers in Genoa and Milan and Rome, flies like a banner across all the front pages. It ripples from kiosks and corner shops. And it isn't alone. There are other headlines, too. Dozens of them, not dictated by the BR.

Terrorists' Demands Rejected. Parties Agree, No Negotiations. Moro Letter Appeals to Government.

The words dog Angela as she walks from the dry cleaners to the florist's, where she has recently picked up a third job. And then from the florist's to the trattoria.

The letter to the government, which was addressed *Caro Francesco* and signed *Most Affectionate Greetings, Aldo Moro*, confused her at first. She knew it hadn't been the one she delivered because the papers said it had been in the same package as the communiqué, which had appeared in all three cities at 8 p.m. It shouldn't have come as a surprise, but for the first time it occurred to her that she wasn't the only one taking buses, walking in the dark, pulling envelopes out of her bag. She wondered how many there were, and felt strange thinking of herself as part of a secret army, a brigade that acted and worked in concert but never saw one another or even knew for sure that they existed. That the other soldiers were not more than mice in a neighboring room.

> *You cannot betray,*
> *Or be betrayed,*
> *By what you do not know.*

Then she reminded herself that she was not one of them. That all she did was cook meals. Walk to a phone booth. Deliver the words *kiss the children for me*. And then only because Antonio asked her to. Only because he beat inside her like a second heart.

Surrounded by large tin buckets, and piles of stripped leaves and the sweet fecund smell of two-day-old lilies, Angela opens the books and adds up numbers and sees that the florist is going, probably sooner rather than later, the same way as her father's shop. Without really meaning to, she finds herself trying to think up ways to stave off yet another mushroom cloud. Could they have specials on day-old carnations? Or overgrown pots of African violets? Could they offer two-for-one deals the way the supermarkets do, but on dying lilies instead?

She likes the florist's, but of her three jobs, the one at the trattoria is her favorite. Usually she is there alone except for the owner, a tall man with stooped shoulders who hums as he lays the tables and argues with the greengrocer about the menu. In the dark back office where she sits with the TV turned off, she can pretend the world really is about the availability of asparagus. Or the supply of the first small, pungent melons. Or about arguments over the price of green beans and the firmness of tomatoes.

Outside, on the streets, walking to and fro, or even at her other jobs, or at home when the television is on, it's not so easy. The bodyguards bother her most.

Oreste Leonardi. Domenico Ricci. Giulio Rivera. Raffaele Iozzino. Francesco Zizzi.

Their names appeared in the papers and on posters, in boxes lined in black. On the day of their funerals, both the dry cleaners and trattoria closed out of respect.

"They were just men doing their jobs. And for that, they're dead. They had wives. Children. Those bastards can keep their revolution."

The dry cleaner shook his head, pulling the shutter down over his shop.

At the florist's they sold more flowers than in the whole week before. Bouquets were tied to railings, and left by fountains and on the steps of churches even though they had not been frequented, or perhaps ever even visited, by any of the five men. And that was nothing, nothing at all, compared to the drifts of blossoms and ribbons and gifts that were left on Via Fani.

Angela sees it on television—a tide of flowers surging across the pavement, spilling down to the bus stop and climbing the iron railings opposite the intersection where Aldo Moro's car stopped and the shooting began.

His driver, the papers say, kept driving even after he was shot. Had been trying to maneuver, twisting the wheel and stamping on the pedals, when the fatal bullet hit him. The guard beside him had thrown himself over the seat and onto Moro. Had shoved him down, covering Aldo Moro with his own body as he died. The three men in the following car never had a chance. They were hit by a barrage of bullets, semiautomatic fire. Two had been killed instantly. The third died moments after arriving at the hospital.

A cross has been set up, a worn beret tied to it, medals pinned to the brim. Two students from Foggia stand hand in hand and tell the television reporter that they have come to Rome specially, to see the spot where the five policemen died. Where they were murdered for doing their duty. A woman calls them heroes. Another woman stands with her child, who is fingering the big bows on the bouquets, pulling petals off the occasional flower and shifting from foot to foot as his mother tells the reporter that she has brought him here "because we have to learn something."

<hr>

The next time Angela sees him, he doesn't look well. The collar of his shirt is grubby. A button is missing, and he hasn't shaved. Or been allowed to shave. She really doesn't know. There is a toilet in a sort of closet behind a screen at the back of the room—she'd noticed it and looked away, embarrassed—but no sink.

She stands just inside the door holding the plate. It's lamb, with peas and the first baby carrots, and she realizes that she wants him to say something, or at least smile at her. His smile is soft and although his eyes are dark and her father's were blue, there's something about them that is similar. There's a new pad on the desk, and several more books about Marx and Lenin.

"I have to read them," he says when he sees her looking at them.

He is sitting on the edge of the bed, his hands dangling between his knees as if he is too tired to do anything else with them.

"I have to read them to understand what I have done. For my trial." He looks up at her, and it seems as if his face has sagged even more. As if the lines have deepened so they might cut into his flesh, carve his features away. "Did they teach you Lenin in school?" he asks.

Angela shakes her head. They didn't, although she can remember Barbara's father talking about him over Sunday lunch. "That which advances the revolution is moral!" he had shouted from the head of the table, his words slurred. Barbara's mother had rolled her eyes. They had been eating beef and Angela can remember the spots of gravy that dotted the starched linen cloth as Professor Barelli waved his fork. "That which does not advance the revolution is immoral. Elegant!" Barbara's father had thumped the table, making the plates rattle. "The truth is always elegant!" he had announced, reaching for the bottle. The wine had spilled, dribbling down the side of his glass. Barbara had kicked Angela under the table.

Angela pushes the books aside, knocking one onto the floor. She puts the food down and bends to retrieve the dog-eared paperback. Her hand closes over it, but all she can see is the old beret, the faded ribbons of the medals, the too big bows and surging tide of flowers.

That evening, when she gets home, she tries hard to remember. She stands by the calendar that hangs on the kitchen wall and puts her finger on the box that is March 16. She presses so hard her nail leaves a tiny sickle moon. But it's no good. Time has both slowed down and speeded up and she can't sort out the days. Or maybe she can. She tells herself she remembers. That she's sure of it. That on that Thursday, she and Antonio had breakfast together. That they sat at the little table and she rested her bare foot on his while they watched the sun finger the thyme and rosemary she is growing in the window box.

The next letter isn't a letter, it's a box. Quite a big one. Wrapped in brown paper, it will barely fit in her bag.

Several days have gone by. She has made meals on almost every one, but Antonio has taken them himself, so she has not had to go to Via Montalcini, which, honestly, is a relief. If she does not have to go into the apartment, if she does not have to wait while Antonio unlocks the door and then step inside that little room, which, although it has a fan of some kind, is hot and smells sour and close—if she doesn't have to do that, she can almost forget why she's making extra food. Why Antonio has asked her to go out and buy a razor, and a toothbrush, and a comb.

This time she is to arrive at the phone booth at eleven p.m. And although she's only done it once before, the bus ride seems almost familiar. She gets off at the same stop with two other people, a couple. For a moment she's terrified that they will walk in the same direction, that they will live in the house opposite the booth and stand and watch her, or, worse, want to use the phone. But they don't. Holding each other's arms, they laugh and run across the street and by the time the bus doors hiss close and it rumbles away, she's alone.

The phone booth looks just the same. Even so Angela slows down. A block below it, she finds herself looking either way, peering into the gaps between the buildings and the shadows thrown by the trees. There are fifty thousand policemen and soldiers and carabinieri looking for Aldo Moro. She pulls her bag closer to her, as if a hand might reach out and snatch it. But nothing moves, and there's no sound except her footsteps and the faint rustle of spring in new leaves.

Angela makes her pretend call. The phone box smells the same. The only thing that's different is that someone's written "Laura" and a phone number in blue magic marker on the back wall. She hangs up and places the box on the top of the telephone. Then she walks quickly away up the street, eager to put as much distance between her and it as possible, telling herself that whatever else she does, tonight she will not stop. She will not look back.

But she does. As she reaches the pillar and the edge of the wall, she can almost feel the shadows of the trees pulling her in, wrapping her in their darkness. She hesitates, then turns and rests her back against the wall again, feeling the stones finger her jacket and hair.

This time it's five, or maybe seven, or eight, minutes before the woman comes. She's walking faster, as if she doesn't give a damn anymore about trying to look normal. She doesn't even pause, never mind look both ways before she crosses the street. Instead she walks diagonally. There's a desperation in her step, a slight stagger that makes Angela think she's crying. A moment later, when she's halfway across the road and caught in the glare of the streetlight, she reaches up and wipes her face with the back of her hand.

It's warmer tonight. She isn't wearing her green scarf, and her coat is unbuttoned, and Angela is certain, although it has not been very long, that she is bigger, that even in this short time the baby she carries inside her has grown. The woman pauses for a moment as she steps up onto the pavement. Then she shoves open the door and grabs the box on the top of the telephone with both hands. But this time she doesn't whirl away or run. Instead she stands there as if she can't move. Then, very slowly, she lifts the box and holds it against her face.

In Twenty Days They Killed a Leader, La Repubblica cries. *The Destruction of a Man,* writes *Corriere della Sera.* "If they had killed him, I could have understood more easily," one of Aldo Moro's colleagues says. "But not this."

Yet again packages have been left in Genoa and Milan and Rome. Yet again newspapers have received telephone calls telling them where to find the latest communiqué, and the most recent letter. In this one Aldo Moro begs the government to bargain for his life—to exchange him for other political prisoners. He doesn't say so, but everyone knows he means Renato Curcio and the others standing trial in Turin. *"I am a political prisoner and am being subjected to a difficult political trial with a political outcome,"* Aldo Moro writes. *"Time passes fast. Any moment,"* he warns, *"could be too late."*

Angela tries not to read the headlines, or anything else, on her way to the apartment at Via Montalcini. And fails. She knows now that the box she delivered was a tape, a recorded message from Aldo Moro to his family. All the papers say so, although they will not say what it said. Not that it matters. It isn't the words, she thinks, it's the timbre and touch of his voice. The caress of that familiar sound. That's what his wife and children crave.

Standing in the street, holding her basket, looking at the little printed words on the newspapers, she hears her father's whistle. The aimless scattered pebbles of his tune that was not a tune at all, just the sound he made in the world. She never heard her mother's voice. Or if she did, if there was a second, nothing more than the space of a heartbeat, when Annabeth spoke to her, she cannot, of course, remember it. But she is certain, nonetheless, that she would know it. That her mother's voice is lodged in her like a splinter. Finally she pulls herself away and walks on. But all the way to Via Montalcini she feels a weight, the palm of her father's hand, resting on the crown of her head.

Antonio has not said so in so many words, but Angela knows he's worried. The police have knocked on either fifteen, or twenty, or fifty thousand doors in Rome, depending on which report you want to believe. As time goes on the chances can only get greater that they will knock on one that will somehow lead them to Via Montalcini, and what the papers are now calling "the People's Prison." Last night Antonio told her to be careful of what she wears. That it should be as drab and as ordinary as possible. *Don't stand out.* No pretty summer dress for the sudden surge of spring weather. Nothing brightly colored. Nothing memorable. If she meets anyone in the lobby or the street, she should be pleasant and smile. She should not walk too fast, or move too slowly.

Be ordinary.

Be one of many.

That is the best way to disappear.

He also told her not to take the same route, that she must do something slightly different every time she makes the trip. So it takes her longer to get to Via Montalcini than she should, and by the time she does get there the food is cold. There are no mouse sounds from the other room. The apartment feels abandoned. Antonio looks tired when he opens the door, and for an awful moment, as she steps inside, she thinks, *Something terrible has happened. He's choked, or had a heart attack. He's dead.* But it isn't that. As she goes into the stuffy little room carrying the plate, the plastic knife and spoon shoved in her pocket, Angela sees that it isn't that at all. Although a part of her thinks it might as well have been.

She hasn't seen him for a quite a while and his color is horrible. Pallid. Aldo Moro's cheeks have stretched downward, and he's gray. All of him. His face is gray and his hands are gray and his shirt is dirty. His hair is disheveled, as if he's been running his hands through it over and over, and although she knows they have allowed him a razor, he hasn't shaved. But for all that, it's his eyes that upset her most. The last time she was here, his smile didn't reach his mouth. Now it doesn't reach his eyes, either. They are as dull and still as stagnant water.

She glances over her shoulder. The door is ajar as usual, but she can't see Antonio. She senses that he's not standing guard out in the hall, but has gone somewhere else in the apartment. For the first time, she and Aldo Moro are alone together.

"I've brought parmigiana," she says. "The first eggplants are in." And tries to smile, the way she's seen people smile when they are tempting children. But she has never had a child. It strikes her quite suddenly, standing there, that she has never had anyone, not really. Except her father and Antonio.

"If there's something special. Something you'd like me to make."

She's afraid her voice is shaking. He looks up at her dully. There are papers scattered across the bed and on the floor. There's no sign of the Lenin books. There are no books at all, just pages and pages of scrawled writing. He's barefoot, and the room is closer and smells worse than usual, as if there might be something wrong with the toilet behind the makeshift screen.

"You have to keep your strength up," she says. "You have to eat."

He stands up, like a child obeying an order, and sways slightly, then looks at her, as if he's just realized that he knows who she is, or has at least seen her before.

"I love my country," he says suddenly. "But it apparently does not love me."

"They love you."

The words are out of Angela's mouth before she even realizes she's said them. He shakes his head. The smile plays around his mouth now, but it's different, like a reflection, as if he's angled a mirror down inside himself.

Angela glances at the door. It's still ajar, and there's still no sign of Antonio. She puts the plate on the table, rustling the papers, pushing a pad aside to cover her words.

"They love you," she mutters. "Your family loves you."

His face sharpens.

"You've seen them?" The question is a hiss, nothing more.

Angela takes the plastic knife and spoon out of her pocket. "Your daughter." She breathes the words as she puts them down. "Your daughter loves you."

Then she backs out of the room, her heart hammering as if she has just run the fastest mile of her life.

That night Antonio brings his shirt home. Angela washes it, standing at the kitchen sink, rubbing a bar of soap up and down the collar and the cuffs. She rinses it in the plastic bowl and watches the water swirl down the drain. Then she fills the bowl again and does it over. Finally the water runs clean. She finds a hanger and hangs the shirt up in the little bathroom. When she steps out, Antonio is sitting on the ratty old sofa they bought in the market for nothing because someone was going to throw it away. He sticks a foot out, in a mock gesture to trip her. She is supposed to stumble and land in his lap, but she doesn't. Instead she stops and looks at him. He's exhausted. His eyes are red rimmed.

"Why are you doing this?" she asks. She can hardly believe that the words are coming out of her mouth, but they are, and once they start they don't stop. "What good is this doing? And you? I don't care about the others. But you. Why? What is it for?"

Antonio looks up at her, and for a second she thinks he isn't going to answer. *Ask me no questions, I'll tell you no lies.* Or that he's going to spout some revolutionary nonsense at her, quote one of the endless statements about the proletariat that the Brigate Rosse has been blurting and babbling and hammering everyone with for years. Or perhaps he'll be like Professor Barelli and shout, and thump his fist to make himself right.

But he doesn't. Instead he says, "You know why." And Angela feels something inside of her crack.

"You can't believe," she shouts. "You can't believe that doing this will bring him back!"

Antonio is looking at the television, but he isn't seeing it. She knows that. She understands that instead of the endless parade of images—something about car racing and a fire—he's seeing the building out beyond the Darsena with its narrow balcony and the laundry flying like flags from the rails. He's seeing the view from the window of his nonno's farm where the fields are now fallow and the pond overgrown with bullrushes. He's hearing his father's voice, telling him that university is pointless. And Piero's telling him it isn't. And his own telling them they must ask not only for bread, but for roses.

His hand is clutching, and letting go, and clutching again at the old maroon blanket that she keeps folded over the arm of the sofa. Angela kneels on the cushion beside him. Teetering, trying to keep her balance, she puts her arms around him. Antonio has done everything for her and there has been so little she has been able to do for him.

She holds his head against her shoulder. She presses her fingers into his beautiful black curls. She whispers something that is nothing at all, just a sound in the little room.

❦

There Will Be No Secret Negotiations. The Trial of Aldo Moro has begun.

It's badly printed and blurry and lying faceup on the desk, but he doesn't seem to care. Today he is very angry. His voice quavers. Spittle hangs at the edge of his lips.

"They are saying"—he gestures at the newspaper page—"the

government, my friends! Are saying that I was against negotiating for the release of Mario Sossi. They are saying that I didn't agree to talk, and that I wouldn't agree now. It's a lie!" He looks at her. "It's a lie. I told them we have to have a heart. We have to compromise. We have to learn to talk to one another or we are lost. It isn't just bullets that kill people." His dark eyes are swimming as his voice drops. "It's silence. Refusing to speak. Sossi's life—" His voice drivels off. "A man's life," he says a moment later, "is sacred. It's God's to give and take away. We have no power if we do not have humanity."

He turns his back on her. Leaves her standing there, holding the plate.

"That's what I told them," he mutters. "Anything else is a lie."

Antonio took his shirt the morning after she washed it. He's wearing it now. Standing this close in the tiny room she can smell the soap, the same bar she used this morning in the bath. His shoulders heave, in anger or resignation, she's not sure.

"My family," he says, and Angela feels her stomach tighten.

As usual the door isn't quite closed, and also, as usual now, Antonio is not standing right outside. He seems to have decided she doesn't need his protection, that she can be trusted to walk into a space the size of a broom closet and give a sixty-year-old man, who has no shoes or belt or anything but a pen and papers, a plate of food. She can see why. The mention of Mario Sossi's name reminds her of the photographs she saw of him, of how small and inconsequential he looked in his prison. The same thing is happening to Aldo Moro. Once she had thought that Mara Cagol, the Red Brigades, made people disappear like smoke. *Sparito nel nullo!* Now she understands that it is not that simple. That they do not vanish all at once. Instead, in the shadow of the five-pointed star, they shrink. Shrivel like dying flowers until nothing is left but petals and dust.

"Have you seen them?" The whisper is desperate. As faint as the hiss of air seeping out of a balloon.

Angela shakes her head. She pushes aside a pen, a pad of paper, unlined and unmarked, its pages blank and white and empty, and sets down the plate. She has brought him a blue cloth napkin from the linen she packed up and carried away from Via Vittoria, and she is folding it and laying out the plastic spoon and knife the same way they do in the trattoria, when his hand closes over hers.

It takes her a moment to understand. He is pushing a scrap of paper into her palm. She doesn't look up. She doesn't meet his eyes as she shoves her hand into her pocket and backs out of the room.

⁓

71 Via Forte Trionfale. Angela is not sure what she expects it to look like, but she understood at once, as soon as she got on the bus home and pulled the smudged tiny scrap out of her pocket, what it was. This is where Aldo Moro lived. This is the home where his family waits for him.

She had stared at the cramped handwriting, the four words of the address, as the bus lurched along, feeling something like panic, as if he had given her a bomb. A tiny incendiary device that could explode at any moment and ruin her entire life. Kill her. She had crumpled it up and held it, balled in her palm until she got off. Then she had dropped it in the first litter bin she passed and vowed to forget it.

But it was not that simple. She heard the words the next morning, beaten out in the tattoo of her feet as she walked to the dry cleaners. She heard them in clink of glasses and the rattle of plates as the tables were cleared at the trattoria after lunch. The next morning at the florist's she heard them in the whisper of cellophane wrapped around blooms. *Have you seen my family? Have you seen my family?*

And then, two days later, walking home, there is the newspaper, a special late edition. People are lining up to buy it at the kiosk on the corner. They turn away and open it there on the pavement, read, their heads bent, as the pages flutter in the April evening wind.

Angela stops. There was a time when she paid little attention to the papers, when they were a backdrop on the far horizon of her life, removed from everything that counted—her father, the shop, Antonio, Barbara, how fast she could run a mile. Not anymore. Now she feels they are written to her. Personal messages that might as well carry her name. She sidles around a large man in a jacket and flat cap until she can see the poster pasted to the kiosk's signboard, read the ugly black letters:

Red Brigades Communiqué Number 9
The Interrogation of The Prisoner Aldo Moro Has
Been Completed.
There Are No Doubts, Aldo Moro Is Guilty and
Therefore
Is Condemned To Death.

When she gets back, Antonio is not home. The little apartment seems to close around her, its walls collapsing until it feels no bigger than a broom closet. A utility room. One more People's Prison.

Finally, at seven o'clock, she can't stand it any longer. Angela snatches her jacket and her purse, and runs down the stairs, almost afraid he'll arrive and stop her. She studies the map in the bus shelter. Via Trionfale snakes high above the city, and there, off of it, is Via Forte. She can figure out the stops and bus lines, but she has no idea how long it will take her to get there, or when she will get back.

In the end she walks what seems a long way. A few times she

stops and looks back at the lights of Rome burning in the spring night. The neighborhood is unlike anywhere she has ever lived. It is as different from Trastevere and Ferrara and the ghetto as it is possible to imagine. None of the buildings are old. They look like the shoe boxes out at the Darsena, except they are bigger, and set back from the street, and most of them have balconies. Greenery flows over the railings like Rapunzel's hair.

Lights glint through the tresses of ivy. Trees cast shadows against the concrete walls. Angela knows when she finally finds the right street because there is a crowd, a blob of people in the soft dark. She can hear them murmuring and shifting, stamping like anxious horses. A line of policemen stand facing them. Several more stand on the pale stone steps of the building. One turns toward the glass door and Angela sees the outline of the gun he carries.

As she sidles into the crowd it becomes clear that most of them are journalists. They rustle and twitter among themselves and strain at the fact that they are not allowed to surge across the street and into the building, ride the elevator up and storm the doors of the penthouse apartment where someone has muttered that the Moro family is hiding. Angela leans back, cranes upward. But there is nothing to see, just tiny glints of light escaping through what are obviously closed shutters.

When a few minutes later a car comes down the street and is waved to the door and a woman gets out, the crowd trembles, taut as hunting dogs. A couple of the journalists shout questions. "Have you spoken to your mother?" "Has she had word from your father?" "Has there been another letter?" The woman runs up the steps, her head bent, and Angela finds herself leaning forward, standing on tiptoe, straining to see her face, and her belly. Suddenly she is consumed by the idea that if the woman will only look this way, will only stare for a moment into the crowd, their eyes will meet and they will know each other. But when she turns around at the top of the steps, it is clear that she is not pregnant.

She raises a hand. Stillness falls as quickly and completely as if she was the pope. She doesn't even have to raise her voice.

"Pray for my father," she says.

Then she's gone.

It is four days before Angela goes to Via Montalcini again, and in the meantime things become very strange. The president of Italy pleads for Aldo Moro's life. "A sense of humanity may induce them to a gesture of repentance," he says. Aldo Moro's wife, Eleonora, goes to a special mass and kneels side by side with the political leaders she has attacked because they will not bargain, dice, and deal with the Red Brigades for the life of her husband.

Watching on TV Angela studies Signora Moro as she comes out of the church. She has read enough of the papers to gather that it was Agnese she saw on the steps, his daughter who is not pregnant. But other than that she doesn't know what she's going to say. How she is going to tell him that she saw nothing but a building, a crowd in the dark, some policemen, and a woman begging them to pray? Then it appears she may not get the chance to do even that, because two days after her trip to Via Trionfale, a reporter at the newspaper *Il Messaggero* receives a telephone call telling him to look in a garbage can, where he finds a statement entitled *The Trial of Aldo Moro*. The text is intoned on the radio, flashed across the television screen, and printed on front pages, not only in Italy, but around the world.

We announce that we have carried out the execution by suicide of Aldo Moro,
president of the Christian Democrats. We consent to the recovery of his body

by making known the precise place where it rests. The
body of Aldo Moro is
immersed on the slimy bottom of Lake Duchessa.

There is footage of helicopters taking off, and of commandos
standing in the snow of the high Abruzzi, which stretches, white
and untouched, save for the footprints of boar and wolves. Frogmen crack the ice of both Lake Duchessa, and of a smaller lake
in a neighboring valley. But the bottoms, although undoubtedly
slimy, yield nothing.

❧

"Is it true?" Angela's voice sounds very small, even to her.

Antonio is sitting on the sofa staring at their television, which
is always on now, as if the only way they can be sure of what is
happening is to see it on the screen. He looks up at her as she
speaks and shakes his head. Then, a little to her surprise, he gets
up from the sofa and comes and puts his arms around her. It's
the first time since the night she shouted at him.

"No, Carina," he says. "It's not true. We don't even know who
sent it. It's a fake."

He smoothes her hair. His hand on her cheek, the feel of his
chest and shoulders, his chin as it nudges her forehead is like air.
She has been slowly suffocating without it.

"We're not barbarians," Antonio says. "No one is going to kill
him."

Angela looks up at him.

"I promise you," Antonio's lips brush the top of her head. He
takes her face in his hands. "No one is going to kill him. I promise you, Carina. I promise. But we have to make the threat—to
force them. To be recognized. To get their attention. They'll give
in," he says. "They'll take us seriously. You'll see. They'll give in."

"And if they don't?"

"They will." He kisses her. "They will," he says. "We're not the killers. They are."

*

The next day when she arrives at the apartment, there are the usual mouse sounds, scrabbling and rustling from behind the closed door, as if whoever is in there is burrowing away, afraid of Angela's eyes. Afraid that if she so much as glimpses them they will go up in flames, or fly apart in tiny pieces.

As usual Antonio is waiting for her. After she has unpacked the basket, he packs it again, loading in two of her baking dishes from previous meals. As he goes to the cupboard for a plate and plastic utensils, she lifts the lid off the top dish and sees that, as usual, it has not been cleaned. Lentils in tomato sauce line the bottom, and there are still chunks of onion and pork. Angela lifts one out and eats it absently, watching Antonio as he searches through drawers for the box of spoons.

The taste brings her father back with a jolt. Suddenly she is standing again in the kitchen in Via Vittoria, dicing carrots, the knife rising and falling above the old chopping board while he stands swirling oil in the cast-iron pan, seasoning it with peppers. She eats the remaining two pieces, making sure to catch some of the lentil sauce, wipes her hands, and puts the lid back on the baking dish, which she will have to scrub and scour after she's lugged it home on the bus. So much for proletarian equality. She's half tempted to march over and bang on the closed door. Shout through the keyhole that doing dishes is moral, and thus good for the revolution.

After the plastic spoons are finally located, Angela takes the meal. She watches as Antonio unlocks the door, then steps into the tiny room. The first thing she sees is the front page of the newspaper, carefully clipped and lying on the desk. In the center of it is a photo of Aldo Moro. Wearing the same white shirt, and freshly shaven, he sits in front of the five-pointed star holding a copy of the morning edition of *La Repubblica*, which bears the banner headline *Moro Assassinato*. Moro assassinated. His head is tilted. He has his quizzical little smile on his face, the same one he has now as he sits on his bed watching Angela.

He looks much better than when she saw him last, as if the anger has left him and even he has found this last episode—the slimy lake, the frogmen and helicopters and reports of his suicide—almost funny.

"What have you brought me?" he asks, and it takes her a moment to realize that he is not talking about the bowl of risotto she holds in her hands.

He stands up in his stocking feet as Angela bends to put the bowl down. They are so close they are almost touching. The door is ajar. She can hear Antonio in the main room, talking in low tones, presumably to one of the mice who has emerged now that she is safely out of sight.

"Agnese," she whispers, and his hand reaches out and closes over hers.

Angela looks down at the pale soft nails, the long elegant fingers and narrow bones so unlike her own father's, and doesn't have the heart to tell him that that's all. That she took the bus and walked up the street and stood inside a crowd, and saw nothing except a glimpse of one of his daughters and tiny slats of light escaping through the penthouse shutters.

"And your wife," she murmurs.

"Noretta?"

The hand tightens. Angela nods. Then she lies. She whispers everything she can remember about Signora Moro from the television. What she was wearing. Her silver hair. Her glasses.

When she stops, his eyes are shiny and far away.

"Your grandchild," she whispers. "He's getting bigger and bigger. He's waiting for you to come home."

"Anna."

Angela has no idea if this is the pregnant woman's name, but she nods anyway.

"She was wearing a green scarf."

"Maria Fida, Anna, Agnese, Giovanni," he whispers.

The names of Aldo Moro's children flutter in the fetid air. Angela nods. He turns away, and she reaches into her pocket and takes out another linen napkin, and a twist of salt that she lays carefully beside the bowl.

"What is your name?"

She looks up. He's watching her. Angela swallows. Part of her would like to, but she can't look away from him.

"Angela," she whispers.

He nods. The voices beyond the door have stopped. Angela glances behind her, but before she can turn to leave, he reaches out. His thumb presses her forehead. He makes a small cramped cross, and whispers, "Don't let them take your heart, Angela."

⁓

The sickness hits her like a punch. By the time she gets home, she is doubled over, can barely creep up the stairs and let herself into the apartment. With very few exceptions, Angela has been blessed with rude good health. While other children succumbed to flu, tonsillitis, winter colds, and even things more serious, Angela barely ever spent a day in bed. Once, when she was eight, she had been pushed over playing in the Piazza Lampronti and had skinned both knees, gotten a bloody nose, and sprained her wrist, necessitating a week's worth of wearing a brace and much attention from Nonna Franchi, but that was about it. So she is wholly unprepared for the waves of nausea punctuated by pains in her stomach as sharp as knife jabs.

When Antonio comes home and finds her curled on the sofa, her face pale and sweating, he calls the doctor, a round, smooth-faced man in a suit whose shoes make a squeaking sound and who comes right away and pronounces that she is neither pregnant nor has appendicitis, but has probably eaten something that doesn't agree with her, and will almost certainly feel better by morning. She does, but not much. Antonio goes to explain to the dry cleaners, and the trattoria, which sends him home with a jar of soup, and the florist's, who add a bouquet of day-old lilies. When he comes back, he holds her hand and smoothes her hair and tells her to sleep and leaves her tucked up on the sofa in the old maroon blanket.

Angela does sleep. Almost as soon as she hears the door close and his footsteps echoing on the stairs, she feels herself sinking, being pulled down into some place so dark and empty it feels like death. She is not alone in this well of dreams. Voices flutter around her—her father's, her mother's; their words finger her cheeks. She hears the shuffle of worn shoes on cobbles and the rustling of prayers. Once, the darkness parts and she finds herself on Via Vittoria. It is night. The street lamp is hazy and the familiar houses rise on either side of her, cradling her in the deep womb of the ghetto. She stands at the corner and watches while ahead a figure moves away from her, a man whose footsteps ring words she can hear but not make out, and whose shadow looms in a five-pointed star.

She wakes up sweating, and pushes the blanket aside and realizes that it is dark. The summer night has dropped over Rome. When she sits up her head swims a little, but not too much. Antonio is not in the apartment. Her mouth is dry and her tongue feels swollen. Her bare feet are strange on the floor and unreliable, but she goes into the kitchen nonetheless and makes herself a cup of tea, and opens the window and listens to the horses shuffling in their stables while the last shreds of cloud fade in the sky.

Feeling better she rinses the tea mug and goes back into the sitting room and turns on the television. A crowd is gathered at St. Peter's, a sea of heads and shoulders sparked by the candles some of them are holding. The pope has made an appeal.

"I beg you on my knees, free the honorable Aldo Moro, simply, without any conditions, not so much because of my humble and loving intercession, as by virtue of his dignity as a common brother of humanity."

Despite the warm evening, Angela pulls the blanket back over her. This time she is not sure if she sleeps or not. She seems to drift on the noise from the television. Words form and break before she can get ahold of them. When Antonio finally comes home, she keeps her eyes closed, her face buried in the cushion. She feels him bend down, brush her hair aside, put his hand on the hot damp back of her neck. He kisses her shoulder, then turns off the television and goes to sleep in the bedroom.

The pope's appeal does seem to have some effect. The next day the Red Brigades issue a specific demand for the first time. They will free Aldo Moro in exchange for thirteen prisoners, among them Mara Cagol's husband and another man who was one of the kidnappers of Mario Sossi.

Aldo Moro writes another letter begging the government to agree. It is delivered in what is now a regular pattern—to Milan, Rome, and Genoa. Angela dreams of this. Of people who look no different from herself dropping his words into dustbins. Slipping them through the open windows of cars. Tucking them into the cracks of phone booths and shutters of shops.

Let the Will of God be Done, Aldo Moro writes. *We are almost at Zero Hour. It is more a matter of seconds than minutes from the end. We are at the moment of slaughter.*

It is a few days later when Angela forces herself into the kitchen, when she takes down her knives and strops them on the whetstone and begins to dice the veal she has asked Antonio to buy.

She is doing this, not because he asked her, but because Antonio has told her that Aldo Moro is refusing to eat anything they bring him. He has accused them of drugging him and trying to poison him, when he will speak to them at all, which is not often now. The government has refused to release any prisoners, and Brigate Rosse is refusing to speak to the Catholic organization, Caritas, which has offered to negotiate. Neither side will recognize the other. Neither side will speak to the other. And Aldo Moro's words do nothing. He is caught in the middle, stranded in silence.

Let the Will of God be Done, his latest letter said. Angela who, unlike him, does not believe in God—or at least a God who, as far as she can see, has any discernible will—considers what this might mean as she adds the tenderest baby carrots, the newest peas, the soft furred shells of tiny artichokes to the oil that is spitting in the pan.

Via Montalcini feels different from the moment she walks through the door. There is a palpable sense of disarray. Usually the entrance and the kitchen, which are really all she ever sees, are neat to the point of barren. Now there are books and papers lying about. A huge wicker basket sits by the table. There are glasses and knives and forks and plates in the sink. Antonio has to wash one before she can dish out the veal.

The sauce is heavy and velvety and pale, exactly the way her father taught her to make it, and as a treat she has brought rice, too, the thick kind more usually used for risotto that she has steamed so it sticks together. She makes a well of it, and suddenly wishes she had remembered to bring parsley, to sprig the edge and sprinkle across the top.

Angela picks up the plate. Antonio unlocks the door to the little room, then turns away and goes back into the kitchen, letting her step inside alone.

He is sitting on his bed, his hands between his knees again, almost exactly the way he was the first time she saw him. She doesn't know if they've taken the razor away or if he has just decided to stop shaving. And possibly stop washing. That's how it smells. She tries not to let this register on her face as she sets the plate down.

"I've brought you veal," she says. But he doesn't say anything. He doesn't even look at her, or seem to be aware that she is in the same tiny space, that she is standing not a few feet from him.

"I cooked it myself. There's nothing in it." When he doesn't reply to this, she adds, "I made it specially. For you."

Angela lays out the plastic utensils, the napkin, another twist of salt, and still he doesn't look at her. There is no sound from beyond the door. She has no idea where Antonio is, or what he is doing. A pall of helplessness descends over her, thickening the air, making it hard to breath or move. Finally she steps around the desk and sits down on the narrow bed beside him. The mattress is thin and hard, and she thinks it must be uncomfortable to lie on for one night, never mind the seven weeks they have kept him here. The fan set high up in the wall has developed a whine.

"Your grandchild." She reaches out and takes his hand, which is limp and alarmingly cool. "Anna's child," she says. "You'll hold him soon. You have to stay strong enough to hold him."

He shakes his head.

"I'll never hold him. They're going to kill me."

"They won't kill you. I promise." Her words are sharp, as if she is spitting them. Slapping them into his face the way you slap someone who is fainting. "They've told me they won't. They won't kill you. I know. I promise. You will go home."

Something in this seems to touch him. Very slowly his head swivels. When he looks at her, she realizes he has become familiar, the soft mouth, the folds of skin, the eyes that are black but not like river stones. Black instead like midnight.

"You have to try. You have to eat. Please." Her pleading melds with the high-pitched mew of the fan. "You have to try. What is your favorite? What do you eat at home, with your family? Tell me, and I'll make it. I'll bring it to you. No one else will touch it. I promise."

"Do you know what I miss?" he asks, and when she shakes her head she is sure he is going to say his children, or his wife, or all of them—his family. But he doesn't. Instead, he says, "The sky. It has been forty-eight days since I have seen the sky." He smiles. "Angela." She feels a slight, returning pressure on her hand. "Tell me," he says. "Tell me what the sky looks like today."

So she does.

She whispers that it is very blue, because there are no clouds at all. That in the morning it was as pale as the veins that run under a child's skin, and that now it is darker, more like the breast of bird, the kind you see in paintings, and that at sunset it will turn the color of the inside of shells.

When she stops talking, he nods.

"Thank you," he says, and she realizes that he is crying, that thin glassy tears are running down into the folds of his whiskered cheeks. "Come to my funeral, Angela," he whispers. "I only want people who love me to come to my funeral."

When Angela leaves the room, she is shaking. She feels weak and sick again, and it takes her a moment to realize that no one is there. That Antonio is not sitting at the kitchen table. That he doesn't get up and come to the little room and turn the battery of locks.

She stands, confused, then she realizes that the door to the room off the kitchen is open, too, and that there is no noise coming from inside. She tiptoes over and peers in, her heart banging. There are mattresses, and stacks of books, and clothes hung over chairs. Angela turns back to the kitchen. Sun is pouring through the huge window over the sink and spilling onto the unswept floor.

She whirls around. Before she knows what she is doing, she is back in the horrid, stuffy utility room. She is taking his hand. She is pulling him up off the little bed, and dragging him past the desk to the open door.

He comes with her obediently, shuffling in his stocking feet. Angela pauses, listens. But there's nothing. So she leads him out, and into the kitchen, where they stand like children, holding hands and staring out of the window.

There's a park across the street. They can see the feathery tops of the trees and a single puff of cloud, the kind Nonna Franchi used to tell her were angel's kisses. He turns his face toward the sunlight that hits the dirty dishes and the rimes of food and the glasses that have lip marks on them, and as he does Angela looks behind them toward the entry hall and the front door, which she realizes is ajar.

She has no idea where Antonio has gone, but she knows the way out of here. She knows the elevator—she could push the button in her sleep. She knows how many steps it is to freedom.

She walks into the entryway. She can see a sliver of the landing. No shadows fall across the floor. The only sound is her breath, and the scrabble of her heart, and she has begun to turn around, begun to go back, and grab his hand, and lead him to the elevator, when footsteps sound on the stairs.

The door flies open, and a man Angela has never seen before strides in. He is shorter than Antonio and has dark hair and a mustache and glasses and is wearing a striped shirt with a linen jacket over it and walking so fast he almost slams into her. For a moment they stand paralyzed, staring at each other. Then he shoves past her into the kitchen, swearing as he bangs against the wicker basket.

Angela feels her head spin. People say that, but this time it's true. She will say, she will say—she has no idea what she will say. Then it flicks across her mind that there are two of them and one of him, and if they are quick, if they can find a knife or—

But the kitchen is empty. The spot in front of the sink where Aldo Moro had been standing, his face bathed in sunlight, his eyes fixed on the trees and the puff of the cloud, is filled only by dust motes.

The man she doesn't know is already around the corner. She follows him in time to see, even before he reaches for the handle, that the utility room door is closed. When he opens it, Aldo Moro looks up. He is sitting at the desk, has a plastic fork in his hand, and has speared a piece of veal. His head is tilted, his smile is quizzical as his eyes meet Angela's. Then the door is slammed and the locks are turned.

"Goddamn it!" the man explodes at Antonio as he walks in to the entryway. "Where the hell were you?"

Antonio shrugs.

"An alarm went off, in the garage. I went down to check." He takes a gun out of his pocket and places it on the table. "It's OK," he says, nodding toward Angela. "You can trust her. I told you. Nothing happened, right?"

"She didn't lock the door."

Both of them are talking about her as if she isn't there, as if she isn't standing two feet from them. Antonio shrugs again.

"I'm sure she was about to." He comes and puts his arm around her. "Weren't you?" he says, and from the pressure of his hand, from the rigid way he is standing, she realizes that whoever this man is, Antonio hates him.

She nods. Antonio leans down and kisses the top of her head.

"You can trust her," he says again. "I told you."

Angela leaves a few minutes later, carrying the basket, the cloth folded over the top of it. As soon as she gets into the lobby, even that feels heavy. It must show on her face, because Antonio, who has come down in the elevator with her, says, "Don't mind him. He's an asshole."

She nods. She wants to ask about the gun. She wants to know how long he has been carrying it, and if he always sat out there with it, if the trigger was unlocked and his finger was on it while she was laying out plastic knives and forks and whispering the names of Aldo Moro's children. She wants to ask what he would have done if—

But she doesn't. Instead she smiles and lets him kiss her and tell her he'll see her tonight before she walks back out onto the street where the sun hits her like a slap and makes her eyes water and where she starts to shake so badly that as soon as she gets around the corner she has to cross into a bus stop and sit down on the bench and put her head between her knees.

⌒

April is over. Angela's twentieth birthday is coming up. Four days before it, on Sunday morning, Antonio says he has a surprise. He is going to take her to Ostia.

"But we have no car."

The little Fiat broke down some time ago, shortly after they arrived in Rome. They sold it to a junk man because they couldn't afford to fix it and, as Antonio said, you don't need a car in the city anyway. He beams at her across their rickety table that even putting coins under the legs won't fix.

"Yes, we do," he says. "For today."

It is a red Renault, and Antonio has already put everything they will need into it. Her basket, which he has packed with a bottle of wine and glasses and food for a picnic. Their bathing suits, rolled in towels. He has even bought her a new pair of sunglasses, fancy ones she admired once in a magazine. They are in a case on the passenger seat with a ribbon tied around them. At the last minute, as he is starting the car, Angela shouts,

"Wait, there's something we've forgotten!" And runs back inside and upstairs and grabs the old maroon blanket so they will have something to sit on at the beach.

The road to Ostia is straight and feels as if it runs slightly downhill, unspooling like a long gray ribbon. They turn on the radio and sing along. Antonio reaches out and takes her hand and squeezes it, and for the first time in a long time they feel as if they are themselves again. As they drive away from Rome, the last fifty days melt. They fade and dissolve. Flake away. Angela leans back in the seat and thinks that this is how she used to feel when she ran.

At the ancient port, which is now not very near the ocean in much the same way that Ferrara's Darsena is not very near the Po, they park under the pine trees and wander among the ruins of the Roman city. They walk into houses, step over crumbled walls into people's kitchens and bedrooms and storerooms. They lean down and trace the outlines of mosaics of dolphins and sea monsters and ships and climb up the steps and sit on the warm stone seats of the amphitheater. Then they get back in the car, and follow the river to the sea.

⌒〰⌒

The blanket is spread on the soft loamy earth where the pines meet the sand. They change behind their towels and run, holding hands, into the soft, sloppy waves. Antonio swims and dives, while Angela only paddles up to her waist, until he attacks her from behind and pulls her under, sucking her down like a sea monster. Later they drink the wine and stretch out on the blanket, feeling the sun dapple their wet skin. Antonio rolls over lazily and licks the inside of her arm and the well of her collarbone. His tongue is warm and smooth and when he kisses her, his lips are salty.

"I love you, Angela," he says. And a little later he takes her hand, and presses her palm to his mouth. Then he reaches back into the basket and pulls out a tiny box.

The ring is gold. A very thin band with a tiny emerald, her birthstone, set into it. Antonio slides it onto her left hand. Then he folds her fingers around it and says, "Marry me."

And Angela says, "Yes." "Yes," she says again, just to hear the word, and despite everything that has happened in the last weeks, she thinks she has never been happier in her life.

There's traffic and the drive home takes longer than they would like. So by the time they get back to Trastevere it feels like forever since they last felt each other's skin, disappeared inside each other's taste and touch. When they finally find a parking place and get back to their building they are so impatient that they run inside and upstairs, and it is only late at night, after Angela has fallen asleep and woken up and they have made love again, that she remembers that although they grabbed the basket and the towels, they have left the blanket, covered in sand, in the back of the red Renault. She means to fetch it the next morning. But when she wakes up, Antonio is already gone and the car is gone with him.

Monday passes in a blur. Angela has time to make up at her jobs, from when she was sick. Antonio has said he will take her ring, sometime next week, and have it engraved with the date, May 7, 1978, and she decides that she will not tell anyone that they are getting married—not that she has anyone to tell except the dry cleaner and the florist and the man who owns the restaurant—until after. Until she can put it on her finger and never take it off.

Somewhere in the back of her head, she knows that what she really means by this is, until after all of this is over. Until the mice decide they have tortured the country and extracted their pound of flesh from Aldo Moro, and they let him go, and dismantle the

People's Prison, and the apartment at Via Montalcini is no more. She senses that this will be soon—that that is why Antonio has asked her to marry him now. That it's his way of telling her that any day they will have their own lives back, their own future, and that all of this will be nothing but a bad dream. In the meantime she threads the ring onto her gold chain and wears it with her locket, next to her heart.

That night Antonio brings her a bouquet. Pink roses. She knows they are a few days old—this is the bad side of working at the florist's, she understands which blooms get discounted and when, and will never look at bouquets with the same eye again—but she doesn't care. They are the first flowers he has ever brought her. She puts them in water with a crushed-up aspirin—another recently acquired nugget of wisdom, along with how to fold shirts and napkins—and makes him a special dinner. They share a bottle of wine and talk about when they will go to Mestre to tell his parents, and do not even turn on the television. The next morning, Tuesday, May 9, Antonio gets up very early, at six a.m. Before he leaves the apartment, he holds her face in his hands while she is still in bed and whispers, "I love you Angela Vari." Then he kisses her, and she closes her eyes and drifts back to sleep.

It is seven hours later, just after half-past one that afternoon, and Angela is sitting in the back room at the florist's trying to understand how things could possibly have gotten so out of control, how this mushroom cloud could have grown quite so fast and under her very nose, when a woman screams.

The sound is high and shrill, and by the time Angela and the florist have rushed out of the shop and into the tiny piazza that fronts it, it has wound down to a kind of keening wail. A crowd is bunched around the fountain, and within seconds the wailing grows as if it is being passed from one person to the next.

"What? What?" people are asking, the people who are not already wailing.

A man turns away, his face ashen, his hands twisting.

"They've done it," he says. He stares blankly at Angela and the florist, who is now clutching Angela's sleeve. "They've done it," he says again. "They've murdered Aldo Moro."

Angela hadn't believed it. She found herself shaking her head, saying first to herself, and then out loud and over and over again, "No, it's not true. It's not true. No, it's not true."

But it is. And now she knows it, because she is standing in front of an electronics' shop with a clutch of other people watching the television footage from Via Caetani, where, at one o'clock this afternoon, the body of Aldo Moro was found in the back of a car.

There is footage of the street, which is clogged with policemen and carabinieri. There is a blurred shot of an ambulance flying by, and the high whoo-whoo of sirens. And then there is a color photograph. It was taken by a photographer called Gianni Giansanti, who looks no older than Angela and caught the break of his life when he happened to be around the corner at one p.m.

Gianni Giansanti is still talking about this, describing how he had his camera and turned and sprinted, when the photograph he took fills the screen.

Aldo Moro lies twisted, his head on his shoulder. He is unshaven and wearing his navy blue three-piece suit, the pants he always had on and the jacket and waistcoat Angela saw that first day draped neatly over the back of his chair. He has been shot ten times in the chest and one of his hands is curled like a baby's over his heart. Several policemen are trying to stop people getting too close to the open back of the car, which is a red Renault.

A carabinieri officer is reaching for the edge of the maroon blanket that Aldo Moro is lying on, and that has obviously been his shroud.

The street tilts. Angela reaches for the wall of the shop, but she doesn't feel the rough brick beneath her hand. Instead she feels the worn wool that all her life was folded at the foot of her parents' bed. That she slept coddled in for the weeks and months after her father died. That Antonio covered her with when she was sick. That he laid her on while he licked the sea from her skin, and kissed her. That she felt rough and sandy against the back of her legs as he opened the little box and slid the ring onto her finger and asked her to marry him. The maroon blanket that, in her fever for him, she forgot to bring from the back of the red Renault they drove to Ostia.

She's lucky there's a dustbin a few steps away. She gets to it, and is sick. Once. Twice. A third time.

Via Forte Trionfale is a river of light. A thousand flames, perhaps more, flicker from the candles that the silent crowd stand holding. Stars fallen to earth, burning for the memory of Aldo Moro.

Angela stays there all night. She couldn't think of anywhere else to go. Already posters are tied to railings and the backs of benches and the sides of rubbish bins. Some have flowers looped through the strings and ribbons that hold them in place. Aldo Moro's face stares out from them. Underneath are printed the words, *Egli Vivra Nei Nostri Cuori. He Will Live in Our Hearts.*

The family has issued only one statement, that they do not wish for any officials, any members of political parties to be present at his funeral. In the early hours of the morning, it begins to rain. People tent the candles with their hands, trying to keep them from going out. Some sputter and die anyway. Some people melt away, too. But many stay, standing mute and wet, their mere presence the strongest rejection of the Proletarian Revolution—of the Communiqués, and *gambezzati*-ing, and the ranting, and the bullets—that they can think of. Angela looks at their faces and feels his thumb on her forehead.

Near dawn, it begins to rain harder, and a ripple runs through the crowd. The funeral has been moved forward. He will be buried today in Torrita Tiberina, where the family has a country house. Angela has no idea where this is, but she knows she is going to get there. She takes one last look at the closed shutters of the top floor apartment. They are shiny in the first gray light. Today the sky will not be the color of a baby's veins, or of a bird's breast, or of shells. Rain pours off of the balconies, tangling the long strands of ivy, and tips into the street, and flows like a river to Rome.

She finds an open bar, buys herself a coffee and a roll, and sits at a table by the window looking at nothing. When the kiosk next door opens, she gets a map and a bus plan. Torrita Tiberina is not so easy to get to. It takes her almost three hours. When she arrives she finds she is not alone. His family has said they do not want any outpourings, any national demonstrations of grief. Even so bunches of people stand outside the church. They watch as the pale wood coffin is carried inside, and follow at a distance like wary sheep as it makes its way to the cemetery. Later Angela will read that crowds gathered at crossroads and threw hydrangeas into the path of the funeral cortege. That when it stopped at a light, a truck driver climbed down from his cab and hurried across three lanes of traffic to press his lips to the side of the hearse.

After the prayers have been said and the coffin has been placed in the vault, there is nothing left to do. Angela doesn't even have any flowers to leave. She watches as the family files away—Anna, Agnese, Giovanni, Maria. The names that fluttered in that tiny awful room, their wings beating the stagnant air.

A half hour later when she gets to the bus stop and sees that the last bus going in the direction she needs to go has already gone, she isn't even surprised. It's somehow inevitable that she'll have to walk. Eventually, she supposes, she'll come to the next town south and perhaps there will be a bus from there and perhaps there won't be. She no longer understands whether or not she cares. Bowing her head against the rain, she pulls her sodden bag across her chest, digs her hands into the pockets of her jacket, and begins to make her way back to the city.

Monica Ghirri stopped at a bar after the funeral. She had thought Giovanni would say she was crazy, last night when she insisted on going and standing outside of the building on Via Forte Trionfale, but he didn't. Ever since that terrible March morning he has been quieter, and more understanding. She knows that he has always loved her, just as she has always loved him, even if the spark between them died some time ago. Two children, jobs, bills, schools, in-laws, will do that for a couple. But since the kidnapping, since that morning she stood on the pavement and watched five men die and another vanish, something new has flowed between them. An unspoken anguish. A sadness that dwells somewhere beyond the realm or remedy of words. It's like an underground river they find themselves in, side by side up to their knees steadying each other, and that Monica suspects may, in fact, be nothing more than the underpinning of life. So, when she said she needed to go to Via Forte, and then this morning announced that she was taking the car and driving to Torrita, her husband didn't argue or ask why. He just said he'd take care of the children.

She closes her eyes and remembers that the first thing she thought was *Fireworks.*

Then she realized fireworks didn't go off on Thursday mornings in March in the middle of Rome, and didn't come from men jumping out of Fiats. Or from Alitalia stewards, who a moment before had been lounging in the sun beside the bus stop and were now pulling guns out of their bags. And firing through car windows again and again and again.

She opens her eyes, but she can still see it. Sometimes she's afraid she'll never stop seeing it—the driver sprawling into the road, his hands flying up, as the car's back door is yanked open and a man wearing a black suit and clutching papers in his hands is dragged out. He stumbles, his foot catching. Then, as they pull him forward, his head jerks up, and his eyes meet hers.

Monica dreams of those eyes. They are still and dark as night, and in her dreams he looks at her and silence ticks like a clock and she realizes that his suit was not black, but dark blue, and that his hair is a crinkly iron gray touched with silver. And that his lips are moving. That, as they drag him away, he is speaking. To her.

Then she wakes. She bolts upright, her hands wound in the sheets, lips cottony and tongue swollen and tears running down her face because he was trying to tell her something. But between the breaking glass and the bullets and the screaming, she couldn't hear him.

Doors slammed and tires screeched and then, suddenly, there was nothing. Except the damn honking of that horn that went on, and on, a street away. Monica felt something and looked down. Her shoes, which were new and suede and she had paid too much for, were covered in blood. Blood spattered up her legs, and clung in thick drops to her stockings. It dripped from an arm dangling out of a car, and leaked from the man who had fallen into the street and lay in front of her, his knees bent and arms outstretched and head tilted at a strange angle in the blood that pooled around him. It ran in rivulets through a field of broken glass, and flowed like a river to Rome.

She knocks back the brandy that came with her coffee, and wonders what she's going to do. Not in the next ten minutes, or half hour, or hour after that—that's simple. She'll get in the car and drive home. Make dinner. Tuck in her kids, maybe read them a story. Brush her teeth, have sex with her husband. No, what she means is what is she going to do in the next day, and week, and day after that. Because since the moment she saw Aldo Moro dragged from his car, since the second he looked up at her, and their eyes met, and his lips moved, since then she has felt his heart beat inside her.

Sometimes she was sure she heard his voice. Felt his hunger, or anguish, or exhaustion. She marked the days on a calendar. Every one. All fifty-five of them. She read every word that was printed, all the letters in the newspapers.

I am a prisoner.
I kiss you for the last time.
Give a kiss to the children.
We are almost at zero hour.

And now he's dead. And there is nothing but a dull, reverberating emptiness.

Monica stands and takes her bag off the table. She brushes spilled sugar from the strap. Her shoes are wet through and ruined. Just rain this time, thank God. She pushes the door open and hears the voices in the small fuggy bar cut off as it snaps closed. Her umbrella wasn't much use at the cemetery, the shoulders of her coat and her blouse are soaked. There doesn't seem much point in hurrying as she makes her way to the car.

The heater fogs up the windshield. Waiting for it to clear, Monica turns on the radio. Then she can't stand it and turns it off again. She isn't sure what they are having for dinner. Perhaps she ought to stop and get something. She can't remember what's in the refrigerator. The wipers snap back and forth. If anything, it's raining harder now. She turns the defroster up to a roar and watches as the little puddle of clear glass spreads slowly upward. When she can see, she pulls out and winds her way through the narrow streets. She's gone a few miles when she sees the girl.

Hunched, hands in pockets, plodding along the side of the road, she's so wet that her dark hair is plastered to her skull. She doesn't even look up when Monica pulls out to pass her. All the same, Monica recognizes her. She saw her last night at Via Forte, and again today outside the church. A fellow pilgrim.

Monica pulls into the side of the road, stops, and watches as the blurred figure gets larger and larger in the rearview mirror. The girl doesn't run, or even look up, or seem to care that the car is there. Finally Monica has to roll the window down and call out to her, or else she'd walk right by.

"Ciao! Ciao, hello!" she calls. "I was at the funeral. Can I give you a ride?"

The voice startles Angela. She slips on the muddy verge and puts her hand on the car to steady herself. The Mercedes is warm. Steaming, as if it's alive.

"I'm sorry?"

The window is half open, rain spattering in, and the woman is talking to her, maybe asking directions. She's small and doll-like and blond, with curly hair not unlike Angela's own.

"A ride," The woman says. "I'm going back to Rome. I saw you last night. And at the funeral. Can I give you a ride?"

Angela is about to shake her head, to say no, she's fine, even if she isn't, or if she doesn't know what she is, when she hears something in the woman's voice. The offer is less a question than a plea. Angela frowns. Her brain doesn't seem to be working correctly. *Don't let them take your heart, Angela.*

She hears his voice all the time now.

"I'm very wet."

She looks beyond the woman to the car's leather seats, to its fancy interior, with wood on the dashboard. She has never ridden in a car like this, and surely, soaked as she is, she'll ruin it. The woman shakes her head, she actually lets out a little laugh that seems almost relieved.

"Well, it's raining," she says. "It would be strange if you weren't." Then she leans over and opens the passenger door. "Come on, get in."

So Angela does. The seat cradles her like a hand. She places her muddy, squidgy shoes carefully on the navy blue carpet and puts her soaking bag beside them, which seems like the best place for it. When she closes the door, the car surges forward without a sound.

At first Angela doesn't dare lean back against the padded headrest, then, little by little, as the heat courses through her, she can't help herself. Rain streams down the windows. The clack and slap of the wipers push time away. Angela closes her eyes and feels like she's melting. She is almost asleep when the woman says, "I saw it."

Angela looks at her.

"I saw it," the woman says again. She glances at Angela, then back to the road where a truck is putting on its brake lights, slowing for a puddle that has spread like a lake across the tarmac.

"When they took him. I was there. On the pavement, beside the bus stop. I'd just taken my kids to school." She shakes her head and laughs, then reaches up and wipes her cheek with one of her tiny hands, and Angela realizes she's crying.

"I was just standing there, you know, waiting to cross the street—we live right across—and I saw the cars, the accident. When they stopped and made his car run into them. And I remember, I just thought, 'Oh how stupid. Bad drivers are so careless.' Then there was shooting."

They've slowed to a crawl, are nosing their way through the gray sheets of rain, following the red wolf eyes of the truck.

"I'd never heard a gun go off before," the woman says a second later. "I thought it was fireworks. Isn't that stupid? Isn't that the stupidest thing you've ever heard? Fireworks at nine in the morning. But now I hear them all the time. Every bang. Even if it's just a door slamming, I think it's a gun. And I see it, those men dying. I see it every day. Isn't that crazy?" She glances at Angela again. "That's crazy isn't it?" she says. "That's what crazy people do. Play movies in their heads like that. Over and over and over." Damp curls bounce and cling to her cheek. "They didn't even have time to get out of the cars. Those men. Only one. He fell, and lay there in the road. His blood—"

Tears are streaming down her face now. They hit the high collar of the silk blouse that pokes above the neck of her coat. Ahead of them the truck has cleared the lakelike puddle. As they drive through, Angela feels the Mercedes's tires slip, then take. A fin of spray rises up.

"They just reached in and took him," the woman says. "As though they had the right. Just to take him like that. Pull him off the face of the earth because they wanted to. And you know the strangest thing? He didn't even fight. Or try to get away. He didn't do anything. Except look at me."

They have come into a town. There is a sign Angela can't read, partly because it's graffittied and partly because of the rain. Grimy buildings, their windows black and slick, slide by.

"He looked at me," the woman says. "And since then, nothing's been right. Nothing. Because he said something to me. And I keep thinking, I'm certain, that he was asking, begging me, to stop it. To save him. But I couldn't." She takes a breath and her voice drops. "I couldn't," she says. "I was standing right there, but I couldn't do anything. Nothing. Nothing at all. And now they've killed him. I'm sorry."

She reaches out and touches Angela's thigh, her jeans that are so wet they're a second skin.

"I'm sorry," she says again, looking back at the road. "It's just, you were there. You know? Like me. Last night. And at the funeral. It's good to talk to someone who—" She shakes her head. "I'm forty years old. I have a husband and two children, and I can't stop. I dream about it, every night." She puts both hands on the wheel and frowns as her voice breaks again. "I couldn't hear him. I couldn't do anything. I couldn't do anything at all to stop it."

"No one could have stopped it."

Angela's voice sounds strange and far away. Hollow, as if it's coming from a tunnel somewhere deep inside her. "No one could have stopped it," she says again. "No one could have saved him."

"What kind of people?" The woman shakes her head. "What kind of people do that?"

Her voice dribbles off, replaced by ragged breathing, as though she's been held underwater.

"I'm sorry," she says again. "I'm sorry." Then she pushes her hand through her hair and makes an effort to smile. "Where would you like to go?"

They have reached the outskirts of Rome. Torrita Tiberina is only thirty-five miles north of the city, nothing in a car. What took hours this morning, changing buses and waiting for new ones, has flashed by in barely thirty minutes. Angela looks at her and almost laughs. Then she realizes she can't say "nowhere," and feels a faint nudge of panic.

"Anywhere," she says. "Anywhere is fine." The woman looks as if this is the wrong answer.

"I can get a bus," Angela adds. "Now that I'm back in the city."

"But I can drive you. Really. It's not a problem."

"No." Angela shakes her head. "I'd like to be alone for a while," she adds. "You know, before I go home."

The woman nods, but even as she says it, Angela knows it isn't possible. That she no longer has a home. She wonders if she ever did. Or if the last few months have just been borrowed, weren't really ever part of her life at all. Is that what Antonio planned, somehow, from the very beginning? From that day in the orchard? That it would always be like this? She reaches into her jacket and feels through the soaked cotton of her shirt, her fingers finding the hard nub of the ring that hangs around her neck, no date engraved inside the band. She wonders when he bought it. Or if it was borrowed, too, like the red Renault.

They have come into the city and are winding through the modern expensive suburbs with their balconies and concrete walls and trees. Looking out the window, Angela half expects the phone booth to flash by. To see a woman wearing a green scarf, life swelling inside her as she hurries down the pavement, clutching a box of words.

"I'm sorry?"

The woman has said something to her, but she has no idea what it was.

"I live just here. Up the street. Look—" They have stopped at a light. "If you'd like to come in." The woman looks at her, her blue eyes searching Angela's face. "If you'd like get dry, have a meal. Or if I can help you. I could—"

Angela looks out and sees a sign that says Via Stresa. Another says Via Fani. Across the street a triangular neon light spelling BAR, TAVOLA CALDA sparkles in the rain.

"This is fine." She picks up her sodden bag. "Here is fine. Anywhere." Angela looks across at the shelter. "I can get a bus."

The woman nods reluctantly.

"Well, OK," she says. "If you're sure."

Angela opens the Mercedes's door.

"Thank you." She gets out, feeling her shoes squish with rain.

Then before she closes the door, she leans back into the car. "The men?" Angela asks. She can feel traffic behind them, sense the light about to change. "The men who took him that day. Did you see them?"

The woman nods. The look in her eyes suggests she has seen them every day and probably most nights since. And that she will go on seeing them. Possibly forever.

"They were dressed as Alitalia stewards," she says. "You know, in the uniform. One had a mustache and glasses. The other was taller. Quite a lot taller. Dark hair."

"Was it curly?"

The light has changed. A scooter shoots by. A car hoots.

"I'm sorry," the woman says, leaning toward the open door. "I didn't hear—"

"I asked—" Angela smiles. "It doesn't matter," she says, and closes the car door.

The woman is staring at her through the window. She is saying something. Then another car honks, and another, and finally she is forced to move off. Angela watches the Mercedes turn into Via Fani, and then turn again, and slide into the mouth of the garage below the building on the corner.

She stands there for some time, on the far side of the stream of traffic, looking at the last things he saw before he was pulled out of the world and dropped into the People's Prison. The buildings are tall and dull. There are some magnolia trees in bloom. Oleander leaves drip beside the bus stop. A few ragged fingers of late forsythia reach through a fence. She seems to remember reading somewhere, in a magazine or the newspaper, that on the morning of March 16, the sun was shining. She might be making that up, but she hopes it's true.

The light changes and changes again before Angela finally crosses the street and stops at the memorial to the five bodyguards. She is a little surprised that she can recite their names.

Oreste Leonardi, Domenico Ricci, Giulio Rivera, Raffaele Iozzino, Francesco Zizzi. The tide of flowers has receded, but the cross she saw on TV is still there. And the beret, the medals with their faded ribbons pinned to its brim. A few remaining bouquets are piled on the pavement, some newer than others. Rain beads their cellophane wrapping. The flashing neon sign from the bar across the street catches the drops and makes them glitter. Red. Pink. Green. Red. Pink. Green.

Angela doesn't know how long she sits in the bus stop. Later, when they ask her—because they ask her every tiny thing, even the most embarrassing, even the most intimate, things—she can't tell them. Just as she can't tell them what time, exactly, it is when she gets up and walks down the street. It is certainly after dark, certainly after the time when Antonio will be back in the little apartment, will be turning on the television and wondering where she is and what has become of her. Or perhaps he already knows, and the apartment is empty, and after he kissed her and held her face in his hands and told her he loved her, he never planned on coming back there again. She doesn't know. Any more than she knows if he stood at the bus stop in a stolen airline uniform, or if he pulled a trigger, and if so, which one. Which bullet he fired. All of them? Any of them? None of them? It doesn't matter. Any more than it matters that she believed him when he promised her Aldo Moro wouldn't die, told her they weren't killers.

The rain has eased. It falls now in showers, bursting and splatting as the wind picks up. Angela reaches inside her collar. She feels for the clasp her father's fingers could not manage and undoes the gold chain. The locket is soft. She slides the ring over it, feeling the sharp edges of the stone, then reclasps the necklace and tucks it away.

The tiny emerald winks in the light of a passing car.

"I couldn't stop it," the woman with the blue eyes had said. "I couldn't save him." And Angela had replied from far away, "No one could have stopped it. No one could have saved him."

But that was a lie.

It isn't just bullets that kill people. It's silence.

All it would have taken was a phone call. An anonymous note. *Via Montalcini.* Two words for a man's life.

Angela leans forward and drops the ring into the gutter. For a second, the gold glints. Then it is sucked in to the thin, dark torrent that runs down the storm drain, and is lost.

The officer on desk duty looks up as the door swings open. It's been a long bad day in a string of what now seem to be endless long bad days, and he hopes, he really hopes, that this woman isn't another nutcase who has come down here to tell him she's had a dream and knows where the kidnappers' prison is, or that Aldo Moro is sending her secret messages spelled out in the hairs in her curlers, or that she's always thought that jerk Guido her sister married was strange and there's something they should know. It's happened in police stations all over the city, but especially here, so close to Via Fani. Then, with something that feels like a punch, he remembers that it probably won't happen much anymore. And if anything, that's worse.

She's very young, this one, and soaked to the skin, and looks confused, standing there clutching her bag.

"Can I help you?" he asks, and she looks at him as though she's surprised he's here.

"Signorina?" he asks again, and begins to wonder if something really bad has happened to her. Or if this is one for the trash bin—not that they're mutually exclusive.

"Signorina?"

She steps to the desk, still clutching the bag, and places her free hand, her left one, flat on the wooden surface and studies her fingers, which are bare—no rings—and look cold and white. When she finally looks up, the expression in her eyes is enough to make him reach down and feel for the butt of his gun.

"Can I help you?" he asks again.

And he's about to push the button under the counter, thinking *To hell with her, I'd better help myself,* when she nods, and says, "I killed Aldo Moro."

Part V

Ferrara, 2010
Tuesday, February 9

Anna woke with a start. Her head was on a pillow, her hands underneath it. There was the garish green stripe of a quilt, a piece of blue carpet. For a moment, she didn't understand. Then she remembered, and sat up.

Enzo Saenz was sitting on the opposite bed, watching her. Something told her he'd been sitting there all night—or all early morning—or all dawn. Whatever you wanted to call it since she'd stopped talking.

"Are you hungry?"

Anna ran her hands through her hair, catching the tangles in the ends, looked at the red chafe marks on her wrists, and nodded.

"I think so. I'm not sure."

Shards of dreams—of the inside of her father's ruined shop, of the bicycle with the torturous seat, of the long pale road stretching through nothingness and the crack-crack of bulrushes as the bird rose out of them—glittered around her. She heard her own voice calling for Antonio, then winding through the dark as she sat here on this bed, telling this man she didn't even know her life. Letting it spill through her like a dam that had finally given way.

She felt dizzy. And must have looked it, because he was off the bed, shoving her head between her knees, the palm of his hand on the back of her neck.

"Breathe," he said. "Just breathe."

She did. But not fast enough to stop the tears.

"It's going to happen again, isn't it?"

"No. No, it isn't." Enzo crouched in front of her, his hands on her shoulders, bracing her the way you might brace a wall or rickety fence that's about to tip over on top of you. "We can stop it," he said. "This time we can stop it."

Anna looked at him.

"Listen to me," Enzo Saenz said. "You have to tell me the rest. About the phone call. From Antonio. You have to tell me everything about it. Every single thing, even if you don't think it's important. He's only called you once, is that right?"

She nodded. "At the Excelsior. During breakfast. After I left the message on Kristin's phone."

"Tell me exactly what he said."

Anna closed her eyes. She felt the phone in her hand, heard the chink of silver and glasses. The tap of footsteps on the marble floor.

"I'll kill her, Carina. If you say a word, just one, this time, to anyone. I will kill her. Do you believe me?" he had asked. *"Do you think I'm lying?"* And she had answered, *"No."* No, she didn't think he was lying. *"Good. Then come and find me. Because I love you. I have always loved you, Angela. Ti possiedo, per sempre, Carina. And you owe me. You owe me a life."*

"He wouldn't let me talk to Kristin." Anna took a breath. "He said I had to believe him, that she was alive. He said it was just between us, him and me, this time. That I could make it up to him, but that if I said anything to anyone, he'd kill her. He said I should turn my phone on twice a day, at seven and seven, to see if I had a message from him. Then he laughed, and said we were playing hide-and-seek, and it was my turn now. He'd come to find me when he left Padua. Now I had to come and find him."

She opened her eyes and stared for a moment at nothing. "When I asked him how Kristin was," she said finally, "when I asked Antonio if she was all right, he said she wanted her teddy bear. That's all." Anna Carson looked at Enzo. "That's all," she said. "After that, he hung up."

Enzo Saenz no longer thought she was lying about Rome, about what had happened. He had already called Pallioti and told him as much while she had been asleep. But he did not think she was telling him the truth now. He had seen it before, in the faces of the desperate, the terrified, the cornered. People who had nothing left—except the tic, the hard leftover lump of scar tissue, the something to hold back. One final bargaining chip.

"All right," he said. "That's why you brought the bear. What else?" He studied her face, hoping they could do it this way, and not a worse way. "Antonio said something else. One more thing, didn't he?"

Anna Carson looked at him for a long time. Then she nodded.

"He said he loved me, and that I owed him a life."

"And?"

Her eyes slid away. Enzo could feel it, stuck in her throat like a bone. He was not a hard man, but if he had to, he would. He would reach down and jerk it out.

"Anna," he said, "I can't help you if you don't let me."

She looked back at him.

"He asked me if this time I believed him, because he lied to me, about killing Moro, and I said yes. And then he said that he would never lie to me again. That he was sorry. And he was telling me the truth, and to make sure I paid attention and worked hard. I had a deadline."

"A deadline?"

She nodded.

"They were always doing that. In their stupid communiqués. They were always setting deadlines. If something didn't happen by such and such a time, they'd kill Sossi, or they'd kill Moro or—"

"He'll kill Kristin?"

Anna nodded. Enzo felt himself go cold.

"When, Anna?" he said as softly as he could. "When is the deadline?"

"A week. Antonio said it was a gift, because he loved me, that it was that long. He said he would give me a week. Then he'd kill her."

While Anna Carson took a shower, Enzo called Pallioti again. Then, after he had brought him up to date and Pallioti had announced he was on his way to Ferrara, Enzo called room service and ordered breakfast. He kept his eye on the bathroom door. There was no window, and he didn't think she was a suicide risk—she was driven too hard to make up for what she had not done before, to find the girl, or, rather, help them find her the way she had not helped anyone find Aldo Moro—but even so he didn't trust her. Desperation made people very unpredictable. Anna Carson would use him just as he would now try to use her. If she thought it was working for her, she'd cooperate. If she didn't, she might do anything. It was going to be a very long day, and what they needed first was food.

Enzo Saenz had been awake, or at least not asleep, all night, propped against the headboard of the second bed, one eye on the woman's sleeping form. He loosened his ponytail and ran his hands through his hair. His face looked back from the mirror that hung over the trendy metallic set of drawers, and he wondered who he was seeing. Not Giulia with her broad, high bones. Not his grandfather, with his long face and straight patrician nose. Someone he had never known, and would never know. The father whose genes he carried inside him like a secret code he couldn't read. He crossed to the window and pulled back the heavy curtains. Behind the dark shape of the Castello the sky was turning the color of roses. Any moment the bells would begin to ring. It was seven a.m. on Tuesday morning.

"A week" was Thursday. The day after tomorrow.

⁓

Sixty miles to the west, Hedwige Aarlheissen reached across the bed, felt her hand meet empty air, and snapped her eyes open. She had not even undressed, had allowed herself to fall asleep last night after the nightmarish dinner party, convinced that she was only taking a nap and would wake up to either find Barbara beside her or hear her downstairs, banging about, searching for leftovers.

A glance at the undented pillows and a second of listening told her neither was true. Hedwige could feel the emptiness in the house, the undisturbed air. She swung her legs over the side of the bed.

The clock in the hall started to chime, running through its carillon of bells. Most mornings Hedwige didn't notice it. Most mornings she didn't drink coffee, either.

Padding downstairs, she caught sight of herself in the glassy reflection of the kitchen window. Her hair was standing on end. She had raccoon eyes from sleeping in her makeup, and something that was probably a combination of drool and lipstick smeared the collar of her white silk shirt.

Priming the Bella Machina, Hedwige made herself a double espresso, then carried the cup, sipping as if it might be hemlock, as she patrolled the house—checked the locks and back entry and office, confirming what she already knew. Not only was Barbara not here now, she had not been here. She had not come and gone in the night, gathering papers and leaving hastily scrawled notes, as she sometimes did in the middle of a case, or when she had to get to some prison or police station at some un-godly hour.

Her patrol completed, Hedwige put the now empty cup down on the kitchen counter. After hosting what had turned out to be a perfectly dreadful dinner party alone, she'd cleaned up. But not very well. Crumbs and bits of food littered the polished stone. A cherry tomato had rolled under the edge of the fruit bowl and squashed itself there. Hedwige regarded it for a moment, as if the pattern of little yellow pips might tell her something. Then she pulled her phone out of her trouser pocket where it had nestled all night like a baby possum.

She'd left the ringer on, and turned up loud, so she knew there were no messages before she even checked. All that was in the log were the four calls she'd made to Barbara. Two yesterday evening before the party, and two afterward, all unanswered. She tapped the speed dial number again. This time Barbara's number didn't even ring before her voice cut in, demanding that she be left a message. Hedwige didn't bother. The phone was turned off. Barbara would see her number and know what she wanted— *Where the hell are you? Are you all right? Has that son of bitch laid a finger on you?*—when she turned it on again. If she ever turned it on again.

The thought bloomed like a sick black flower in Hedwige's head before she could even begin to stop it. Its smell, fetid and sweet, filled her nostrils and made her stomach heave. She dropped the phone and gripped the edge of the counter, hanging on until her eyes watered. Then she gave in. Hedwige Aarlheis-sen did not cry. Despite appearances to the contrary, she was the tough one. The strong one. The one hard as nails. So the sound that came from her throat was unfamiliar. It took her a moment to even understand what it was.

After hearing from Enzo, Pallioti had been tempted to grab the first car he could find in the police garage and fling himself onto the motorway. Then he'd realized he'd probably be more effective if he got his ducks in a row first. The primary duck was James MacCready, to whom would now fall the unenviable job of convincing Dr. Kenneth Carson, yet again, that the very best thing he could do was stay put and shut up. Give them just another few hours. Another day.

Enzo believed Anna Carson. She had been very young and very much in love, trapped between needing to believe in Antonio, who was all she had left in the world, and betraying him. In the end, perhaps inevitably, she had done both. Aldo Moro had died anyway. And Antonio Tomaselli had spent half his life in jail. He had thought about it for years, and now he was having his revenge. On Thursday, the day after tomorrow, if he hadn't already, he'd kill Anna Carson's stepdaughter. And, Pallioti suspected, if he could manage to lure her to him, probably Anna, as well. And then, almost certainly, himself. If he couldn't get his Angela back even for a few precious minutes to punish her by killing her—well, then he'd very likely just settle for the next best thing. Killing himself and Kristin and making all that her fault, too.

Unless they found him first.

What was it Barbara Barelli had said? Love drives us all to the biggest screwups? Something like that. Pallioti allowed himself a single roll of the eyes. *Jesus,* he thought. *What an unholy mess.*

Pallioti liked James MacCready, not least because he didn't have to waste breath explaining to him exactly how delicate this was. They had brought Anna Carson, like some renegade spy, in from the cold, and now nothing must be done, by Kenneth Carson or anyone else, to break the nebulous bond Enzo Saenz had somehow established with her. Neither he nor Pallioti had a clue where Antonio Tomaselli was, but he was fairly certain,

from what Enzo had told him, that Angela Vari did. Even if Anna
Carson didn't realize it.

It felt to Pallioti like that silly party game in which a whisper
is passed from ear to ear, only now it was traveling through
decades—Antonio to Angela, Angela to Anna, Anna to Enzo—
and they had to play it fast. If they could keep the meaning in-
tact, the prize was not a bottle of wine, or a kiss, or a piece of
cake, but Kristin Carson's life. And probably Anna's and Antonio's as well.

He wanted to be in Ferrara by lunchtime. When he finally
stepped out of the elevator into the police garage, Pallioti saw
the car Guillermo had ordered waiting for him already running, as if the officer on duty expected him to leap in and
fly up the ramp like something out of *The French Connection*.
The young man scurried to take the overnight bag Pallioti kept
packed in his office. He placed it carefully on the backseat,
then jumped to open the door, standing so straight Pallioti
felt he ought to salute. He thanked him instead, slid into the
driver's seat, and had just finished adjusting the mirrors when
his phone rang.

Anna Carson leaned against the cold glass of Enzo Saenz's passenger window and watched the countryside she had ridden
through at such cost yesterday fly by. The same way she had
watched it all those years ago from Antonio's Fiat. The same
way she had watched the sodden green of Torrita give way to
the outskirts of Rome from Monica Ghirri's car. All of them in
other lifetimes, shuffled and falling back out of order like a badly
played card trick.

"This may be a stupid idea."

She said it without looking at him.

"It's not."

They had talked more over breakfast. Anna wasn't certain how she felt about the fact that he'd called his boss, the long-faced man in the black suit who looked like a well-dressed member of the Inquisition, but she supposed it was inevitable. It was only in the movies that the Daring Guy and Spunky Gal went solo and caught the dastardly villain all on their own. In real life you reported in, and did as you were told. Which they were, more or less.

Pallioti had said Florence would square things with Ferrara—thank them for their help and tell them they no longer needed the CCTV tapes, giving the distinct impression that everything was cleared up—and that he would come straight to the hotel where they should expect him around lunchtime. He had not said what they would do then. Or, at least specifically, that they should sit in the room waiting for him. So when Enzo had asked her what she had planned next to find Antonio—beyond waiting for him to call or send a message so she could beg him to tell her where he was—she'd told him. Then she'd reached for her coat as he picked up his car keys.

"Are we sure it's open? That we can get in? Today? In the winter?" Anna asked again, even though she knew the answer. She'd been sitting across from Enzo at the room service breakfast table when he'd made the arrangements. The words were just something to say. Something to stop Angela Vari from creeping into the car. Not that that was possible. She couldn't stay away. Pomposa had always been one of her favorite places.

They saw the campanile first. It rose like a needle from the gridwork of winter fields, a beacon to the weary and the faithful. To pilgrims, and robbers, and those simply in need of succor, material or otherwise, for over a thousand years. The day Antonio had finally kept his promise, bringing Angela after he showed her his nonno's farm, the tower had seemed to waver in the thick summer sun. Now it shimmered. The pale stone was almost pink, and glowing, as if a giant mirror had been placed at its feet, gathering light from the sea.

Antonio's father and grandfather had known the abbey when it was still a living community, before it became a tourist attraction run by the state. They had bought honey from the monks, and the herbal teas and fruit pastes Antonio's grandmother loved. Rumor said the monks had supplied other things, too. That the campanile had been used as a watchtower, and the storerooms as a weapons dump by the Partisans during the war. That there had been coded messages sent in the ringing of the great bells. Which now, Anna thought, were almost certainly programmed, machines ringing out the notes that had first been named and written down here.

The caretaker was waiting for them. One of the perks of those credentials Enzo carried seemed to be that when he said "jump," the only answer was "how high?" Anna glanced at him as they got out of the car. As far as she could tell his outfit—the jeans, the leather jacket, and certainly the sneakers—hadn't changed. But he no longer felt or looked like a policechild.

They shook hands with the caretaker quickly. The small man in his padded coat was obviously both eager to know what this was about, and determined to keep his dignity by not asking. When it became clear that Enzo wasn't going to say anything, he led them to a side gate. Anna supposed she must have come here on a weekend when she came with Antonio. Or perhaps back then it had been open all the time. Now it was only Friday and the weekend. Even if she had thought of coming here yesterday and managed to actually do it, she would have found locked doors.

Arches rose around them as they stepped into the long cloister. She remembered the library, and the refectory painted by students of Giotto who had wandered down from Padua, and the mosaics. The colors that had still been bright after a millennium, or perhaps they had only seemed that way because it had been summer, and she had been with Antonio, and everything had been bright. The caretaker paused, and produced more keys, and opened the door that let them into the bell tower.

Light fell through the narrow casements, but between them it was dark, and the steps were worn. Anna, never fond of heights to start with, kept her eyes on the caretaker's back. His feet moved quickly, his small ungloved hand barely touching the guide rope. He could probably navigate these steps in the dark, and perhaps he did—climb up on full-moon nights and gaze down over the fields that melted into canals and merged almost seamlessly with the sea.

It was probably some kind of miracle that the abbey itself was still standing. Some divine hand must have guided the builders to this piece of solid ground, because the area was a notorious marsh, inhabited largely by seabirds and the few remaining fishermen who netted for eels in the brackish, muddy water. Their shacks were almost impossible to get to if you didn't know the paths and causeways. Holding her around the waist as they stood in the top of the tower, Antonio had pointed out the almost invisible rush walls and roofs, and whispered in her ear the stories his nonno had told him, about how the shacks had been used by the Partisans during the war, providing a camouflaged web of all but unreachable hiding places.

The idea hadn't occurred to her before, but it did now. If Antonio had gone there, out to one of the huts, they would never find him. They could look forever. There would be no more possibility of finding him out there than there had ever been of finding Aldo Moro innocent. And maybe that was the point—what he intended all along. They had liked to talk a lot, the Red Brigades—about the unfairness of the Establishment, the State, whoever it was they had been so damned oppressed by. But, she thought sourly, they'd always made sure they played with a stacked deck.

Then she remembered another piece of litany. It came back, unbidden and whole.

The simplest option is always the best—
The least likely to go wrong.
Never be complicated.
Keep the variables to a minimum.
Stay clean and fast.

To come out here, to hole up in one of the eel fishers' huts, Antonio would have had to have brought in supplies, probably by boat. Which would have been possible, but far more likely to go wrong. And way too risky and exposed once he had Kristin. And he would have had to stash the car somewhere, or get rid of it. Enzo said it hadn't been found, at a station or airport or burned out or abandoned. So unless it was in someone's garage, which was unlikely because it would mean he was working with someone, which she was almost certain he would avoid—*Each shall see and hear according only to his need*—he must still have it. Which meant he would have chosen somewhere where he could hide it on-site. Not a marsh. Somewhere with a barn or an out-building and reasonable access to a road, to get Kristin in. And himself out.

Or perhaps not.

She realized suddenly that she'd understood, from the very beginning, from the second she'd seen the photo on that girl's phone, that this time he did not plan on escaping. That there would be no more disappearing like smoke. For either of them.

"*Va tutto bene?*"

Anna did not realize she had stopped. Enzo's hand was on the small of her back. He asked again if she was OK. The temptation to say no was almost overwhelming. Instead she nodded, and started climbing again, following the caretaker who was now nothing more than footsteps above them.

As they came out onto the top of the campanile, Enzo registered the fact that Anna Carson didn't look well. Her face had paled and pinched in on itself. The cheap sweater was too big for her. The neck coddled her chin and the sleeves came down over her hands, cuffs sticking out from the equally cheap black coat she'd bought. He reminded himself to ask her where she'd dumped Kristin's things—the down jacket and red pack and Graziella Farelli's wallet. It probably wouldn't be difficult to get them back.

Below, in the car park, it had been still, but up here a breeze was kicking. Enzo pulled a glove off, reached into his pocket for the binoculars that had come equipped in the car, and handed them to Anna. She took them without saying anything, looped the strap over her head, and pushed her hair out of her face. The light was clear and harsh, and for the first time Enzo noticed the lines at the corners of her eyes and mouth. Half a century had left its mark on her, after all. It wasn't unbecoming, just a blueprint of her life.

The abbey was surrounded by what, in the summertime, must be a lush windbreak of trees. Beyond that, the land was barren. When Anna had suggested coming here, Enzo had honestly thought that it was probably pointless, and had only agreed— told her it wasn't stupid—because he hadn't had a better idea, and couldn't stand the idea of just sitting around and waiting for Pallioti. Now he realized that she had been right. It was better than any map.

You could see for miles. In another season, the occasional lines of trees might screen drives or tracks or back roads or buildings. Now they were nothing but thin gray fretwork against the faded greens and duns of the fields. To the east, canals spread in a broken network of veins across the marshes. Anna held the glasses in that direction for barely a minute, then swung around and looked inland.

The caretaker had gone back into the staircase. Enzo could hear him scrabbling like a mouse in the wall as he fiddled with whatever it was he was doing. He moved to the balustrade beside Anna, trying to understand what, exactly, she was looking for, and even as he thought it, knew what her answer would be. That she had no real idea—just something, anything, that might feel like Antonio.

"Pomposa," she'd said this morning, putting her coffee cup down. "His grandfather used to take him there when he was a boy. They could hear the bells, on the farm. Antonio thought it was the most beautiful place in the world."

His nonno had been right, Enzo thought. Perhaps it wasn't superlative, but it was extraordinary. A lightship built, not for boats, but for souls. A calling to God here in this empty no-man's-land between earth and sea. For the first time he wondered if Antonio Tomaselli had a soul after all, and, if so, what had happened to it.

"There."

Without lowering the glasses, Anna reached out and touched his sleeve.

"What?"

She was looking due southwest over a particularly barren stretch of fields beyond the road they had come in on. Enzo could only see a few tracks, a black lace of trees against the silver sky, and the metallic line of a stream or small river threading its way through the irrigation ditches. Then he got it. The nothing Anna was pointing toward was actually a cluster of buildings, low and pale and nearly lost in the grays of winter.

When he took the binoculars, they jumped like pop-up cards. Enzo could see the cube of a farmhouse, and an outbuilding that stretched beside it. There was a single large tree. No sign of any cars. Or for that matter, any life at all. He followed the track back. It curved and almost disappeared, lost in the dead uncut grass before it met a one-lane secondary road that ambled toward nowhere.

There were no telephone poles near the property, which meant no power. Which meant the farm was not in use—at least not much. Even if a generator had gone in, they were too expensive to run full-time, except possibly as storage for a larger operation somewhere nearby. Enzo couldn't see well enough to tell whether the buildings were in good repair or not, if there were holes in the roofs or shutters hanging from the windows. He lowered the glasses.

"What makes you think so?"

Anna shrugged. She was staring intently toward the tiny fading outlines.

"Abandoned," she said. "The outbuilding—for the car. Close enough to a road that he could get in and out without too much trouble. The drive's long, and there's nothing else around. Look."

He did. She was right. There wasn't another building within what had to be a mile.

"There are a couple of other places that are possible. Maybe. Over there."

She pointed north toward a bigger road. The roofs of several cars flashed in the hard light. A village, probably not more than a cluster of houses and a post office, squatted off toward the sea.

"Maybe," Enzo agreed. "But a bigger road means too many cars. And houses. Too many places to run if you got away."

Anna looked at him and nodded.

"Would Kristin fight?"

Enzo dropped his voice to a murmur. The caretaker hadn't come out, but he'd stopped scrabbling, which meant he'd either left, or was hovering just inside the stairwell desperate to know why it was that the police had called on a Tuesday morning in February demanding access to the campanile and were now standing scanning the surrounding countryside like bad caricatures of spies. Anna nodded again.

"If she can," she said. "Once she realizes—what's going on."

Both of them knew, she meant once she realizes this is no lover's bolt-hole. Once he stops sleeping with her, or at least making love to her. Or even stops being nice. But neither of them said it. Enzo saw a flicker of pain cross Anna's face, and was amazed all over again at how impervious love was to reason. And time. And even self-preservation—all the parameters of what was generally considered life.

He raised the binoculars again and took one last swing across the empty landscape.

"I think it's the place. I'm probably wrong," she muttered. "It's just." She shrugged. "A feeling. And it's not more than a couple of miles away from his grandparents', as the crow flies."

"Is that important?"

"I think so."

Enzo didn't look at her as she spoke, but kept scanning for buildings, tracks, they might have missed.

"I told you, he used to—Antonio, when he was little," Anna said. "He and his grandpa used to walk up to the top of the hill where you could see the campanile and listen for the bells. At sunset." Enzo could feel her looking at him. "I think he'd want to hear them again," she said finally. "I think that would be important."

The remark annoyed him, although he wasn't sure why. He stared through the glasses for a few more minutes. Then he dropped them onto his chest and zipped up his coat.

"Come on," he said. "Let's go."

〜

They drove north first, following the bigger road they had come in on, branching down single lanes and inevitably dead-ending at well-kept, or not so well-kept, groups of buildings. A barn, a house, a shed. Sometimes there was a barking dog and curtains at the windows. Sometimes not, but all of them were obviously inhabited. And not by Antonio. There wasn't as much as a whiff of a black BMW.

Since the car hadn't turned up anywhere, Enzo, like Anna, figured Antonio still had it. If he didn't, he'd had to have gotten ahold of a new one, and that probably meant he had an accomplice—somebody supplying him, covering for him, planning with him. And what that meant—Enzo didn't even want to think about what that meant. A lone kidnapping lunatic was one thing. A pair, or God forbid, a group, of kidnapping lunatics was entirely another. *Il passato scompare, viene poi di nuovo, come la luna.* The past disappears, and comes again, like the moon.

He thought they might have gotten lucky once, when the track they were following crested a rise and ended up in a semicircle of abandoned sheds with an old cottage crouched behind them. But a second look revealed holes in the roofs, collapsed walls, and no sign of habitation beyond the snow-dampened remains of a bonfire and a pile of rusting beer cans. Finally they turned around and went south.

The first road they found themselves on was small and narrow enough. The one they branched off on was barely one lane, little more than a track, the tarmac cracked and falling away at the sides so severely that in a few years it would be gone altogether. If Enzo had needed more proof than the lack of power lines that the farm Anna had latched onto was abandoned, this was it. It probably wasn't even used for storage. Tractors, trailers, all the paraphernalia that went with growing and harvesting, had not been coming up and down here with any regularity. They wouldn't have tires left if they did. He swerved for a pothole and nearly went into a ditch.

Neither of them had spoken since coming back past Pomposa. Anna was staring straight ahead, chin sunk into the neck of her sweater, hands clutched in her lap, chewing at her lower lip, which was already chapped. Enzo slowed almost to a crawl, watching the sides of the road for the entrance of the track that would serve as a drive, and for anything else. When he saw it, he braked hard and Anna jerked against the seat belt.

"What? What is it?" she asked, getting out of the car.

Enzo, who had leapt out almost before the car had stopped, waved her back.

"Please," he snapped, "don't come any closer. Go and get back in the car."

She stood still, but ignored the second part of the order, watching as he crouched on the edge of the crumbling pavement, staring at what looked, on first glance, like an empty, frozen verge. Then she saw what he'd seen. Tire tracks. Wide ones, from a fairly big vehicle. They were deep, meaning it had been parked here for some time.

"When did it last snow?" Enzo looked back at her. "Has it snowed since you've been here?"

Anna nodded.

"The first night. Sunday. But out here, I don't know. It can be different."

Enzo stood up. He walked a wide circle. A business card with, say, a name and phone number on it, dropped in the ditch would be a little too much to hope for. But a cigarette butt might not be. A gum wrapper. There wasn't one. And of course, he could be wrong. Kids could come out here to smoke dope and make out and drink themselves silly every weekend. But there were no condoms or cheap vodka bottles in the dead grass— and they'd definitely leave cigarette butts.

The tracks were recent. There had been slight melt, some sun when the car had parked here, and the wind had not yet broken down the ridges. If he knew more, if he was a real motor head, he might even have been able to tell what kind of tires they were—Pirellis, or Firestones, or whatever. He would take a bet on the car, though. It had been something very heavy. Longish.

Probably four door. Like, for instance, a big black BMW sedan. Enzo frowned.

He walked down the road slowly, got about thirty yards before he found the entrance to the track, and stopped. It was rutted, and deep, and had recently thawed enough to be muddy. Which might prove there was a God after all. Because the footprints were dead clear. Someone had walked down here, recently.

Enzo crouched and looked more closely. There were tire tracks, too. Recent ones. Motor head or not, he'd put money on the fact that they were the same tires, from the same car that had parked back down the road. He stood up, reached for his cell phone, then stopped.

"Let me see your shoes."

"What?" Anna was standing behind him.

"Let me see your shoes!"

She looked at him, confused, almost started to laugh, then registered the look on his face, and put her foot out. She wore expensive American running shoes. Enzo didn't even need to lift them up to know that the tread was completely different from the shoes—or more likely, winter boots—that had made the tracks on the drive. He tried to remember if Anna had been wearing running shoes the night before. She had. She'd dropped almost silently through the hatch in the butcher's shop, and when she'd kicked him, catching him just once in the shin before he got her on the ground, it hadn't hurt. The realization that she hadn't lied about where she'd been yesterday brought a pang of relief. Then something else.

"How big are Kristin's feet?" he asked. "Are they bigger than yours?"

Still watching him, Anna shook her head.

"No," she said. "They're a size, maybe a little more, smaller. Why?" she asked a second later. "Do you think she—?"

"No."

Enzo was looking at the drive again, at the tire tracks, and the footprints, which were definitely smaller than his own, but larger than Anna Carson's. He turned around and took her by the shoulder.

"Get in the car," he said, hustling her down the road. "Go get back in the car. Now."

On the way back to Ferrara, Enzo figured he broke just about every speed limit in Reggio, from the back road ones, to the motorway, to the old city street that led to the hotel parking. Anna Carson said nothing the whole way. Once or twice, he glimpsed her, out of the corner of her eye, studying her shoes, trying to understand what he'd seen.

At the hotel Enzo parked abruptly, and was surprised to feel relieved at the sight of another set of Florence plates on another immediately recognizable unmarked police car. Taking Anna by the arm more roughly than he intended to, he pulled her out of the car and trotted up the hotel steps, pushing the sleek glass door into the lobby and causing it to jam because he was too impatient to wait for it to slide open automatically.

Pallioti met Enzo halfway. So it was not until they had nearly run into each other that Enzo realized that he was not alone. That Pallioti, too, had a woman with him—a tall, statuesque blonde wearing jeans and a bright red parka with a fur collar who sat with a coffee tray in front of her, looking as if she had recently been crying.

Enzo had no idea who she was. Right now, he didn't care. Still hanging onto Anna's arm, he turned away from her, and said to Pallioti, "I think we've found it. A farmhouse out toward Pomposa. We need to check it out, see who owns the property, how it's registered. There's no power. If he's out there, he may have a generator. And there's a problem."

Pallioti said nothing. He stood with his head bowed, listening.

"A car drove in," Enzo went on, dropping his voice to something barely more than a murmur. "Recently. Just one. Something fairly big, probably sometime after noon on Monday when it was warmer—thawed enough to leave tracks. Whoever it was sat and waited by the road before. For some time, by the looks of it, so I doubt it was Tomaselli. I think the driver walked in first, probably looking around. Doing a recce. There were footprints. Either a small man's or a large woman's. Then they went back to the car and drove in. Only one set of tracks, so whoever it was is still in there. Meaning either Signor Tomaselli has a friend. Or we have another hostage."

"Yes," Pallioti said quietly. "I know."

Hedwige Aarlheissen had flung open the front door the moment he pulled into the drive, causing him to wonder if she'd been standing behind it since she'd called and told him Barbara Barelli was missing.

Getting out of his car Pallioti had seen at once that the serene doe-eyed Amazon he'd met less than twenty-four hours earlier had vanished. In her place was a haggard, teary woman who had obviously slept—or, he suspected, not slept—in the clothes she was wearing. Her black trousers were badly creased. Smudges of something, makeup probably, darkened the collar and shoulder of her cream silk shirt. She'd turned and led him into the family room without speaking.

The dinner party had obviously taken place, and been only marginally cleared away. Serving plates with bits of food clinging to them were piled by the sink. Place mats, coasters, and scrunched-up napkins littered five of the places set at the glass dining table. The sixth place, at the head, was untouched, its napkin still rolled in a silver ring. Tears welled in Hedwige's huge eyes. She wiped her nose with the back of her hand.

"Like I told you on the phone," she said. "She went off yester-day. About a half hour after you left. I thought she'd be back. I didn't know what else to do. You said to call if—"

Pallioti nodded.

"I think, perhaps," he said. "I had better make us some coffee. Then you can tell me exactly what happened."

Pallioti was not good with things mechanical at the best of times. He had approached the gigantic Nespresso machine that crouched on the countertop with genuine trepidation. Hedwige had murmured something about changing out of these things and taken herself upstairs, leaving him to peruse the terrifying display of dials and levers. He'd finally pushed and pulled several of them, then found a bottle of grappa in the glass-fronted bar behind the dining table as he listened to the sounds of running water and footsteps overhead. He'd been quite proud of the fact that, by the time she came back down in fresh jeans and sweater, her face as scrubbed as a schoolgirl's, he'd produced two decent cups of espresso. A hefty shot glass of grappa accompanied hers.

Hedwige had looked at him gratefully, then sunk down on the sofa, cradling her cup. Pallioti sat opposite her in a leather arm-chair so large and squashy it threatened to swallow him whole.

"Now, Signora Aarlheissen," he said.

"Hedwige. Please. Signora Aarlheissen is my mother. I haven't spoken to her in twenty years." She glanced at Pallioti over the rim of her cup. "She didn't take well to having a gay daughter."

Pallioti nodded.

"All right, Hedwige. I would appreciate it if you would simply tell me the truth. Or at least as much of it as you know. It will save us a lot of time, which, just now, is one of the things we don't have."

She bowed her head. Blond hair fell over her eyes. Hedwige pushed it away with her free hand, then said, "If she knew, Bar-bara would kill me."

Pallioti had wondered if he really needed to point out that Barbara Barelli did not know—at least for now—and that if Hedwige did not tell him, the chances were fair to good that Antonio Tomaselli would kill her. Apparently not, because she looked at him and nodded.

"All right," she said. "It all began, I don't know, about five years ago, I suppose."

Pallioti frowned.

"What began, Signora?"

"This—" She was agitated enough to overlook the "Signora." "This whatever it is that scumbag has on her."

The words had taken Pallioti by surprise. He put his cup on the coffee table and leaned forward.

"You are telling me that Antonio Tomaselli has something, on Dottoressa Barelli, his lawyer?"

Hedwige nodded.

"And what makes you think this?" he asked.

"I don't think it," she snapped. "I know it."

"Yes," he murmured. "Of course. I'm sorry. Please go on."

"Well, about four years ago, the way she treated him changed. It became almost as if, I don't know. Almost as if she was afraid of him. Besides, if it hadn't been true, she'd never have agreed about the farm. Never. Although that was later. About two years—I don't know—maybe eighteen months ago. And the weird thing is—" Hedwige looked at him and blinked, her eyes welling up again. "She hates him. I mean I knew she never liked him. But Barbara had a thing. Guilt, whatever the fuck. About the Red Brigades. She bought into that crap, about what they did being society's fault, whatever the fuck that means. So, yes—she defended him. But she never liked him. And now she hates him. I mean really hates him. I kept saying to her, 'drop him, then. Find someone else to represent him.' But she wouldn't."

Wouldn't or couldn't? Pallioti wondered. And what on earth, he asked himself, could Antonio Tomaselli have on Barbara Barelli? And how—given that while he was in prison she would have been his main conduit to the outside world—had he gotten it?

He'd ask her, if he ever got the chance. But, for now, the other tidbit Hedwige had just dropped interested him more.

"The farm, Hedwige?" he'd asked. "What are you talking about when you say 'the farm'?"

She'd picked up the grappa glass and downed half of it. Then uncurled herself from the couch. "Come on," she said. "I'll show you."

Launching himself, with some difficulty, out of the chair, Pallioti had followed her across the entryway to a closed door where she'd pushed a series of numbers on a security pad.

"Bar's never, officially, given me the passcode to her office." Hedwige glanced over her shoulder. "But for a really smart woman, she can be remarkably dumb. It's the date plus the distance of the first international race she ever won."

"Dotoressa Barelli?"

Hedwige nodded as she stepped inside and turned on the lights.

"Sprinter. Bar represented her country for three years, right after she came back from college in the States." She shrugged. "No reason why you'd know. She messed up at the Olympic trials, then quit when she started practicing law. But she was good," Hedwige added. "Almost very good."

Pallioti had the idea that "almost very good" would probably not have been anywhere near good enough for Barbara Barelli. And in some ways, worse than bad.

The room Hedwige showed him into was lined with bookcases and cabinets. A large desk sat in the center of it. A screen filled half the opposite wall.

"Video conferencing." Hedwige waved at the screen. "Without it Bar would have to traipse up and down the country and God knows where." She'd dropped to a squat and began fiddling with the combination lock on the front of one of the cabinets. "She didn't take a briefcase or anything like that yesterday. Just her handbag and her coat. That's why I was so sure she'd be back. I mean she does have to go quickly sometimes. She keeps an overnight bag packed—if someone's arrested or something. I just hope the damn papers are still here," she added.

Watching her, Pallioti wondered exactly how much time she spent breaking into her partner's world, and if Barbara knew about it and tolerated it, or was simply clueless when it came to what was obviously one of her lover's favorite pastimes. He would have used Hedwige as a safecracker any day. Her fingers moved with such dexterity, her head cocked so acutely, listening to the inner clicks of the combination lock, that she seemed almost as good as Enzo Saenz.

At the thought of Enzo he pulled his phone out and glanced at it, but there was no message. Pallioti didn't know whether to be reassured by that or not. He slipped it back into his pocket. When he looked up, Hedwige had the door open and was rifling through a series of manila files.

"Oh, thank God," she said. "It's still here. I was afraid she might have taken it with her."

She lifted a file out, crossed to the desk, which was as barren as Pallioti's own, and spread the contents in front of him. They appeared, on first glance, to be the deeds, sales, and purchase papers of a property. Pallioti glanced at Hedwige.

"Two years ago," she said, nodding. "When it started to look as though he really might get out, he called Bar and asked her to come and see him." She waved at the empty screen on the wall. "Usually she'd just talk to him through that, save her the drive. But he insisted she actually go to him. So she did." Hedwige shrugged. "I told you, she'd changed. At least as far as Antonio was concerned. Before she would have put her foot down, told him he could talk to her here. Not anymore. He says 'jump' and she says 'how high?' There's no one else on this earth she does that for. Including me. That's how I know," she added. "I told you. He has something on her. I can't think of any other reason."

"Did he call her, or did she call him? Yesterday, after I left?"

Hedwige shrugged.

"How the hell should I know? She locked herself in here. Then she just left. She barely even spoke to me."

"But you think she's gone to find him?"

Hedwige looked at him as if he was stupid.

"Don't you?"

Pallioti nodded. He did. Whatever she might have felt or not felt about the Red Brigades, Barbara Barelli had been extremely upset when she'd heard about Kristin Carson. Now he was very much afraid she had gone off to be an Avenging Angel.

"Anyway," Hedwige said. "About two years ago she came back after that visit. Upset."

"Upset, as in angry?"

Hedwige had thought about that for a moment.

"Yes," she'd said. "But not really. I mean, underneath, it was almost more as if she was—depressed. Resigned. As you can imagine, Barbara's not passive, but—in any case," she went on. "It was a couple of months later when I finally wheedled it out of her. Antonio had asked her to buy a house for him."

Pallioti raised his eyebrows. He knew that many lawyers were deeply committed to their clients—but there were requests, and then there were requests.

"And this is it?" He turned and looked more closely at the papers, at the plan and photographs attached.

Hedwige nodded.

"She set up a dummy company. She didn't want her name on it. I don't think it was expensive, it looks—I mean it's apparently almost derelict. A farm, abandoned when the family couldn't make it anymore, and for sale when they couldn't pay the taxes on the land. I think it's somewhere outside Ferrara."

Now the same photos were spread across the hotel room bed. Hastily shot, and slightly blurry, they showed a solid cube of a house and a long outbuilding fronting a yard shaded by a single tree. Overgrown fields stretched on either side. The photographer seemed to have been standing in the drive, which looked to be little more than a thin broken track. Both Enzo and Anna were quite certain it was the same property they'd seen from the top of the campanile at Pomposa.

When she heard about the tire tracks and the footprints, Hedwige's eyes welled. Her voice sank to little more than a whisper.

"Do you think he's killed her?"

She was sitting in the ugly armchair by the window, still wearing the red parka, which Pallioti guessed was Barbara's. Looking at her, Pallioti saw the girl underneath—a big rawboned teenager, too good at sports, at odds with her family, and perhaps even with herself. He wondered what meeting Barbara Barelli must have meant for her, and realized he knew the answer.

"No," he said firmly. "He has no reason to kill her," although he could think of plenty. "No," he repeated, and didn't add, *He's inked that in for the day after tomorrow.*

"Ciao," Kristin said. "Wait for the tone. Then tell me everything."

The first time Anna had heard the message, barely a week ago, she'd found it annoying. Its fake coyness. Its little-girl sexuality. Now it made her queasy. She blinked, and saw the wink of an emerald. A flash of gold in dirty water. And heard his voice. *"Ti possiedo. Óra, tu sei mia, per sempre."* It was a whisper, so close and tangible that for a second his body was on hers. Weight and heat. And the taste of earth.

After talking it over, they had decided not to wait until seven, decided they couldn't leave it up to Antonio to contact her. Or not. Looking up from where she sat at the hotel room desk, the phone pressed to her ear, Anna Carson met Enzo Saenz's eyes. All of them were watching her intently. Enzo, the woman Barbara loved, and the man in the black coat whose name Anna had trouble remembering. She nodded as the beep of Kristin's voice mail sounded, and felt the room waver and fade, become as insubstantial as this ghost of herself she kept coming face to face with.

"Antonio," she said. *"Ho sentito le campane da Pomposa."*

I've heard the bells from Pomposa.

After she cut the connection, the room felt somehow more crowded. They had come upstairs because they could hardly discuss Antonio and Barbara Barelli and Kristin standing in the lobby while half of Ferrara passed in and out of the sliding doors and drifted like pilot fish to the bar.

At first the conversation had been confused. Having barely skimmed the background Anna provided all those years ago, Pallioti had gone to see Barbara Barelli thinking she was merely Antonio's lawyer. That fact alone had been surprise enough for Anna. But on hearing it, she had understood immediately why Barbara had done it—had seen her leaning in the kitchen doorway, watching Nonna Franchi polish the shoes her father would be buried in, learning about the favors you did for the dead, and applying them to her friend Angela Vari. Who fell downstairs and was laid to rest at the chipped foot of the stone angel.

The shock had obviously been similar for Hedwige, who had looked at Anna with barely concealed dislike, as if she was the unwelcome piece of a puzzle that had finally slotted into place.

Anna had wanted to ask her how Barbara was. Had wanted

to ask if Hedwige had a photo in her wallet—so she could see the woman, and look for any trace of the girl she'd known. Barbara Barelli, with her long braid and her crooked teeth. And later her braces, and her swearing, and her smile. But she hadn't dared. She had no right to ask. She'd surrendered that. Shed it like a skin when she walked into the police station off Via Fani. Then shed it again almost a year and half later when, having exhausted Angela Vari, having hollowed her out—mined her life and heart and soul and bartered them for salvation—Anna had discarded her like a husk as she stepped between two federal marshals onto a plane at Ciampino, and watched out the little window as first Rome, and then Italy, grew smaller and smaller.

She got up and went into the bathroom. Locked the door and ran the taps, both of them, on full, and looked into the mirror, almost expecting to see nothing there.

Forty minutes later when her phone rings, Anna is sitting on one of the beds holding Kristin's bear. She feels Pallioti's hand on her elbow as she stands up. He still looks less to her like a policeman than an undertaker. Or a priest. With gold cuff links. And a gray tie, flecked with silver, as if he's going to a wedding.

"Remember," he says. And she nods.

As if he has to tell her. As if she doesn't know—have it running like rats through her head—along with all the other little verses from the Book of Hours.

The best lie is almost the truth. Just trimmed—to change the shadow it throws.

"Si, sono sola," she says after she pushes the green button on her phone. *"Cèrto, che sono sola, Antonio. Non ti ho mài mentito."*

Yes, I'm alone. Of course I'm alone. I've never lied to you.

Pallioti is surprised at how untouched her accent is, as if her own language has been sleeping inside her all these years. He watches Anna Carson as she bends her head, holding the phone. As she tells Antonio that she understands. That she's sorry. That she has thought about what he said, and knows she owes him, and that she will do anything.

It's not just her voice. Her face changes, too, and suddenly he realizes he's seeing Angela Vari. Surfacing like a drowned body. One that has rocked, and chafed, and finally slipped the weights that held it down.

"What do you want me to do?" she asks. "Just tell me. Just tell me, Antonio, and I'll do it. I'll do anything." She pauses. Then winces, and whispers, "I love you, too."

There is a silence. Pallioti feels his heart shrink. He does not need to hear what she says next. He already knows, they all know, what the price will be.

"*Sì. Sì,*" Anna Carson says. "*Cèrto.* I promise. I'll come. I'll be there, tomorrow. Alone."

"I can't do it. You do know that?"

It was a question, but didn't sound like it. Enzo looked at Pallioti and said nothing.

He was right, of course. They could no more let Anna Carson walk down that farm track than fly. Even if they did believe Antonio would do as he said—send Kristin out of the house, set her free as a bird the second Anna reached the front door. The second, he'd said, that she came close enough to kiss.

Anna had not been able to ask about Barbara without giving herself away, and Antonio had said nothing about her, one way or the other. Neither Pallioti nor Enzo seriously thought she was an accomplice, but the truth was they didn't know. Any more than they knew whether she was alive or dead or somewhere in between. Or even there. Technically the same could be said of Kristin. Anna's request for proof of life had been laughed off. *Don't you trust me, Carina?* Antonio had asked.

In the movies they would creep across the fields by night, have Anna distract him, and with the magical help of the Angels, or some other squad cobbled together and rushed to Ferrara in secret, ambush the farmhouse. Free Barbara Barelli and Kristin and whomever else might be in there without harming a hair on anyone's head.

But this was not the movies. It was the overlit hallway of a hotel in Ferrara some twenty miles from a frozen field in the middle of nowhere where an almost certainly armed, definitely angry, possibly crazy, man who had probably killed before at least once was holding one, and more likely two, women hostage in a derelict farmhouse.

Pallioti sighed. It was the very scenario he had hoped somehow to avoid. Hoped he could twist and turn his way out of. But it was no good. He and Enzo had come to the end, and both of them knew it. The irony was that they would be congratulated. They'd found Kenneth Carson's wife and his daughter. They'd established contact with the probable abductor, and determined his price. In short they had set the game in motion. Now it was time—and perhaps, to be honest, well past time—for them to step back and let the professionals do their job.

DIGOS, the special intelligence police, would be alerted. There would be a SWAT team and, because television expected it, and it would cover their asses afterward, a hostage negotiator. There would probably be helicopters. And combat uniforms. And night vision goggles. And stun grenades. And then, just before dawn, there would be silence.

Followed by a lot of noise. Most of which would be shooting.

The hall carpet was slightly stained, as if someone had tipped over a room service tray, spilled dregs of coffee, or possibly red wine. Somewhere near the elevator a lightbulb was buzzing. Enzo nodded.

"Are you going to call Rome directly?" The words felt sticky on his tongue.

Pallioti gave a sour little smile.

"*Cèrto.*" He shrugged, his shoulders jumping under the black coat that was so attached to him it was a second skin. A veritable cashmere pelt. "They'll know in five minutes anyway." He began to punch the number. "And insist on taking over. So," he asked, putting his phone to his ear, "what's the point in wasting time?"

In the end, Pallioti was able to arrange for them to be there. His clout, it seemed, extended that far.

Having Anna Carson on site might be necessary in any case, and he had argued that it was inhumane to make Hedwige sit by herself in a hotel room waiting to hear whether Barbara Barelli was dead or alive. Inhumane and not very intelligent. Barring locking her in a cell in the Ferrara Questura—an option the fat man seemed to have considered—it was better to have her on site where they could at least control her. Make certain, for instance, that she was not using the hotel switchboard—Pallioti had politely but firmly confiscated her cell phone—to wake any number of Barbara's legal colleagues, or the local television correspondents. The fat man had made his humming sound, and Pallioti suspected it was the logic of this argument rather than any appeal to the human heart that triumphed.

"We get in, we get out. We get it done before anyone knows it's happened. Then it never did," he announced.

That was how it was going to work. The farmhouse would be taken just before first light. Even Kenneth Carson would not know what was going on until shortly after breakfast, when his wife and daughter were returned to him. The happy family reunited. As for himself and Enzo, they would be observers only. Privileged to answer the questions asked of them, then shut up and step back and watch how it was done in the big, wide, real world.

Hearing that, Pallioti had barely suppressed a snort. Holding his tongue had been too much to ask.

"Well, old friend," he'd snapped, "in that case let's just avoid justice, and hope it all runs ticktock, like clockwork. Let's hope there's nothing nasty. No little corrections. No salt sprinkled in the wounds."

"Don't be petulant, Sandro," his friend had replied. "It doesn't suit you."

Anna and Hedwige now had their own rooms. Pallioti had been given some sort of penthouse apartment on the roof, either because of the sheer impressiveness of his credentials or the cut of his suit. Enzo figured it was fifty-fifty either way, but was leaning toward the latter. The more banal truth was they probably just had nowhere else to stick him. The hotel wasn't as big as it looked and there seemed to be some sort of mini-convention going on. When they finally went downstairs, the bar was so crowded that Pallioti took one look at it, shied like a nervous horse, and announced he was taking a walk. Enzo watched him through the glass doors. A freezing fog had lowered over the city. The fur coats scurried back and forth. Pallioti passed through the castle floodlights, black as a crow, and disappeared toward the cathedral.

Enzo had not been tempted to join him. He couldn't in any case. Someone had to keep an eye on Anna Carson. There was, after all, no guarantee that Antonio Tomaselli wouldn't decide not to wait until *domani*, but would simply come to Ferrara and fetch her. That he hadn't sensed a trap and would move first. He might have some trouble finding her, but he wouldn't have much. Especially if she called Kristin's phone and left a message telling him where she was.

The thought turned Enzo toward the elevator, and made him fidget on the ride up. He'd checked on Hedwige an hour earlier. She had ordered dinner and said she just wanted to watch TV. Propped against the headboard with the remote in her hand, the meal untouched on the desk, she'd looked at him with a vacant stare that suggested she wouldn't be seeing much of anything, except the movies that ran in her own head. He'd opened his mouth to say he was sure everything would be fine, then had thought better of it and backed quietly out of the room. Now he stopped outside Anna's door and listened. Then he raised his hand.

Anna heard the knock. It didn't occur to her for a moment that it was anyone but Enzo Saenz.

She had thought she wanted to be alone, and was surprised to find out she didn't. When she opened the door, he stood with his hands dug into his pockets. She had seen him without his leather jacket last night, but he looked more like himself with it on. As if it was attached to him, the way some people's sunglasses were attached to them. Propped on their heads even when it was raining or dark. She undid the chain, then stood back to let him in.

As she did, she caught a glimpse of herself in the big mirror over the hotel dresser. Ferrara's damp had turned her hair curly again and the dye had made not only it, but her eyes, a different color. Darker. Greener. For the first time in thirty years, an older version of Angela looked back at her.

"Have you called him? You might as well tell me."

Enzo had taken her BlackBerry, but there was a perfectly good landline sitting on the desk. Pallioti had ordered the switchboard to block outgoing calls, but you never knew. Everyone was open to persuasion. Anna shook her head. It was pointless to admit she'd thought about it.

"Where do you get them?" she asked suddenly. "Your eyes? I've never seen that color before. From your mother?"

"Father."

Enzo turned to the window, pulling the heavy curtains that were already closed tighter, then pulled at the edges, overlapping them as if he was afraid the fog might creep in like a vampire.

"Your nose, too?"

He nodded, his back still to her.

"Are they going to kill him?"

Enzo's hands stopped moving. The words felt like bubbles of glass. She hadn't meant to let them out.

"No," Enzo said. "Not unless he forces them to. They're not the BR. They don't carry out executions. All they want to do is get Kristin out."

"And Barbara."

"Yes, and Barbara. If she's there."

"She's there."

He turned around.

"How do you know? Did he say something? Something you didn't tell us? Think. It's important. It could—"

"Save people's lives?" She smiled, looking up at him from where she sat on the bed. "Are you telling me my speaking up could save someone's life? Is that what you mean?"

"No," he said. "No. I'm sorry."

"Antonio didn't say anything," she said a second later. "About Barbara. I just know. I don't want him to die," she added. "I never wanted anyone to die."

"No one will die," Enzo said. "We aren't Brigate Rosse." She looked at him. "This is different, I promise."

Her bark of laughter was sharp and unexpected.

"Don't," she said. "Don't make promises you can't keep."

Wednesday, February 10

It was half past three in the morning. Darkness hung across the fields and rose from the bend of the stream. Shreds of fog wavered at the edge of the headlights as they crept up the road.

They had passed barricades as soon as they left the larger two-lane highway—a series of sawhorses bearing the neon logos of an electricity company, and highway signs announcing NIGHT WORK ROAD CLOSED, and pointing toward a detour and apologizing for any inconvenience. There was even a number to call in case of complaints. Pallioti imagined an ancient black phone perched on an unmanned desk somewhere in the bowels of Rome ringing unanswered into the dark.

The men who waved them through wore overalls and jackets bearing the same logo, their faces barely visible under the hard hats, the earpieces they muttered into almost certainly not connected to a work crew. Or at least not the sort one might expect. A helicopter flyby had taken place a half hour earlier. It had been calculated that they could risk one, and was generally agreed it had been worth it. There were no lights visible in the farmhouse, but the infrared picked up bodies. Three of them in separate rooms. Two upstairs, one down. Which meant Barbara Barelli was alive. They already knew she was there. Casts had been taken just before midnight from the verge of the road. The tracks matched her tires.

Half a mile inside the barricades, Pallioti left his car as instructed. Then he, Enzo, Anna, and Hedwige were ushered into an electricity van. It rumbled down the road for five minutes before stopping. When the door opened, the man who climbed in did not introduce himself. He shook hands with Pallioti and Enzo, nodded at the two women, then moved to a control panel with a series of screens on it, and flipped a switch. A picture faded in, blurry and greened. They could see the house, its bottom row of windows shuttered, the top ones staring down onto the empty yard. A single tree stood to one side, its naked branches resting on the roof of the long, low building to the left. The man tapped it with his finger.

"Here," he said. "The barn. That's where we assume the cars are. From the plans we were able to get ahold of—they date back twenty years to when it was last lived in—there's no access from the house. So unless he's busted a hole in the wall, Tomaselli will have to come out the front door if he tries to get to a vehicle."

"What about the back?"

The man nodded at Pallioti and flipped another switch, bringing up a second screen that showed the back of the house.

"There's a door into what we assume is still the kitchen," he said. "There's no record of any work being done, so unless he's turned himself into a master builder, the plans we have are basically good. The stairs run up from the kitchen. The front door leads to an entryway between the two main rooms, kitchen right, sitting room left. We're guessing the women are upstairs. So we go in both doors at once. Three men each. Assuming the downstairs body is Tomaselli, the back team goes straight up and gets the women out, while the front team subdues our friend. Or vice versa." He shrugged. "Doesn't matter much. We have someone on the roof of the barn. Another two guys on the hill in front of the house, and two more below the berm of the stream behind." He turned around. "So it should be neat and clean. Everyone's getting into place about now. It's a little tricky because there's not much cover, but believe me, these guys know what they're doing. Give us a half hour, ladies," he added, smiling at Hedwige and Anna, "and we'll have your loved ones safe and sound."

He stood, gave a little bow, and ducked out the back of the truck. The driver slid from the front and took his place at the screens. Hedwige moved over beside him, mesmerized by the wavering green images that made the farmhouse and the tree and the barn look as though they were in outer space, or part of one of those villages flooded by reservoirs. As if water or sci-fi goo swirled around them instead of air. Pallioti followed the man out the door. A moment later Enzo Saenz followed him.

It was refreshingly cold after the stuffy interiors of the car and the van. Pallioti was standing on the narrow road. Ahead of them two more vans were pulled up, both bearing the power company's logo. Enzo wondered if they used it for all of these situations, or if they had others. Plumbing companies, or perhaps pest removal firms. He hoped there was a power line around here somewhere, in case anyone did come by. Or at least an underground cable.

Pallioti shivered inside his coat, flexed his gloved hands, and started down the road, heading for what was obviously the command vehicle. Enzo started to follow, then thought better of it, and turned back and opened the van door.

Hedwige was still sitting beside the driver, watching the screens intently, as if she could pull Barbara out of the house by sheer willpower. Anna sat on the hard bench that ran along the opposite side. She glanced at Enzo as he sidled past to bend between Hedwige and the driver, watching the screen over their shoulders. All at once the pictures flared—the yard, the farmhouse, and the twisted outline of the tree jumping like startled animals.

A swarm of dark figures, ant men, appeared from nowhere, running. Then, as the second team hit the back door of the farmhouse, the front door burst open. A man pushed a girl out. He had one arm around her neck. With his other hand, he held a gun to her head.

"Antonio."

Enzo heard the whisper behind him. At the same moment Hedwige started, gripping his arm. On the other screen, Barbara Barelli was being hustled out the back of the house, held by both arms and half dragged toward the edge of the picture. The front team of ant men had stopped dead and were backing toward the tree. As the man's mouth moved, shouting something at them, Enzo felt a blast of cold air. He spun around. The van door was open and Anna Carson was gone.

At first he couldn't find her. He looked left, right, up, and down the road. Then Enzo let his eyes sweep over the rutted darkness of the overgrown field that stretched toward the farm. She was already halfway across it, running hard. He leapt the irrigation ditch he had almost driven into the day before. Enzo was fit and twenty years younger, but Angela was fast.

She felt her blood pumping. Felt her heart and arms, her back and legs in every stride. The earth was frozen and stubbled. Her feet hit cracked ice, imprinted frost, but she kept her eyes ahead, focused on the fading dark. In the thrumming of her breath, she heard it over and over, and over again—*Antonio, Antonio, Antonio*—and knew she was running the race of her life.

Enzo felt himself struggling. He started to call, then decided not to waste the breath. She was hardly going to stop and he had no idea how many people were really creeping around these godforsaken fields carrying who knew what kind of weapons and grudges. He dug out an extra burst of speed from somewhere, and felt it pay off. Her figure was silhouetted now against the glow of lights trained on the farmhouse. Enzo pushed himself again, forced his feet to turn over faster, his thighs to burn. And thanked God, because she stumbled.

He caught her around the waist and lifted her off her feet. Then he slapped a hand over her mouth. She twisted like a snake, but Enzo held on. A second later she went limp. He lowered her feet to the ground, but didn't let go.

In front and slightly below them, they could see the farm lit up like some sort of bizarre film set. The men in black—there appeared to be four of them now—had stopped at the tree. Antonio was standing with his back to the wall of the house, far enough away from the front door and windows that he couldn't be reached. He had Kristin in front of him. She was gagged with what looked like a piece of duct tape. Her hands were cinched behind her back. Antonio had one arm around her neck and held a gun to her temple.

Anna let out a small moan.

"Sssh." Enzo tightened his hand. They were outside the lights. He had no idea who else was standing in the dark with them.

"Let her go, Signor Tomaselli, and no one gets hurt."

The call came from a megaphone somewhere beyond the tree. Antonio didn't move.

"Let Kristin go, and we can talk this out."

Enzo thought he saw Tomaselli smile at that one. He was sure he saw him shake his head.

"Where is she?" he shouted back.

"Where is who?" the megaphone asked.

"Angela!" Antonio bellowed into the dark. He grabbed Kristin tighter. "Angela," he screamed. "You promised me!"

Anna thrashed and kicked. Enzo felt his hand fall away from her mouth.

"Antonio!" she screamed. "Antonio! I'm here!"

At the sound of her voice, his head whipped around.

"You can let her go!" Anna shouted. "I'm here!"

As he peered into the dark, searching beyond the wall of lights, Antonio's arm loosened, and Kristin staggered forward. Released, she stumbled, then fell to her knees on the cobbles. But Antonio didn't seem to care. He dropped the gun, and turned away from her.

"Angie!" He stepped toward her voice. "Angela! Where are you?"

"I'm here," Enzo heard her say. She began to walk forward, and in that moment, he saw it.

Antonio had moved away from the farmhouse. He was peering into the darkness as the sniper rose from the barn roof.

Enzo threw himself forward. He caught her by the shoulders and spun her around as the shot went off.

She hears herself scream. Then she hears Enzo Saenz's voice. And feels his hands, pressing her head, hard, into his shoulder.

"Don't," he is saying. "Don't." It's a murmur in her ear, an instruction straight to her heart. "Don't look. Don't look."

He is holding her neck, cradling the back of her head, pushing her into his own body so she cannot see what is in front of them in the dead white circle of light.

"Remember him. Do it," Enzo Saenz says. "Do it now. For Antonio. Remember him the way you loved him."

And so she does.

She closes her eyes, screws them tight, and clings to the shoulders of his jacket, her fingers digging into the soft leather, and feels herself flying. Back past the beach at Ostia. Past the sand and the taste of salt, past *Marry me, Angela,* to the tiny cramped kitchen in Trastevere where sun spills into the scratched sink and they sit across from each other, her bare foot on his. While Enzo Saenz holds her, while he presses his chin to the top of her head, she flies past the campanile at Pomposa where she stands with all the summer world below her and Antonio's arms around her. She flies past the bedroom under the eaves, and the cleared pane of glass that bears the imprint of his hand. Past the Montagnola, and the Angels' Gate, and the ghosts of the old men under the street lamp in Via Vittoria, to August. To the prickle of orchard grass and the mingled buzz of bees and laughter and the tight, bursting skin of an apple that Antonio holds in his hand and stretches toward her as he smiles, dappled with light.

Epilogue

Monday, February 15th

PALLIOTI ALLOWED VALENTINE'S DAY, that most gruesome and unlikely celebration of lovers, to pass before he returned to Bologna. It only seemed fair.

Although, he had to admit, he was finding fairness a stretch these days. It didn't interest him much, or at least as much as he suspected it should. This, for instance, was essentially an ambush. Or perhaps, he thought, as he got out of the car and crunched across the expensive gravel, it wasn't. He found it hard to believe that a woman as intelligent as Barbara Barelli would be surprised to see him.

Antonio Tomaselli had held her against her will. He had threatened her with a gun, tied her up, and locked her in an upstairs room. That much was true. But it was also true that she had gone to the farm of her own free will, and that when Antonio opened the door and let her in, she had stepped over the threshold announcing not only that she knew Kristin Carson was there, but that she refused to leave without her. A fight had ensued. Tomaselli had won.

Pallioti did not know, when it came to it, if Antonio would have killed Barbara, or Kristin. He probably didn't want to. But then again, he probably hadn't really wanted to kill Aldo Moro, either. It was hard to know exactly what was in people's hearts.

Or what they would do when they could not get what they wanted—whether it was political recognition, thirteen comrades freed from jail, or one last chance with the woman they loved. Pallioti was sure Antonio Tomaselli had wanted that. The past returned and Angela Vari with it.

Like all attempts to unwind time, and every love story ever written, it was, he thought, that simple. And that complicated.

This time the bells ran through their full chime before anyone opened the door. When she did, Hedwige Aarlheissen was barefoot and, somewhat disconcertingly, wearing purple fuzzy leggings and a very long and equally fuzzy purple sweater. Pallioti thought she looked like a large moldy grape. As she waved him in, he heard Barbara call from the family room.

"Is it the wine order?"

"Sadly not."

Barbara looked up at the sound of his voice. She was stretched on the couch, a book in her hand. Giorgio Bassani. Very fitting. *The Garden of the Finzi-Continis*. Pallioti wondered if she was merely suffering from a fit of nostalgia, or if the text held a deeper and more immediate resonance for her. He smiled.

"Dottoressa."

Barbara nodded and said nothing, her eyes following him as he came in, turning down the coffee Hedwige offered. The truth was, he would have loved an espresso. But this wasn't that kind of visit.

"I was wondering," he said to Barbara, "if we might have a talk?"

She dropped her eyes, as if she was hoping he would go away, or had come for something else. When she looked up and saw him still standing there, she put the book down and nodded. Barbara Barelli swung her legs off the sofa slowly. She was barefoot. A thin gold chain glittered around her left ankle.

"I think," she said, "it would be better if we went into my office."

Pallioti felt Hedwige's eyes on his back as he followed Barbara across the entryway and into the locked room.

Barbara Barelli closed the door. Then she looked around her office as if it was unfamiliar to her—the big desk, the wall-mounted screen, the rows of cabinets and shelves. The blind over the window was half lowered. She didn't raise it. Instead she gestured Pallioti to what was obviously the client chair.

"Please," she said, and sat down behind her desk.

Pallioti let a few seconds of silence beat between them while she gathered herself.

"How did you know?" she asked finally, folding her hands on the blotter.

"The magazine article."

She nodded.

"The publication," he said, remembering the files he had picked apart over the weekend. "The American one, what is it called—"

"*Runner's World*. April 2006." Barbara swallowed. "Yes," she said. "You see, I went to college, in the United States, on a track scholarship. So I still get the American edition. You know, to keep up."

Pallioti nodded.

"It was—" Barbara cleared her throat. "There was an article. Because New York was coming up, the marathon, and one of the contenders had been operated on by a Dr. Kenneth Carson. He does miracles, apparently. On a routine basis. So they did a profile on him. And there she was."

Pallioti folded his hands and leaned back in his chair.

"There she was," he said.

The conversations he'd had with Anna, and with the US Federal Marshals, in the course of the weekend had yielded startlingly different results. For their part, the marshals insisted—and their statistics agreed—that they had never lost a member of the Witness Protection Program, provided the witness in question obeyed the rules. The cardinal one was no contact. No anonymous postcards, or wordless phone calls. No backward glance. No last look.

If the break with the past was clean, they kept people safe. If, on the other hand, there was the tiniest chink of light, the tiniest tipping of the hat to the past, then all bets were off. So, according to them, since Antonio Tomaselli had clearly known all about Anna Carson, it must have been her fault. She must have done something, however unwitting, to alert him to who and where she was.

But she hadn't. In the last five days Anna had not wanted to say much of anything to anyone, even Enzo Saenz, but she insisted on that. She had kept her locket, with the picture of her father and mother in it, and she had kept running. But that was all. And in the end, Pallioti thought, it had been enough.

"Go on," he said.

Barbara shook her head. She passed a hand over her eyes and looked up at him.

"I couldn't believe it, when I saw it. Her. Or, I don't know, maybe I could. I never really felt that handful of sand, or whatever it was we buried that day, was Angie. I know it sounds strange, but I never felt her leave. You know?"

Pallioti nodded. He did know. He remembered quite clearly the moment his mother died. He had not been allowed upstairs in to her room, but had been sent out in to the garden and told to play. Standing on the clipped grass, his toy army dutifully arranged at his feet, he had felt suddenly as if a vacuum had been attached to his stomach. As if all of his blood and his heart and organs had been sucked out, leaving him weightless, with nothing holding him to the earth.

"But Antonio." Barbara shook her head. "Antonio did believe it. And it devastated him. He was angry of course, or disappointed—I don't know—about what she did. About what he called her betrayal. At least at first. Later I think he almost found it a relief. To stop. Tell the story. Pay his dues. Whatever. I'm not sure he ever knew what he was doing, really, back then, or why, exactly. He kept talking about bread and roses, but when I asked him, he could never tell me what it meant. I think perhaps he wanted to explain that to Angela, or hoped someday he'd have the chance. I don't know." She shook her head. "But I do know that he loved her. I don't even like him. I never did." Barbara looked down at her hands, still folded on the blotter. "But I will give him that. He loved Angela. I think perhaps she was the only thing he ever did truly love, except for his grandparents, and his brother—and in some warped way he thought the future would be better for them, I don't know, if Aldo Moro was made to stand trial. That it would be some kind of correction. Justice."

Pallioti grimaced. There was that word again.

Barbara sighed.

"Yes. Whatever the hell that is," she agreed. "In any case, when he heard that Angie had been killed, it broke his heart. I saw him first at the funeral. My parents, well, my father, was still living in Ferrara then, so I heard and I went and I felt sorry for him." She looked up at Pallioti. "I represented him, yes, because in some way, I suppose, I did understand what they'd done, even if I didn't agree with it. And because someone had to. But I did it mostly because it was something I could do for Angie. I remember, once, right after her father died—" She shrugged. "It doesn't matter. The point is, I thought she would have wanted me to. Help Antonio. It kept me close to her. I loved her, too, you know."

Pallioti nodded.

Barbara smiled. "Odd, isn't it? That Antonio Tomaselli and I should have that in common." She looked down at her hands. "Anyway," she went on when she looked up again, "I suppose I wanted to be near him because he was the last living trace of her on this earth. Or so I thought."

"Until you saw the magazine?"

"Until I saw the magazine."

"And you showed it to Antonio?"

She nodded.

"Yes," she said. "I showed it to Antonio."

Barbara Barelli put her face in her hands.

"I don't know if I wanted to share it with someone," she said. "Or if I did it for him. Or if I thought I was doing it for her. I honestly don't know." She dropped her hands and looked at Pallioti. "I do know I didn't think anything like this would happen. You have to believe that. I just thought, in his place, I would have wanted, no, I would have needed to know." She shook her head. "And I thought—"

Thought, what? Pallioti leaned forward. "Dottoressa," he said. "You are a lawyer. And as such your first duty is to the court. You must have understood, surely, what had happened? That Angela Vari had been made a protected witness? And what that meant?"

Barbara Barelli nodded. She opened a drawer, pulled out a tissue, wiped her eyes, and nodded again.

"I told him he couldn't tell anyone. Couldn't even whisper. That I was only telling him so he'd know she was all right. I thought Angie would have wanted me to. I thought I was doing it for her."

Pallioti stared at her. It always amazed, and often terrified, him that highly intelligent people could be so stupid. Especially when it came it love.

"I think—" Barbara ran her hand through her hair. "I didn't understand at the time—it didn't even occur to me, but I think it made him even angrier with her. That when he found out she was still alive, had been alive all this time, he felt doubly betrayed. Wanted to punish her—not for Moro, for turning him in—but because she never let him know. That she was still alive—that even if they never saw each other again, he wasn't alone in the world. That she was out there somewhere. And that loving him hadn't gotten her killed. He felt so guilty about that. As if he'd killed her himself."

Barbara looked at him and shook her head.

"I just didn't understand," she said. "Not really. I felt sorry for him, but I never tried to know him. He was my client, and I didn't even talk to him. Not really. Then, of course, when you showed up and told me, I understood at once. How he knew the girl's name. It was all in the article, even about how the first wife, the girl's mother, had been killed. It's why Angie married him, the surgeon, isn't it?" Pallioti did not have an answer to that, but Barbara Barelli did.

"It is," she said. "Not because he operated on her knee, but because his little girl had lost her mother. Just like Angie did." She bit her lip. "I can only imagine how Antonio must have used that."

Pallioti nodded. A sour feeling twisted in his stomach at the memory of the emails, how the hook that reeled Kristin in had been baited and set with her mother's death.

"How is Kristin?"

Pallioti was tempted not to answer the question, to snap, "Why should you deserve to know?" then told himself not to be petty.

"Fine," he said.

And it was true. The young were resilient. With help they would bend and not break. So far Kristin had bent admirably, and she would have plenty of help, mostly from her father, with whom she had reclaimed her relationship. It was hard not to think that was all the easier, all this newfound understanding between father and daughter, because Anna Carson—or Angela Vari, as he suspected she would now prefer to be called, and who had never had much help—was no longer resilient, but in a military hospital outside Prato being treated for advanced shock and exhaustion. Which was apparently the current lingo for a broken heart.

After a brief meeting with her husband, she had chosen to stay in Italy and not return to the United States until she was better. Whatever that meant. Pallioti had watched Kristin and Kenneth Carson board a plane hand in hand on Friday morning. Neither father nor daughter had looked back. Kenneth Carson was not a forgiving or an understanding man. He did not deal in shadows, or understand lies, or the past. And finally her stepmother had made it possible for Kristin to get what she had always wanted, her father's undivided attention. Pallioti suspected that from now on the Carson family would be composed of two.

Barbara Barelli opened her mouth and closed it again. Both of them knew she had been about to ask about Angela, and both of them knew he would not have told her.

He had been present during Angela's debriefing over the weekend, and had visited her yesterday with Enzo Saenz, who had taken some long overdue time off. Pallioti was almost as worried about him as he was about Angela. His self-contained world had been pierced. He did not know it yet, but Pallioti understood that Enzo Saenz would never know solitude again, now that he had been introduced to loneliness.

He looked at Barbara Barelli.

"The car," he said. "I take it you won't make me waste the time tracing the holding company that owns it?"

"No." She shook her head. "Antonio asked me to buy the house. That was his price for staying quiet about what I'd told him. And then the car. When he got out. I set up another dummy company—" She waved her hand. "It's all perfectly legal—"

Perhaps, Pallioti thought, in the strictly practical sense of the word. At least as far as the purchases went. But the court of public opinion would be something else altogether. Not to mention the fact that knowingly compromising a witness would, at the very least, mean Barbara was suspended while she was investigated before being stripped of her right to practice. There might well be additional criminal charges—for lying to the police, not cooperating in an ongoing investigation—depending on who was feeling vindictive.

It was a fair guess, given the causes she had chosen to defend, that Barbara had enemies. Probably powerful ones who would be all too happy to get a dig at her. And none of that even began to touch on her moral obligation to her client and his safety. To say it had been compromised was something of a sick joke.

He stood up. What he was about to say gave him no pleasure. Barbara Barelli was a gifted lawyer. The causes she fought for had been the right ones.

"Will you write the letter?" he asked. "Or would you like me to?"

She looked at him for a moment, then folded her hands on the blotter again and shook her head.

"I'll do it," she said. "This afternoon. I'll submit myself for judicial investigation, and relinquish my license. Immediately. Regardless of the outcome."

Pallioti nodded. Then he turned on his heel and started toward the door. He was about to turn the handle when she said, "Dottore?"

He turned around. Barbara Barelli stood up. Her fingertips rested on the blotter. Her dark hair drifted on her shoulders. Looking at her he remembered again how much he had liked, and even admired, her.

"I wondered," she asked, "of course, I wasn't there, but—have you seen the autopsy report?"

Pallioti smiled. There was no humor in it at all.

"The real one?"

She nodded.

A piece had come out in the papers, barely more than a paragraph telling yet another pathetic story about the end of the Red Brigades. Detailing how, after his release from prison, Antonio Tomaselli had been unable to adjust. Had struggled first to find a job and then to build a life, and had finally given up on both when he retreated to an isolated farmhouse outside Ferrara where he had died in an accident involving a gun. Pallioti looked at his watch.

"It should be on my desk," he said, "when I get back to the office."

"Will you tell me what it says? Just for the record?"

His mouth twitched in an unpleasant smile.

"Just for the record."

Pallioti let himself out of the office. Hedwige Aarlheissen was in the kitchen. She leaned against a counter, watching him, then turned away as he left.

⁕

Once again the fat man had been as good as his word. It was strange, Pallioti thought, but there really was a code of honor among thieves. Or perhaps it was something less admirable even than that. And more dangerous. An irreducible part of the arrogance that led to the crime in the first place. He had read once that the spy Kim Philby had kept a framed photograph of a mountain in Russia on the wall of his office the entire time he worked for British Intelligence. The idea made him smile. It was well known that people never really looked at photographs.

He had, though. Last night. He had spent until the early hours of the morning studying the pictures of Angela Vari's funeral. They had worried him from the beginning. It was some time before he finally understood what he was seeing.

Now he tipped them out and spread them across his desk. As

everyone knew, the early hours of the morning were notoriously unreliable. He wanted to be certain, in the cold light of day.

It was not just the number of photos, it was the angles they had been taken from. Far too many. He had realized at once that there had been more than one police photographer in the cemetery. Now he understood why. They were not merely keeping a record. They were setting up evidence. He couldn't spot the shooter crouched behind a crypt. Or shooters—there would surely have been more than one. Or the shoulder holsters worn by the prison guards, whom he now doubted were prison guards at all, but he understood why they had stayed so well back, why they'd taken Antonio Tomaselli's chains off, hadn't even handcuffed him. Not out of respect, but because they'd hoped he would run.

But no one had taken the bait and come to try and set him free. Mara was dead, and the others were locked up, or too smart, or simply didn't care enough anymore. During the war it had been a point of pride among the Partisans that they rescued their own, never handed them over to the enemy. But as Barbara said, Antonio had never quite been one of them, had never quite belonged. To anyone. Except Angela Vari.

Which didn't mean he wouldn't do something very stupid. Take the opportunity of her funeral, for instance, to bolt. Make a dash, conveniently relieved of all restraints, through the crypts and monuments, and vanish into the city he knew so well.

If he had, he would have been dead within seconds. And the whole thing would have been caught on film. All asses amply covered. *Notorious Terrorist Attempts to Flee. Tragic Shooting Assures Safety of Population.*

They must have been crushed when he was too busy grieving, and too many civilians appeared, to carry out plan B—because there was always a plan B. He wondered what it would it have been. Merely knocking him to the ground and shooting him in the head? The priest probably wasn't even really a priest, or, if he was, he was one of ours with bulletproof armor under his vestments. They must have been furious, after going to all that trouble. After all, Angela had no family, how could they have guessed that the Pirottis and the Ravellis would notice that she was dead and insist on paying their respects. Or that Barbara Barelli would be visiting her father? Pallioti wondered if they would have shot her, too, if she got in the way. What did they call it these days? Collateral damage.

Barbara Barelli was right. He hadn't believed it, not really, deep down inside. Then he'd studied the pictures. Pallioti felt a physical wave of disgust so powerful he nearly staggered. He pushed the photos aside and turned to the envelope, the fat man's second little billet-doux he had received this morning.

He didn't know if this was a second autopsy report. He suspected not. Antonio was not Mara. He wasn't a founder of the BR, or a beautiful young woman who had become a media star when she busted her husband out of jail. And he did not have a wife or lover to be outraged, to organize vigils and light candles and call for vengeance for his assassination. He was just a two-bit conspirator, probably a killer. A dried-up terrorist reduced to manipulating teenagers. So Pallioti doubted they'd bothered. No one cared about Antonio Tomaselli. He wasn't worth a fake autopsy report. In fact Pallioti found himself half surprised they'd bothered with an autopsy at all. But they had. That was another puzzling thing about pictures. How often killers took them of their victims. He thought of all the film footage, all the photographs from the concentration camps.

There weren't many pictures in the envelope. He'd seen hundreds of death reports with more. But they were enough. The ones taken from the front were ugly. But not as bad as the ones taken from the back. Pallioti gave a slight shudder. The ammo used in sniper rifles made one hell of a mess. Which was why snipers liked them. If you lined up a good shot, you didn't want to have to take it twice.

As the accompanying notes confirmed, Antonio Tomaselli had been hit squarely in the back of the head. Pallioti wasn't too surprised to read that he'd been hit again just below the left shoulder, probably as he went down. Just for good measure. Just to show off. See if you can rupture the heart while you're at it. Not that it was necessary. The first shot had been a beauty— more or less blowing off the top of his skull.

There were a few scene photos, too, showing the diameter of the spatter marks, which were impressive. Antonio's head had all but exploded. From the looks of the body, he had been lifted off his feet, thrown forward, and had landed face down on the rutted cobbles, his hands outstretched. The gun, the one he'd dropped on hearing Angela Vari's voice, had been so far behind him it wasn't even in the photograph. No second weapon had been found on his body or in the house.

Pallioti had expected to feel sick. He had expected to need a drink, or fly into a rage. Had thought perhaps he would pick things up and hurl them against the wall, indulge in what his mother had called throwing his toys about. But he didn't. He didn't even feel the compulsion to call Rome and shriek down the phone at the fat man, who, either before or after he told him again that petulance didn't suit him, would doubtless remind him that they were all fighting the War on Terror.

Instead he walked to the window and stared down at the familiar view of the piazza, realizing that he ought to be tired. Or at least a little surprised. Barbara Barelli's words came back to him.

You couldn't survive if you really thought that the state—that your beloved polizìa even—might go around eliminating those they find inconvenient. Or just plain don't like. That they might do a little correcting when they think the courts have gotten it wrong.

He looked at the flags—the lily of Florence, the Italian tricolor that flew in front of the fancy new police building—and thought, we lie about what we love. To ourselves and to others. But mostly to ourselves. We lie about it because we are selfish and cowardly and human. And because, sometimes, when we were forced to see what we love for what it really is, we have to give it up.

He walked back to his desk, sat down, and unscrewed his favorite pen.

Fifteen minutes later, when he had finished writing, Pallioti made a copy of the single page on the machine in his closet. He put the original in an envelope and placed it in the center of his desk. Then he gathered up Antonio's autopsy report and the photographs the fat man had sent him, and slipped them, together with the copy, into a large manila envelope that he addressed to Barbara Barelli.

In the outer office Guillermo was bent over his computer. He glanced at his watch, then reached, without looking up, and pushed the intercom button to Pallioti's office.

"Just to remind you," he said, "you have a meeting at three with—"

"Cancel it."

Pallioti's voice was not much more than a murmur, but the tone caused Guillermo to stop typing. He was about to ask if he'd heard correctly when the line went dead. Guillermo looked at the closed door. He leaned back in his chair and felt his mouth go dry. A moment later the door opened and Pallioti came out carrying a large envelope and wearing his overcoat. Guillermo, without being quite sure why, got to his feet and stood as he left the office.

The day had turned windy and bitterly cold. Pallioti pulled on his gloves as he came down the steps.

I am resigning my position because I will not serve a state that kills people.

I am resigning my position because of my severe moral reservations.

I am resigning my position because we've become a murderous, lying, self-righteous shipload of shits I wouldn't trust a gerbil with and I'm sick of it.

Of the wording he'd toyed with, he preferred the last. Although, even in his present state of mind, he realized he couldn't say it. And to be fair, it wasn't entirely accurate. There were many policemen who were neither self-righteous nor liars, and who did their jobs as well as they could, more often than not with bravery and distinction.

A skin of ice slicked the cobbles in the piazza. The fountain hissed and spat, flinging its silver drops about like a child having a tantrum. A few carriages were pulled up near the taxi stand, the horses swaddled in blankets. Behind the glass, the restaurant was full. No one was standing under the loggia or sitting on its steps. Above him the flags snapped and clicked, keeping time as he crossed toward the flower seller's kiosk.

The buckets weren't out. It was too cold, they'd tip over in the wind. Inside the little pavilion, the air was warm and heavy with scent. The flower seller jumped up from his stool when he saw Pallioti. They had been friends for a long time.

"Dottore." He clapped his hands together. "What can I get you? The usual for the signora?"

The signora was not Pallioti's wife, he didn't have such a thing, but his sister. He was in the habit of taking Saffy flowers when he had dinner with her once a week, or went to Sunday lunch, or to a show or opening at her gallery. She was fond of tulips in the spring, and generally of roses. He shook his head.

"Something else," he said. "Today. Something special. White, probably. And that will get through the night. I'm going to a funeral tomorrow."

The flower seller made a face.

"My condolences, dottore," he said. "Not family, I hope?"

Pallioti shook his head.

"No," he said. "Not family."

They were burying Antonio Tomaselli in Ferrara, not far from where they had once buried Angela Vari. He didn't know who would be there. Antonio's father, a cripple, had died while he was in prison. His mother, from what Pallioti understood, was blind and frail and had for many years, ever since the death of Aldo Moro, whom she had considered a saint, claimed she no longer had a son. He doubted the fat man would show up, and wondered if he'd have the nerve to punch him if he did. Probably not, on both counts. In the end, he thought, it would just be Angela Vari and Enzo and himself, a strange little trio, not one of them believing in God as they stood beside the open grave with a priest and a few DIGOS agents reciting the prayers for the dead.

He watched as the flower seller prepared the bouquet, his chapped red hands quick and delicate as he chose blossoms and trimmed their stems, then crimped and wrapped and tied them with a suitably somber bow, and thought of how, in the end, he had taken a page from Brigate Rosse. A prayer from what Angela Vari had called their "Book of Hours." *Keep it simple. Clean and fast.* It was good advice. Finally he'd just paraphrased Barbara Barelli.

I am resigning because when we become Judge and Executioner, there is no difference between Them and Us.

Pallioti handed the flower seller a significant number of euro notes and told him to keep the change. Then he lifted the bouquet, cradling it in his arms as he walked across the piazza. He stopped at the mailbox beside the loggia just long enough to slide the manila envelope into it before he turned down the alley that led toward the river and home.

A NOTE FROM THE AUTHOR

The Lost Daughter is the second novel I've written in a planned trilogy dealing with key moments in Italian politics in the twentieth century. In fact, the last three novels I've written, *The Faces of Angels, Villa Triste,* and *The Lost Daughter,* have all been set in Italy, though I myself had barely set foot in the country before I'd turned forty. I was born in Boston, Massachusetts, and grew up pretty much half and half between the USA and the UK, where we moved for my father's work the first time before I was six months old and later owned a house for thirty-five years. My first encounter with Italy was a two-week vacation of the pretty standard broke-university-student type when I was in my early twenties; the second was a slightly more upmarket vacation in Florence and Venice with my mother that lasted only a week.

So it's not unreasonable to wonder, Why Italy? rather than England? Or America? Or for that matter, France? I've asked the question of myself, not least because the what and where any writer chooses to write about is both defining and revealing—to ourselves as much as anyone else. One of the weird alchemies of writing is that we don't always know what we're doing until we've done it. And sometimes not even then.

To begin to explain, I need to give a little bit of a background. In 2000, my British husband and I bought a group of derelict seventeenth-century barns on the northern edge of Dartmoor in the west of England and embarked on what would become a decade-long building and renovation project. That is how we came to be living in the west of England when the Twin Towers fell on the morning of September 11, 2001.

We spent that day, like most of the rest of the world, glued to the television and on the phone, anxiously tracking down family and friends. It wasn't until dinner that we slowed down enough to ask each other "what this all meant" and, I suspect like many people around the world, "what would happen next."

Over a glass of wine, my husband and I found ourselves asking each other what we would choose to do if the world were going to fly to pieces. I never went to continental Europe as a kid, despite the fact that I had spent every summer and school holiday in England. So it was I who said, "I want to go to the Uffizi. If World War III is going the break out, let's go to Florence." And so we did.

What I remember from that trip is the cold, blowing down from the Apennines, flecking the Arno into whitecaps, and the way the streets, narrow enough to be shadowed at the best of times, turned dark by five, and how the shops spilled light out onto the glassy cobbles. I remember a few warm days, but mostly rain, running down the grim, rusticated faces of the buildings with their gigantic torch rings and doors so huge smaller doors had to be set into them, as if this were a city once inhabited by giants. I remember the crowds on the Ponte Vecchio just before dark, braving the winds to feed the fish who come there at sunset, carrying in the shadows of their fish memory the centuries before when the bridge was the province of butchers who at sunset drew their shutters and threw their spoiling offal and carcasses and hooves into the sludgy water. I remember facing the *Primavera* and thinking it one of the most sinister paintings I had ever seen, stained as it is with Botticelli's madness that seeps like mold up through the beauty. And I vividly remember standing in a darkened room staring at Bronzino's *Lucrezia Tuornabuoni*—first because she had the same name as me, and also because Bronzino gave me the eerie feeling that I had never really seen portraits before.

How do we first begin to love a person, or a place, or an idea? I don't know, but I think that it has far less to do with beauty or even appearance than we are led to believe. Because, I should confess now, I do not find Florence—or even most of Italy—particularly beautiful. Of course there are certain views, vistas, buildings, Tuscan valleys, and cliffs falling into azure seas that are undeniably lovely. The food is good, but, like everywhere else, can sometimes be awful or just mundane. The wine is nice, but for me, France takes that biscuit every time. None of that is what I found beguiling on that trip, or have found beguiling ever since. To me, Italy is compelling simply because it is one of the most intellectually rich, vibrant, and contradictory countries in the world—and from that first visit I knew both that I wanted to try to understand something of it, and that I probably never would.

In the spring of 2002, I returned to Florence alone, rented an apartment for three months, and walked. Accompanied by the tingly awareness that being alone and lonely in a strange city brings, I prowled. And poked. And stared. And, yes, I shopped. I don't know exactly what I had learned by the time my husband joined me at the end of May, but I was undoubtedly better dressed than I had been—although I had a pretty weird haircut—and I had finished my first novel set in Italy, *The Faces of Angels.*

We were lucky in where we lived in England. Not only because it was beautiful, isolated, and usually rather boring—no bad thing if you're trying to be a writer—but also because it was close to a regional airport that EasyJet began to fly in and out of shortly after we arrived. It didn't take us long to figure out that we could be in Milan faster than we could be in London, and that—if we were willing to fly at ungodly hours on odd days of the week at either very short or very long notice—we could do so for approximately the same cost as the train.

And so, for the next nine years, we went to Italy at every opportunity. We went for weekends and weeks and months. We went north and south and even east. We drove and took trains and occasionally flew or took boats, and did not walk as much as either of us now wish we had. We found favorite places, and places we thought were wonderful and then "went off" of, and places we hated at first and then liked better, and a very few places we did not like at all. And when we wanted to go somewhere that felt like home, in the sense that we knew how it would smell and feel and sound, when we wanted a favorite walk, or when we wanted to be surprised yet again at what had been achieved on a relatively small patch of ground by a very small handful of humanity, we went back to Florence.

For all that we found familiar—the same greengrocer, the taxi route from the airport, the place I like where you can get a dish of chicken liver and sage, the dark creepy shadows of the fish—I do not think that there was ever a time when Florence failed to surprise us or remind us of what we did not know or understand. No company will ever bottle that, although I daresay every perfume house has tried—the delight, disappointment, familiarity, and contradiction; the endless refracted strangeness that fills a familiar container we have come to love.

It was on one of these trips, somewhere down the line of years, that I noticed for the first time the plaques on walls. I bumped into one in Florence. Then, once I started looking, I saw memorials to the Partisans in towns of every size everywhere, and I began to understand how little I understood about Italy's experience in World War II. My second novel set in Italy, *Villa Triste*, came directly from my effort to comprehend, both in political and human terms, not only what had happened during the War, but how it had happened.

In terms of Italian history, we all know about the Romans: Julius Caesar and gladiators and horrid stinky vats of oil and fish paste that are periodically pulled off the ocean floor and found to be still edible today. And about the Renaissance: the Medici and Humanism and *The Decameron* and Michelangelo's *David* and Da Vinci's flying machine. After that it kind of dribbles off into one long bleach of Tuscan sun, with spurts of Shelly and Byron and odd goings-on in Venice. Merchant–Ivory films and Vespas. All of which are fine, as far as they go. But like all lovers, I wanted more. And more. Every niggling little bit of history. Which was how I ended up at the Red Brigades.

My family lived in England during the IRA years. I remember photograph after photograph of when the secretary of state for Northern Ireland's car exploded as he was leaving the House of Commons. And the December bombing outside Harrods, where we always had a family day of Christmas shopping. I remember that the horse the IRA did not kill with a nail bomb in Hyde Park was called Sefton. From farther afield I remember news footage of Black September and the Baader-Meinhof Group. But I do not remember the Red Brigades. And I do not recall one moment of the Aldo Moro kidnapping, which, through the series of letters published in newspapers, became nothing less than an extraordinary public dialogue over how terrorists and terrorism should be treated. So, when I came across this most human drama— something that could be playing out today in Syria or Somalia or Afghanistan and raises many of the same questions—I found that Italy had surprised me yet again, and I wanted to know everything I could.

The Moro kidnapping itself proved surprisingly easy to outline in detail. The newspapers were a primary source, followed by the trial transcripts of the Red Brigade members involved in the kidnapping. We know a great deal about how he was taken, how the private messages and tapes and letters were passed to the family, and about the apartment where he was held. All the details down to the giant wicker basket used to transport his body to and from the garage, the furnishings of his room, and that sand from the beach at Ostia found in the blanket he was wrapped in after his death, which for a while led to the erroneous belief that he had been killed there. Eventually, these facts fit together into a mosaic. Filling the mosaics, gaps—some wider than others—in as plausible and emotionally convincing way as possible is the special province of the historical novel.

As with *Villa Triste,* I now had a factual framework. The challenge, again, was to stick to it faithfully. Everything about the Red Brigades in *The Lost Daughter*, where and how Mara Cagol was shot and even the rumors concerning her second autopsy, for instance, are true. I felt strongly that I would find the novel, yet again, in the gaps—the spaces between that can be filled only with "how it might have happened." And, of course, why.

We packed up and went to Ferrara. I chose the city because the Red Brigades were largely a product of the affluent north and in particular of the University at Padua, which has a tradition of radicalism going back four or five centuries and is, relatively speaking, Just Up The Road A Piece. Ferrara was not only close by but smaller and quieter, less a hotbed, which was what I was looking for.

In January the city was freezing and beautiful and haunted by the ghosts of the Finzi-Continis, who never actually had a garden there. Antonio is a composite figure. The farmland in the Po delta is as described, and the factory explosion did happen. Many people were killed, but the brothers, although likely, are a product of my imagination. The character of Angela is based on a real person. One I knew existed, in that apartment in Rome. But that was all. The rest—the woman herself, her life, where she came from, what happened and did not happen to her and the hows and whys of her heart—was a gap.

From the start, I was fascinated by three questions. The first was: How do you come to be an intelligent, well-educated, middle-class, twentysomething native Italian—this is the typical profile of Red Brigade members—in an apartment in the middle of Rome, holding the nation's most famous politician captive? The second was: Once you're there, what do you do? And the third was: If you have been a part of a kidnapping that ends with ten bullets, do you ever stop being a part of that? Do you ever really have "another life"?

In order to write *The Lost Daughter* successfully, to make that convincing case, I needed to know everything I could about the Red Brigades. Not just factually, which was comparatively easy, a matter of public record. But viscerally and emotionally. I needed to understand who they were in their heads, why they did what they did.

That the Red Brigades were more professional than the Baader-Meinhofs, and, even arguably, the Provisional IRA, that they posed more of a danger to the stability of the state than either of those groups said something about them, about their discipline, dedication, and control. In order for Angela to be a viable character in the novel, it had to be possible that her "official version" of what she knew and when she knew it could be true (whether it is or not is up to the reader to decide). To that end, I had to understand how the Red Brigades worked—how they became so disciplined and how the "cells" were set up, the system that dictated and controlled who knew what and when. I put a great deal of time and energy into this, and I became utterly convinced that the possibility of lovers and spouses and best friends being on the most intimate terms, sometimes for years, with best friends and lovers and spouses whom they had no idea were active, long-term members of Brigate Rosse was not only possible, but happened. This was precisely what made them so dangerous.

DISCUSSION QUESTIONS

1. Both Kristin and Angela lost their mothers at a young age. How did each of them deal with those losses?

2. Mary Louise isn't surprised when Kristin asks her for money after their night of bonding, thinking, "However many Kristins there were fluttering around like moths inside that blond, blue-eyed glass, one of them, the biggest, was always and indelibly Kristin Carson" (page 36). How much of Kristin do you think is genuine and how much is an act? Are there other characters who shift between different personas the way Kristin does?

3. Angela and Antonio finally came together after they'd each experienced a painful loss. How do you think this impacted their relationship?

4. On page 341, the author writes, "It was a myth, that love encompassed everything...Like everything struggling to survive, love was selfish, and narrow, and fanatical." What does she mean by this? What do you think of this view of love?

5. Enzo's mother says that many young people "thought they'd been betrayed—been promised a better life, then had it snatched away" (page 118) and that this outrage led to the

formation of the Red Brigades. What led Antonio to join the BR? Do you think he was motivated by that same sense of betrayal?

6. When she goes to the police station to confess, Angela tells the officer that she killed Aldo Moro (page 399). Though she didn't pull the trigger herself, is Angela responsible for Aldo Moro's death? Why do you think she didn't go to the police sooner?

7. Antonio went to great lengths to lure Angela back to Italy. Do you think his desire to see her again was fueled by vengeance or by love? Explain.

8. After Antonio's death, we learn that Barbara was the one who let him know that Angela was still alive. When Pallioti asks her why, Barbara says she "thought Angie would have wanted [her] to" (page 449). Do you believe that Angela would have wanted Antonio to know that she was all right? Is Barbara to blame for the events that followed?

9. When Pallioti puts in his resignation, he says, "When we become Judge and Executioner, there is no difference between Them and Us" (page 459). Do you agree? Were you surprised by his decision?

10. Just as Antonio hid so much of his life from Angela during their relationship, Anna kept her true identity a secret from her husband. How much of their dishonesty was justified in each of these cases? Do you feel that we are required to be completely honest with those we love?

ACKNOWLEDGMENTS

With special thanks to Peter Straus and all the wonderful people at Rogers, Coleridge & White. Special thanks also to Beth de Guzman, Scott Rosenfeld, and everyone else at Grand Central and Hachette Book Group, who work so hard to make their authors look good!

ABOUT THE AUTHOR

Lucretia Grindle was born in Boston, Massachusetts, and grew up spending half her time in the United States and the other half in the United Kingdom. Continuing as she started out, she still splits her time, but now calls the coast of Maine home.